T0194192

—Bloody Oil—

Lev Amusin

iUniverse, Inc.
Bloomington

Bloody Oil

Copyright © 2010 Lev Amusin

All rights reserved. No part of this book may be used or reproduced by any means, graphic, electronic, or mechanical, including photocopying, recording, taping or by any information storage retrieval system without the written permission of the publisher except in the case of brief quotations embodied in critical articles and reviews.

This is a work of fiction. All of the characters, names, incidents, organizations, and dialogue in this novel are either the products of the author's imagination or are used fictitiously.

iUniverse books may be ordered through booksellers or by contacting:

iUniverse
1663 Liberty Drive
Bloomington, IN 47403
www.iuniverse.com
1-800-Authors (1-800-288-4677)

Because of the dynamic nature of the Internet, any Web addresses or links contained in this book may have changed since publication and may no longer be valid. The views expressed in this work are solely those of the author and do not necessarily reflect the views of the publisher, and the publisher hereby disclaims any responsibility for them.

ISBN: 978-1-4502-7016-8 (pbk)
ISBN: 978-1-4502-7017-5 (ebk)

Printed in the United States of America

iUniverse rev. date: 12/3/2010

—— Introduction ——

The final decade of the twentieth century in Russia is sometimes called the Dashing Nineties. Really, Russian history (once again!) took an impetuous zigzag from political totalitarianism and socialism to political freedom and "wild" capitalism. Thus, it is impossible to ignore the fact that the USSR has broken up as the result of contradictions developing inside the Russian empire.

The second factor that influenced the nation's disintegration was the world price of crude oil, which sat at around sixteen to eighteen dollars, sometimes even up to thirty dollars, per barrel. The Soviet Union managed to purchase grain and keep an iron fist over its people as well as over those of so-called countries of national democracy, but when the price per barrel dropped to ten dollars, the USSR broke apart.

The victory over the communistic dictatorship was a victory for all Russians. Millions took to the streets once the long years of oppression ended, not because stores lacked consumer goods, but because people were simply tired of being silent. Many protested the former attempts of communistic ideologists to forge or deform the historical development of human nature. But as the transformation to new life began, attention turned from the construction of a communistic society with a human face to the construction of a capitalistic society with an animal muzzle; the impetuous development of democracy showed that the country required moral values, probably in greater measure than the development of capitalistic relations with those in manufacturing, trade, and financing.

The terms *criminal economy* or *shadow economy* refer to an informal part of the national economy, comprised by activities that are unrecorded in official statistics and, therefore, escape legislation (i.e., the black market). It would seem that under socialistic conditions, in which the state exercises total control, there would be no opportunity to develop shadow or criminal economic relations; however, the deficiency of consumer goods, which is a by-product of socialism, generates all kinds of underground economic activity.

"Shadow people" are always and everywhere, including the developed countries of Western Europe and the United States, existing as a part of the worldwide economic structure. It is estimated that within developed countries, however, black market earnings do not exceed 10 percent of the gross national product. Shadow activity exists in the production of narcotics, textiles, and medical and pharmaceutical products, and in illegal pursuits such as the trade of metals, jewels and illegal migration.

Under the Soviets, these shadow people were sometimes imprisoned and sent to labor camps; at other times, they were persecuted and placed before firing squads. But profits seemed always to overcome any fear of punishment. Illegal operations during periods of irregular inflation, the disruption of established economic relationships, financial-system crises, and bankruptcies created opportunities for reaping excessive profits, leading to the creation and growth of these criminal economies. In fact, the merging of the criminal economy with the state's economy as well as with private enterprises was not observed in any civilized country to such a great extent as during the Dashing Nineties.

The reason for the unprecedented growth of the shadow economy in new Russia lay in the transition from a centralized, bureaucratic, government-controlled economy to a free-market system. Criminal activities in the free-market economy represented great danger, especially with the merging of the "underworld" with the political elite.

The other factor contributing to the growth of the shadow economy during this time was technical flaws in the accounting procedures for both extracted raw materials and finished products. For example, in the petroleum industry, methods for measuring the amount of crude oil that was extracted and transported, both by rail and pipeline, was made by volume; but for accounting purposes, the measurements were recorded in terms of weight. The conversion from one measurement to another opened up substantial opportunity for illegal operations.

An additional key factor in underground activities was that cash had become the basic means of payment; as a result, the basic method of settling of business conflicts became violent coercion—something known as *razborka*. In Russian mobster's lingo, word *razborka* refers to a meeting among members of various gangs, in which conflicts are discussed. Often, these meetings end in bloodshed.

Yet another factor of the growing shadow economy was the state's licensing and quoting of activities by legally registered enterprises. This activity gave corrupted state officials additional opportunities to generate shadow incomes.

As such, the shadow economy had a fatal influence on the development of new Russian society; after the USSR fell apart, the process of privatization was, to a certain extent, criminalized. In fact, according to some sources, the majority of economic crimes were either committed or made possible by corrupted government officials. And as a result, Russian export operations involving metals, crude oil and petroleum products, lumber, and other goods that were in great demand on the world market, if not criminal, were certainly "shady," or in the shadows.

On the other hand, had it not been for the Dashing Nineties, with its formation of capitalism with an animal muzzle, and had it not been for the development of sovereign democracy in Russia, increases in world prices for crude oil might possibly have gone unnoticed. But as it was, by the year 2000, Russia was completely prepared for the gold shower of petrodollars, which changed (once again), the course of modern Russian history.

This era, with its complexity and dramatic nature, can be compared to the troubling times of the seventeenth century, in which the transition from totalitarian management of the country to unlimited freedom (which one cannot refer to in the conventional definitions of democracy) was accompanied by the agony of Russian society. However, because the Dashing Nineties took place so recently, this period in Russian history has neither been completely studied nor analyzed by scholars. Therefore, it will be the duty of future historians to tell the world, comprehensively, about these events and their influence on the further course of Russian and world history.

The events in this novel are based on real events that took place in 1993, at which time the price of crude oil was approximately fourteen US dollars per barrel. (It should be noted, however, that by the summer of 2008, that price exceeded one hundred and forty-four dollars per barrel, but by summer 2010, it was back around seventy dollars.)

A summary, albeit short and superficial, of the historical events that occurred in the summer and autumn of 1993, is that political groups connected to the Russian president Boris Yeltsin were opposed to groups aligned with the Supreme Council of the Russian Federation. The climax of this opposition was bloodshed. In this novel, the author makes no attempt to understand the economic, historical, and political processes of these events, let alone to evaluate their significance; however, it is important to know that during this complex transitional period, the economic life of the country steadily grew—and that growth fueled deadly warfare over the possession of the means of production. From the conflict, a new class of society, called the "new Russians," was born. This kind of people, frequently connected to the shadow economy, would not stop before achieving their goals. They were ready to do anything they could to use privatization to seize former national property. And as a consequence, the blood flowed.

Despite this novel's authentic descriptions of some historical events, the characters and stories herein are the sole product of the author's imagination, and not to be taken as documentary. All names of characters, the descriptions of their appearance and acts, are fictional and are products of the writer's imagination. This includes the descriptions of companies, which have never existed and do not exist now. If someone tries to recognize relatives or friends, the author officially declares that he does not know anybody similar to the characters described in this novel. The author has never met them. In short, this novel is purely fictional, with the sole purpose of providing entertainment to the reader.

1

Frankfurt, Germany
November 4, 1993

THE HUGE, HUMPED BOEING 747, with more than three hundred passengers hammered in its belly, flew over the ocean, as flight attendants pushed their carriages forward, stopping at each row, and with forced smiles, offering drinks.

One attendant, a youthful-looking woman, had by now reached forty-eight-year-old Boris Goryanin, who sat in an armchair on the aisle, absorbed in thought. With a charming smile, she exposed teeth that would be the envy of any gelding, and said to him, "Was möchte, daß Sie trinken?"[1]

"Vielen Dank! Nichts ,"[2] he answered and returned to his thinking.

Soon, the stale air in the plane became overwhelmed with an aroma, followed by a repetitive offer to passengers: "Pasta or chicken?" Then, after a clinical trial of the miracle cookery, innocent victims organized a long line at the restrooms, which trailed down the aisle.

Pretty Woman appeared on the overhead monitors. Over the last six months, Boris had had the opportunity to enjoy this modern day Cinderella story at least ten times, one for each of his trips across the Atlantic. Now, he had no interest in Julia Roberts' shopping spree on Rodeo Drive. Instead, he plunged back into heavy thought.

He never would have believed it if, six months ago, someone had told him that his life would turn upside-down, that he would be kidnapped and almost killed by the Russian mafia, that he would miraculously escape from a gangster's hands, and that he would be rescued from torture and a horrible

---

1   What would you like to drink? *(German)*
2   Thank you. Nothing. *(German)*

1

death by a young, beautiful British woman named Melissa Spencer. But the fact that he, a middle-aged man, had achieved reciprocity from this woman who was almost half his years, and that she, as a result, had gotten pregnant and was now waiting for his child, continued to be unfathomable to him.

"Who is she to me?" he wondered. "The mistress? The girlfriend? It is nonsense! What will happen if my wife finds out about her? Well, what will be—will be. Still, it is a stupid situation: I am in love with my wife, and I am in love with my little Melissa, as well.

"But, what happened in Geneva? Why didn't they even want to speak to me?"

Then the most repetitive thought of the day hit Boris again—"Will I meet my Melissa ever again? What will happen with our child?" Followed by the realization, "I knew it! I should never have trusted that guy Kravchuk. If not him, then who else would try to kill us and get the money? Who is this best friend of mine? Vladislav Yakubovsky or Eddy Pennington?"

Then the monotonous rumble of the engine began to work on him better than any sleeping medication, and Boris closed his eyes.

2

Moscow, Russia
May 20, 1993

THE END OF MAY was Moscow's best season. The soft, warm, damp air was fragrant with the anticipated arrival of flowers and green leaves. And the fluff had not yet begun to fly down from the poplars.

Unfortunately, midway through the previous century, one of the cleverest comrades of city government had issued an order to plant poplars around the dumpsites of Moscow, and, as was to be expected, he did not choose the species based on how well it would correspond to conditions in the central part of Russia; instead, he chose it to catch the eye of his superiors. The folly of his decision, however, had not yet become apparent in late May, when the sun had not yet begun to warm the houses and asphalt-paved streets, forcing people to flee the city.

So in that spring of 1993, if only for the moment, Moscow was all beauty. And this is when the attractive young lady Ms. Lydia Ostapovna Selina[3] arrived. Her business card announcing a PhD in economics and positions as both board member and chief of the Department of Economic Development for the Tyumen Oil & Gas Production Association.

Being young and beautiful, Lydia was welcomed everywhere, and enthusiastically so. While making rounds at the Moscow ministries, somebody advised her to contact some of the newly formed Russian companies, particularly Agroprom.

"There are smart dudes in Agroprom," she had been told. "They will be

---

3   Russian names consist of a first name, a father's name, and a family name. In this case, Lydia is first name, Ostapovna is father's name, and Selina is family name.

interested in what you have to offer, Lyd, and they will figure out who can assist you."

At the time, Lydia was thirty-three. She was of above-average height, with the figure of a fit high-school senior, complete with classical long legs. Her dense hair, slightly twisted and shining with the colors of ripe wheat, was woven into braid and wound around her head. The beautiful, well-groomed nails of her thin fingers showed that she engaged mainly in brainwork. Her thin, gentle sunburned face, with its matte skin, its straight, small nose, and its attractive, kissable lips was dominated by huge, gray, slanting eyes. Her gently prominent cheekbones reflected her Volga-Ural origin. Wherever Lyd Selina appeared, she sparkled with youth and beauty.

This is also how she appeared one nice day, at about lunchtime, when she entered Gavrila Petrovich Kravchuk's reception room. Mr. Kravchuk was the president of Agroprom, a Russian financial-trading corporation. Dressed in a bright blouse and short skirt that fitted harmoniously with her figure, she held her thin, diplomat-sized briefcase lightly in her hands, and her stylish glasses, in their thin gold frame, set off her impressive eyes. She looked like she meant business in a most elegant way.

In his office, Mr. Kravchuk was listening to his young secretary, Valerie, who was informing him that a very beautiful young woman was waiting for him in the reception room. He waited five minutes before receiving her, more out of protocol than from a lack of courtesy.

"Ms. Lydia Selina," she said, introducing herself with a nod of her head, but without the offer of her hand. She spoke softly in a Volga River dialect, with its characteristic open O's emphasizing her lovely mouth.

"Very pleased to meet you!" Mr. Kravchuk blurted. "Please, just call me Gavrila." Then, with the seductive smile of the proverbial ladies, man, he bowed politely to his beautiful guest and said, "How can I be useful to you?"

"For the last few years, I have worked as the chief of the Department of Economic Development for Tyumen Oil & Gas Association," she said. "I have made personal connections throughout our Siberian city of Tyumen. In particular, I have formed strong business relationships with our oilmen, who have given me the authority to represent the workers at the drilling and pumping stations in Tyumen before the officials in Moscow, the capital of our motherland." She paused for a moment before putting a face to her mission. "The people are tired. Their salaries have not been paid for months. And yet they cannot wait any longer to feed their families. And imagine, with winter not far off!"

After letting her compassionate notes resonate for a few seconds, the official representative of the drilling and pumping workers of Tyumen continued. "Therefore, by virtue of the above-stated facts, our trade union and local administration have decided to sell our black gold, so that we may buy food and consumer goods for the workers of the association and for the city of Tyumen itself. Unfortunately," she drew a breath, "we have no direct connections with the appropriate officials in Moscow. In other words, we want to arrange an export sale of five hundred thousand tons of crude oil of the Ural type. I have all the required credentials. I need only to confirm my authority and provide a complete report on the oil.

"My questions to you, Mr. Kravchuk, are these: First, whether you would be capable of and interested in participating in this transaction. Second, if you would be capable and interested, on what conditions." Then pausing, Lydia trained her gray eyes on this ladies'-man president of Agroprom, and finished respectfully with, "I hope I have made myself clear."

Mr. Kravchuk used his usual technique to buy himself time to formulate a response: he walked up and down alongside the large map of the former Soviet Union, which almost covered one whole wall of his huge office, raised his hands as if to heaven, and, sighing dramatically and shaking his head, exclaimed pathetically, "What a great country the bastards ruined."

Before Kravchuk could follow his outburst with a full-blown description of political conditions in Russia and abroad, Selina said, "Ruined or not—and who has done the ruining is debatable—the reality is that we in Tyumen have to live by finding a solution in these difficult economic-political conditions. Simply put, do you have a suitable infrastructure to make this happen, and people who are capable to work on this project where and when it's needed?"

Her straight-talk returned Mr. Kravchuk to reality. He went to his desk and spoke over the intercom. "Val, please ask Nataly, Strelov, Filimonov, Isaev, Popov, and Theodora to step in my office."

Nataly was the first to step in, self-importantly shaking her wide hips as she walked through the door. She was a large and imposing middle-aged woman, a mistress-mother personality who always carried out Kravchuk's instructions precisely. Mr. Kravchuk spoke to her as if he were a doctor dictating a prescription. "Nat, please lay out a table for ten. If we are out of food and drinks, send my driver to buy some. Theodora will give you cash, as much as necessary. She should to write them off under the 'miscellaneous expenses' account. Any questions?"

As Nataly shook her head, Kravchuk waved her off. He was already adding up figures in his head.

"Imagine," he thought. "Five hundred thousand tons of crude oil at one hundred and two US dollars per ton.[4] That would be fifty-one million dollars!"

"Okay," he said, trying to calm himself. "There will be some expenses ... well ... but, there should be a profit as well. Okay. How much will it be possible to take? It will be a lot of money. A lot of money."

Just then, the remainder of the invited associates entered Kravchuk's office one by one, introducing themselves, as was customary at the time, by not only providing the post they currently occupied in Agroprom, but also mentioning, with great pride, the last post they had held under the former Soviet administration.

The first to introduce himself was a tall, important-looking man with unsubtle facial features. "Mr. Isaev, vice president on legal issues."

"Mr. Isaev used to be the head of legal experts in Mr. Gorbachev's administration,"[5] Gavrila added.

Next was Mr. Strelov, a heavyset, middle-aged man who served as chairman of the board of directors of Agroprom. "Mr. Strelov," Gavrila added, "was the Head of the Leningrad City Communist Party Committee during Brezhnev's time, and during the time of all subsequent secretaries general of the Central Communist Party Committee."

The next Agroprom associate to introduce himself and shake hands with the beautiful stranger was Mr. Filimonov, a tall man with the lupine look of an exceedingly clever and skilled Communist Party operative. Unlike his colleagues, and despite the summer heat, he was dressed in an expensive gray pinstriped suit. But just so there would be no doubt left in Selina's mind, he added in staccato syllables, "Agroprom's executive director."

"Don't be shy, Mr. Filimonov," Kravchuk inserted himself, explaining to their charming guest that "during the Soviet regime, Mr. Filimonov held the post of Head of the Leningrad Region Communist Party Committee. Mr. Filimonov was an associate member of the ruling Politburo."

While Kravchuk was involved with fully crediting Mr. Filimonov's accomplishments, another colleague, of medium height, and simultaneously growing gray and bald, had entered.

"Mr. Popov," Kravchuk loudly proclaimed, "is our expert on oil questions, especially unsolvable ones. He is a graduate of the Moscow Oil University, and his entire career has been spent in the petroleum industry." (The unsolvable problems Kravchuk was referring to were not those of a technical nature, but

---

4   At this time, so-called US sweet crude oil was trading for about fourteen to fifteen US dollars per barrel.

5   Mr. Michael Sergeevich Gorbachev was the last head of the ruling politburo of the Communist Party of the USSR, as well as the last president of the USSR.

those that could be dealt with only by virtue of Popov's personal connections with a large number of prominent oilmen.)

"And here is our Mrs. Theodora, our chief accountant." The tall, plump dowager of a woman that Mr. Kravchuk thus introduced was covered like a Christmas tree in expensive gold and diamonds. Mrs. Theodora Vasilieva had enjoyed an important position in the home-based Northern Navy Fleet's Food Procurement department when her husband, a vice admiral, had been Fleet deputy commander, until 1991, when he was dismissed for participating in the coup attempt against President Gorbachev. Later, it was determined that he was not connected to the conspirators, and his military pension and privileges were retained.

All the guests having now arrived and paraded their credentials before the charming visitor, Mr. Kravchuk ceremoniously opened the meeting with a florid greeting of comrades. Gavrila loved such meetings, where he could show off before visitors, putting forth an exaggerated image of his own importance.

"Our Siberian visitor has brought with her a request to assist our Siberian brothers," he announced, and proceeded to outline the opportunity.

When Kravchuk ended, Lydia, who had been silent all this time, outlined her requirements. "In order to manage this project, we will need a skilled operative who has a good track record as a supervisor. For carrying out the project in the field, we will need an experienced, well-educated, and trained colleague who knows several languages and has spent significant time abroad." Then frowning in a way that put little wrinkles in her forehead, she asked, "What candidates can you suggest?"

Mr. Kravchuk, anxious that this gorgeous creature hadn't taken over the meeting, blurted, "We have a man living in the United States who is our shareholder and a member of the board of directors. He knows several languages, and has a PhD in technical science." Then after his definitive response, Mr. Kravchuk leaned over his desk and pressed his secretary's call button. "Valerie," he said importantly, "please call Boris. He should be at his home in California."

"But ... Mr. Kravchuk," Valerie could be heard objecting over the intercom, "it's early morning in California."

"It doesn't matter," Gavrila said. "This is urgent. Very urgent."

"As you say," Valerie answered, and put in a call to the overseas operator.

"Does everyone agree on Boris for this job?" Kravchuk asked.

Isaev smiled and shrugged his shoulders. Strelov and Filimonov nodded.

"Can I conclude that there are no objections on the nominee, Mr.

Goryanin?" Kravchuk asked rhetorically. He was now anxious to get into the dining room from where the food Natasha was laying out on the serving table was sending out delicious smells.

"How long has your colleague been working in America?" Lydia asked.

"A dozen years. Maybe more," answered Kravchuk.

Just then the phone rang. Valerie said loudly, "Mr. Kravchuk! Boris is on the line."

Picking up the telephone, Kravchuk rattled off his message. "Is that you, Boris? I hope we did not wake you. Still working out at the gym regularly? Let me tell you quickly what's going on. As you know, the economic conditions in Siberian city of Tyumen are terrible. The government has allocated an export license to the Tyumen oil industry for five hundred thousand tons of crude oil, but the people of Tyumen don't have access to foreign buyers. Neither do they have connections with the Ministry of Economic Development in Moscow to obtain the allocated export license, or permission to use the main Russian pipeline to transfer the crude oil.

"However," Mr. Kravchuk continued in the same rapid-fire manner, "they have sent us a representative and are awaiting our help. In view of this, could you contact one of the Seven Sisters and present yourself as an exporter? Tell them that we are planning to sell this crude oil directly through you. Further, can you arrange a meeting with a buyer? I am ready to come to the US, along with the minister of fuel and power, and our own team of experts, to enter into negotiations. You, of course, would participate as our representative. He paused, and then said, "That's all. I will wait for your call in Moscow, and, naturally, for results. Please, give greetings to your spouse. Remember, I am waiting for your call. Best regards."

Then Kravchuk hung up without waiting for Boris to say good-bye. After all, the food was on the table and the vodka had already been poured, on the verge losing its potency. Such a scenario was impossible for dear Mr. Kravchuk to countenance.

With a deep sigh, Kravchuk addressed their guest. "Tomorrow, our dear Ms. Lydia, you will start working on documents with Mr. Isaev and Mr. Popov. But now, ladies and gentlemen," he said, turning to the rest of them, "please enjoy this dinner which God has granted to we simple people. To the table, please."

Mr. Kravchuk adored these feasts, and was at his most charming when he was hosting them. As the assemblage basked in his happiness, Kravchuk lifted a full glass of vodka and toasted. "Friends, as they say, money does not bring happiness, but its amount does." And with a wink and a nod, he ended with, "For that, let us drink."

The table was overloaded with green vegetables, potato salad, fried potatoes with chunks of sausages, hamburgers, pelmeny,[6] and bottles of vodka. In no time at all, the partygoers became tipsy, and were soon joined by others who, though uninvited, were already drunk, and therefore nicely fit in. The little doll, Valerie, turned on music, and people began dancing. Then the speakers offered an appropriately off-color pop song:

"I do not believe at all

In the revolution social!

All my dreams and all my thoughts

In the revolution sexual!"

In a word, the party went well, and, in fact, all would have been perfect, except for one minor detail: they didn't have an export license. To be perfectly clear, Agroprom had not been certified to export crude oil abroad. Aside from this trifle, however, everything was just superb.

---

6   An authentic Russian food resembling ravioli, but larger and containing more meat.

3

THE NEXT MORNING, AT five minutes to nine, Lydia was back in Kravchuk's reception room. She was joined a few minutes later by the broadly smiling Mr. Isaev, who invited her to his office to begin their work and then wasted no time in complimenting the young woman on her charming appearance.

After inviting her to sit, he carefully studied the documents she had brought, but then wasn't remiss to also complete a thorough visual examination of her. Lydia made it clear she was indifferent by not returning the interest; she was used to aging men losing their heads in her presence. When Isaev asked her questions about the materials he'd read, she answered quickly and precisely, showing complete mastery of her subject. In the process, though still devouring her beauty, Mr. Isaev also developed a healthy respect for her knowledge and business savvy.

While Isaev was being thus occupied, his boss Kravchuk was greedily gulping down glassfuls of cold water, sharing with a hoarse voice and obvious pleasure to everyone within earshot, "My gridirons are burning." And why wouldn't his gridirons burn, when the night before, after several glasses of vodka to loosen up, he had drunk all by himself an entire bottle of Black Label whisky, and then finished the evening with a bottle of champagne? He had broken the immutable law of drinking: thou shall drink boozes only with progressively greater levels of alcohol.

Nevertheless, despite his disgusting state of health, Gavrila had already instructed the legal department to register a new company, which would be created specially to handle crude oil transactions and called, simply and elegantly, the First Russian Oil Corporation.

It is worth noting here that Kravchuk was a man of unusual features and a distinctive personality. He was two hundred seventy pounds, six foot six, and broad-shouldered. His features were regular, but handsome, including very smart eyes, elegant motions, and an imposing head of thick hair.

And as for his personality, he was extremely generous. Once, being in a Las Vegas hotel and casino called the Imperial Palace, Gavrila had, in passing, casually thrown a dollar into the belly of a "one-armed gangster." To his surprise, the slot machine at once began lighting up and making noises, which soon resulted in money spilling from its mouth. When an attendant brought Gavrila his winnings, which amounted to sixteen hundred dollars, the Agroprom president, without hesitation, divided the money evenly among the members of the crowd with which he was partying. In addition to generosity, he could offer beautiful toasts, make perfect compliments to women, and always function as the life of the party.

Kravchuk had attended the Moscow Historico-Archival University, which, in those days, prepared students for future employment in human resources; in some cases, it also served as a springboard for further education under Communist Party supervision, which often led to careers within the party. In Kravchuk's case, after graduating, he worked a few years in the provinces and then returned to Moscow where he was a graduate student at the Supreme Communist Party School. Then, springing from the contacts he'd made in graduate school, Kravchuk landed a position in the personnel department of the Central Committee of the Youth Communist Organization. While working full-time at this position, Gavrila continued to take correspondence courses through the Moscow Historico-Archival University, where he successfully defended his dissertation and received a PhD in historical sciences.

By 1986, using his experience, personal connections, natural charm, and knowledge of the German language, Kravchuk was sent to work in East Germany. After this excellent beginning, he expected to make a career working with the Ministry of Foreign Affairs, the KGB, or even the Ministry of Foreign Trade; however, when Gorbachev's reforms abruptly changed the course of history, they also changed the course of Kravchuk's life.

In 1987, Gavrila returned to Moscow and assembled a team of business partners. Working quickly, they formed an association that ruthlessly snapped up private shops, stores, and even the first private toilet in Moscow at Kazansky Railroad station. By 1990, they were offering private businesses protection from racketeers, not noticing that, meanwhile, they themselves were becoming just such racketeers.

Although many Communist workers were already fleeing the party, only a few had started private small businesses, and most of them, having formerly been professional government bureaucrats, didn't know what to do except sit around and gossip. But Kravchuk knew what to do. He hired former Soviet

Army Generals and ranking officials of the Communist Party and Soviet organizations; these people were called apparatchiks. Being of retirement age, they were united by their nostalgia for "the former time," still hoping for restoration of the Soviet Union, still refusing to understand that power was now in the hands of a different kind of people—a kind of people that had no intention of giving up their power.

Still, for Kravchuk, these employees held invaluable qualifications: personal connections. Based on this reason alone, they were employed by Agroprom to carry out one task only—to obtain from the government substantial funding for a project of indisputable national interest. For this purpose, a multifaceted program called the Revival of Russia was developed. This ambitious program included, among other goals, relocating former officers of the Soviet Army, constructing affordable housing, increasing the birth rate, improving agricultural methods and productivity, developing small private business, and reviving the role of religion as the moral basis of Russian society. Although some questioned whether the program was a scam, it certainly was not. The issues it dealt with would remain well into the foreseeable future. On the other hand, within the next two years, all of the federal resources allocated to the program somehow disappeared.

These funds were, of course, necessary to support the projects developed by the Revival of Russia, along with the salary of its numerous managers and employees; the cost of daily banquets and receptions for delegations of Cossacks,[7] farmers, officers, inhabitants of the far north and the south; trips to check the performance of order fulfillment; and oversight and control of the use of various financial streams. But after struggling for two years to reach the goals of the Revival of Russia, Agroprom realized that tangible results would not be achieved any time soon.

Meanwhile, the Revival of Russia program operated under the guise of a trading company called Prestige, which Kravchuk's wife Alevtina managed. Prestige was comprised of retailers, fast food chains, and a cafe called Molodezhnoye,[8] which was a great success among the young people, because of the popular bands and other performers who played there in the evenings.

Originally, the management offices of both Agroprom and Prestige were located in private apartments in a residential building at 1 Astrodamsky Street, which was near the Molodezhnoye. But after racketeers threw military

---

7   People of Russian origin who settled on the peripheral regions of Russia. During the tsar's time, they carried out the military service of protecting the Russian border, but during the USSR regime, they were oppressed by the Soviets.

8   Youths *(Russian)*

hand grenades; one into the cafe and one into Agroprom's office—as an unmistakable warning to leave, Kravchuk rented office space in a high-rise at 9 Leninsky Prospect, where, at the time, the Bureau of Government Standards, the Academy of Sciences of the Russian Federation, and some other large organizations and banks were also renting space. Agroprom occupied the entire tenth floor.

Although the building had existing security in place—something that had remained intact since Soviet times—Agroprom added its own force of more than two hundred guards. The man in charge was Colonel Dmitry Cherkizov, a former officer of KGB's[9] 9-th Division, charged for safety of country leaders.

In addition to Agroprom's main offices, a few shops, and a casino inside Hotel Ismailovo,[10] Cherzikov's security force protected a cottage in the Zariadye[11] Housing Estate. One side of the cottage adjoined a summer residence once belonging to the "Best Friend of All People," Joseph Stalin. On the other side was a cottage occupied by Lenin's aged nephew, who took lonely daily walks along the well-groomed paths of the estate—and none of the prosperous new Russians who had moved to Zariadye had noticed him.

So the cottage in Zariadye, its bedrooms and bathrooms equipped with video surveillance and audio monitoring systems, and cleaned by a maid who also prepared breakfast, was kept as Agroprom's private hotel for the most important visitors. Agroprom's guests of honor were also assigned a car and driver. For all of these reasons, Kravchuk invited Lydia to stay there, but she politely refused, preferring to remain in the more convenient Hotel Mir, located near the historical center of Moscow in Bolshoi Devyatinsky Lane, a two-minute walk from the US Embassy and five minutes from Novy Arbat Street, with its modern shops and restaurants.

The Kravchuks themselves lived in a rented house in the gated community of Arkhangelskoe, about twelve miles outside Moscow. The entrance to this community, marked boldly with a "No Entrance" sign, was protected by a

9   From Wikipedia: KGB is the Russian abbreviation for the Committee for State
      Security (*Komitjet Gosudarstvjennoj Bjezopasnosti*), which was the official name
      of the umbrella organization that served as the Soviet Union's premier security
      agency, secret police, and intelligence agency from 1954 to 1991. The largest
      Russian successor to the KGB is the FSB (*Fjedjeral'naja Sluzhba Bjezopasnosti*)
      or the Federal Security Service. On December 21, 1995, President Boris Yeltsin
      signed the decree that disbanded the KGB, which was then substituted by the
      FSB, the current domestic state security agency of the Russian Federation.
10   This huge hotel development was built in the central part of Moscow for the
      1980 Summer Olympics.
11   One of several gated communities outside Moscow designed for the Communist
      elite.

detachment of the Moscow Police's special forces. Kravchuk's house was near the house occupied by the family of then Russian Prime Minister Mr. Egor Gaydar and next door to the house of then Minister for Foreign Affairs of the Russian Federation Andrey Kozyrev. The community tennis court was often used by President Yeltsin.

All large houses in Arkhangelskoe were built on oversize lots and surrounded by high metal fences. In each large, seven-room, brick building, the flooring was made of high-quality oak parquet, the huge kitchen held two giant stoves, and the dining room had seating accommodations for fifty. Each house also held a pool-table room, a bar, a library, and other pleasant amenities.

Besides the usual group of security guards, there was a dog handler who, in the absence of the owners, released onto the grounds a canine security force consisting of three Caucasian shepherd dogs: two bitches and a huge male named Khan. The story was that this same dog team, plus three additional bitches, had previously guarded Russia's large department store, GUM. One night, a group of twelve gangsters armed with knives, who were obviously unaware of the dogs, entered the store to rob it. In the morning, the gangsters were found dead, as were three of the bitches. Khan and his two battle-tested female companions were subsequently given the responsibility of guarding Kravchuk's house.

For transportation, Kravchuk was usually driven in a twelve-cylinder Mercedes S600, while the members of his family were driven in a BMW-525i, and were accompanied by both bodyguards and assistants. Agroprom's senior employees used the prestigious Russian-made car, the Volga. On business trips, they traveled by train in sleeping cars, or by plane in business class.

Agroprom needed an infinite amount of funds for the salary of its employees and security personnel alone, not to mention for the substantial unrecorded amounts of money that were used to bribe various officials. They spent money faster than it came in, which is why the appearance of Ms. Selina was a godsend. The profits from both the sale of Tyumen's crude oil, and the purchase and sale of the foodstuff and consumer goods for Tyumen, could revitalize the existence of Agroprom. Otherwise, the financial-trading monster was close to breathing its last.

4

May 21, 1993

IN THE PRESENTATION FOLDER that Lydia Selina brought to her meeting with Mr. Isaev were the following documents:

> 1. A power of attorney from the Tyumen Oil & Gas Association, authorizing Ms. Lydia Ostapovna Selina, PhD, and a member of the board of directors of the Tyumen Oil & Gas Association "to represent the Tyumen Oil & Gas Association in the matter of the sale of 500 thousand tons of crude oil."

> 2. A copy of the registration certificate of the Tyumen Oil & Gas Association.

> 3. A copy of the land use license, authorizing the extraction of solid, liquid, and gaseous minerals.

> 4. A copy of the license authorizing the firm to sell the liquid and gaseous minerals obtained by the enterprise in conformity with the activity.

> 5. A copy of an extract from the report of the Labor Collective Assembly of the Tyumen Oil & Gas Association, concerning the petition sanctioning "the sale and delivery of 500 thousand tons of crude oil for hard currency, for the purpose of repaying debts consisting of the unpaid salaries of workers of the Association, and also for the purpose of purchasing foodstuff and consumer goods for workers of the Association and members of their families." Also, an

extract of the minutes of the meeting at which these matters were discussed and agreed upon.

6. A letter from the governor of the Tyumen region acknowledging the above mentioned petition of the Labor Collective Assembly of the Tyumen Oil & Gas Association.

7. The official decision of the Central Committee of Trade Unions of Russia supporting the above mentioned petition.

8. Specifications of the crude oil offered for delivery to export.

All of the documents were on official-looking letterheads, complete with dates, registration, and reference numbers, and each had been signed by the heads of the organizations that had issued the documents and notarized with the appropriate seals. All documents also contained approval from the heads of the relative parent organizations.

Isaev read through the documents, paying close attention to each word and punctuation mark. He held every paper up to the light to make sure none had been intentionally altered. Once satisfied that the documents were genuine, he prepared a memo for Kravchuk that confirmed that he, Arnold Isaev, had personally checked all of the documents on the list and had no doubts about their authenticity.

At eleven o'clock that morning, Isaev and Lydia Selina went to Kravchuk's reception room, where Isaev had the secretary go to the copy office and make two copies of each document. At that time, the chief of the copy office also certified that the copies were genuine facsimiles of the originals. When this had been done, Isaev and Selina went into Kravchuk's office.

Once Kravchuk had examined the documents, including Isaev's memo, he called Alexander Popov into his office, handed him the documents folder, and directed him to start working on it.

At this moment, however, Selina, who had, until then, been silent, told Kravchuk and Isaev that, before the project could go forward, it would be necessary to come to an agreement on "mutual interests above and beyond the formal contractual obligations." Kravchuk frowned and put his hand on his forehead, as if the previous day's party were still affecting him, and responded that there was no need to worry, that Agroprom would not offend Selina in any way.

This answer did not satisfy Selina. "What do you mean I shall not be offended?" she asked. "Either we are serious, and we make an agreement about the terms and conditions of our partnership here on the shore, so to speak, before we begin our journey, or I will assume that I have wasted my time with you.

"I think," she continued, "that in the capital of our motherland, there are other little companies like your Agroprom-chik.[12] I think I could easily find another company like yours!"

Kravchuk had turned a deaf ear; he didn't want to even consider losing this project. Instead, realizing the position he was in, he asked immediately, "What are your terms and conditions, dear Lydia?"

And just as quickly, Lydia answered, "As it is customary in our motherland, ten percent from the profit of each sale, or five percent from the total amount of the contract."

A half-hour later, after some sober negotiating, an agreement was reached that Selina would personally receive 8 percent from the total amount of each sale. She then brought up a further requirement: for the consulting services she would provide to Agroprom, a contract would be drawn up stating that she be given an advance of fifty thousand crisp, "freshly green," US dollars.

Without blinking, Kravchuk called his chief accountant, Mrs. Theodora Vasilieva, into his office and asked her to pay Ms. Selina the specified amount.

Just as unblinkingly, Mrs. Theodora Vasilieva looked at Mr. Kravchuk as if he were the village idiot, and asked incredulously, "Fifty thousand of what? Wooden Russian rubles?"

Mr. Kravchuk, with a deeply offended look on his face, answered sadly, "No, dear Theodora, this citizen wishes for American dollars."

"Dollars?" was all she could say. Then, going over to Mr. Kravchuk's desk, she lifted a stack of papers, looked at the empty desk underneath, and, with a questioning look, told the president of Agroprom that she did not see any dollars on the desk.

Mr. Kravchuk, even sadder than before, sighed deeply and said to Lydia, "Do you see? I make a request, but my orders are ignored, and I am told that we don't have dollars in the country."

Ms. Selina answered at once. "I have been at the circus many times, dear Mr. Kravchuk, and know all about clowns." Then, upon seeing on his face that the meaning of her words had sunk in, she continued. "Besides, I am not alone in this matter. I have others with whom I must share. And so, my dear friends, it's either an advance payment or I must be leaving you."

Mr. Isaev leaped in to rescue the situation. After all, he knew better than anyone that the documents were in perfect order, and that the project was a genuine one. He offered to make a personal loan to Agroprom in the amount

---

12   In Russian, the suffix –*chik* is often added to the end of a noun for the purpose of describing the noun as small (e.g., *boychik* would mean little boy).

of twenty thousand dollars at 25 percent interest per year. This was a very generous offer, considering that, at the time, Russian banks were lending money with minimum annual interest rates of 100 percent and, in some cases, as much as 150 percent. Obviously, Mr. Isaev wanted Agroprom to make this very favorable deal.

So, Ms. Selina, Mr. Isaev, and Mrs. Theodora agreed that Lydia would return to Agroprom the next morning, sign the contract for her consulting services, and receive an advance of twenty thousand US dollars.

At the time, however, nobody at Agroprom suspected that this lovely lady already had visited the trading company called Solvaig, owned by Mr. Arkady Fedorov, and showed its management the same documents. And nobody at Agroprom would have guessed that at Solvaig, the management had asked her to wait one day before making any decisions. Apparently, they had needed a day to "collect their thoughts."

5

California, United States
May 20, 1993

THE RINGING PHONE BROKE the dense darkness of the summer morning. As had become his habit, Boris Goryanin reached for the phone in the dark, without opening his eyes.

"Hello!"

"Is this seven-one-four, five-six-three, one-two-one-four?" asked a telephone operator with a strong Russian accent.

"Speaking."

"Please, answer. Moscow is on the line."

Boris heard something squeak and then click. Then, at last, he heard the friendly voice of Mr. Kravchuk's pretty secretary, Valerie.

"Is this Boris Georgievich? Gavrila Petrovich has important business to talk to you about. Mr. Gavrila Petrovich? Mr. Gavrila Petrovich, Boris Georgievich is on the line."

Kravchuk picked up the phone and began rattling away. "Boris? I hope we did not wake you. Are you still working out at the gym regularly? Let me tell you quickly what's going on. As you know, business in Tyumen is terrible. So the government has allocated an export license to the Tyumen oil industry for five hundred thousand tons of crude oil. But people from Tyumen don't have access to foreign buyers, and they don't have connections with the Ministry of Economics in Moscow to obtain the allocated export license, and they don't have permission to use the main Russian pipeline to transfer the oil.

"However," Kravchuk continued in the same rapidfire manner, "they have sent us a representative and are waiting for us to help. In view of this, could you contact one of the Seven Sisters and present yourself as an exporter?

Tell them that we are planning to sell this oil directly through you. Further, can you make arrangements for a meeting with a buyer? I am ready to come to the US, along with the minister of the Fuel and Power Ministry and our own team of experts, to enter into negotiations in which, of course, you will participate as our representative. That's all. I will wait for your call in Moscow, and, naturally, for results. Greetings to your spouse. Remember, I am waiting for your call. Best regards." And Kravchuk hung up, not waiting for Boris's answer.

From the tone of Kravchuk's voice, Boris could tell that a party was already in progress. He looked at the clock. Four thirty. Suddenly, he felt awake. After thinking the conversation over for a few minutes, Boris got out of bed, threw on a T-shirt, and went out into the backyard. He took a deep breath of the cool, fresh air, and began more thinking.

Boris Goryanin and his family had lived in California since 1979. They currently were renting a small townhouse while renting out their own house for an amount that exceeded the combined total of their mortgage and real estate tax.

Except for profits from a small business run by Boris's wife, Ruslana, however, the family had no other source of income. Some years earlier, Boris had formed a small engineering firm that manufactured chemical-processing equipment for the electronics and semiconductor industries. But when California legislators had adopted stringent environmental regulations, they effectively killed such industries in the state; in due course, many manufacturers had relocated to Pacific Rim countries, leaving local companies in ruin and, as a result, tens if not hundreds of thousands of families—including Boris's—without a source of income.

Outside, he could smell the ocean in the cool breeze. It was a quiet morning, with birds singing. On a nearby magnolia, huge white flowers had blossomed, its delicate perfume permeating the air.

At first sight, Kravchuk's proposal seemed tempting. But Boris knew from personal experience that Kravchuk could not be trusted. Kravchuk would walk over anybody he could at the first opportunity. On the other hand, when he and Kravchuk had started putting together a network of American connections, and Kravchuk had wired their joint company two hundred and fifty thousand dollars, it was not only Kravchuk who had wasted most of the money on extravagant partying. And it was said that Kravchuk's character had apparently undergone major changes in the last two years, although who knew what those changes were.

Boris played out various scenarios in his head. In order to be safe, he knew he would need to involve more people from Agroprom, so that it wouldn't be just him and Kravchuk. Strelov was a rascal, but Filimonov, Isaev, and Popov were all trustworthy guys with whom it might be possible to work. And if he would open bank accounts for them in the States as a good-faith gesture, probably, they would work as a team.

A series of clichés then barraged him, all urging him to go ahead with Kravchuk's plan. "Why not? You'll never know if you don't try. There's nothing to lose. You never can tell what will happen."

After his usual stretching and other morning exercises, Boris showered and ate breakfast. As the possibilities of the project started to excite him, he sketched a brief working plan, listing names of some of the largest US oil companies. He then dialed a toll-free number and got the telephone numbers of the leading six. From his years in the States, he knew that the sale of everything, including one's own services, depended on the number of contacts you made.

Next, he composed a simple sales speech, which he planned to repeat word for word to every company representative he spoke to until he reached someone who would understand the significance of his words. He knew it would be less difficult to get through to contacts in the sales departments than to any heads of companies, and so, after reading his sales pitch to assistants in the departments responsible for procuring crude oil, Boris left his number with each one. He would allow two days for his calls to be returned, and would call back each company who did not.

The next morning, at quarter after eight, his phone rang.

"Good morning," a pleasant voice said. "My name is Jonathan Barker. I am returning your call from yesterday regarding the purchase of crude oil. I am the manager of the Crude Oil Sales and Acquisitions department of Global Oil Research and Sales Corporation. Could you please tell me more about your offer?"

Boris told him everything in as much detail as he knew.

"Is this information verifiable?" Barker asked.

"Of course," Boris answered confidently.

"But how do I know?"

"Please, communicate all of your questions regarding this matter to the commerce department at the US Embassy in Moscow," Boris said, with only a slight tinge of sarcasm. "Let them spend the taxpayers' money."

"Okay, I'll do it. I'll let you know. Have a nice day."

"Same to you," Boris said, and then exulted silently, *Contact has been made!* He waited an hour before calling Kravchuk at home. It would be nine in the evening in Moscow, an eleven-hour difference.

"I have good news for you, Mister Comrade Kravchuk," Boris reported with a jaunty air, addressing Kravchuk with both capitalist and Communist salutations.

Boris repeated his conversation with Barker, after which Gavrila said, "Let them check." Then he made a slight growl, as if he were offended by Barker's cautious attitude.

"Can you imagine that he doesn't know about us yet?" Boris asked, a slight laugh in his voice.

"It doesn't matter," Gavrila said. "We can handle him!"

The conversation ended with both men agreeing to wait to hear again from Barker.

6

Russia
1945–93

BORIS GEORGIEVICH GORYANIN WAS born during the final year of the Second World War—the one with Germany, which Russia called the Great Patriotic War. During the war, his father, who had been made a professor while still very young, taught at the military school in Kazakhstan, and his mother was a medical school student. They survived, but their parents, as well as Boris's aunts and uncles, perished either during the German occupation or at the front.

So only after the war, when Boris's sister was born, did life return, more or less, to normal. The family went back home to Moscow, where Boris's father taught as a professor at the Academy of Economics. But when Stalin, in the late 1940s, began to wage war against the so-called rootless cosmopolitans, someone suggested to Boris's father that he slip quietly out of town to look for work. Taking the hint, the family moved to Kazan, the capital of Tatarstan.

Boris's father was named head of the economics department at Kazan University, but that didn't last long, because, in the aftermath of shenanigans associated with a traditional and very boisterous students' holiday called Kill the Goat, some leading faculty were dismissed from the Communist party for refusing to divulge the names of the worst offending revelers. And, naturally, dismissal from the party meant dismissal from his post.

The family then moved farther south to the small Ukrainian Black Sea town of Nikolaev. Soon after, however, Boris's father died, not yet forty-eight; his health had been undermined by the emotional and physical stress he had undergone over the past few years. Boris's mother, who had worked in Moscow and Kazan as a local family doctor, continued to do so in Nikolaev. In any weather, good or bad, she visited patients at their homes, wrote out medical reports, and prescribed medicines that were permitted by the guidelines of the former Soviet Union; or rather, medicines that the pharmacies had in stock.

Boris was a good student, and after his parents' insistence, had taken up the violin. By the time he was fifteen, he was also working, thanks to a neighbor's referral, at one of Nikolaev's canneries as a mechanic's apprentice. Boris was actually lucky to work at a factory in which the manufactured product was food, because soon after getting acquainted with his fellow workers, he felt comfortable enough to steal cans of food that had not passed quality control. At times, it was even possible to steal bones, as the factory also processed meat in addition to vegetables. The method was simple: Boris and a friend of the same age would throw a bag of bones over the fence whenever they knew someone wasn't looking. Owing to such good dining at the factory, Boris grew to over six foot tall by the time he reached seventeen. And by working out, lifting weights, and doing other body-building exercises, he had pumped up some decent muscles. And that is how he, his mother, and his sister survived in Nikolaev.

Boris continued his education at night school, but it didn't prepare him adequately for passing the first entrance exam at the local university. The second time around, however, he was better prepared, and was accepted by the Nikolaev branch of Odessa Polytechnic University.

The summer after his first year at the university, Boris and his classmates were formed into a construction brigade and sent to work on undeveloped land in North Kazakhstan. There, he got to know a skinny, nice-looking girl with large, gray eyes. Her name was Ruslana Katushkina, and she was a student at the Odessa University of Business and Economics. They fell in love at once, and married in November 1963. Ruslana then left the university as a full-time student but continued her education by correspondence. She also took a job as a bookkeeper. In July 1964, their son Anton, known as Tony, was born.

In the same year that Boris transferred to Odessa Polytechnic, he began working in a foundry shop. His job was to shake out aluminum and pig-iron castings from their molds after forging. Because they poured only every other day, Boris was able to incorporate the work conveniently into his university schedule. On a normal day, he would arrive at the foundry after classes; change into a heavy-duty, lined uniform, and put on special protective gloves. His work consisted of pouring water over the still hot forms, overturning them, separating the castings from the sand-based molds, and shaking out the loose sand. Then he would knock off the metal runners and gates, separating any rejected castings and collecting them into a pile. After that, he would again pour water over the hot sand. It was physically hard, but by eight o'clock in the evening, Boris was finished.

There were few competitors for this position, since not everyone had the physical strength. But the work suited Boris. It took little time, and the additional one hundred rubles a month allowed him to continue his studies.

Meanwhile, Boris was falling increasingly in love with music, and so, in addition to his work in the foundry, his studies at the university, and his time with his new wife, he took to practicing the violin for at least one hour a day. In fact, Boris had learned to play the violin at such a high amateur level that, had fate decreed, he could have become a professional musician.

Boris was never drafted into the army because the university had its own military faculty. Consequently, Boris was able to concentrate on his grades and was awarded an increased stipend to support his studies. This meant he could continue working in the foundry, but now as a pregraduate student, focusing on research. As such, Boris developed an express test procedure for identifying the level of internal stress in the castings of multicomponent alloys that were of great importance to the aerospace industry — aluminum, magnesium, titanium, and zirconium. Test results would, in turn, help to determine which heat-treatment processes should be used to minimize fractures. Quite simply, it meant preventing midair accidents—a definitively important job.

Boris' undergraduate faculty mentor and advisor, Professor Pavel Khristichenko, believed his student's efforts could be carried over into conventional PhD work, but when Boris received merely a good grade for the project, instead of an excellent one, he was denied a diploma with honors. In other words, his road to postgraduate study had been blocked.

After graduating, Boris could not get a job for some time. Of course, through bribery or connections, it would have been possible to get a decent job, but Boris knew no one, and had no money. Finally, he landed a position as the assistant to the foreman of a metal-processing plant, but he thought this was the worst job possible: lots of responsibility, but no authority.

Understanding that any hope for work at Odessa, even though he qualified, was futile, he quit his job and moved to the city of Togliatti, where the new automobile plant was hiring just about anybody. At first, he lodged in a hostel with five others. Later, when he was allocated a separate room, Ruslana and their small son joined him.

In the ensuing three years, Boris passed all of his PhD tests. In 1971, he began postgraduate study at the technical institute in Tver. Then in 1975, he received his PhD after successfully defending his dissertation in molecular physics, regarding the development and implementation of a unique device to produce so—called Water-2. This water, which could be found in condensation on the walls of capillaries thinner than human hair, had properties different from those of common water.

The existence of Water-2 had been theoretically predicted by the Institute of Physical Chemistry, which was part of the Academy of Science, but producing it, collecting it, and conducting experiments on it was not possible until after Boris' research. Yet, again, despite his outstanding record of success, he began to hear the same tunes playing over again: "You have to understand why you can't get this job," or "Without me, you couldn't get this kind of job." Finally, Boris asked himself how long he was willing to put up with such unfair treatment. His answer was never again.

So in 1979, Boris Goryanin, his wife, and their son have left for the United States. At Moscow's International Airport, customs had prepared a special farewell for them. First, for the luggage check-in: though this involved only two suitcases, the customs inspector provided quite a show when he shook out their contents, apparently in search of diamonds, and then tore open two pillows, sending feathers afloat all around the customs hall.

But that was not the end of the fun. During registration, the airline announced that the plane was overloaded, which meant Boris' family was allowed only one carry-on. They had brought three. One contained sandwiches and dry soups. Another was a briefcase with three bottles of champagne, three cans of caviar and two cartons of cigarettes. The third was Boris's violin. The inspector decided that Boris could take only the briefcase. The sandwiches were dumped into the trash, and the violin was left with a stranger who had come to see off his relatives.

Boris faced different challenges in the United States, but overcame them. During his first five years, he worked as a freelance engineer for different firms, eating lunch in his car during deliveries to and pick-ups from his clients. After work, for two hours each day, he studied English and gained a decent knowledge of the language. Then he began moonlighting, preparing drawings for engineering equipment companies. Eventually, Boris saved enough to buy a house and a small start-up business for Ruslana.

In 1989, the seductive goddess of travel and an irresistible desire to make money inspired Boris to return to Russia. He contacted old acquaintances and made new connections. He also started working on engineering development projects for private companies at a time when American know-how was necessary to Russia.

Gradually, Boris developed a closer relationship with Kravchuk who had a gift of vision and, as Kravchuk himself said, contacts within the Kremlin. There was a red phone on Kravchuk's desk that apparently connected to a special, internal line, on which he could directly — that is, bypassing secretaries — contact the country's most influential political and economic leaders, including the president, ministers, members of the joint staff, financiers, and so on. It seemed to Boris that Kravchuk was acquainted with the most influential people of Russia, and that if even the smallest part of his ideas were realized, the country would become a better place for the "simple people," and Kravchuk would become one of the Russian oligarchy.

At the same time, Kravchuk possessed less impressive characteristics, and these Boris also understood too well. In short, Kravchuk did not acknowledge the existence of basic human decency, and he could not be trusted at all, not even for one minute. With Kravchuk, it was possible to go on a scout's mission only one time—the last time.

And so Boris Goryanin had to ponder whether, for him, it was to be, or not to be.

7

May 24, 1993

REGISTERED IN CYPRUS, THE trading company Solvaig, headed by Mr. Arkady Fedorov, was within walking distance of Agroprom. One had simply to walk along Leninsky Prospect down to the Octobersky Square and turn left, pass by the Hotel Warsaw, the main entrance to Gorky Park, and the Crimean bridge, and then cross to the opposite side of the Zubovsky barracks. These were the directions to Solvaig's beautiful corner in old Moscow.

There, inside a courtyard, was the three-story "little cabin" building of forty-two thousand square feet that had been constructed by some Russian count right after the 1812 Russian—French War. Mr. Arkady Fedorovich Fedorov, former deputy minister of rural construction,[13] rented it from the city of Moscow at the end of 1988. At this time, smart apparatchiks could see the approaching decline of the economy, so Fedorov signed a ninety-nine-year lease agreement at a rental rate of seventy-four rubles, fifty-eight kopeks per month.

The lease with the city included a provision that all involved parties honor the full term of the lease, as long as payments were made on time. Well, four years later, Fedorov paid off the full amount of the lease, which was just over the eighty-five thousand rubles. The money had been paid according to an invoice issued by city of Moscow and had been deposited in the city's account with the Savings Bank of Russia. And thus, since at the time, one US dollar was equal to five thousand Russian rubles, Fedorov became the full owner of the former count's palace for only seventeen US dollars.

But the most interesting point was that the agreement allowed the lessee to renovate the building and surrounding property in order to increase its

---

13   The USSR had ministries for everything!

usable square-footage. Considering the building adjoined a number of illegally built garages, this gave the lessee a potential of almost five acres; oh, what great economic opportunities were sometimes concealed in corners of old Moscow!

Solvaig exchanged everything: crude oil to the Ukraine in exchange for canned green peas and other vegetables, which Solvaig then sent to buyers in Siberia. (It's not clear what Siberia had to give in exchange, but Solvaig collected eventually.) When working in Tanzania on the development of kimberlitic tubes, Solvaig found diamonds and other precious stones that turned out to be exactly like those usually found in Siberia, opening up another trading opportunity with that area. Solvaig also traded lumber and plywood to Scandinavia.

Solvaig worked on a barter basis, and business was prosperous. Although transactions were always on goods-for-goods concept, somehow, at the end, Solvaig wound up with hard currency, which ended up in their bank accounts in Cyprus and Switzerland. In turn, they collected currency on these special accounts from selling diamonds on the Amsterdam Diamond Exchange. Some deposits had been made in Cyprus, where their model YK-40 corporate jet used to land "for refueling" (although the plane was equipped with an additional fuel tank, allowing it to fly up to eight hours at a time). The plane had sleeping places for twelve passengers, a kitchen, and a meeting room. The plane had two safes: one for weapons and ammunition, and the other for money and jewelry.

In addition to guarding the company's premises and personnel, Solvaig's security department handled all payment problems. Its head was a former special airborne regiment commander, Colonel Vladimir Shkolnikov, who began his army career in 1973 at the Ryazansky Military College of Airborne Military Commandos. In this school, in addition to the required subjects, he paid special attention to learning English and boxing. Each day, he would learn a few new English words, using the tape recorders in the language lab. In his senior year, he began to study Spanish. And when he wasn't studying English or Spanish textbooks, he'd spend his free time pumping iron in the gym.

After graduating with honors, Shkolnikov was assigned to the newly formed Special Operation Forces division because of his knowledge of foreign languages and his outstanding athletic skills. In Then in December 1979, as part of a forty-three-member team called Alpha, Shkolnikov participated in the capture of Amin's palace in Kabul, the capital of Afghanistan. For this operation, he was awarded the Order of the Red Star and was promoted to the rank of captain. After serving in Afghanistan for one-and-a-half years,

Captain Shkolnikov was ordered to Nicaragua where he was promoted to major and awarded a second Order of the Red Star.

Later, after graduating from the military academy, Colonel Shkolnikov was named commander of the airborne regiment. In August 1991, he volunteered to protect the Russian White House, but by the end of 1992, after disagreeing with his superiors over their handling of the Chechen conflict, he submitted his resignation and was transferred to the reserve. At that point, one of his former military comrades recommended him to Solvaig.

It turned out that Fedorov needed someone who was young, strong, and capable of making quick decisions under pressure, and Shkolnikov was the perfect candidate. When Solvaig needed payments from clients, Colonel Shkolnikov never allowed matters to get to the point where he had to use force. In fact, Colonel Shkolnikov could solve all problems peacefully, without inflicting violence and humiliation.

Shkolnikov, however, had a vulnerable spot. As was true of many former Russian military officers, he had no place to call home besides a one-bedroom apartment rented for him by Solvaig—or, to be exact, by Fedorov. Conveniently located near the metro station Profsouznaya, it satisfied his bachelor's needs. Shkolnikov also had at his disposal a new V-8 BMW 540.

In Solvaig, Lydia Selina was not received as delightfully as she had been at Agroprom. From the moment she entered Fedorov's reception room, she felt sparks of jealousy radiating from Fedorov's personal secretary, Mrs. Tamara Boykova, who wagging tongues said sometimes stayed late in her boss's office. What the tongues did not say, however, was that after such sessions, Mr. Fedorov would take a shower and go to sleep in an adjoining private recreation room. Nor did they say that Tamara, after her shower, did not sleep, but had a cup of coffee and a cigarette, while pondering the meaning of life.

But Tamara was suspicious not only because she disliked such a beautiful woman working on her turf, but also because she thought she saw through to Lydia's real intentions. Still, she let this stranger into Fedorov's office. After all, her papers had been in order, and all that remained to do, it seemed, was to arrange the details of the barter, which was routine at Solvaig.

Selina made a better impression on Shkolnikov than she had on Tamara. At thirty-nine, he was not married, but only because he had not had time to start a family. Still, he could not take his eyes off of beautiful women, and was planning, when he had enough money, to marry one of them.

It's true that Shkolnikov could not be considered handsome, but he had a strong, well-formed body and a great posture, and he was always cleanly shaved and neatly dressed. Despite his minimally acceptable height of six foot in the air commandos, he had won several heavyweight-boxing championships in the districts he had served. He ran no less than five kilometers every day, and, out of habit, continued to lift weights. He was highly structured and disciplined, having remained very much the military man.

Shkolnikov, who served Fedorov loyally and reliably the way he had once served the motherland, was the only person on this trip to whom Lydia had offered her hand after introducing herself. He, not possessing any training etiquette, gobbled up her small girl's hand in his big paw, squeezing and holding it until her face reddened in a very becoming blush. She immediately felt that she could be confident and peaceful with him. She was not only impressed by the strength of his character, mind, and body, but also convinced that, were it ever necessary, she would be able to count on his support.

8

IT WAS ALMOST MIDDAY when Selina left Agroprom. After spending the whole morning there, disappointed by Kravchuk's actions, she left the Committee of State Standards building and headed for Oktyabersky Square. In response to her driver's questions about why she wanted to walk when she had the use of a car, Lydia answered that walking was good for her health, and that she'd be back in three hours. If she didn't return, she added, it meant that she had met her girlfriend, in which case the driver was to meet her at the Warsaw Hotel at nine p.m. and drive her to Hotel Mir.

Selena's low-heeled shoes made walking much more comfortable without spoiling the effect of her magnificent legs. On the contrary, Lydia looked even more feminine and lovely in them. The weather was perfect, and after a thirty-minute stroll, during which she kept an eye out for anyone who might be following her (at one point, she stopped at a newspaper stand, bought a soda, went into the Hotel Warsaw, and left again, without noticing anything suspicious), she reached Solvaig.

Lydia was accepted at Solvaig politely but with reserve. She figured that Fedorov's secretary had probably talked to her boss by then, in an effort to relieve her anxiety, but then that mattered little; deep in her heart, it was Fedorov whom she did not trust. In any case, as soon as Lydia entered the reception room, Tamara immediately let her boss know that Ms. Selina had arrived.

As usual, being occupied with his daily routine, Fedorov had not yet had the time to run Selina's proposal past his experts. So, when she entered his office, the first thing he asked was whether she would like to have some lunch. Refusing to take her no for an answer, he called in his chief of security, Mr. Shkolnikov, and asked him to take Lydia to the Metropol, one of the most famous restaurants in Moscow. Fedorov promised to give Lydia a final answer upon her return.

Normally, Fedorov would have invited Selina to lunch at Solvaig. Solvaig's chef, who served the company's management and visitors, went to the farmers' market daily and bought the freshest produce to prepare home-cooked meals. The kitchen, adjacent to a large dining room, had been, during the recent renovation, equipped with the most modern European appliances. Today, however, Fedorov needed time to discuss Selina's proposal with his experts — and naturally, without her being present.

So that's how it happened that Lydia and Mr. Shkolnikov went to lunch at restaurant Metropol[14]. Vladimir was pleased to become further acquainted with this charming lady, and Lydia, who had taken notice of this strong, confident man upon their first meeting, was in good spirits. Passing a flower shop, Vladimir stopped and bought Lydia an elegant bouquet of fresh, long-stemmed roses that were subtly colored and filled the car with an intoxicating fragrance.

When Lydia saw Shkolnikov with the bouquet, she asked him sarcastically, "Was purchase of the roses were included on the list of your daily assignments?" A bit hurt, Shkolnikov responded, "I bought the roses on my own initiative. I do only so whenever I am feeling attraction to someone." On that Selina asked with a gentler, teasing tone, "Should I regard this compliment as a declaration of your true love?" Shkolnikov answered, looking straight in her eyes, "If you are thinking such a thing would be appropriate to do, then I have done so with all my heart and I would be delighted to seal it with a kiss." Slightly confused, Lydia said, "I am personally not against a kiss … if it wouldn't go any further." Shkolnikov suddenly felt embarrassed and then surprised that, for someone whose life had trained him not to express his feelings so easily, he was able to kiss her lightly on the cheek. Lydia appreciated this gallant gesture, realizing she was beginning to like her lunch companion more and more.

After salad and shish kebabs at Metropol, they returned to Solvaig and headed straight for Fedorov's office, where Mr. Fedorov offered them seats around a coffee table, took out a documents folder, and announced that Solvaig had made a decision not only to accept Ms. Selina's offer but to start work on it as soon as possible. Explaining in more detail, Fedorov said that Solvaig was prepared to pay all charges connected with the purchase and resale of the crude oil, and to take care of any payments to the suppliers and intermediate partners for the purchase and delivery of foodstuff and other consumer goods.

Then, after a brief pause, Fedorov asked Selina how she saw her role in the project. Lydia kept silent for a few seconds, more out of courtesy than out

14   It is one of the oldest and best Moscow restaurants.

of a need to think about the answer, since she had long ago decided what she was going to say.

"Although intermediaries usually charge three percent of the transaction," she said finally, "if Solvaig is ready to consider a down payment, then I am ready to take two percent and a down payment of one hundred thousand dollars. I would take the remaining nine hundred thousand when the contract was complete."

Asked why she wanted to structure the deal that way, Lydia explained that she was obliged to share her take with those in Tyumen who had organized the project. She answered that she needed fifty thousand to pay her confederates, and another fifty thousand to purchase a two-bedroom apartment in Moscow, which she would then have to renovate and furnish. And that was the truth.

Shkolnikov was impressed by the speed of Lydia's response, as well as her clear, decisive answers. And after her most recent comment, he felt certain that this young but obviously savvy woman wanted as part of her plan to stabilize and improve her position in life by settling down and starting a family. He, even though ten years her senior, had been dreaming about the same, and therefore, decided to do everything he could to win Lydia's respect and friendship — with the ultimate goal of marriage.

Fedorov thought her purchase of an apartment in Moscow would, at least symbolically, tie Selina to Solvaig. And quite possibly, he could replace Tamara with Lydia, who was younger and much better looking.

Thus, inside Solvaig a situation was being played out in which each participant believed he — or she, as the case was, was pulling the wool over the others' eyes. But just as much as Lydia and Vladimir were both free, available, and attracted to each other, Fedorov and Tamara were both married and cheating on their spouses; therefore, the interests of each couple were antithetical.

Arkady pressed the call button and asked Tamara to direct the company's chief accountant to come in. The chief accountant was an elderly woman who possessed immense professional experience and worked on the company's most complex accounts. The six accountants under her could barely keep up with all of the payroll calculations, postings, reports, audits, and payments, not to mention the all-important tax-inspection requirements.

While it may sound impossible, in the mid-1990s, the combined federal and local taxes that businesspeople had to pay exceeded 100 percent of their revenues.[15] As a result, weekly reports had to be made to regional tax inspectors, and only the chief accountant could represent the firm at the

---

15   From 1992 to 1999 in Russia, the total amount of business taxes was 102 percent of revenue (not profit). This sounds unbelievable, but it is fact. Because of that, nobody paid taxes!

inspection — an awesome and exhausting task. The chief accountant's post may have been rather low—paid, but it also enjoyed a level of responsibility equal to that of the head of the company. Therefore, the influence of the chief accountant on the company's activities was essential. Which is why now, in the presence of his two guests, Arkady Fedorov, asked whether his chief accountant could find a hundred thousand dollars for Ms. Selina.

"Sure," the answer came. "If it's necessary, we will find it."

Fedorov kept silent, doing mental calculations. Then after a moment, he asked the chief accountant to prepare the necessary documents to compensate Ms. Selina for her services.

When the chief accountant left, he called Tamara and asked, "Where is Kasimirich?"

When Tamara answered that he was scheduled to return from Yakutia[16] in two days, Fedorov asked Lydia whether she could come back in three to review the documents; if she approved them, he said, he would finalize the contract. And so they agreed to meet on May 30, at ten a.m.

Lydia and Vladimir Shkolnikov left Fedorov's office together. Vladimir touched Lydia's hand and told her, "If you are planning to go somewhere, I would be more than happy to take you there." She replied, "Yes, I would appreciate that. You can take me to the nearest metro station." In the car, he asked Lydia, "Do you have any plans for the evening yet?" The young woman looked at Vladimir, and replied to his question with one of her own. "What might your offer be?"

Realizing it was best to ask her straight out what he had on his mind, Vladimir told Lydia, "I found you very pleasant, and I would like you to go out with me. By spending time together, we could become better acquainted." Pleased by his straight shooting, Lydia agreed, and they decided to meet at five thirty that evening at the place he was to drop her off.

Having reached the Octyaberskaya metro station, Shkolnikov parked, opened the door for her, and extended his hand. She took it, and shook with a businesslike squeeze. Thus, a kind of relationship was established that went beyond what was normal between a company's consultant and its chief of security.

At 5:25 p.m., Vladimir was back at the metro, and five minutes later Lydia appeared, precisely on time. Vladimir opened the passenger door and helped her into the car. Once behind the wheel, he asked her how much time she had. Lydia answered that her driver was to pick her up at nine.

Vladimir suggested they go to the viewing platform on the hills near

---

16   A province in central Siberia and the coldest region of the world, except for the South Pole. One winter, the town of Oimyakon recorded a record low -69° C.

Moscow University, and then have dinner. Lydia liked the plan, and so they took off, talking about the usual things of interest on a first date, then gradually discussing matters of a more personal nature. Neither Lydia nor Vladimir hid the fact that they were interested in the other. And it was clear that, besides their mutual interest, they were drawn to each other by the stage in life they had both reached, and their corresponding hopes for the future.

The weather that summer evening was perfect. The down from the poplars had not started to fly. The trees were green. The only things that spoiled the view were the peddlers' booths, set up in the most impossible places, accompanied by dirty streets, drunkards, homeless people, and just in-and-out tramps, none of which made Moscow more beautiful. And that wasn't to mention the children, maybe ten years old and older, rushing up to the cars driving by, offering to wash the windows with their dirty water.

There were only a few people on the viewing platform. Moscow's famous ice cream had been sold out. A photographer with a Polaroid camera offered to take a picture as a souvenir. From one of the old women selling flowers, Vladimir bought Lydia a lilac branch. When he offered it to her, he touched her hand, and she enjoyed the feeling. Soon, they were strolling the long platform, hand in hand.

After the hills, they went to an area near the metro station, not far from where Vladimir lived, to a small authentic Georgian restaurant he knew. They ordered cheese, vegetables, an assorted meat platter, and a bottle of Kinzmarauly,[17] a famous Georgian red wine. It was obvious to both that they felt comfortable with each other, and to tell the truth, they did not want to part. For the first date, it was a very good start.

Driving Lydia back to Hotel Warsaw, Vladimir, surprising himself, impulsively asked Lydia to go with him to a birthday party in honor of his former division commander. It was a tradition for all officers to go, with or without their wives, but certainly without an invitation. This year, he told her, many veterans of the war in Afghanistan would also be there, at this "family" celebration.

Lydia asked Vladimir whether it would be proper to go after just one date, but then she quickly decided that it would be much better than sitting alone in her hotel, especially since it would mean spending the evening with a man to whom she was increasingly becoming attracted. At the same time, it would be a chance to get to know his friends. So, they decided to meet the next evening at five, at the entrance to the Hotel of the Academy of Sciences, building number three, on Leninsky Prospect.

She did have one condition: that Vladimir drink as little as possible, so she wouldn't have to worry about him driving. He promised her that in order

17 Joseph Stalin's favorite wine.

not to offend their host, he would drink one glass of wine, but that he would drink one glass only. Leaving the car, Lydia touched Vladimir's cheek with her hand, and kissed him on the other cheek, signs of gratitude for their friendship and the pleasant evening. She left and, after a few steps, looked back. Seeing Vladimir watching her, she waved to him, and then turned the corner.

Lydia passed her driver, who was waiting for her near the hotel, walked into the hotel lobby, and, after making sure that Vladimir had not followed her, came out again. She double-checked that he was not still watching, and then walked back to her car. The driver greeted her and asked whether she needed his help. Receiving a negative answer, he started the engine, and they drove to the Mir Hotel.

9

Mr. Fedorov arrived in his office at eight, which was earlier than usual. He had spent almost the entire night on the phone, dealing with a situation in Tanzania. Bank accounts there were empty. A lot of money had been wasted. Things were so bad that he couldn't even think about any return on the investments they had made. Heavy equipment stood idle and rusted, and the results of geological exploration and analysis gave no hope that the reports, which had attracted lots of investors in the beginning, would yield positive results. They were lucky that the investors were mostly Canadians. If they had been Russians, they would already have been at each other's throats.

Arkady Fedorov sat silently in the armchair, deep in thought about Selina's proposal to sell crude oil; this was not typically something that Solvaig got involved with. And though he had enough money to pursue the project, he was not comfortable with the level of risk. To move five hundred thousand tons of crude oil by rail, he would have to tie up more than eighty-five hundred railroad tankers, each with a capacity of sixty tons. And at current international prices, payments for the crude oil would exceed fifty million dollars.

He wondered how this young woman had made connections at such a high level. There had to be powerful people behind her to make it work. But if that were the case, then why didn't they go directly to the government? It was a question he had to have the answer to, and not from Ms. Selina, but from a more reliable source. In fact, he had such a person at his disposal.

He heard someone moving around the reception room, which meant Tamara had arrived. He pressed the call button. "Toma, please come in."

Tamara flitted into her boss's office, closing the outer door tightly and locking the inner door with a key. "Why didn't you let me know, Arkady, that you would be coming in early?" she said, coquettishly swinging her hips and putting on an adorable pout. "Are those black Tanzanian girls better than me?" Then without waiting for an answer, and hardly expecting one, Tamara approached her boss, and quickly began undressing both him and herself simultaneously.

"Let's see how you missed your little Toma," she continued as she pulled Arkady into his private recreational room, chattering all the while. In about ten minutes, she obtained proof that even had Arkady not missed her, he had at least not forgotten how to be with her.

Exhausted, he fell asleep on the open sofa bed. Tamara moved silently through the room, trying to not wake him. She picked up the scattered clothes, and then having dressed and straightened her hair, she carefully folded his things and laid them on the back of a chair. Looking around the room to make sure all was in order, she then left his office quietly, tightly closing the second door and locking the outer door.

After a fifteen-minute power nap, Fedorov awoke, continuing to lie a minute to clear his head, and then went to the shower. There, under the jet of water, he remembered that he had needed to ask Tamara to find Mr. Peter Veresayev as soon as possible, but had been distracted by her charms. "What a wench," he thought. "Where does she get the strength to do it all?"

Peter Kazemirovich Veresayev, still tall and straight at sixty-seven, and still fond of drinking, worked as the chief geologist for Tanzanian Diamonds International, Ltd. Registered in Cyprus in 1990, however, TDI, unlike Solvaig, generated no income. Though Veresayev did not feel that the absence of diamonds was his fault, he still felt responsible for what was going on at the company. As a result, Veresayev never objected to tackling Mr. Fedorov's assignments, even if they did not fit into his job description.

"Kazemirich," as Mr. Fedorov called him, had repeatedly told his boss that it wasn't a good idea to pursue the industrial development of diamonds in Tanzania, but his boss continued to bring in Canadians and even clearly unsavory investors. After describing glowing prospects, Fedorov showed the investors unpolished samples of raw diamonds, which he said had been found "by chance," and put them side by side with cut and polished diamonds from South Africa and Yakutia. The visitors would be swept off their feet, and leave with visions of megaprofits dancing in their heads.

Eventually, dredges, lorries, conveyors, crushing equipment, and sorting machines of various types were shipped to Tanzania. Since their arrival, however, they had been left outside, unused and unattended, to face the elements. Only when they started to rust did pre-manufactured modules for erecting the new industrial facilities begin arriving.

Fedorov's son Ivan, his wife Valentine, and his little daughter spent much of their time in Tanzania. Still, Ivan's relationship with his wife was not in good shape. They constantly quarreled in public, Ivan drank, and Valentine - either out of boredom or a desire to humiliate her husband - slept openly with the security guards. As a result, her father-in-law took his granddaughter away from her parents, put the little one in the care of her grandmother, and sent Valentine back to the industrial city of Tula from where she had come.

Though their difference in years was significant, Ivan Fedorov and Veresayev were both alumni of Moscow Geological Survey University, and had become fast friends.

After graduation, Veresayev was assigned to the Tien-Shan Mountains in Central Asia, where he had previously lived for fifteen years in the settlement of Majli-Saj. His geological survey work, during which he found mercury, uranium, asbestos, and other nasty chemical resources, gave him useful experience and helped him develop an intuitive sense of both geology and people.

Later, Veresayev had moved to Yakutia to supervise a geological services team, and met Ivan, who had been assigned there after graduation. At that time, Veresayev was the senior manager, but now, having retired, he continued working for Fedorov Jr.

Fedorov Sr.'s plan was to assign "Kazemirich" to take command of the transport and delivery of the crude oil, from supervising the work at the well to loading the crude in the railroad tankers. This work would include handling contracts, identifying and getting to know (and bribe) key people, and tracking the progress of the tankers. But his most important task would be to answer two questions: who was standing behind Ms. Selina, and how could these people be contacted directly without her knowledge?

For this latter purpose, "Kazemirich" was to get in touch with former classmates, colleagues, and acquaintances, who, as a conglomerate, would know just about everybody and be able to size up the situation rather quickly.

Mr. Fedorov had already formulated a mental plan of action: First, they were not to rush into the business with Lydia, and second, they were to keep her under constant surveillance so that when "Kazemirich" reported his findings, Fedorov could quickly finalize a decision.

Mr. Fedorov pressed the call button. "Toma, I need you to find 'Kazemirich.' It's urgent."

"He's in Cyprus."

"When will he be back?"

"He will be flying directly to Yakutia, and then back to Moscow. He will be back …" he could hear her thumbing through her calendar, "no later than Sunday, June 6."

"Okay, let's wait until Sunday," he said, shaking his head, and then he chewed his lower lip. "And where is Ivan?"

"He'll be back in a few minutes. He took a drive somewhere." Tamara answered.

All of Solvaig knew that Tamara was serving both Fedorovs; father and son. Both father and son knew it, too, but neither took offense. After all, they were relatives. And Tamara would not be so easily used up; there was plenty of her for the both of them.

—————— 10 ——————

AFTER WAKING, LYDIA LAY in bed a few minutes longer than usual. Her clock read 6:25 a.m. As she reflected on the previous evening with Vladimir, she was reminded her of her upcoming date with him, that very evening. She sprang out of bed, put on her sports suit and gym shoes, and went outside. Reaching the street, she inhaled a few times, invigorated by the fresh air of the Moscow morning, and began running along the embankment of the Moscow River. She circled the Russian White House for about twenty minutes before returning to her hotel room.

She unwound her braid and enjoyed the pleasure of a quick shower. Lydia's skin was clean, light tan, gentle, and smooth; it was the skin of a young, healthy woman. She thoroughly soaped herself in the shower, paused when she reached her breasts, noting with satisfaction their firm, youthful shape. Then while washing her legs, she noted that a manicure and pedicure would be in order for that night.

11

Russia
1937–86

LYDIA SELINA CAME FROM the "new" industrial city of Togliatti. She lived with her mother and grandmother in a nearby settlement called VSO-5 (Army Settlement No. 5).

Lydia's father Ostap Selin, served as a noncombatant in an army unit whose responsibility was to guard prisoners. Though he wasn't directly responsible for guarding prisoners, his terrible childhood—born in a labor camp, raised in an orphanage, and then always surrounded by either prisoners or guards - made him feel perpetually angry and resentful, as if he himself were an inmate.

As a result, Lydia's father was an alcoholic monster. He died drunk in 1971, only thirty years old, when Lydia was eleven. He'd been on his way home from work one winter evening when he fell and froze to death in the street, only a hundred feet from the barrack in which they lived. After his death, however, peace came to their household. Nobody got drunk anymore, and nobody held a belt and threatened her mother anymore.

Lydia's mother Fatima worked as a nurse in the medical unit of the prison in which Lydia's father was a guard, which is where they had met. She was a kind-hearted woman, but had been broken by life. She was so busy that she had almost no time for her daughter. After her husband's death, although she was only twenty-seven, Lydia's mother never remarried; she continued to live with her mother-in-law and daughter in the same barrack. By contrast, Lydia's grandmother, Elizabeth Zeldina, or Grandma Liz, adored her granddaughter. She taught little Lyd how to read, write, and do arithmetic, and often interceded for Lydia with her parents, covering up or making light of her childish tricks and pranks.

Elizabeth had grown up in the city of Kalinin, where, in 1937, her parents had been arrested and sentenced to twenty-five years in Stalin's labor camps. Meanwhile, fourteen-year-old Elizabeth was sent to a camp for "children of the people's enemies" in the city of Izhevsk. She became friends with another fourteen year old; a poor girl named Bella Kozitsky, and soon fell in love with Bella's older brother, Joseph Kozitsky, whose nickname was Osya. He, too, fell in love with Elizabeth, with all his heart and soul, and they pledged that when they were released from camp, they would marry.

When Osya finished high school, he was released from camp and entered a trade college, where he could get professional training in the oil industry. When the USSR-Finnish war began in 1939, however, Joseph was sent to the front. After a year of service, Joseph received five days' leave and went home in search of his Elizabeth. The children's camp allowed her two hours away with him, so the two set off for a photography studio to have their picture taken as a souvenir. But when Joseph and Elizabeth arrived at the studio, they found that they had come during a lunch break, and they had to wait in the street for an hour. As a result, Lisa returned to camp one hour late. For this tardiness, she was put in solitary confinement for three days.

Joseph, having gone right back to the front, had no idea that she'd been punished. He also had no idea that the next day, an inspector had visited the camp, and a camp chief, in misunderstanding Elizabeth's delay, described her tardiness as an attempt to run away. As a result, because she was already seventeen by this time and considered an adult, she was sentenced to twenty more years in the adult labor camp.

As if that weren't bad enough, on her way to the labor camp on Kolyma River (one of the worst in the Gulag), the seventeen-year-old beauty caught the eye of the head of the transit camp in Stavropol-on-Volga. He raped her, but kept her in the camp and did what he could for her. In the beginning, he gave her a relatively easy and clean job; she was to work in the bakery on the bread-slicing machine. But when her pregnancy became obvious, he transferred her to the accounting department in the mess hall. Then, in 1941, at eighteen, Elizabeth gave birth to a boy whom she named after her first and truest love, Joseph or, as Ukranian version of his name - Ostap.

At first, little Ostap lived with his mother in the camp, but was soon taken from her and placed in a nursing home for small kids. Later, Ostap was transferred to a camp for children, and eventually, he was placed in a foster home. Only in 1956, when Elizabeth was released from prison under amnesty, did she obtain the right to take her son home. She learned that Ostap, while in the foster home, had graduated from high school.

Just before her release from the Gulag, before receiving her first passport (prisoners then did not have the right to have even an internal passport), Elizabeth had changed her last name from Zeldina to Selina by changing the letter Z to S, and omitting the D. She entered her son's name onto her passport the same way. That's why his first name was Ostap, the paternal name Alexeevich, after the monster, who raped his mother, and his family name became Selina. Elizabeth and her son lived in the small settlement near Stavropol-on-Volga that subsequently became the large city of Togliatti.

Many years after the labor camps were gone, Lydia's grandmother continued to be a bookkeeper in the mess hall where she had previously worked. There was only one difference: the mess hall was now called Cafeteria No. 5.

Elizabeth's work, along with Lydia, were what made her poverty-stricken existence bearable. Whenever she could, she would brighten up her favorite granddaughter's life by giving her candy, or perhaps a pencil and paper on which she could draw.

Lydia did well in school. Sometimes, influenced by other kids, she became lazy, but in the matter of her studies, her grandmother was adamant. She wouldn't let Lydia go to sleep or to the neighbors' house before she had finished her homework. In fact, until her senior year in high school, Lydia had prepared all of her homework with her grandma. But in the middle of her senior year, Elizabeth became seriously ill, took to her bed, and never recovered. At the time of her death, Grandma Liz was only fifty-six.

Fourteen years had passed since then, but Lydia still missed her grandma. By then, her mother Fatima had also passed, so Lydia was completely alone. She had neither sister, brother, aunt, nor uncle. She had only one girlfriend her age, Ira Sedelnikova. Ira's mother, Svetlana Alexandrovna, had been a student at the university when she became pregnant with Ira; the father had been a classmate from Bulgaria. They loved each other, but in the USSR in those days, marriages with foreigners were forbidden. So, the boy returned to Bulgaria, and Svetlana was assigned to the city of Stavropol-on-Volga. Later in life, she married Mr. Sedelnikov, who adopted her child. But he started drinking, and eventually disappeared.

Svetlana then began working as a programmer, and was eventually promoted to chief of the computer center at the Togliatti Research Institute. She taught both her daughter and Lydia about computers and the basics of programming. Although Lydia never directly used her skills and knowledge in programming in her career, she understood what computers were about.

After Lydia's graduation from high school in 1979, the same year her grandmother died, she entered Togliatti Polytechnic University. She graduated in 1984 with a degree in mechanical engineering, and was assigned to the Engineering department of Tyumen Oil & Gas.

Lydia knew she was pretty. Therefore, in her youth, she was not in a rush to marry. She was also particular about whom she dated, and rarely went to parties because she knew that most of them ended in drunken orgies.

At twenty-seven, however, she found herself tired of feeling lonely and living on her own in dormitories. She foolishly married the local geologist, not out of love but out of boredom, although she did like the way he sang folk songs and played guitar. But after spending only three weeks with her new husband in a dormitory for newlyweds, she returned to her former room; Lydia remembered how her drunken father had abused her mother, and she did not want to suffer the same fate.

Fortunately, she had not become pregnant, though her chances of doing so had hardly been possible. After the wedding and subsequent festivities, her husband had never gotten sober; in fact, he had remained drunk until the divorce proceedings began. Afterward, he came to Lydia and asked for her forgiveness, but by then, it was far too late.

12

AFTER THE SHOWER, LYDIA dried her hair. Since it had grown to her waist, it had demanded special care. She'd been wanting to get it cut, but hadn't found the courage. Today, she decided, she would leave it unbraided. After carefully combing, she wound her hair into a ponytail, secured it with a rubber band, and put it up with a hairpin. Next she worked on her fingernails and toenails.

Finally, she chose an outfit that would be appropriate both for her afternoon at Agroprom and later, for the party with Vladimir and his military friends. She donned a black jumpsuit and a white shirt that partially revealed her shapely, high breasts and emphasized her velvety skin. Then she slipped on a pair of low heels. In this ensemble, tall and straight, with her ponytail, Lydia looked younger than her age.

She grabbed a medium-sized handbag and put in a light nightgown, a change of underwear, and a bra, along with her comb, toothpaste, hairbrush, makeup kit, scissors, and nail file. She did this, as they say, just in case. She then checked herself in a mirror, and, being satisfied, proceeded to the hotel dining room.

After a light breakfast, at about ten, she walked outside to wait for the car, in no particular hurry, and by the time she arrived at Agroprom, it was almost midday. She was pleasantly surprised to see Isaev and Theodora waiting for her.

Selina read through the contract, and all was as they had agreed, so she signed it, after which Isaev also signed on behalf of Agroprom. Then grabbing her copy with one hand, Lydia held out her other and was handed twenty thousand US dollars.

Lydia's insides jumped with joy, but careful to keep cool on the outside, she simply asked Mr. Isaev if she could make a few phone calls. Arnold told her that he was leaving for lunch and said that his office was at her disposal.

Sitting behind Isaev's desk, Lydia phoned the deputy to the general director of the Tyumen Oil & Gas Association, Mr. Joseph Klementievich Kozitsky. After reporting what had just happened, she promised to call him every day to keep him posted. Then Lydia retrieved her address book from her purse and dialed the real estate agency with which she had discussed the purchase of a two-bedroom apartment.

The Aeroflot real estate agency was located on New Arbat Street in a high-rise building where the former ministry of the coal industry was once located. This building was being rented out as office space for various businesses. The advantage for renters, compared to other premises, was that the Committee of Veterans of the Afghanistan War had rented one of the offices, which, at the time, was excellent protection against organized crime. On the second floor, the Aeroflot Bank had its offices, and the Aeroflot real estate agency was one of its subsidiaries. A Russian-British joint venture formed to exploit the real estate market newly created in post-Soviet Russia.

Aeroflot used to trade apartments, but now, they prefer to lease the office spaces in the term of forty-nine years from scientific research institutes, warehouses, and factories. These larger premises were then subdivided into small offices, and after undergoing cursory renovations, were leased out for one year at a rental price a hundred times greater than what Aeroflot paid. The apartments were used to bribe officials in other organizations, and less valuable apartments were resold on a commission basis.

Valentine, the agent, answered the phone, almost as if waiting for Lydia's call. Selina introduced herself and reminded Valentine that they had met recently in her office. Valentine remembered perfectly and told Lydia that she had something for her-an apartment on the seventh floor of a brick building located on Cherepanovs' Drive. Valentine explained that because the neighborhood had been built by the Ministry of Defense, its apartments had been upgraded with high ceilings and parquet flooring.

The owner was planning to go abroad, the agent said, and was therefore ready to sell his apartment for a reasonable amount: "twenty-five thousand greenbacks. And including the agency's fee and closing costs, the total should not come to more than thirty-five."

The apartment was in good condition, needing no repairs, and the purchase price included furniture, which, although not great, would be quite enough at first.

Lydia wrote down the address and directions that Valentine gave her, and said she was ready to leave in ten minutes. She left a note on Isaev's desk, thanking him for his kindness, and then closing his door behind her, handed his office key to Valerie. Lydia was subsequently delighted to read the memo from Valerie confirming that she had been hired by Agroprom as a consultant. The job would be effective May 1, with a monthly salary of twenty-five thousand Russian rubles.

Lydia proceeded to the accounting department to get a copy of her employment contract. While there, she was also paid her salary for the first half of May: the twelve thousand, five hundred rubles.

Pleased as a child about the previous few days, Lydia got into the waiting car and gave the address of the apartment to her driver. When they reached Building Three at Cherepanovs' Drive, Valentine was waiting at the entrance.

From the moment she entered, Lydia noticed the wonderful high ceilings and the large entry hall. Directly opposite the front door was another doorway leading to a spacious kitchen that contained a stove, a large refrigerator, modern cabinets, a large countertop, and a small breakfast table with four chairs.

The more Lydia saw, she more she liked. There were two rooms, one with two hundred and forty-eight square feet and the other with two hundred sixty. The balcony provided a panoramic view of the city, which Lydia loved in addition to the fresh, clean air—not at all like the foul air downtown. The bedroom floor was covered in oak parquet blocks, and the furniture, about which Valentine had been right in telling her, was not new, but would be enough at first: there were two beds (one in each room), a sofa, a nut-wood wall unit, a desk, and in a living room the second dining table with chairs.

Walking back through the kitchen, Lydia saw that it was equipped with all kinds of utensils, as well, including knives, forks, pots, and pans. There was even a broom. Really, it would be quite enough for the beginning. And after that, she thought, who knows what would happen? Lydia caught herself mentally asking Vladimir's advice, and smiled. She wanted him to like this apartment.

"I like what I see," Lydia told Valentine, "and I'm ready. I have twenty-five thousand cash, and can have the rest within two or three days." Valentine said she would start on the paperwork, and then asked Lydia if she had a job. Lydia answered proudly that Agroprom had just hired her, and pulled the employment contract out of her bag.

In the elevator, on the way down, Lydia asked Valentine again whether it was necessary for her to make a down payment or deposit in advance. Valentine told her that she would prepare all of the documents within the next two days, but that, even then, Lydia should only pay the seller, and then should do so directly in front of the notary public in his office. The agency would not expect to see its commission until after Lydia received the title.

"If you want to privatize the apartment by purchasing it outright from the government," Valentine added, "I can help you take care of that, as well, for an additional payment."

All of this not only suited Lydia; it seemed to put her on top of the world.

By the time she had returned to Leninsky Prospect, it was already ten minutes to five. Vladimir was probably waiting for her. She asked the driver to let her off at the last streetcar stop before Shukhov's TV Tower,[18] from which it was only a short walk to the hotel at the Academy of Sciences. She grabbed her bag, took down her driver's phone number in case she needed him that evening, and left.

Lydia blended into the crowd of other women carrying their bags with food and other stuff. Nobody even suspected that she had thousands of dollars and rubles on her, or she would have certainly been a goner.

When she reached the hotel, Vladimir was standing next to his car dressed in his colonel's full-parade uniform, which was decorated with military awards, medals, badges, and two diamond-shaped pins testifying to his graduation from the military university and academy. He was holding a bouquet of red carnations.

Lydia approached him, shyly smiling. She had not expected such a reception. When he greeted her with a sweet smile and a presentation of the flowers, she said, looking him in the eye, "Oh, you shouldn't buy so many flowers! You have probably spent too much money."

Now Vladimir was flustered. "First, it was not a lot of money. Second, I wanted you to feel special. It's not every day that I am dating such a beautiful woman."

He opened car door, then softly closed it after Lydia was sitting, holding both her bag and the flowers on her lap. She sat there, frozen, until he had put the key into the ignition. Then she stopped him by putting her hand on his.

"Let me ask you three questions," she said. She waited for his nod and then said, "First, should we call each other *Ti* or *Vi?*[19] Second, should I wear my hair in a ponytail for the party, or braid it like I did yesterday? Third, you weren't thinking of going to the party empty-handed, were you? We really should stop somewhere to buy a gift of some kind, and also maybe some flowers."

---

18 A tower built in Moscow by Russian engineer Shukhov as a radio and TV transmitter before WWII.

19 The diminutive form *Ti* is reserved for informal relationships, while *Vi* is used for formal ones.

Vladimir, who was not used to thinking about such domestic details much less discussing them with a near-stranger, no matter how beautiful, answered a bit awkwardly. As for her first question, he had the deep feeling that the diminutive *Ti* seemed appropriate, even though they hadn't participated in the prerequisite traditional ritual of toasting each other with intertwined wineglasses. Still, he couldn't bring himself to answer that one quite yet.

His answers to the other questions came easier. "I like all your hairdos," he said, "but for the party, a braid will be better. Regarding the third question," he said with a smile, "I already have everything we need in the trunk."

Lydia then looked at him coquettishly. "Please, Dyadya,[20] do not think bad about me, because I am a decent girl. But since we haven't toasted each other yet, I'd better let you kiss me now so we can call each other *Ti*." And she looked at him with mischief definitely sparking in her eyes.

Vladimir was flabbergasted, but after quickly regaining his composure, he turned to Lydia, put one hand gently on her shoulder and, with his other, turned her face to his, softly kissing her on the lips. Then feeling her immediate, warm response, he showered her face with kisses.

"Volodya, Volodya!"[21] Lydia said, laughing, but he continued until he had satisfied his impulsive desire. Then he turned on the engine and drove away.

Lydia, smiling all the while, watched him without a word. Then she turned and put the flowers on the backseat. She took a hairbrush and hairpins from her bag, put the bag on the backseat, and, unwilling to part with her flowers, she grabbed them back and lay them across her knees. She opened the mirror in the passenger's seat visor, and then letting down her hair, turned to Vladimir, addressing him with *Ti*, and asked him if he liked her this way.

He looked upon her with a long glance, and said, also using the affectionate diminutive, "I like you better this way, but the braid will be better for this occasion," and then begged, "but after the party, let your hair down. You are so beautiful when your hair falls over your shoulders!"

Lydia knew Vladimir was right. She really looked great with her hair down. Nonetheless, she acquiesced to his request and, with long-practiced movements, wove her beautiful hair into a golden braid.

While this most common of a woman's chores was going on, Vladimir couldn't help stealing glances at Lydia. It was more than exceedingly pleasant to have such a companion; he felt certain that she was his reward for the seemingly endless loneliness he had endured throughout his life.

---

20   Uncle (Russian)
21   Informal nickname for Vladimir (Russian)

With her hair finished, Lydia put the hairbrush into her bag and took out a pink lipstick, with which she lightly brushed her pouty mouth.

And when Vladimir looked at her again, he wondered at the miracle. Right before his eyes, Lydia had transformed into a stunning beauty.

In accordance with long-standing tradition, Major General Michael Petrovich Potapov extended an open invitation to his officers each year to celebrate his birthday; no RSVPs were required. The general lived in the large four-bedroom general's apartment in the so-called KGB building on Alabyan's Street. Descendent from a long line of soldiers, he took good care of the officers under his command, and though he was moderately strict, he always tried to be fair. His wife Irina was always with him, except during his years in Afghanistan, which she spent in Moscow caring for their children. She had never graduated from a university and never had a job. Irina devoted her life to her family and to the care of her husband and children. Now that their children were grown, Irina led a quiet, peaceful life, her husband's position allowing her to avoid domestic drudgery.

Vladimir drove down Leninsky Prospect and parked along Alabyan's Street, a short way from the large building that was Potapov's home. Lydia helped him retrieve a bag of food and gifts, as well as a bouquet of flowers for the general's wife, from the trunk, and they walked toward the entrance, where a few paratrooper commandos were stationed for security. One of them approached, saluted, and politely asked for their documents. Vladimir produced his passport, after which the officer found Vladimir's name on the list of visitors, but saw that it described him as a single man. Vladimir noticed this with a smile; when the list was made, of course, he had been single. The officer saluted Lydia and asked to see her passport. She opened her handbag and retrieved it for him. After checking their documents, the officer again saluted them and asked if they knew where to go. Vladimir said that he did.

In the lobby, the couple saw two more commandos holding short-barrel machine guns.

"I wonder what's happening here," Vladimir said to Lydia.

The mystery deepened when they knocked at the door, and were received by an officer in the rank of captain. He asked for their names, and then led them through a hall into a dining room, which was occupied by a group of officers in parade uniforms. Among them was the commander of the paratrooper forces of Russia, a three-star general, Pavel Ivanovich Sedykh. In a corner of the room, away from the officers and soldiers, a group of women, including the general's wives, were talking among themselves.

To Vladimir's surprise, General Potapov's full-dress uniform sported the epaulets of a lieutenant general. Vladimir soon learned that Potapov had recently been named chief of staff to General Sedykh. In precise military fashion, Vladimir saluted the three-star general and introduced himself. Then he saluted Lieutenant General Potapov, wished him a happy birthday, and congratulated him on his promotion.

After Vladimir had turned to Irina and informally introduced Lydia, Potapov approached and embraced him. Then he looked closely at Lydia and, with admiration in his voice, whispered to Vladimir, "Are such beauties now being distributed in the civilian sector? I don't remember that in our garrison we could find such pretty ladies, even with a bonfire."

Irina, who had known Vladimir since he was a second lieutenant, broke the ice by asking him to take his bag to the kitchen. Then, she took Lydia under her wing and started a quiet conversation.

Upon his return, Vladimir approached every officer he recognized, usually someone with whom he'd served in Afghanistan or elsewhere. They would heartily embrace, ask the other about his life, and engage in the usual chatter of friends who had not seen each other recently.

After mingling for some time, Vladimir noticed Lieutenant General Potapov summoning him. As Vladimir approached Potapov, who was standing with the three-star general, the lieutenant general proceeded to tell his comrade that Colonel Vladimir Shkolnikov was the officer he had been talking about. General Sedykh eyed Vladimir and then said to Potapov, "While the ladies are setting the table, can we use your office? I would like to ask the colonel a few questions."

After they had followed their commander into the office, the lieutenant general began with, "Gentlemen, there is something I do not understand. Why is Colonel Shkolnikov, who is not a mere colonel, but a seasoned officer who speaks several languages, working as the chief of security for a private company? How can such a thing be possible?"

"It's true," Vladimir answered, avoiding the generals' questioning looks. "When I handed in my note of resignation, they fired me."

"What do you mean, they fired you?" Potapov asked in a steely tone. "Why didn't you come to see me, my boy? You know, I do not hand over my sons so easily."

Vladimir lowered his head. "I didn't feel comfortable seeing you - I was embarrassed," he said quietly. "It was not fair what they did to me."

"You were offended by paratroopers?" General Potapov raised his eyebrows; obviously, he was not appeased. "You know what they say? Those who are too easily offended will wind up working for others." Then, after having reproached his "son," Potapov turned to the commander. "Comrade General, if Colonel Shkolnikov will not be reinstated, then there is no place in the army for me either."

Now it was the three-star general's turn to become indignant. "You're both too sensitive," he spluttered. "One does not feel comfortable talking to his superiors, and the other gets hysterical! Okay, tomorrow, be at my office at ten o'clock sharp. I will sort things out with both of you. Understood?" And without waiting for a reply, the commander put one hand on Potapov's shoulder and the other on the colonel's, and led them out to see the guests.

Meanwhile, Lydia was making the acquaintance of many and receiving nothing but compliments on her youthful appearance. And though she was glad to help her hostess in the kitchen, wherever she was, she tried to be close to Vladimir, and he to her. At dinner, they were seated next to each other, and throughout the evening, Vladimir took care to look after his girl by giving her special attention. There were lots of toasts, for Mother Russia, for the paratrooper commandos, for the women. But, though they consumed a lot of hard booze, nobody seemed drunk. And Vladimir kept his word to Lydia, having only one drink.

At eleven o'clock, when the visitors started leaving, Vladimir and Lydia said their good-byes. On their way out, the commandos, still on their watch, saluted Vladimir and escorted the couple to the car, opening the door for Lydia and then closing it behind her.

After starting the engine, Vladimir asked Lydia if she'd like to stop at his apartment for coffee. Knowing what her acceptance of his invitation might lead to, Lydia gave Shkolnikov a little warning. "I will go with you, but please, don't change your ways with me. Continue to be as tender and attentive to me as you have been. And please don't offend me today, or ever. I can be a very good and loyal friend whom you will always be able to rely on."

As a token of his acceptance of this serious new note in their relationship, Vladimir embraced Lydia. He went to kiss her on the cheek, but a mosquito appeared next to her ear, startling her, and when she moved, Vladimir, instead of her cheek, kissed her directly on the lips. Lydia responded in kind, after which they embraced and settled into a long, deep kiss, as if sealing the contract for their life together.

Then taking off, they drove quickly through the dark, empty streets of Moscow, going from Alabyan's Street via Sadovy Circle to the neighborhood of the Profsousnaya metro station in fifteen minutes. When they entered the lobby of Vladimir's apartment building, the heavy smell of cats struck them, but that was nothing new. All of Moscow's lobbies were like that, with smells and broken doors clapping, as they swung open and shut. Decay, stench, and dirt were everywhere.

His apartment on the third floor was a typical bachelor's pad— not dirty, but somehow devoid of warmth.

"This can be fixed," Lydia thought, as she walked to the bathroom, unwound her braid, and lightly combed her hair. Then she returned to the living room where Vladimir was, shaking her head and running her hand through her hair, letting it cascade enchantingly upon her shoulders. "Better?" she asked.

Vladimir smiled at her and took off his uniform jacket, and then he got busy in the kitchen. He set the table with two mugs, two small plates, and two wineglasses. Then he laid out a tray of sweets, a chocolate cake, an almost full bottle of Cameo cognac, and an unopened bottle of Amaretto. The teapot was boiling on the stove.

As he busied himself, he continued to think about Lydia's question, and now finished, he turned to face her. "That's it," he thought, "this woman has to be my wife." Still, he said nothing, but continued just to look at her with admiration.

Unable to stand the silence no longer, Lydia clapped her hands in glee, and broke the silence. "I insist that we continue the party!" So they sat at the little table.

She politely refused his offer of cognac, but could not resist the Amaretto. They toasted, and took tiny sips.

"Volodya," Lydia said, "tell me about yourself."

"There is not much to tell," Vladimir answered. "After high school, I went to military school and then into the service. That is my story."

"I did not mean that. Please tell me about your childhood, about your parents, your sisters and brothers. Tell me about you!" And so they stayed up talking until it was almost dawn.

"Vladimir," Lydia said suddenly, "don't you have an appointment with the general at ten?"

"No," said Vladimir. "I'm not going. Look, my life is half over and I still don't have anything to call my own, no corner to live in, no family, nothing."

"Don't worry. We will have everything," Lydia said confidently.

"So, you're ready to become my wife!" Vladimir exclaimed joyfully.

"Didn't you already ask me about this, Colonel?" Lydia whispered with mock pouting lips. Then Vladimir knelt before her and, theatrically, and with great sincerity, proposed. How this ended, it is not difficult to guess, but when they awoke at just after eight, neither of them went out to run; they simply had no energy left. Lydia fixed him a breakfast of oatmeal, which he ate with sausage and washed down with strong tea. Then Vladimir put on his military uniform and left for the commander's office.

Lydia walked around, examining Vladimir's apartment for a while. Then she resolved to get to work. Starting in the kitchen, she did a thorough cleaning, wiping counters, washing utensils, and mopping the floor. Then she washed the linens and the dirty laundry, hanging them out on a clothesline on the balcony. In the main room, she dusted and swept the floor. Then she carefully hung Vladimir's dry clothes in the wardrobe.

Finally, she bathed, dressed, and went across the road to a little farmers' market, buying cabbage, a few potatoes, and other sundry vegetables. In the store next to the market, she found fresh bread, a cut of meat, a small container of sour cream—and a payphone. Lydia called Valentine and asked whether she could show the apartment to her young man. Valentine obliged, so they agreed to meet there at six o'clock.

Back at the apartment, Lydia had just started preparing cabbage soup and cooking the meat, when Vladimir arrived, absorbed in thought. But he snapped out of it as soon as he saw the apartment in such excellent shape, and Lydia cooking dinner in the kitchen. He felt that now, she really needed him, and he knew without a doubt that he really needed her—not only as a companion, but also as the future mother of their children. The thought warmed his soul and he felt good inside, as if he understood for the first time what it meant to be human. It calmed him. He approached Lydia and spoke words of gratitude to her having appeared in his life.

"And in my life," she whispered back, "I am grateful for you, my darling."

And with that, Vladimir looked Lydia in the eye and told her that his former commander, General Potapov, had made him an offer, and that it had been approved by the commander of the Russian paratrooper forces.

However, he explained, because he was not active duty, but in the reserve, they would have to call him up through the regional military office. Only then could they give him the title of major general. Then after six months of special training, they would name him deputy chief of operations for the general staff of the paratrooper forces, and give him the duties of a lieutenant general. He had twenty-four hours to decide.

"You must accept it, Volodya," Lydia said quickly. "Take it. You are a military man. That is your destiny. Don't worry about Solvaig. They can find another chief of security."

"But the army has no housing for us. And the salary will be less than I am making at Solvaig."

"Okay, Volodya," Lydia said peremptorily and then, changing the subject, "take off your uniform. We will eat, and then we will go … somewhere, and you will see … something!"

"Where? What?" Vladimir asked.

"Okay, you got me," Lydia answered, mischievously and mysteriously. She left the room for a moment, returned with the bundle of money, and told him about the apartment. Vladimir looked admiringly at Lydia. Here was the woman he had always dreamed of. Then he told her that, in addition to her money, he could add twelve thousand dollars, which he had saved over the past few years.

After Vladimir changed, they ate quickly and rushed off to meet Valentine at the apartment. And after having seen the place— something that neither of them would have even dreamed about until the day before—Vladimir decided he would accept the commander's offer to rejoin the military. Now, he would have it all—a job in which he belonged, a beautiful woman and girlfriend in Lydia, an apartment that they could buy together—and still have enough money left for a car. They asked Valentine to write up the title as soon as possible.

If Vladimir had been on aimless autopilot, he now felt a surge of strength and energy. He felt as he had after military school, like a young wolf ready to fight passionately to, first, establish and then, second, care for his own wolf pack. This time, though, Lydia was the heart and soul of the pack, and he was ready to do whatever it took, even if that meant cutting someone's throat, to be close to this wonderful, enchanting woman. His woman.

On the way back to Vladimir's, the couple decided to keep their relationship secret from Solvaig's employees as a precautionary measure. They also agreed that Vladimir would, after returning from the commander's office tomorrow, submit their marriage application to the recording office. That way, the title to the apartment would be vested in the name "the Shkolnikovs." Although they had come to know each other very quickly, they both trusted their hearts.

At home that evening, they made their bed on the floor, and when they lay down, Lydia shyly whispered to Vladimir, "Volodinka. I want a baby from you." Then she opened herself to him, devouring him totally, and giving body and soul without reserve. Vladimir received her gift with gratitude, conscious of the implied responsibility, not only to Lydia, but also to their future children and to the children of their children.

Next day, they left to fly to Tyumen, where Lydia wanted Vladimir to meet an old friend, practically a member of her family, whom she called Grandpa. Grandpa met them at the Tyumen Airport and took them back to his apartment, where they all sat at a table that Grandpa had festively decorated and chatted the hours away. It was after midnight when the old man became tired enough to go to bed. Lydia and Vladimir cleaned everything, washed the dishes, and discussed the events of the past few days while making plans for their future.

It was clear that Lyd's Grandpa and Vladimir liked each other. The old man even became a little sad that, after their departure, he would be alone again. But the new couple agreed that, as soon as possible, they would buy an apartment in Moscow for Grandpa, too.

Before they boarded their flight, Grandpa made Lydia promise to call him every day at nine p.m., Tyumen time. Lydia promised, and with that, they parted.

Lydia and Vladimir returned to Moscow glowing with happiness.

13

DURING THE TIME WHEN Khruschev's economic reforms led to the merging of many smaller enterprises, certain oil-refining factory became part of the Tyumen Oil & Gas Association, and with it, an employee named Joseph Klimentievich Kozitsky. Several years later, in 1964, when the manager of the association's commerce department retired, Kozitsky took over his post.

After some time, Kozitsky was again promoted, this time to chief deputy of the general director. The general director depended on Joseph for all serious decision-making. Due to the influence of Mr. Kozitsky on the association's internal policies, and considering the plans he approved were not only always successful but also carried out on time, leading to exceptional results, the deputy general was widely respected. In fact, this was why, in the succeeding twenty-six years, Tyumen Oil & Gas gained a reputation for invariably fulfilling their promises, and always providing employees with due bonuses.

Joseph, however, was so self-effacing that his photo was never displayed on the board of honor in the entryway to the association's main office building, and very few people had ever seen him face-to-face.

Joseph Kozitsky's parents had moved to Petrograd[22] from the Ukraine right after the Bolshevik Revolution. In Petrograd, Kozitsky's father received

---

22   After the Bolshevik Revolution, the city of Saint Petersburg was renamed Petrograd. Later, after Lenin's death, the city was named Leningrad. Then, after the disintegration of the USSR, the original name, Saint Petersburg, was restored.

an economics education and worked as, first, the senior and then the chief economist at a Baltic shipyard.[23]

In 1922, his son was born, whom, in honor of Comrade Stalin, he named Joseph.[24] But in 1934, when Joseph (or Osya, as his mommy and daddy called him) was only fourteen, his father was arrested in connection with the Promparty case,[25] declared an enemy of the people, and summarily executed. Joseph's mother was arrested the day after, and nobody ever saw her again.

Osya and his younger sister Bella were sent to a "re-education camp," in the city of Izhevsk, which had been designed for such children of enemies of the people. Here, among the children of former party and financial leaders, actors, Red Army commanders, and other so-called enemies, Osya and Bella spent four years. Osya made friends with many of those children who, later in their lives, would, like their parents, become prominent national figures, regardless of the hardship they had been forced to endure as teenagers.

Among his friends was a girl who had arrived in a new group of children in the middle of 1937. Elizabeth Zeldina was his sister Bella's age—fourteen—with large gray eyes. Not only were he and Bella friends with Elizabeth; Osya was also in love with her. He had fallen for her the moment they met, though he was careful not to show it. Then, in the spring of 1938, just before graduation, he found himself alone with her, and he could not resist embracing and then sweetly kissing her. At once, Joseph regretted his impulsive action, but Lisa, crying, suddenly opened her heart to him, saying that for a long time she had been in love with him too.

Their happiness was short-lived, however, since—though they occasionally enjoyed brief, secret meetings—even friendship between boys and girls was strictly forbidden. Eventually, they joined a theatrical club together, but both had so little talent, they were soon asked to leave. Then final exams made meeting nearly impossible, unless it was done in public. Despite everything, Joseph and Lisa continued to love each other, and pledged that, when they were grown and had finally been released from camp, they would marry and live a long, happy life together.

Upon graduation from the camp's high school in 1938, Osya was accepted by the city of Ufa's[26] Technical College of Petroleum. Joseph's studies took two years, during which he sent Lisa the one letter per month that she was allowed to receive; likewise, she sent him the one letter per month that she was allowed to send.

---

23   One of the largest Russian industrial factories.

24   In those days, it was customary to name children in honor of the country as well as the Communist party leaders.

25   A major political case, after which Stalin took over as dictator.

26   A large city in the Ural region.

When Joseph graduated, he was called into the army, and in 1939, he was sent to the Russian-Finnish war[27] with an armored tank brigade. Soon promoted to lieutenant, he served as a deputy commander whose platoon was responsible for maintaining tanks and supplying crews with ammunition, fuel, and lubricants. Then in 1940, Joseph received three days of leave plus six days' travel time. Naturally, he used it to go see Lisa and Bella—the only people in the world to whom he was close.

It took Joseph almost four days to travel from Karelia to Izhevsk, which meant that he arrived on the morning of the fourth day of his leave, and so would have to start his return to the front that very day. If he were even a little late getting back, he might be considered a deserter and threatened with a court-martial. And during those days, that could easily mean being convicted and sentenced to the firing squad.

Since Joseph was a frontline Red Army officer, the camp authorities had been willing to schedule an appointment for him inside the camp, with Lisa and Bella. Joseph's fondest wish was to have a photograph taken of him and Lisa, so that each would have something by which to remember the other.

The camp prohibited both girls to leave the camp at once, so Bella insisted her best friend go. Since Lisa had recently celebrated (if you could call it that in a camp environment) her seventeenth birthday, the outing would be Bella's gift. Lisa was granted two hours away.

The photography studio was closed for lunch when Joseph and Lisa arrived, however, so the lovebirds returned to camp one hour late. After escorting Lisa back, Joseph had to rush off to catch his train on time, and did not have the chance to say good-bye to his sister. Joseph also did not have the chance to stay and see that Lisa was put into a special cell for three days as punishment, and that during her confinement she was sentenced to another twenty years in the labor camps.

As the convicted prisoner waited for her assignment to the next camp, the photo of her and Joseph arrived in the mail, and it was the only possession that Lisa took with her when she left.

At about the same time, somewhere near the front line, Joseph received an identical photo. He didn't find out until later (thanks to a letter from Bella) what had happened to Lisa, but by then, what he could do? He wrote, searched, and asked, but it seemed useless. Lisa was gone.

Joseph spent the remainder of the Great Patriotic War, as World War II was called in Russia, commanding a platoon on the second line of defense. And after the war ended, he arrived in Poland with the new rank of captain. He was decorated with several orders and medals, although he hadn't really done anything heroic, except for the time in Belarus, at the beginning of

27 The 1939–1940 war between the USSR and Finland over a border dispute.

the war, when his brigade was surrounded. They'd had to break out of the encircling German forces with terrible fighting, and suffered heavy losses. Joseph was lucky that despite his long service at various fronts, he not only survived, but also did so without injury.

After demobilization in 1946, he found his sister Bella, who had been released from labor camp and was working at a factory in Izhevsk. They hoped to settle down in Leningrad where they'd lived with their parents, but when they got there, they learned that strangers had occupied their family's apartment. So their next stop was the city of Kuibyshev.[28]

Wherever they went, Joseph and Bella continued to search for Lisa Zeldina, though it was futile. It was obvious that Lisa was gone forever. Joseph often looked at the old photo, thinking that if it had not been, his Lisa would not have suffered. Yet he understood that it was not the photo that had caused their misfortune; the Soviet regime was the reason for all their problems.

Then one day, at the railroad station, Joseph, by coincidence, bumped into a former college classmate, who told him that the city of Tyumen[29] had jobs available for trained oil workers. So, Joseph and Bella took off for the city, where Joseph—with his training, intelligence, and resourcefulness, along with his intuitive ability for building and maintaining productive relationships among the government, the oil workers, and the industrial manufacturers—not only landed himself a job at an oil refinery, but also, soon after, a promotion.

Of average height and strong build, Joseph wasn't classically handsome, but he was attractive. And being always well-dressed, smoothly shaved, and generally tidy, he was popular with the local women. While in Kazan[30] in 1956, he became acquainted with a fellow student, a Tatar, and subsequently took great interest in his younger sister, whose beautiful Tatar name was Igul. They soon married and spent their honeymoon in a boarding house on Lake Baikal.[31] When they returned to Tyumen, Igul got a job in the planning department at the factory where Joseph worked, and the newlyweds lived in a factory barrack until the company granted them a three-room apartment. The young couple lived amicably and happily, but was not blessed with children. Igul was examined for her barren condition, but the prescribed treatment did not help her.

---

28 A large industrial city in the Mid-Volga River region, formerly known as Samara. After the death of one of Stalin's flunky's, Valerian Kuibishev, Samara was renamed Kuibishev. Later, the name Samara was restored.

29 The Siberian city that is considered the capital of the Russian oil industry.

30 A large industrial city in the Mid-Volga River region, and the capital of the Tartar Republic (part of the Russian Federation.)

31 A stunning Siberian lake that is also the largest body of fresh water on Earth.

Joseph and Igul lived peacefully and happily together for thirty years until, in 1986, Igul was diagnosed with cancer and, soon after, died at the age of fifty-six; Joseph was then sixty-four. Shortly after, Joseph's sister Bella died.

Now, less than two years after the deaths of his wife and sister, in the winter of 1988, Joseph and a beautiful young woman from his company, Lydia Selina, occupied the same compartment on the express train from Tyumen to Moscow.

———— 14 ————

LYDIA WAS ON A routine business trip to the USSR Ministry of State Supply's logistics and planning committee, after which she would visit a factory in Riga[32] to attempt to expedite its delivery of equipment to Tyumen Oil & Gas. Joseph Kozitsky was on his way to meet officials at the USSR Ministry of Oil and Gas.

Despite the fact that they worked for the same corporation, Joseph and Lydia did not know each other. Lydia had seen the deputy once or twice among the upper management, during meetings or holiday celebrations, but he had never visited the engineering offices where she worked. Now, having spent two days in the same compartment, they had the chance to learn much about each other, and became fast friends. So upon their arrival in Moscow, Joseph and Lydia exchanged numbers and agreed to meet again when they were back in Tyumen.

Upon her return home, Lydia learned that the deputy had called and asked to visit her. Lydia had not forgotten about this old man, to whom she'd been able to pour out her heart. And as for Joseph, having experienced life in all its many dimensions, and being skilled at understanding people, saw in this badly dressed young woman a smart, kind-hearted, sympathetic person overwhelmed by life. He also saw something in her appearance that he could not ignore.

Lydia did not go to see Joseph right away. Instead, she waited several days, so that she could pull herself together after what had been a very tiring business trip. On Sunday, the day before she was to return to work, she went

---

32   This city is the capital of Latvia. It used to be one of republics of the USSR. Now, Latvia is an independent country and it is an EU member.

to a sauna during the day and took a bath in the evening, which helped her feel much more like herself. On Monday morning, she put on her best clothes and some light makeup, and, at nine thirty, entered the reception room of the deputy to the general director. The deputy's secretary told Lydia that she knew Mr. Kozitsky had been expecting her, but that, at the moment, he was in a planning meeting, and it would be better if she could come back at eleven thirty. Exactly at eleven thirty, Lydia returned, and though there were others waiting before her, the secretary told her to go right in. It felt a little awkward doing so, but Lydia felt better after crossing the threshold into Mr. Kozitsky's office.

Joseph stood and offered her an armchair. Then pressing an intercom button, he told his secretary that he would be busy until one o'clock and to tell everyone waiting to return then. He would see everybody, he promised, but only after lunch, and she was to distribute lunch coupons, so that they could eat in the dining room.

Then turning to Lydia, Joseph noted with pleasure that she appeared rested and energized, unlike how she had seemed on the train.

"Well, how was your trip?" he asked, looking her in the eye. "Have you been back long?"

"Not too long," she answered, suddenly uncertain about being there.

"Don't worry," Joseph assured her, sensing her confusion and worry. Then to put her at ease, he told her a story about a business trip he had taken when he was young, in which he had not been able to handle a simple assignment. As he talked, he watched Lydia gradually calm down. Color returned to her cheeks, and she even began to smile.

"Do you want to eat?" he asked. "It's lunchtime, and according to the labor law, everyone must break for lunch."

"Oh, no, thank you," Lydia said. "I'm not hungry."

"That's not possible," stated Joseph, with a hint of a smile. "According to the union's laws of hospitality, if you are here at my request, I can't let you be hungry. Please, do me this favor," he said, and in a gallant gesture, invited Lydia into the small room behind his office.

Inside, a table had already been set for two. And as it turned out, Lydia was hungry. She often didn't eat breakfast, because the kitchen in the hostel where she lived was so overcrowded, and this morning had been no exception. In addition, as she ate their simple lunch of cabbage salad, chicken soup with vermicelli, and Chicken Kiev with a garnish, she relaxed and began to feel more comfortable.

After lunch, Joseph offered her tea from the samovar,[33] along with cookies

---

33 A traditional Russian device for boiling water, which consists of a metal urn with a spigot, and an internal heating tube.

and candies. Joseph liked Lydia a lot. He enjoyed the company of this young, beautiful woman, and her large, gray eyes reminded him his youthful love, Elizabeth. Lydia, once she had warmed up to him, enjoyed his company, as well; she felt oddly at ease with this older person.

They talked over tea until the hour hand on the large floor clock had almost reached the one, then Lydia stood to go, when Joseph said, "You know, Lydia, despite the difference in our ages, you and I share something in common. We are both very lonely. If you would not mind spending time with an old man, I'd like to invite you to meet me on Sunday and walk on our skis."

"And why not?" Lydia thought. Joseph was a nice, respectable man, who would never try to take advantage of her, and it would be much better than spending the weekend alone in her stinky hostel room, which she shared with four girls. Besides, as it had turned out, Joseph lived in the three-story management building adjacent to dormitory where Lydia lived, since both properties belonged to Tyumen Oil & Gas. And so she agreed.

When they met Sunday morning, it was, as usual, a frosty minus twenty degrees, but it was sunny. The two hooked onto the steel ski track that went directly past Lydia's dormitory on its way to the park. Then after walking and circling the park, they stopped, and Joseph dug a thermos with hot cocoa from his bag, poured a cup, and offered it to Lydia. She drank it with great pleasure, and Joseph followed suit.

They walked over to a pond and watched some kids playing ice hockey, then after a while, they slowly made their way toward their respective homes. By the time they arrived outside Joseph's building, it was already one thirty, and seeing Lydia shiver, Joseph very politely invited her to come to his place. She agreed at once. It was becoming more and more interesting and pleasant to be with this person who knew so much and had so much influence not only in the corporation, but also in the city.

Joseph's apartment was on the top floor, and had been formed by combining two smaller apartments, one with two bedrooms and the other with one. The result was a spacious living area with two bathrooms; three large bedrooms; a living room, dining room, and kitchen; Joseph's small office; and a small storage room, which housed a washing machine and a second refrigerator. Everything was neat and clean, and quite cozy, making Lydia feel very much at home.

At Joseph's suggestion, she decided to take a hot bath to warm herself. Inside the guest bathroom, a large clean towel, a warm bathrobe, and warm socks were hanging on a hook on the door. Lydia filled the bath with hot water and plunged in, her whole world at once becoming warm and comfortable. After a ten-minute soaking, though, she felt it was time to get out. She would have liked to stay there all day and lose herself in the serenity, but she felt somewhat awkward leaving her host alone. She dried herself and put on the socks and bathrobe. She felt so good and peaceful, and was glad that everything was going so nicely.

When Lydia walked out of the bathroom, Joseph, dressed in a woolen sports suit, was in the kitchen, skillfully laying out pickles, salads and other delicacies on the table. He had obviously prepared the meal in advance. There was red caviar in a small crystal bowl, and on the stove, pelmenies were boiling in a little pot. Seeing the caviar and pickles, and catching the fragrant smell of the pelmenies, Lydia realized that she was as hungry as a lioness. Before eating, however, she asked Joseph if she could help him, to which he answered, "Thank you, Lyd, but everything is ready. Except, wait, I wanted to take out something to drink."

She stopped and looked at him for a second. He had called her by her childhood name, and so naturally that it somehow relaxed her. She smiled as they sat down to eat.

The meal was delicious and beautifully presented, unlike those at the hostel. They drank Posolskaya vodka, straight up, from beautiful crystal liqueur goblets, rather than in cheap glasses stolen from the dining room.[34] Lydia devoured the pickled mushrooms, tomatoes, cucumbers, and cabbage salad, and she marveled at how the caviar had been perfectly spread over the rich, buttered bread.

All through dinner, they talked about literature and politics, both feeling that the difference in their ages and positions was unimportant. Then, after the pelmenies, Joseph went to the refrigerator and took out a chocolate layer cake (How did he know it was Lydia's favorite?), which he served with cups of tea.

After dinner, Joseph suggested that Lydia rest in front of the TV, but she vigorously protested, saying that he had set the table and served the meal. So Joseph agreed and put the leftover food in the refrigerator, while Lydia washed the dishes.

When they finished, Joseph again suggested that Lydia rest in the large armchair, and then turning to leave the room, said he would return in five minutes. When Joseph got back to the living room, his guest was already asleep in the armchair, her legs folded underneath her like a baby's. Looking at this young woman, admiring her beauty and purity, Joseph sighed. Then he quietly covered her with a plaid blanket and left the room.

When Lydia awoke, the room was dark. A digital clock on the table showed it was almost four o'clock.[35] She had slept for about half an hour, and

---

34   An old tradition of people living in hostels was to take dishes from the eatery.
35   In Tyumen, during wintertime, it gets dark very early.

felt very warm and cozy. She got up and tiptoed to Joseph's room. He was asleep in his bed, with one hand cupped under his head. Hoping not to wake him, she quietly closed the door and returned to the living room.

Feeling right at home, Lydia took the liberty of scanning the books that filled a Scandinavian wall unit. Cocking her head to one side, she browsed the titles, moving from one shelf to the next. On one shelf, some photo albums caught her interest, so she took one down and flipped through it. There were several photos of Joseph and a woman, perhaps his late wife. Lydia then noticed an album with older photos, which she took off the shelf. When she opened the front cover, she saw a familiar-looking photo of a young officer wearing lieutenant's stripes, looked lovingly at a young woman. It was … it was … her grandmother, Liz.

Lydia let out a cry, unaware that Joseph was watching her from his bedroom door. Then upon seeing him, she wanted to talk, but the words seemed to stick in her throat. Instead, she made a kind-of helpless gesture with her hands, until finally, she had recovered enough from her shock to say, "Where did you get this photo?"

"Why, Lyd?" Joseph asked. "What photo?"

"Here," she said, showing him the photo. "Who is this man?"

Joseph looked at it, amazed that she had asked him who the officer was, but not the girl.

"It's me," Joseph told Lydia. "But tell me, do you know this girl?"

"Yes, she is my grandmother," Lydia said in barely a whisper and promptly rushed to the bathroom, where she put on her ski suit and ski boots. Then, seizing her woolen hat, she ran out of the bathroom, and out the front door of the apartment, trailing the words, "I'll be right back."

After a few minutes, she was standing before Joseph, holding a small photo album in her shaking hands. "Look," she said, holding out the album and then opening it to a page that contained the exact same photo. "The girl," she said breathlessly, "is my grandmother."

"What? What did you say?" Joseph was practically shouting. "Is she your grandmother? She's your grandmother? Where? Where is she?"

Lydia looked down, and said quietly, "Grandma Liz died fourteen years ago."

"Died?" Joseph said, then repeated, "She died?"

Lydia, seeing that he could not hold back his tears, also began to cry.

"Liz, Liz, Liz," Joseph repeated with a faraway look in his eye, as if addressing someone who was not in the room. "At last, I have found you, but you are not here anymore. No, no …" he repeated, nodding his head in step to his words.

Then finally he looked Lydia. "Lyd, your grandmother was my first love.

My first love," he said, and told Lydia everything that had happened between them in Izhevsk. He explained how he had searched for her grandmother for sixteen years and, not having found her, finally married Igul in 1956.

Shocked and overwhelmed, a suddenly exhausted Lydia slumped onto the sofa, and Joseph sat down opposite her in the armchair. Lydia felt sorry for her grandmother's ruined life. And she felt sorry for this unfortunate man who had suffered so much from their separation.

Lydia told him everything she knew about her grandma. She told him that Elizabeth had been raped by the supervisor at the labor camp that, as a result, her father had been born and her grandmother had named him Ostap and called by his nickname Osya.

"Yes, yes," he said, "that was my childhood name, and Liz used to call me Osya."

Lydia went on to tell him about the poverty-stricken life that they had been forced to endure and about how her grandmother had sometimes spent hours holding the photo in her hands, silently crying. Joseph deeply sighed when she said this, and wiped tears from his eyes.

Joseph now understood what had attracted him to Lydia; she had something of the features of his Liz Zeldina. He also could see the resemblance in their last names.

"Move into my apartment, granddaughter," the old man said somberly. "I have no relatives. Come and live with me, my girl. There is a lot of room for both of us. I could not find my Liz, but God has sent you in her place. For you, Lyd, I will do everything I can."

Seeing his deep sincerity and trusting it implicitly, Lydia embraced the old man. And, as such, they sat—as close friends do upon meeting after a long separation—embracing and silent, incapable of expressing their feelings with words.

Then at last, Lydia broke the silence. "But what will people say? What they will think?"

"What they will say?" Joseph responded. "Nothing."

A few days later, the newsletter distributed by the Tyumen Oil & Gas Association ran a biographical article about the deputy to the general director—how he had met his first love, how he had searched long and wide for his intended bride, how she had been raped in a labor camp, and how, after many years, her granddaughter Lydia Selina had accidentally met the deputy on a business trip for the association.

Soon after, Lydia moved into Joseph's apartment. She had her own separate bedroom and a private bathroom, but, most important, she had the company of a person whom she knew she could trust.

15

ONE EVENING, ABOUT TWO weeks after Lydia had moved to Joseph's apartment, the two were having dinner when the conversation shifted to Lydia's future.

"Lyd," Joseph began, "please listen to me carefully. I want to prepare you for an important career. I hope, granddaughter, that you do not object to this proposition, because it seems that you have the potential, granted you by nature, to become a top executive. If you agree, I suggest that you begin taking advantage of this opportunity. Or, life will pass you by if you do not decide quickly."

"Yes, Grandpa, I agree," Lydia answered sincerely. "Thanks to you, of course. You have already done so much for me. I am so grateful to you."

"Lyd, it will be in memory of my Liz. Don't forget I am still planning to go to Togliatti with you to visit Liz's grave, when the snow melts in the spring."

Next day, Joseph called the regional Communist party's special warehouse and scheduled a trip to purchase personal items that Lydia needed.[36] When the day came, he and Lydia went to the warehouse in his personal chauffeur-driven car.[37] Joseph told her not to worry about price or quantity, adding that she could take everything she liked. The situation felt awkward, until Lydia decided that she would eventually pay Joseph back for whatever money he spent on her. Then she chose everything from a Canadian sheepskin overcoat

---

36 During the Soviet era, there was a shortage of everything, so community leaders, upper managers, and party bosses shopped in special warehouses, where purchase prices were much less than in regular stores (although regular stores were empty most of the time anyway).

37 In those days, a privilege of upper managers.

to a woman's briefcase, getting input from Joseph about everything but the bras and underwear.

Finally, loaded down with bags and packages, they returned home, where, all evening long, Lydia tried things on and showed them to Joseph. Both of them were delighted that everything both suited and fit Lydia.

Lydia kept her word, giving practically all of her earnings to Joseph except what she needed for daily expenses. To her surprise, he accepted this money from her, though, she would learn later that the old man was putting it away in a savings account for her to use on a "rainy day."

A week later, Lydia was transferred to the association's department of Procurement and Sales and made a project planner. She also began taking English and philosophy at Tyumen Polytechnic University, to prepare for the entrance exams to the PhD program. And after studying every night after work, Lydia passed the entrance exams in May with flying colors.

With the coming of spring, Joseph prepared the necessary documents for he and Lydia to take a business trip to the Novokuibyshevsky oil refinery. As they flew together to Kurumoch, the airport serving the cities of Kuibyshev and Togliatti, Lydia could hardly hide her joy at returning to the city where she had spent her childhood. She showed Joseph the VSO-5, where she had lived with her grandmother, as well as the place where her grandmother had worked. Joseph was even able to find some long-time workers who remembered Elizabeth and to ask them questions about her.

Finally, the two visited the cemetery where Elizabeth was buried right next to Lydia's parents. The deteriorating headstones needed serious care, so Joseph negotiated with some workers to put the gravesites in order. He also ordered one large headstone for the three plots, and made plans for Lydia and him to return in a month to ensure that the work was complete and to offer compensation.

Visiting Elizabeth's gravesite was a deeply emotional experience for Joseph that he appeared to age overnight and, in the ensuing weeks, to have lost his energy. Although he continued to spend about twelve hours a day at the office, his demeanor had changed. He became not only increasingly sentimental, but also more attached to Lydia.

By the late summer 1988, Lydia was accepted into a PhD correspondence program at Tyumen Polytechnic. She started to accumulate data for her PhD dissertation, which focused on the economics of the petroleum industry. Her mentor for the dissertation was an internationally renowned authority in the industry, not to mention the head of the university's chamber of economics.

Incidentally, by year's end, the explosive growth of large and small firms with a wide range of specialized services and products began to change the landscape in Tyumen as well as in the country at large.[38] Unfortunately, however, this progressive new development did not influence the food industry, in which, somehow, the availability and quality of products went down, and consumer goods and foodstuff began promptly to disappear from store shelves. Although Joseph and Lydia, whose supplies came exclusively through the Communist party distribution system, experienced no problems obtaining food and other consumer goods, average workers at the association increasingly asked management to take aggressive measures to correct the situation. In response, Joseph began contacting national enterprises that depended on lubricating oil and crude oil byproducts for manufacturing machinery and cars, offering them substantial discounts for cash purchases.

Part of the association's assets consisted of storage tanks that, combined, could hold a million tons of crude oil. A less obvious asset consisted of the heavier parts of the crude oil (the hydrocarbons), which mixed with residual sand, clay, and stones that settled on the bottoms of these storage tanks, to form sludge. Recovering these heavy hydrocarbons from the sludge was not considered cost-effective because it involved such considerable labor that it was never recorded in the association's official books. However, Joseph said that if workers were willing to contribute their labor, he would try to sell the recovered hydrocarbons to manufacturers with whom the association had existing working relationships. Since these manufacturers usually had cash on hand (because they sold on the open market, where transactions were typically made for cash), Joseph explained that the cash could be used for purchasing foodstuff and consumer goods for employees.

Director General Sviblov supported Joseph's idea, as did the trade unions, so, throughout the spring and summer of 1988, workers removed the sludge from its storage tanks and recovered the valuable hydrocarbons. As it was crucial to load, ship, and deliver the asset as quickly and inconspicuously as possible, since officially they did not exist, Joseph assigned the job to Lydia.

The deputy was ready to back her up, using his influence and authority, if needed, but Lydia managed the complex task exceptionally well, moving more than ten thousand railroad tank cars to the loading docks within six months, and then filling about two hundred heavily loaded trains with approximately six hundred thousand tons of recovered hydrocarbons—all without any hitches.

In fact, the plan went so smoothly that the association's shops were soon filled with foodstuff and other consumer goods. The people of Tyumen praised the initiative that had made it possible for them to survive the winter.

"Good for you, granddaughter," Joseph said with great pride to Lydia.

---

38   Gorbachev's reforms began during this period.

"Your performance has exceeded all expectations, and has earned you political credit, as well; management will not object to assigning any task to you."

So in the first quarter of 1989, Selina was appointed manager of the sales department, an impressive position, considering she was only twenty-nine. Lydia understood, however, that without the support of "Grandy," as she sometimes called Joseph in private, her success would not have happened. Lydia was grateful beyond measure for everything he had done for her.

Almost a year had passed since she had met her grandmother's childhood friend, and even she could fully appreciate how much she had changed. She had grown up since the time she was a little office worker and was now a department head. She was neck-deep in her work on an economics dissertation. And she had started to take better care of herself, improving her appearance and wardrobe. She visited a beauty salon every week for a hairdo, manicure, and pedicure; began to use expensive cosmetics and skincare products; and attended the newly instituted yoga classes. At Joseph's insistence, she also exercised every morning and took healthy, cold showers. As Lydia continued to follow the instructions of her mentor, she saw the positive results multiply. Even as her language changed and became more businesslike, Lydia was transforming herself into a successful businesswoman in the best sense of the word.

As positive political changes spread throughout the country, everyone seemed to be starting businesses. Lydia often suggested that Joseph do likewise, perhaps starting a retail store or video game arcade. He listened to her ideas, but never with interest.

Then one day, during one of their political discussions in which Lydia was arguing that people usually take advantage of an improving political situation, Joseph stopped, and after thinking for a moment, said, "As a matter of fact, Lyd, I don't trust the current buzz about where we are headed. I imagine that our leaders will get what they want, but I don't know how, and I don't know in what way it will affect us. Basically, I have to admit, it is impossible to trust them."

"So, instead of starting a small business, as you sometimes mention, I will tell you a secret—the association's executive management is considering privatization by the workers. So, here's what we need from you, granddaughter: an analysis, from an economist's point of view, of the entire process of obtaining, transporting by pipeline and rail, and selling the crude oil. And, please pay special attention to quality control, the relationship between weight and volume, how precisely both can be measured, and the official procedures under which companies must conduct any export and import activities, in particular the licensing, quotas, and permits requirements for the sale abroad."

"But crude oil production is on the decline," Lydia responded. She didn't understand the direction Joseph was headed.

"Unfortunately, that's true," Joseph agreed. "But if you remember, we emptied all the storage tanks and are only now gradually refilling them. A lot of this crude oil has not been recorded—the oil that has not yet reached the pipeline. So according to the books, we may have relatively little crude oil, but in reality, we have a good amount. And the cash value of that oil is increasing. If we were to privatize the association, then, this oil would belong to the workers instead of the state. And the approval for privatization, if business continues as it is, could happen within the next twelve months. I think you understand. Only one thing, granddaughter—don't reveal this conversation to anybody. It is a great secret."

Actually, there was one more thing, but Joseph withheld this bit from Lydia; the local mobsters also had their eye on the association. But as yet, they didn't dare wage war against management, and gangsters from larger circles, who might be willing to take aggressive action, would first have to deal with the locals.

Over the next several weeks, Lydia diligently studied the association's start-to-finish process, and to her surprise, found an inconsistency in the way crude oil was measured. When measured for the purposes of the extraction and transportation, calculations were made in terms of volume; when measured for the purpose of payment, however, the oil was recalculated in terms of weight. The problem with this was that the hydrometric devices used at the time for measuring volume could yield results that deviated as much as 1 percent from results gotten from weight-measuring devices. In fact, the combined margin of error of all measurements might reach as much as 2 percent, which was significant, considering these parameters were used to determine crude oil's value during sale. It was also significant considering the association extracted and transported about twenty million tons of crude oil per year; 2 percent of that would come to five hundred thousand tons. Lydia estimated that at the current price of about fifteen dollars per barrel, that was an error of almost fifty million dollars a year. Now she understood why Joseph didn't want the information to be public.

A second problem she discovered had to do with obtaining legal sales documentation. Though many seemed to talk about the purchase and sale of crude oil, only a few actually did so according to government guidelines. So, while the association was able to pump the crude oil through the pipeline to the loading dock in the harbor, turning the oil into hard cash was another matter. It required connections in certain quarters of Moscow, to which no one at Tyumen Oil & Gas had access.

This wasn't to mention that, at the same time the crude oil was being sold and presumably turned into cash, someone had to purchase foodstuff and consumer goods for the workers—and both of these tasks required government licensing and quotas, something not accomplished overnight. So Lydia cautiously, so as not to bring attention to her actions, started making plans.

By 1992, Lydia had all but finished her dissertation, while continuing to successfully supervise the sales department. In everything, she displayed a high level of professional skill, and served well by her years of study and supervisory experience, she eventually was able to speak briefly but persuasively at employee meetings about the privatization of Tyumen Oil & Gas. Further, after privatization was completed, and the necessary documents properly registered, Lydia joined the board of directors. Meanwhile, as always, Joseph remained in the background.

The summer of 1992, however, the problems with mobsters became worse. One gang offered the association protection from other gangs, while the others, who were also more arrogant and powerful, openly aspired to take over. The director general and his deputy were spending nearly all of their time just deferring the mobs.

As anxiety at the company rose to a fever pitch, however, they continued to pump oil. The only question left was where this oil would go. So once more, the association cleared the sludge from its storage facilities and sold the recovered hydrocarbons for cash, which they used to purchase foodstuff and consumer goods. But, still, the workers were not being paid their wages and bonuses.

That fall, Lydia successfully defended her dissertation, and the paperwork and documents were sent to the supervising body in Moscow for accreditation. Three months later, her PhD was confirmed.

In the winter of 1993, storage tanks were again filled with crude oil, including five hundred thousand tons that were not recorded by the state; the question about licenses and quotas for sale abroad had not yet been solved.

By spring, it had become obvious to everyone that the association would not maintain its independence and that, only in the very best-case scenario, would a gangster takeover occur without bloodshed. Thus, the director general negotiated an agreement that, in the summer of 1993, the employee-reserved foodstuff and consumer goods would be delivered to the warehouses, and he and his deputy would both retire. This complex decision was agreed to by the city and regional governments after the association promised that, in exchange for their support, it would make a portion of the foodstuff and consumer goods available for public consumption.

Once that was settled, and with it some breathing space, the board of directors sent Lydia to Moscow to quickly turn the crude oil into hard cash. She was equipped with the necessary references, documents, and authority to sell five hundred thousand tons. Only three people knew that an additional unrecorded five hundred thousand tons sat in the storage tanks, and that they would sell in parallel, distributing the proceeds among the workers. These three were Director General Sviblov, Deputy Joseph Kozitsky, and the executor, Lydia Selina.

Before Lydia's departure to Moscow, Joseph had a long conversation with her, expressing grave concerns for their safety. During her negotiations, he said, Lydia would be safe, but once the sale had been concluded, gangsters would feel free to confiscate the cash, and very likely the lives of Lydia and Joseph as well.

"Once the crude oil begins flowing through the pipeline," he said, "we had better leave town—and quickly."

He also gave her advice for her stay in Moscow. He recommended that, initially, she stay in the Hotel Mir, located close to the US embassy; the rooms were clean, the dining was good, and the building was protected by Russian military police. He gave her the address of Cyprus Bank, where he had opened a joint checking account for them, which was set up to accept wire transfers of the proceeds from the crude oil sales. This checking account already contained two hundred thousand dollars, which, Lydia was surprised to learn, had come from the money she had been giving him to pay back her shopping splurge, plus his own contributions. He had converted all of this money into hard currency and transferred it for safety to Cyprus.

Joseph also suggested that Lydia purchase a small apartment in Moscow, where they could hide out if necessary, and urged her to think about other ways to secure their physical safety. In this matter, he was not an expert but relied on Lydia who was, in his opinion, completely capable of acting on her own.

"As always, be extremely careful," he said in closing. "Stay in constant touch with me, either by phone or fax. And one more thing …"

"Yes, Grandpa?" said Lydia.

"Trust no one."

16

Washington, DC
July 17, 1993

ALMOST TWO MONTHS AFTER Kravchuk had called Boris in California and directed him to organize a meeting between the Russian minister of the power and fuel industries and the Global Oil Research and Sales Corporation, Boris Goryanin arrived in Washington, DC on Delta Airlines Flight 1892 from Atlanta.

After retrieving his garment bag, Boris went to the Avis desk to pick up his reserved car. He politely refused the offer of additional insurance, took the keys to his Pontiac Firebird, and boarded a shuttle to the parking lot.

As he drove along Route 267, Boris admired the green exuberance of the surrounding area. In a city built on what was basically a swamp, it was amazing to see so many maples, magnolias, acacias, and other large trees. Everywhere, huge subtropical bushes caught his breath with their strong aromas, and he quickly understood why the air in America's capital was so damp, heavy, and sticky during summer.

About thirty minutes later, he pulled off of Tyson Boulevard into the Ritz Carlton. In the empty hotel lobby, Boris checked in, and then, politely refusing the clerk's offer to have his luggage taken up, he went in search of the elevators.

The Ritz Carlton may have been the only hotel chain in the States to be given a rating of five stars, and Boris could now see why. The floors in its entryway and lobby were covered in dark marble and expensive wall-to-wall carpets. Its walls were inlaid with stained cherry wood, and finished with fine wallpaper and original oil paintings of English country life, including landscapes and hunting scenes, along with portraits of the hotel's owners.

Everything about the hotel said money, riches, and luxury. Boris had never stayed in such a hotel, and he devoured every detail.

After being whisked to the top floor, where his room key was then required to run the elevator up to the twenty-third, Boris stepped out into a magnificently decorated lobby. Exquisite small tables lined the walls, while a huge table in a corner was laden with dishes containing delicacies and fruits. Along one wall was a bar. Its shelves displayed at least forty varieties of vodka, cognac, whisky, and other liquors, and its clear-fronted refrigerator was filled with soft drinks. On a separate table, toward the center of the room, cakes and torts were set out on elegant silver trays; and next to them, carafes with different grades of coffee, and a pot of hot water for tea.

Goryanin gasped as he opened the door to the huge, two-room suite that Jonathan Barker had reserved for him. In the first room were a large desk and a leather armchair. A leather sofa and loveseat, and a small coffee table were arranged along the opposite wall. And completing the furniture set was a TV with at least a five-foot screen.

A thick Persian rug lay atop the wall-to-wall carpet, and a refrigerator held drinks and wonderful things to eat. Beautiful limited-edition serigraphs of modern paintings, signed by the artists, decorated the walls. And when Boris drew back the lovely, heavy curtains, Washington appeared before him in a stunning panorama, with the tall, concrete Washington Monument—one of the most powerful symbols of the US capital—at its center.

The second room was a bedroom with a king-size bed and, on the opposite wall, a cabinet that opened to reveal a large-screen TV. On the floor lay another thick Persian rug. A door on one wall led to a walk-in closet with built-in shelves and a safe. A second door took Boris to the spacious bathroom, which, he guessed, occupied about two hundred square feet. There was a huge bathtub, a separate stall for the shower, and a porcelain sink surrounded by granite countertops, which held small bottles of liquid soap, shampoo, and cologne, as well as bags and boxes with various toiletry items.

Boris showered and returned to find that someone had come in and laid out the latest editions of several newspapers on the coffee table. Maybe, for the first time in his life, he felt the pleasantness of having money.

Just then, the phone rang.

"Mr. Goryanin?" said the man's voice on the other end.

"Speaking."

"Good afternoon, Mr. Goryanin. Do you have a minute?"

"Sure."

"My name is Mr. Eddy Pennington, Mr. Goryanin. Mr. Jonathan Barker gave me your name and room number. I will be participating in your meetings with the Global Oil Research and Sales Corporation, as soon as all the parties arrive. As the matter of fact, could you tell me when you expect them?"

"Tomorrow afternoon. I will be picking them up from Dulles."

"Great. By the way, what are you doing tonight? Are you available for dinner?"

"Yes, I am available."

"Great. I hope you will join my girlfriend and me."

"With great pleasure. Do you have some wonderful place in mind?"

"The Maestro, the hotel restaurant, is excellent. What about six o'clock?"

"Done. I will wait for you in the entry hall of the twenty-third floor, Mr. Pennington."

"But how we will recognize each other?"

"One fisherman usually recognizes another fisherman from a distance."

"I get a good feeling from you, Mr. Goryanin. I look forward to our meeting tonight."

"Likewise, Mr. Pennington," Boris said, and then hanging up, he thought, "So far, all goes perfectly." Then, without anything else to do, he turned on the TV and dozed off.

Boris awoke just before five and stepped into the bathroom to refresh himself. To his surprise, someone had completely cleaned the bathroom while he'd been sleeping. He shaved and used the cologne in the small bottle. Unsure how to dress for the occasion, he decided on a light gray suit, but skipped the tie, since he had the feeling that dinner would be informal.

At five minutes to six, Boris was back in the impressive hall. There had been a change of dishes, and some rearrangement of the tables. A window view of Washington caught his attention for a moment, until a youthful, perfectly dressed, average-height guy entered from the elevator. Boris knew it was he.

"If I am not mistaken, Mr. Eddy Pennington?" Boris asked with a smile.

The man smiled back. "And you are Mr. Goryanin?"

"Like I said, fishermen recognize other fishermen," Boris said as they shook hands.

"Lady Melissa will join us in a few moments," Pennington said.

A minute later, a woman came into the hall. She was a little above average height, about twenty-six, and, as Boris saw at once, extraordinarily beautiful, exuding an almost tangible warmth, perhaps, from the light of her soft, radiant, gray-green eyes or from the way her dark copper hair fell down around her shoulders.

She was wearing a simple black dress with spaghetti straps, completely open to her shoulders and neck, the latter of which graced a thread of delicate pearls. Against the black of the dress, her soft, pink, slightly matte skin shone, devoid of the spots and freckles that often marked British women; though, directly under her left ear was a small birthmark, and above her upper lip on the right side, another, but these only made her seem all the more romantic. In each ear and on her right index finger were ornamental pearls, and on her beautifully shaped, well-groomed nails, a pale shade of pink. She wore black shoes and carried a black evening purse, and her short skirt left no doubt about the perfect shape of her long legs.

Mr. Pennington made the introductions. "Lady Melissa Spencer, Mr. Boris Goryanin."

"How do you do?" the young woman said with a quaint British accent as she smiled and extended her hand toward Boris as an aristocrat would—not for a handshake but for a kiss. As she did so, she cocked her head slightly to the left, a gesture that made her completely irresistible.

"How do you do?" Boris answered, smiling. He did not kiss Melissa's hand, however, but touched it briefly, unsure what to do.

All three of them pretended not to notice his awkwardness, but Mr. Pennington spoke up to preempt any feelings of tension. "So, let's go downstairs to the Maestro!" he said, and with that, the trio got into the elevator.

The presence of Lady Melissa struck deep into Boris's heart with the impact of a lightning bolt. Such a shiver ran through him that he was afraid he could not maintain an outward appearance that would deny his powerful attraction to this woman.

"The name Spencer is rather popular in England, is it not?" Boris asked to fill the silence. "I know one very famous lady with the name: Princess Diana."

"Do you know Princess Diana?" Lady Melissa said, flashing a charming smile. "I am a distant relative of hers. Very distant."

"Really?" Boris said, genuinely stunned. For the first time in his life, he was meeting a real aristocrat. Though he had never felt shame for his proletarian origin, he was now profoundly flattered by the respect and dignity bestowed on him by Lady Melissa and Mr. Pennington.

They got out at the mezzanine and went into restaurant, where, by the manner of the maitre d' approaching them, Boris could tell he knew both the lady and Pennington. Not a moment later, the maitre d' confirmed his suspicion.

"How are you, Lady Melissa," he said, nodding her direction, "and you, Mr. Pennington?" Finally, he nodded to Boris. "And how are you, sir?"

The Maestro was magnificent. Its walls were trimmed in dark-stained cherry wood panels, with inlays of various kinds of wood, the combination of which had been selected with perfect taste. Thick, dark-toned carpets muffled all but the softest sounds. Schoenbeck chandeliers hung from the ceiling, shining with Swarovski crystal suspension brackets. The small dining tables were strategically spaced among the dimly lit room to create a mood of intimacy. Like the hotel, the restaurant was saturated with the feeling of old money, every detail meant to emphasize wealth and luxury.

Not knowing what to order, Boris read the menu while sneaking looks at his companions—as if he didn't have enough trouble keeping his eyes off of the young woman as it was. Aside from her beautiful face and figure, she was charming, spoke in soothing tones, and wore a wonderfully gentle fragrance.

If Boris liked Lady Melissa, however, he thought that her companion had something about him that signaled extreme caution. Dressed in an expensive dark blue blazer, with a dark-claret shirt and dark gray trousers, all perfectly matched, Mr. Pennington seemed pleasant enough, at least on the surface. Nevertheless, Boris got the sense that he was the type of businessman who would, in the name of profit, step over live bodies to walk on corpses. His thin lips seemed those that would speak about secrecy and greed.

Under normal circumstances, Boris would not have been friends with this guy, but he understood all too well that you can't always choose your business partners.

Boris was relieved when Pennington offered to order for all of them. They started with an Italian tomato salad with cheese and olives, and a bottle of a California cabernet sauvignon from 1990. Then for the main course, they had beef carpaccio with pasta, accompanied by a 1989 California merlot.

Since the young woman drank very little, the two men quickly polished off the bottles of wine. For Boris, the amount was rather normal, but for "Eddik," as Boris began to call Pennington in Russian parlance, it seemed enough to cause him to talk more freely. Consequently, Boris learned that Eddy owned a company in Switzerland that traded primarily in oil, but also in metal and foodstuff, which had generated, in the past year, a turnover in excess of one hundred million British pounds. Boris also learned that he and Lady Melissa were engaged but could not marry, because Pennington did not possess a corresponding title. He had purchased an estate, however, that was a three-hour drive from London, since this would be appropriate for his anticipated rise to a noble status; you see, Pennington was in the process of arranging a meeting with Her Majesty's chief of staff to discuss the procedure necessary for obtaining the title of baron—and subsequently receiving the queen's blessing.

Deeply moved by the wine, the surroundings, and Eddie's story, Boris remembered the difficulty with which, after graduation from Polytechnic University, he became the assistant to the foreman, whose duty it was to oversee worker production. A proud young graduate, he carried the forged pieces of metal in a wheelbarrow to the machines' benches and earned a salary of one hundred and ten rubles,[39] which barely paid for his food. He remembered, too, how before that time, as a freshman at the university, he could not invite girls to go out during the winter because his overcoat was fit only for begging in front of the railroad station. On the other hand, though, Boris had thought, "Riches are crying, too …"

If you had said that the dinner was delicious, you would not have begun to describe how absolutely superb it all was; more, it was capped off by an after-dinner cappuccino. Boris made a clumsy attempt to take the bill, but the aspiring baron could not be swayed. So, having stood, the two men shook hands and left, without so much as discussing their next meeting.

It was about nine when Boris returned to his room. Realizing it was too early to retire to bed, Boris remembered a social obligation and called Maria, his wife's niece, who lived in town. A man answered, and when Maria got on the phone, she told Boris it was her boyfriend, from Paris, whom she had met just after moving to DC. She apparently had met him while working at the World Bank, in the department in charge of Kazakhstan.[40]

Upon hearing about Boris's trip to Washington, Maria said she would like to see him and introduce him to her boyfriend. Boris explained that he had to meet a delegation from Moscow after lunch the next day, so they agreed to meet at the hotel before that—at eleven thirty. Then having said their good-byes, Boris went to bed, satisfied that he had fulfilled his social duty.

Lying on his back, Boris looked at the ceiling and thought about Lady Melissa. He couldn't get over the warm aura that seemed to surround her. Her voice and mannerisms echoed in his memory. Having been married for almost thirty years, Boris loved his wife not only as a spouse but also as a woman. Together, they had raised a son who was now older than Lady Melissa. But the lady was something else. She seemed from another world, a world of dreams and fairytales.

For another five minutes or so, such thoughts consumed Boris, until he drifted off to sleep—and when he did, it was with the innocent intensity of a baby.

---

39   In 1969, a salary that would have approximately equaled three hundred and thirty US dollars.

40   An independent state in Central Asia and a former Soviet republic. Comedian Sacha Baron Cohen, in the movie *BORAT,* created his comic character as a Kazakh reporter to portray the deep underdevelopment of this country.

17

July 18, 1993

LADY MELISSA'S FATHER MAY have been related to the centuries-old noble family of Spencer. After all, the first mention of William Spencer, the founder of the line, was in 1330, more than a hundred years before the Tudor period. But Charles John Spencer, Melissa's father, was not a member of the nobility, and it was neither known (nor possible to document) whether he was a member of any noble line, although he always mentioned his relationship to the royal family and called himself Sir Spencer.

It had not been possible to document Charles John Spencer's noble standing because, in the middle of the nineteenth century, a fire had destroyed his great-grandfather's country house, and along with it, all of its furnishings and other various belongings, including any documents that may have related the family's hereditary ownership of the land and property.

After the incident, Charles's great-grandfather approached Sir John Points Spencer, the fifth Earl, for help. Sir John took the tragedy to heart since it had happened to a possible family relation, albeit a distant one. As a result, Sir John, or his secretary, wrote a letter to Melissa's great-great-grandfather expressing his sympathy, ordering restoration of their title to the land and property, and offering enough money to restore their lives to normal.

The Earl of Spencer's wife, the beautiful Charlotte Seymour, was also moved by what had befallen the family. So she took the children under her wing, and sent them to a school where they not only received a good education, but also learned good manners, in a way appropriate to their standing. She watched with pride the progress of her protégés, and they, in gratitude, were quick to do what they could to please her with their successes.

Being thus watched after by the earl and his wife, the distant relatives raised their quasi-noble standing to the point that they were added to the mailing list, and all of the Earl's messages to them began, "Dear cousin ..." Although the relationship did not go beyond letters, Melissa's family was included each year in the annual birthday greetings. Therefore, when she had told Boris that she was a distant relative of Lady Diana, she had been speaking honestly.

Charles John Spencer received an excellent fine arts education, with a focus in theater and poetry. He joined a Shakespearian club during this time, as well, which he attended on a regular basis. Later, Charles inherited more than adequate money and assets, but was a bad businessman and managed to spend practically everything he had.

Being, by nature, a kind person, he genuinely concerned himself with the problems of others, frequently participating in fundraising events for the needy. However, he never seemed to notice that he, too, was among the needy, having few means with which to live. To solve his own problems, he had neither the time nor interest.

After he married Melissa's mother—who had gotten a large inheritance from her parents, as well as substantial bequests from numerous childless and spinster aunts—Charles John took refuge in working for the public good, and left domestic matters to his wife. He rendered her formal signs of attention, such as flowers, but it was soon all too clear that he was incapable of normal family life, including the necessary duties of raising their daughter. Melissa's mother knew that if something happened to her, her husband could not be relied upon to take care of her. So she put two million pounds of sterling into a trust for Melissa and expressly appointed her bank, and not her husband, as executor of her will. As such, the provisions of the will would be strictly regulated by law and overseen by a board of trustees; in other words, Charles would not be allowed to touch Melissa's money.

In fact, neither could Melissa receive the entire inheritance until she reached the age of thirty-five. Until that point, she would receive monthly payments just sufficient to pay her expenses, and only then if she became a full-time university student. No limits were put on how long Melissa could study, however, or, within reason, how generous the expenses could be; and they were to be enough for a comfortable existence, given the recipient's reasonable behavior.

When Melissa was six, her mother's second pregnancy became ectopic, and when peritonitis set in, and treatment came too late, Melissa's mother died.

Little Melissa, having lost her mother, was sent to Switzerland to a boarding school for girls from prosperous families, and in accordance with the school's common practice, began to be called Lady Melissa. In addition to general subjects including English, French, German, basic Italian, and religion, the girls were taught art, dance, music, and choral singing. They also learned the basics of etiquette, posture, proper dress, comportment, and health and fitness. And not the least of their lessons concerned the domestic arts: housekeeping, family finances, and childcare.

Discipline was strict but fair. The girls were allowed to visit museums, and to attend the cinema and the theater (for "decent" productions only, of course), but these outings were to be taken under the auspices of the school, and in groups of three under the supervision of either a teacher or parent of one of the attending girls.

In such fashion, Melissa's childhood flew by. Occasionally, she visited her father during vacations, and, occasionally, he visited her; however, she spent more time with the families of school friends than with her own, preventing a warm relationship to develop between father and daughter. Only after leaving school did Melissa begin to understand her father better, and as a result, became closer to him and more tolerant.

Soon after graduation, she was accepted into the London School of Economics, one of the most prestigious educational institutions in the world, from which she graduated with majors in international economics and business management. She then received a number of interesting job offers, among which she chose the Swiss company Pennington International. Pennington, located in the center of Europe, would afford Melissa the opportunity to travel, and offered her a salary that would be more than sufficient for a comfortable existence.

As her main responsibility was to prepare business contracts and oversee their execution, she was required to go on many business trips. During these trips, the company paid for all of her personal expenses, practically without limit, including first-class flights, the best hotels, and expensive dining. As an additional bonus, Pennington paid Melissa an annual twelve thousand British pounds for the purchase of clothes and cosmetics.

After her first year with the company, Melissa had learned how to prepare contracts and understood the methods and matters of Pennington's business. By her second year, Melissa managed to have saved forty thousand pounds, and began to feel more confident than ever, although in some ways, as she would soon learn, she remained an inexperienced and vulnerable young woman.

It just so happened that on a trip to South Africa to negotiate the delivery of industrial lubricants for heavy mining equipment, Lady Melissa was seated next to Mr. Eddy Pennington, the owner of the company. She had met him before, as Mr. Pennington had sometimes participated in business negotiations or in meetings with his partners. He was unfailingly polite and seemed to take particular care to maintain a proper business relationship with Melissa. Now, on their long flight together, Melissa dozed off and unknowingly rested her head on Mr. Pennington's shoulder.

Breathing in the pleasant fragrance of Melissa's hair, Eddy found himself excited and overcome by a passionate desire to possess her young body. So he let her head remain where it was, and indulged in a series of romantic fantasies.

After a while, she awoke, and noting her position, immediately apologized for any inconvenience she caused him. Instead of accepting her apology, he simply asked her to call him Eddy, "even in the presence of the queen of England."

At the Johannesburg Airport, Eddy took charge, for the first time, of both his and Melissa's luggage, and arranged for its delivery to the hotel. Melissa took note of it, but she was not interested in a relationship. Still, she didn't mind being paid such flattering attention. When they arrived at the hotel, she simply thanked him for his courtesy, said good-bye, and went up to her room.

In a little while, she was dozing in bathtub, smiling as she reflected on what had happened in the airplane, when it dawned on her. "What the hell?" she thought. She would soon be twenty-five, and almost all her girlfriends from school were already married and had children. Although Mr. Pennington was somewhat older than she, he certainly had an important position. Why not at least allow him to pay attention to her?

Melissa was still in the bath when the phone rang. It was Mr. Pennington. He invited her to join him for dinner.

Dinner was marvelous. The food was delicious, and Eddy invited her to dance. He held her so close that she could feel his tangible excitement pressing stiffly against her. Suddenly, she was scared; she had never been so close to a man. They returned to the table and drank a little more wine.

Next morning, she awoke feeling slightly dazed and completely naked. Eddy was next to her in her bed, also naked, his hand lightly cupping her breast. Suddenly wide-awake, Melissa could not remember what had happened. She was horrified to look down and see that her stomach was bruised, and that the badly wrinkled sheets were stained with blood.

Eddy was very polite and tender, however. He helped her stand and get to the shower, and when she came out, he kneeled gallantly on one knee, kissed her hand, and proposed marriage.

Melissa accepted and then, seeing Eddy come toward her, requested not to make love again, because she was still very sore.

As if he hadn't heard her, he threw her roughly on the bed and penetrated her painfully, all the while pinching her nipples as seemingly hard as he could, piercing the girl's body. Each time Melissa screamed in pain, Eddy reveled in ecstasy.

From that moment on, Melissa's fiancé had sex with her at every opportunity. Gradually, she became used to his ways and learned to feel pain without making a sound. But although she accepted Eddy's sadism, she never experienced any ecstasy of her own.

Six months before their meeting with the Russian delegation in Washington, DC, they traveled to London to visit Melissa's father, after which Eddy's parents came to Geneva to visit them. Despite the positives of marrying Eddy, three problems bothered Melissa. First, she was not in love with Eddy. Second was that everything had happened so quickly. And third, she felt uncomfortable with the sadistic tendencies he displayed during sex, which made her even more curious about why she, to this day, couldn't recollect a single detail about that night in Johannesburg. And Melissa was no prude; she would have been delighted to wind up in bed with a man she actually liked.

That spring, however, on a trip to Germany, she uncovered something that might address her third problem, and quell her curiosity. After Eddy had left their hotel room, she casually sorted through his things, opening his accessories bag and finding, among the bottles of cologne, deodorant, and other toiletries, a small bottle of dark blue pills labeled "Rohypnol." Melissa had heard about this medication, but could not remember what it was.

She put everything away, hung Eddy's clothes in the closet, and went down to the hotel drugstore. She asked the clerk if he knew what Rohypnol was, and he explained that it was a prescription medicine, not approved in the US but approved in Europe for the treatment of high blood pressure. Additionally, because it lowered judgment and behavior, and often caused memory loss for anyone under its influence, it had become fashionable to use, among more shady types, for the purpose of sexual assault—in fact, for this reason it was often referred to as the "date rape" drug.

In shock, Melissa suddenly understood what had happened in Johannesburg. And after crying alone in their hotel room, she decided that what had happened, had happened, but that from then on she would have to act with great caution. She could never again trust her fiancé, Mr. Pennington. Otherwise, she might receive another dose of Rohypnol … or worse.

18

BORIS WAS ON A couch in the Ritz Carlton lobby, waiting for Maria. The daughter of his wife's sister, Maria was an attractive twenty-seven-year-old, whose artist parents were, as the majority of people in their trade, both highly talented and practically helpless. Fortunately for Maria, she always excelled in school, and eventually graduated from a private Catholic institution in New York. After that, she was accepted to Stanford University, in Palo Alto, on a full scholarship.

Graduating with honors from Stanford, where her PhD dissertation dealt with international politics, Maria was then admitted to the prestigious Paris Institute of Political Studies. After training there for a year, she began working for World Bank. Her department was responsible for the Central Asian republics of the former USSR, including Kazakhstan.

Now, arriving a few minutes late, as usual, Maria greeted Boris and introduced her boyfriend as Morris de Monier. Hearing the prefix *de-*, an amused Boris asked about the young man's proletarian origins. Morris, appreciating Boris's sense of humor, explained that he was "only" a viscount.

When Boris invited them to have lunch, they seemed delighted to accept. And after a fulfilling meal and lively conversation, the couple toured Boris's room, and told him that they were ready to move in with him and stay in this hotel for the rest of their lives.

Boris then told them about the friends he had met the night before, and Morris, in order to quell any similar concerns Boris might have for his relationship with Maria, told him that his own parents had already agreed to their marriage; since there was no longer a king of France, Morris assured him, no royal consent was required.

After Boris congratulated the pair on their forthcoming wedding, they began to chatter away in French, and Boris understood that meant it was time for them to leave. Maria gave Boris her business card with phone numbers in Washington, DC, and Alma-Ata.[41]

Boris looked at his watch. It was already time to leave for the Airport. He had to meet the Muscovite contingent in thirty minutes. Since the hotel provided transportation, Boris engaged a forty-foot stretch limousine, which took him directly to the entrance he needed.

Arriving at the baggage claim area, Boris quickly spotted Kravchuk, Isaev, and Popov. With them was a man he had never seen before. Rather unprepossessing and middle-aged, the man was nonetheless well dressed, and held an erect posture and wide smile. Kravchuk introduced Boris to this man by explaining that the representative of the Ministry of Energy could not come, and that his replacement was Mr. Vladislav Ivanovich Yakubovsky, a representative of the Russian Ministry of Justice.

Shaking hands with each of them, the man said, "Here, as in the US, however, it is not customary to use the patronymic. Please, just call me Vlad."

Having collected their luggage and loaded it into the limousine, the men left for the hotel. With no line at the main desk, they registered in little time, receiving keys to their separate rooms, which, they were informed, were all in a row on the top floor.

Boris amused the Muscovites by showing them how to use the elevator, so they arrived on their floor laughing, and as each stepped out, he expressed delight at the exquisite interior and the magnificent view of Washington.

Mr. Jonathan Barker made a reservation for the corner suite for the Russian Minister of Energy. Now, Kravchuk, as the head of the delegation, occupied this suite. Boris followed Kravchuk to his corner suite. It was the same size unit, but two windows next to each other on perpendicular walls opened an unobstructed view on the surrounding hotel area. Boris showed Kravchuk how to use the various conveniences, and then agreeing to a meeting in half an hour, Boris left to assist the others.

Boris knocked on the next door. It was Yakubovsky's room. He let Boris in, and with a broad smile asked him, "Is Kravchuk suite has windows on all exterior walls?" Not understanding the nature of the question, Boris answered positively, and Yakubovsky continued. "I am certified claustrophobic, and I have to swap my room to his. But, please, go ahead and show me all those goodies."

As with Kravchuk, Boris showed him how to use the blessings of

---

41   Then, the capital of Kazakhstan. The current Kazakhstan capital is a super-modern twenty-first-century city, called Astana.

civilization, all of which seemed to please the representative of the Russian Ministry of Justice. But then suddenly he said to Boris in a lowered voice, "I'm sure there must be some listening devices here."

"Well, let them listen," Boris answered. "I don't care."

"And what about the American democracy you always brag about?" continued Vlad, sounding a mock patriotic note.

"Well, why should I care?" Boris said, hoping to drop the subject.

"Because it's not a proper way of conducting affairs. It could go too far this way. Democracy is getting rotten!"

"Maybe it's getting rotten," Boris said, laughing, "but you'll have to agree that it smells very pleasant. And sometimes, it doesn't smell at all." With that, Boris considered the matter closed.

"By the way," Vlad asked, "I noticed the limousine—did you have problems renting a car?"

"No, I rented one. Unfortunately, I didn't know that the hotel provided its own limo service. Otherwise, I could have saved some money."

"Then," Vlad continued, "may I borrow the car? Mr. Popov is here for the first time, and I'd like to show him some of the sights. He's going to be doing a lot of work, so it would be a shame if he didn't see America at all."

Boris was a bit surprised. "Are you going to go with Mr. Popov?"

"Yes," Vlad said brusquely.

"Then, of course," Boris answered in the same manner. "When you will need it?"

"Oh, let's say every day."

"Well," Boris said, taking the car keys from his pocket and handing them to Vlad, "don't forget to fill up the tank with gas when you're through."

"Your car, my gasoline," Yakubovsky said and laughed.

Thirty minutes later, as agreed, Boris and the Muscovites met in the hallway. In the large room outside the elevator, the bar had been well-stocked and the tables pushed together for their convenience. On the larger serving tables, a delicious feast awaited them. So for several hours into the evening, the group sat around, enjoying an extended dinner that included a great deal of attention to the contents of the bar.

At one point, during an interlude between dinner and dessert, Vlad reminded the Muscovites of some money he had given them before boarding their flight from Moscow, and asked for its return.

"The money is for a fur coat for my wife," he explained to Boris. "We did not know how much money the airline would allow each person to carry without having to declare it."

"Up to ten thousand dollars," said Boris.

Yakubovsky collected and counted the money. It was, he said, exactly twenty-five thousand. He looked back up at Boris. "You said up to ten thousand?"

Boris nodded.

"Good, since sixteen will be enough for a fur coat, I will return with nine—the money will be useful there, too."

Nobody commented on Vlad's financial dealings or asked any questions. They just sat in the pleasant aftermath of dinner, talking about nothing in particular. After dessert, considering what they had in store the next day, they were glad to say goodnight to one another and retire to their separate rooms.

Boris had already showered and was coming out of the bathroom with a towel over his shoulder when he heard a knock at the door. It was Yakubovsky.

Vlad apologized for intruding, and then asked permission to come in; all the while noticing that on Boris's right elbow there was a birthmark resembling Australia.

"Do you have, by any chance, a plastic garbage bag?" Yakubovsky asked Boris. "I need one to wrap the fur coat in."

"Come on," Boris chided. "You know when you buy a fur coat, they always give it to you in a special bag."

"We are simple people," Vlad said, feigning humility. "The garbage bag will be fine for us."

"I'll see what I can do," Boris said, suddenly understanding that Vlad had no intention of purchasing a fur coat. But then, closing the door behind him, he thought, *To hell with him. So he wants a plastic bag. Let him do whatever he wants.*

Then, something occurred to him. He put on some clothes, left his room, and knocked at Kravchuk's door. Yakubovsky opened it. "Is Gavrila available?" Boris asked him. "Yes. But we swapped rooms already. He is in the one that used to be mine."

Boris left Yakubovsky's room and knocked on the next door. Once inside, Boris asked, "Who is this Vlad? Could he be from KGB?"

"Well … what are you thinking?" Kravchuk answered.

"I was thinking," Boris said, "that you could find your way to Washington without their help."

"Yes," Kravchuk admitted. "We can live without them. The question is whether they can live without us. Anyway, without their help, I couldn't have obtained a license and quotas for trading crude oil, not to mention the necessary papers to export it." Then Kravchuk sighed deeply, as if he had no interest in this conversation.

They remained silent for a while, each doing his own thinking, until

Kravchuk sighed again, and explained. "He was forced on us, you know. In fact, I was specifically told, 'If you want the papers and you want to go to the US without problems, take him with you.'"

"Are they at least paying his expenses?"

"Quite the opposite. We had to take the jerk at our cost. And now we have to find ways to keep away from him."

"Or help him," Boris thought, but only sighed in resignation.

"I know what you're thinking," said Kravchuk. Then he thought for a few minutes and continued, "Let me bring you up to date on the political situation."

And with that, Kravchuk laid out the following scenario:

"After the breakup of the USSR in 1991, new states came into being. One of them was the so-called new Russia, whose president became Mr. Boris Nikolaevich Yeltsin, and whose parliament became the Supreme Council of the Russian Federation. These developments did not diminish the struggle for power, however, let alone make it disappear. On the contrary, the power struggle grew; it just developed in new ways. Beginning this last summer, the political elite divided into two groups of politicians, and they are now fighting each other for supremacy.

"The first group included President Boris Yeltsin, Minister of Defense Pavel Grachev, Minister of Internal Affairs General Erin, Chief of Security General Barsukov and his assistant General Korzhakov, the Head of the Federal Agency for Government Communication Mr. Starovojtov, as well as some other members of the government, including Prime Minister Victor Tchernomyrdin and Minister of Foreign Affairs Andrey Kozyrev.

"The second group included, first of all, Russian Vice President General A. Rutskoy, Chairman of the Supreme Council Mr. Ruslan Khazbulatov, and deputies of the Supreme Council of the Russian Federation—General Valery Barannikov, A. Dunaev, V. Anchalov, and others."

Boris listened to Kravchuk's story with a great deal of attention. And Kravchuk had continued.

"Now that the confrontation between the administration and the council has pretty much reached critical mass, the question is, who will come out on top? The president's supporters are planning to dissolve the Supreme Council, and in order to suppress possible opposition; the government also plans to take over the Russian White House, where the Supreme Council is now in session. So perhaps," Kravchuk concluded, "you can now understand why it is so important that we, the businessmen, have our finger constantly on Russia's political pulse. Sigh as much as you want, it is out of our control. It may be out of everybody's control."

"Is it really that serious?" Boris asked.

"Oh yes, it is very serious," Kravchuk answered. "By the end of summer, beginning of autumn, we expect a full-blown civil war."

Kravchuk sighed again and stretched his hand toward Boris, who shook it, wished Kravchuk good night, and went back to his room.

As he was opening the door, the phone rang. It was Alex Popov. He asked Boris in a sheepish and yet irritated voice, "Is it necessary for me to be present at tomorrow's meeting?"

"Do you have a more interesting offer?" Boris asked, jokingly.

"I just don't get it, that's all," Popov said. "We come to America for meetings with Global Oil, but Yakubovsky says I have to go with him—somewhere else. He won't tell me where, but he says that Kravchuk knows about it, and knows where we're going, so that's all that matters."

"I beg your pardon," Boris interrupted, "but I am not your boss. If Kravchuk and you feel that the meeting can go on without your professional advice, for God's sake, so be it."

"But that's not up to me," Popov protested. "Yakubovsky just told me that we must leave for a short while and that, when we return, I must examine the documents and make any changes I think necessary. It's very important, because Pennington's secretary—this girl who takes care of his contracts—is not a simple Pennington's secretary. She's a graduate of the London School of Economics, and apparently an expert in contracts concerning the trade of crude oil."

"Okay, well," Boris said, trying to calm down Popov, "if that's the way it is, let's not make it any more complicated. When you return from your outing, we'll simply go over the documents again—and if possible, without Yakubovsky."

"Thanks," Popov answered with relief in his voice.

Boris hung up, surprised to learn that Melissa was a world-class economist, and perhaps much more. On the other hand, it would have been foolish of her to announce it from the rooftops, so to speak. Memories of Melissa then stirred in his mind, but a mere few minutes later, he was fast asleep.

That night he dreamed that he was going somewhere with Melissa, holding hands, when suddenly, something frightening appeared and they started running. As the "something" chased them, trying to kill them, they fell down and began to kiss.

Boris woke up, gasping for air. The room had become hot and airless. He got up and turned on the air conditioner, then looked at his watch: 3:30 a.m. He thought he could taste Melissa's lips and tongue on his, but just as he was trying to get rid of such a silly thought, he fell back asleep—this time, until morning.

19

THE MEN MET BACK in the hall the next morning at seven thirty, quickly finishing breakfast before heading down to the lobby, where Mr. Jonathan Barker, Mr. Pennington, and Lady Melissa were already waiting.

Boris enjoyed seeing Lady Melissa again. He would like to be able to see her again and again, and to feel her close to him. He was attracted to her presence the way a mountain climber might be attracted to a mysterious new peak. She had taken hold of his imagination; even now, he was thinking about the strange dream he had had the night before.

After rounds of introductions and handshakes, the group stepped outside, where a minivan sporting the emblem of the Global Oil Research and Sales Corporation was waiting. Boris opened the side door to a luxurious interior, and helped in each of the Moscow delegation. When Lady Melissa approached, Jonathan and Eddy were back at the hotel's entrance, engaged in energetic discussion, so Boris offered his hand. She not only accepted it, but also, Boris was sure, lightly squeezed it as she stepped in. Boris responded in kind.

Once the minivan was underway, Boris glanced occasionally at Lady Melissa. Her eyes looked forward, and he noticed an almost imperceptible smile on her lips, as if she were far away in a dream of her own.

Soon after exiting on Tyson Parkway, they reached Gallows Road and pulled into the world headquarters of the Global Oil Research and Sales Corporation.

The group went into the main building, passed through a metal detector, and found themselves in the spacious lobby where a registration table had been set up for their arrival. They signed in, giving their name, date, and time of arrival, and then walked to the wing that held the conference rooms.

Their host, Mr. Jonathan Barker, asked a waitress to come in and take their orders for coffee, tea, and soft drinks, after which they were surprised to learn that the official interpreter had been taken ill. Boris, however, who was delighted at the prospect of remaining in the exciting presence of Lady Melissa, not to mention compelled by his sense of duty, offered his services as translator. His offer was unanimously accepted.

Kravchuk spoke first. In fact, he spoke for almost an hour. His topic was, "Russia, the sleeping oil giant."

"Gentlemen," he said, "to begin this historic meeting, I would like to briefly review the petroleum industry in Russia. That means both the economic situation in which it currently finds itself, and the prospects for its future in the context of the Russian Federation's economy overall.

"The oil industry of the Russian Federation is right at the beginning of a much-needed reorganization, which was made possible when the former USSR collapsed. At the present time, the leading role has been assigned to the Ministry of Energy and Power. In fact, Mister Minister promised to take part in our meeting, but to our dismay, his plans changed at the last minute, and he was unable to come.

"The new Russian government is paying very strong attention to a part of the country's industrial complex which, at present, is a liability. In fact, I would say that now the Russian oil industry is not merely in stagnation, it is in shock. Judge for yourself; to sell even one drop of oil abroad, it is necessary to receive a license for the export of crude oil, which is attached to very cumbersome quotas—bureaucratically determined sets of documents ranging from technical analyses of the raw petroleum to detailed requirements for making payment arrangements. A special commission makes all decisions regarding the makeup and approval of these quotas. However, as you, oil experts know, the commission isn't performing its duty, and, perhaps, is waiting for the outcome of the political straggle for power. This commission, however, simply does not give out quotas. As a result, both the oil-drilling companies and the oil refineries have no money with which to pay their workers, let alone modernize their manufacturing equipment, not to mention supply the basic production resources of their enterprises.

"Fortunately, the situation shows signs of becoming more organized and orderly. According to Decree No. 1403, dated November 17, 1992, recently signed into law by the president of Russia, the process of privatizing the joint-stock companies of existing state enterprises, including the oil industry's research and development, drilling, refining, and distribution systems, has finally been regulated. More recently, on April 22 of this year, a government order created a state company called ROSNEFT, which has been directed to coordinate the drilling and refining activities of the oil companies, and to carry out direct commercial management of the shareholdings of their joint-stock companies.

"The Russian power and energy complex has, as in all oil-producing countries, been an essential part of our national economy. During the Soviet reign, more than twenty percent of the state budget was spent on developing the oil sector. Now that the budget represents approximately thirty percent of Russia's total industrial production, we need to raise the basic production capability by a similar percentage. Before the disintegration of the USSR, the petroleum industry consumed approximately ten percent of industrial production, twelve percent of overall metallurgical production, and two-thirds of pipe production. As a result, the oil sector was responsible for more than half of all of its exporting costs. Its funding will be looked at closely, and almost certainly be restored to adequate levels as a result of the reorganization of the oil, petroleum, and refining industries in the new Russia.

"The economies of the oil, petroleum, and refining industries also influence demographic processes like regional and local rebuilding activities, and will be a major influence in determining both the domestic and foreign policy of the country. The Soviet Union was able to keep itself going as long as the price of oil remained at about fourteen to eighteen dollars per barrel, but when the price dropped to ten, it simply no longer could survive. This critical, life-or-death influence of the oil industry on government may not have been widely publicized, but it continues today, and will do so for some time, because oil remains an irreplaceable industrial resource. Just consider that more than ninety percent of the oil and gas we produce is being used for our electricity and transportation, including gasoline for automobiles.

"Turning to a global perspective, the international demand for oil within the last years has increased one-and-a-half percent annually. But in light of growth rates in China, India, Brazil, and other developing countries, demand for oil in coming years will increase at a significantly higher rate. I will be surprised if the price per barrel during the next ten to fifteen years does not increase to at least eighty to one hundred dollars per barrel, and quite possibly higher. And, of course, world events will cause these prices to fluctuate, which means that countries such as Saudi Arabia, Nigeria, Kuwait, and Gabon will strengthen their influence, since price increases will enable them to boost production. I cannot emphasize enough that, for Russia to take advantage of the potential of this growing market, we must begin to plan and invest today; otherwise, our manufacturing capability, plain and simple, will not be able to grow—and we will be left behind by the competition.

"One final example of how real the competition is: according to available data, oil reserves in Venezuela exceed those in Saudi Arabia. In fact, Venezuelan reserves amount to approximately eighty billion barrels of light and two hundred fifty billion barrels of heavy oil. As a result, their position in the global petroleum industry will undoubtedly play a large part in their foreign policy and could easily cause unpredictable consequences, including changes in foreign policy and in the country's domestic situation. However, Venezuela's ability to develop its oil-production industry and, at the same time, raise the standard of living, as domestic politics often demands, will require an investment of about fifty to sixty billion dollars. That is a much, much higher investment than required by Russia's oil industry. To boot, Russia is more politically stable than Venezuela; we are already in the process of changing tax and investment laws to reaffirm a leading role in the global economic system.

"Under these conditions, the global role of the new Russia can become more significant," reiterated Kravchuk. "I confidently predict that, in the near future, the return on our investment for modernizing the oil industry in Russia will be three to five times that of similar investments in Saudi Arabia, Venezuela, or Kuwait. But we are confronted with the challenge of speed—we must not only develop new fields, but also exploit existing reserves very quickly. Unfortunately, due to outdated technologies and incompetent management, the losses that Russia is even now experiencing—during the drilling and transportation of crude oil, and the production of oil products—has created crippling problems for both its production and sales.

"So think about this. If we put aside all organizational problems, focusing only on the technical side, the primary problem of the oil industry is its lack of modern technology. Secondarily, we don't currently have large oil reserves ready to go. Our main goals, then, are to update the more expensive equipment, obtain the necessary modern technologies, and then develop new fields in remote areas such as Siberia and the Far North.

"In today's Russia there are three major oil areas—the Volga-Ural, the Tyumen-Pechora, and the West-Siberian. The largest of the three is the West-Siberian. Its enormous petroliferous pool is located in the areas of Kurgan, Novosibirsk, Omsk, Ekaterinburg, Tomsk, Tyumen, and Chelyabinsk, and in the Altai and Krasnoyarsk regions. This pool covers about three-and-a-half million square kilometers, and most of the reserves lie at a depth of two to three kilometers.

"These crude oil stocks, formed during the Jurassic and Cretaceous geological periods, are characterized by relatively low contents of sulfur—up to one point one percent—and paraffin, less than point five percent. Their relatively high petroleum content ranges from forty to even sixty percent. The West-Siberian deposits currently constitute Russia's major source of oil, which, by 1993, is expected to reach approximately two hundred fifty million tons. Of this amount, twenty-five million tons will be extracted by conventional shallow-surface drilling. The remainder will be extracted by deep-level pumping.

"In Western Siberia, there are ten large oil fields. Among the best-known deposits are Megion, Samotlor, Ust-balyk, and Shaim. Practically all these fields are in the Tyumen region, which occupies an area of 1,435,000 square kilometers; that accounts for almost sixty percent of the area of Western Siberia. Seventy-five percent of the oil in this area is produced by five associations: Kolm Oil & Gas, Nizhnevartovsk Oil & Gas, Noyabrsky Oil & Gas, Yugansk Oil & Gas, and Surgut Oil & Gas. The largest of these is Nizhnevartovsk. The remaining twenty-five percent of crude oil is extracting by smaller associations.

"Production at all of these fields, however, is suffering from a shortage of financing, and from slow delivery or non-delivery of equipment and supplies, all of which is related to maintaining the necessary quotas. As you all understand, this situation must be changed. But I am glad to say that one important indication of a new beginning is our presence here. We are those first swallows without which spring does not come.

"Despite such tempting prospects, and you may not believe this," continued Kravchuk, "but during recent years, not one drop of oil has been sold by private enterprise. The reason is simple: there are no quotas for the export of crude oil. Fortunately, we are in a uniquely favorable situation. The thing is, we are officially registered as a private joint-stock enterprise with the express right to export crude oil and oil products. Our company, the First Russian Oil Corporation, is registered in Tyumen. A license to export crude oil for sale abroad has already been issued to us, and we are working to meet the quota of five hundred thousand tons of crude oil sold by the end of this year, an amount equal to about three-and-one-half million barrels of crude oil.

"As you gentlemen already know, we are ready to sign a contract for the delivery of these five hundred thousand tons of crude oil today. But there are some unresolved questions. Up until now, we have not been able to agree on how to set a price for our crude oil, which is known as 'Urals oil' or, by some, as 'the Soviet blend.' The task of our technology experts during this meeting is to establish a formula for calculating the price of one ton of crude oil, depending on its properties. At the same time, our financial experts will discuss questions regarding financing. So my recommendation is that we waste no more time talking; let's start solving problems."

On this inspiring note, Kravchuk finished his review. The conference room was silent until Mr. Barker stood and congratulated their speaker, after which there was a round of applause. Then, as the manager responsible for the procurement of crude oil at Global, Barker described what happened in

Russia whenever Global Oil entered negotiations with representatives of the Russian petroleum industry: each time, he said, they ran up against a wall of misunderstanding concerning the price of Russian crude oil as compared to the price of a similar product on the London market. He then particularly noted that the Russians refused to acknowledge that, as the quality and properties of crude oil varied, so must its price. Instead, he said, Russian negotiators wanted to sell their Urals-type crude oil, with its relatively high sulfur and paraffin, at the same price as what was commonly called the "sweet blend," with its substantially lower amounts of these contents.

"I am confident," finished Barker, "that with mutual understanding and a constructive solution, we shall be able to produce an acceptable formula for calculating the price of crude oil. I am also confident that we can resolve the matter of financing, including your requirement that one hundred percent of the agreed-upon payment be made in advance." And with that, the morning session ended.

Kravchuk wanted to taste a real American hamburger, so he, Jonathan, and Eddy went to visit a nearby McDonald's. Meanwhile, Melissa, Boris, and Arnold Isaev stayed to begin assembling a draft of the contract for the delivery of crude oil.

—— 20 ——

EARLIER THAT MORNING, YAKUBOVSKY had waited in the hotel lobby until the minivan was out of sight, then he went to the parking lot and found the white Pontiac Firebird that Boris had rented. He drove a few blocks from the Ritz Carlton, where he parked, waited a few minutes, and then left again, all the while checking his mirrors for anyone who might be following.

Eventually convinced that he was not being tailed, Yakubovsky turned his attention to the road ahead until he reached the drugstore with a telephone booth outside. He drove a little ways past it, parked, and then walked back to the booth. He inserted in a few coins and then dialed a number, leaving the following message, in Spanish, on the answering machine:

"Hola, Señora Vargas. Este es Señor Don Francisco Alvares. Soy un amigo de Señor Gerardo Gomez. Vine de Adjuntas del Rio. Mi numero de telefono es cero-cinco-dos, cuatro-uno-ocho, siete-cuatro-cinco, uno-dos-dos-ocho. Muchas gracias. Tenga un dia de la reja."

In English, this message was, "Hello, Mrs. Vargas. I am Mr. Francisco Alvares. I am a friend of Mr. Gerardo Gomez. I come from Adjuntas del Rio. My telephone number is zero-five-two, four-one-eight, seven-four-five, one-two-two-eight. Thanks a lot. Have a good day."

Yakubovsky had constructed the message in code so that, even if someone listening understood that a meeting was being suggested, it would be difficult to identify the place and time of the meeting, as well as the person arranging it.

In this case, Yakubovsky informed Mrs. Vargas of the place of their meeting via the first three numbers of his phone number, zero-five-two, which was the international telephone code of Mexico. The three subsequent numbers were chosen for two different reasons. On the one hand, they corresponded to the code of city—in this case the small town of Adjuntas del Rio in the province of Guanajuanto. On the other hand, the first number minus two signified the day of the week when the meeting was to take place; when the number four was specified in this case, it meant four minus two, which signified the second day of the week, or Tuesday. The second of those three digits, one, signified the purpose of the meeting—in this case, the transfer of money and information. The third of the three digits, eight, gave the exact place of the meeting—in this case a particular bridge.

The next set of three numbers in his phone number—seven-four-five—signified the time of meeting minus four hours. So seven forty-five minus four hours would be three forty-five in the afternoon.

The final set of four numbers conveyed the following information: "one" symbolized the color of his car (in this case, white); "two-two" was for its American make; and "eight" was for the Pontiac brand.

To make his car more easily identifiable, Yakubovsky had purchased one of the small American flags that were for sale in every corner drugstore, which came with special brackets for easy installation in one of the side windows. It was convenient because it identified the car, but was also easy to make disappear; if the driver suspected an observer, it took only an imperceptible second to lower the window to which it was attached, sending the flag off onto the road. If the unexpected disappearance of the reference point could distract a spy's attention even for a minute, it would be enough to let the driver escape.

Then back in the hotel parking lot, Yakubovsky parked, went to his room, and fell asleep.

21

USING GLOBAL OIL'S STANDARD contract for the delivery of crude oil, which Melissa had brought, Boris began drafting a new agreement on his laptop. The task proved difficult, however, as he was distracted by the presence of Melissa and Isaev. Under different circumstances, Boris would have liked very much to be distracted by Melissa, but in this case, it was the work that demanded his undivided attention. So finally, he plucked up his courage and asked whether they wouldn't mind leaving him, perhaps going for a walk.

At five o'clock, when Isaev and Melissa returned, the three of them agreed that Boris and Popov would work on the basic provisions of the contract tomorrow, and then enter them into the computer in both English and Russian; only after those steps were taken could they bring in the others to identify specific details. Boris also received permission from Barker to return to Global Oil, feeling that he and Popov would work better there than at the hotel. Then, after tying up a few loose ends, Boris stuck his laptop and documents in his briefcase and, with Melissa and Isaev, signed out on the security sheet. Before the three of them left, Boris also ordered passes for Popov and himself for the next day.

The minivan, as expected, met them in the lot, and once back at the hotel, Boris phoned the others and arranged to meet for dinner at seven.

As Boris readied himself for dinner, he couldn't get the dreams of the previous night out of his head. He tried to distract himself by singing loudly, and, in the shower, alternated between hot and cold water. Luckily, his excitement subsided to a reasonable level.

After dressing, he went out into the hall, where others were starting to gather. By seven, all had arrived except Eddy and Melissa. A few minutes later, when Eddy did come, he informed the group that Melissa was tired and had asked them to pardon her absence. Boris was relieved; he had not been looking forward to attracting the attention of the others with his frequent glances at the lady.

They dined at the restaurant where Melissa, Eddy, and Boris had feasted the night before, this time on caesar salad, lobster soup, and filet mignon. Although everything had been perfectly prepared, Kravchuk insisted on loudly telling everyone that "the food they have begun serving in the restaurants of white-stoned Moscow is becoming better and better. Many of the new restaurants," he claimed, in fact, "are even serving traditional Russian cuisine." Absorbed in their meals, nobody took exception to his remarks.

Then at one point, Barker raised a glass of water and offered a toast "to the beginning of a great and long relationship." Kravchuk responded by pouring vodka into Barker's glass. He explained that this was the standard toasting beverage in Russia and then asked Boris to make a toast of his own that would "knock them dead."

Boris filled his glass with vodka and requested the others do likewise. Then he stood up and said, "One of the best Russian poets, Fyodor Tyutchev, wrote a four-line piecework expressing his love to the motherland. I shall take a liberty to rephrase it as follows:

"The brightest mind isn't enough

To comprehend the Holy Russia.

The straight yardstick isn't enough

To measure the size of Mother Russia.

She has the secret place in heart.

You may just trust in might of Russia!"[42]

"And to conclude, let me quote Mr. Barker: To the beginning of a great and long relationship."

Yakubovsky, who had an expert command of English, translated each of Boris's words for the Muscovites, after which Isaev, with great deal of enthusiasm, declared, "Yes, Boris, yes! You did it our way. And to drink to holy Russia, we all shall stand!"

With that, Kravchuk stood and topped of his water glass with vodka. Once everyone else had gotten to their feet, he lifted his glass and downed its contents in a single gulp. Then approaching Boris, he hugged him and kissed him in the Russian fashion, three times on both cheeks.

---

42   The poem was written on November 28, 1866. This poem was translated from Russian into English by the author of this novel, and is not really corresponding to its original.

"You did it just as the doctor prescribed," Kravchuk said. "You are a good fellow."

The filet was charred slightly, but the meat in the center was blood rare. And the steamed vegetables framed what, all would have agreed based on their obvious delight and healthy appetites, was a miracle of culinary art. Also obvious was that to consume such a miracle without vodka would have been a sin, which, besides, nobody had the slightest thought of committing. At the end of dinner, huge pieces of chocolate cake and steaming cups of hot English tea were served, the latter of which was to help cope with the excessive pleasures of the stomach that each diner had courageously experienced.

When the waiter brought the ticket, he handed it to Mr. Barker, announcing that the bill was on Global Oil.

"Such small pleasures always enhance our lives," Kravchuk proclaimed in gratitude, although he was so stuffed, he could hardly get the words out.

After dinner, the group went for a walk, during which Kravchuk, Popov, Isaev, and Boris discussed details of the contract. Barker, Yakubovsky, and Pennington, however, seemed to be discussing unrelated matters. By ten o'clock, Isaev and Popov were in their rooms making calls to Moscow, and Boris had excused himself, citing the need for sleep to be fresh for work in the morning. Only Yakubovsky and Kravchuk remained in the hall, where they finished the evening by draining the bar.

The next morning after breakfast, Boris and Popov, unconcerned with the others' activities for the day, went immediately to Global Oil to continue working on the contract. When they checked in at the security desk, they found that Barker had assigned them to a small room where they could work undisturbed—and that they did, laboring nonstop to polish every last word. They paused only for an occasional cup of coffee, or a roll or cookie from the small table of refreshments that Barker had provided in their room.

By noon, with the first draft complete, Boris called the hotel and asked and asked Kravchuk and Isaev to come down to go over specifics. They arrived thirty minutes later, and in no time at all, the four men were deep in discussion.

At six o'clock that evening, Boris called Barker to notify him that the first draft was ready, and that he would translate it into English the following day. Barker came in and brought Boris two more entry passes for the next day, adding that Boris could leave the documents and his computer there, so that, tomorrow, he could get right to work.

Back at the hotel, Boris found that his shirts had been washed and ironed, and that his second pair of trousers, also ironed, looked good as new. It was pleasant to stay in such a place, Boris thought, especially when Global Oil was paying for it.

Hungry, Boris went out to the hall, where the Muscovites were sitting around a small table, paying undivided attention to a generous selection of Japanese sushi. Soon, they had all come to the conclusion that the sushi would go well not only with traditional Japanese sake, but also with the Russian national drink, which would both elevate the flavor quotient and support the independence of the Kuril Islands, located on the west side of the Pacific Ocean. Someone recollected a popular phrase in Moscow regarding President Boris Yeltsin's position on Japan's request for the return of the Kurils:[43]

> *"Whenever Boris would make a deal,*
>
> *There would be no Russia without Kuril."*

With that, the revelers promptly finished a bottle of Russian Stoli. Then, observing the neutral politics of internationalism, they happily opened and quickly polished off a bottle of Swedish Absolute. Excited by the alcohol and having paid more than adequate tribute to Japanese cuisine, Boris and the other Muscovites went for a walk around the hotel, until they remembered the Russian saying that, "For free, even vinegar is sweet," at which point, they returned to eat more. The sushi had been removed, but in its place were trays of delectable small pastries stuffed with meat, cheese, and other fillers. The pies were tasty and the vodka fresh. In a word, the evening was not passed in vain.

Next morning, Boris got up early, had breakfast in the hall, and then went downstairs, but the minivan was not waiting. Neither was the Firebird in its usual spot. So Boris asked one of the attendants to get him a limousine and thus arrived at Global Oil on schedule. He worked the entire day in the same small room, translating the Russian contract into English, and returning to the hotel just before five. The Muscovites were nowhere to be found, so Boris took out his computer, connected it to his portable printer, and printed both the Russian and English versions of the contract for the next day's meeting. He then went downstairs to the business center and made eight copies of each version.

By six, the Muscovites had returned, announcing that they had spent the day sightseeing. They had seen the White House, the Capitol, the Washington Memorial, the National Art Gallery, and other sites. They seemed overwhelmed by their impressions, but not so overwhelmed that they were not more than

---

43   The USSR took these islands from Japan after World War II, resulting in a strained international relationship that remains today. Yeltsin's position was to return the islands, the value of which includes a two-hundred-mile zone into the Pacific Ocean.

ready to repeat the escapades of the previous evening. And after having another perfect evening, all returned to their rooms.

After breakfast the next morning, as they were walking out to the minivan, Yakubovsky asked Boris if he could take him and Kravchuk to the airport to catch their day-after-tomorrow flight to Moscow.

"No problem," said Boris, though he had thought their flight was for the following day. Yakubovsky, apparently noting Boris's surprise, told him that the situation had changed, and that he and Kravchuk were scheduled to fly out that afternoon, but that Isaev and Popov would stay to sign the contract. Boris continued to wonder about Yakubovsky's strange behavior, but kept reminding himself that it was not his problem; it was Kravchuk's concern. "Let them do what they want," Boris thought. "My responsibility was to work on the contract, and that's done." A few minutes later, however, Boris noted with curiosity that Yakubovsky and Popov did not get into the waiting minivan, but went right to the rental car and drove away.

After they had all arrived in the meeting room at Global Oil, Boris handed each participant a copy of the contract. Everyone started reviewing the text and making notes on the paper that had been lain out for them.

During the ensuing discussion, Boris intermittently glanced in the most casual fashion at Lady Melissa. A few times, their eyes even met; but conscious of Eddy's presence, Boris was careful not to show an interest. Then again, regardless of Eddy, why show an interest? Boris was ashamed to be so attracted to her. After all, who was he? A married man at least twenty years her senior, and, in addition, a penniless pauper! The situation was simply absurd. And having thus resolved the matter in his mind, he stopped even glancing in her direction and deeply immersed himself in his work.

By one o'clock, their discussion was complete. So, while the others went off to eat at McDonald's, Boris stayed to make everyone's final corrections.

— 22 —

July 21, 1993

AFTER LUNCH THE NEXT day, when Yakubovsky picked up Popov from Global Oil, he explained that, today, Popov would be driving the car and that Yakubovsky would be occupying the passenger seat. Back at the hotel, Yakubovsky then explained in some detail where they would be going.

Some hours later, they left the hotel as planned. Yakubovsky nervously watched the mirrors and windows, to make sure nobody was following them, as they drove to the drugstore where Yakubovsky had made his call a couple of days earlier. They drove into the parking lot, drove back out, made a U-turn in the street, and returned to the lot, finally leaving it for good when Yakubovsky was satisfied that there was nothing suspicious.

He then directed Popov to drive in the direction of Global Oil. But after turning left on Gallows Road, they drove past the Global Oil building and continued toward the small town of Vienna. When they had reached the intersection of Gallows and Custis Memorial Parkway, approaching the bridge over Gallows Road, Yakubovsky ordered Popov to stop. He looked at his watch: 15:44. Then after exactly one minute, Yakubovsky got out and pretended to check one of the rear tires. A white Toyota 4-Runner pulled up and stopped approximately sixty feet behind them.

Yakubovsky got back in, and fastening his seatbelt, said, "Alexander, do you remember how to drive back to the hotel?" Popov nodded, and Yakubovsky told him to drive that way. In about ten minutes, they were back at the hotel's parking lot.

"Alexander," Yakubovsky commanded, "park the car. I'm going to get out and go up to my room. In exactly six minutes, you have to drive out of the parking lot. Go to the right. Continue clockwise on Tyson Boulevard and

Gallery Drive, and on International Drive up to Tyson Boulevard, as agreed. When you have driven that route twice, return here and wait for me. Right here. Do you understand what you have to do?"

"Understood," Popov quietly responded, though what he really understood, of course, was that he was in deep trouble and that there was nothing he could do about it.

Back in his suite, Yakubovsky retrieved a camera with a large 300 mm telephoto zoom lens. He used the camera optical viewfinder as field glasses to watch Popov. From two windows in his corner suite on the twenty-third floor with almost a 270-degree view, beside a parking lot down below, Yakubovsky could observe practically all streets surrounding the hotel and even 495 Freeway.

Now, he was ready for the driving experiment. A minute later, Yakubovsky spotted the white 4-Runner, and in a minute and a half, as had been agreed, Popov pulled out of the parking lot and turned clockwise onto Tyson Boulevard, quickly followed by the Toyota. Suddenly, another white SUV, a Ford Explorer, caught Yakubovsky's attention. It wasn't following Popov directly, but was moving in tandem with the 4-Runner, about seventy-five feet behind.

Yakubovsky moved to the window on the perpendicular wall. After a few minutes, the Explorer moved to the right lane, and pulled to a stop at Park Run Drive, but at the same time, another SUV, a black Chevrolet Suburban, took up the pursuit, turning left onto Tyson behind both Popov and the 4-Runner. Yakubovsky returned to the first window At the next crossroads, the Suburban turned right, and simultaneously, a black Explorer joined the cavalcade. The three cars proceeded in a line until the second traffic circle they came to, at which point the black Explorer turned off, onto Park Run Drive, only to be replaced by the original white Explorer.

Yakubovsky knew that surveillance was being conducted and that, although he was not being watched, the 4-Runner was, which meant that the person with whom he had made the appointment was under surveillance. Experience told Yakubovsky that he shouldn't go down, that he should just let Popov drive; not knowing what to do, Popov would certainly return to the hotel. But then Yakubovsky would not be able to transfer the money—and wouldn't be able to keep the nine thousand dollars. If he were to change his flight from Friday, July 22, to Thursday, July 21, however, the surveyors would not have time to find him. Anyway, Yakubovsky reasoned, his contact had already been exposed. There was nothing he could do to help him now.

Yakubovsky closed up his camera, retrieved the plastic Sears bag with the money and went downstairs where, as he'd expected, Popov was waiting for him in the car. They took the same route as before, but on Galleries Drive, they drove into the Sears parking lot.

Having parked, Yakubovsky left the car and walked toward the store, with his plastic bag in hand. Popov, holding an identical Sears bag, got out, walking about thirty feet behind him. One of the 4-Runner's doors then opened, and a man of average height and unremarkable appearance—except for a small mustache—got out. He, too, clasped a plastic bag with the Sears logo, and headed for the entrance behind Yakubovsky, but in front of Popov.

Yakubovsky entered the store, followed by the stranger. Popov, however, was not as successful as he stumbled and dropped his bag. In bending to pick it up, however, he momentarily blocked two agile, young men from entering. While Popov was apologizing for his clumsiness, Yakubovsky and the stranger brushed against each other, exchanged their bags, and went their separate ways—Yakubovsky toward the men's fitting rooms, and the stranger toward the restrooms. The unfortunate Popov, who was by now furiously cursing the whole world, and who never quite managed to get into the store, returned to the car's passenger seat, where he turned on the engine and waited for Yakubovsky.

Yakubovsky returned a few minutes later, and taking the driver's seat, stormed out of the parking lot, going opposite the way from which they had arrived. From there, it was but a short trip to the airport, where Yakubovsky would change their tickets.

On the trip to the airport, and later, back to the hotel, Yakubovsky watched his rearview mirror to ensure they weren't being followed. Fortunately, all seemed clear. And once at the hotel, Yakubovsky and Popov took some much-needed relaxation after their stressful adventure. They did so with Kravchuk, who happened to arrive at the same time. At a free lunch buffet set out by the hotel, they gobbled up all kind of snacks and did their best to drink the bar dry.

23

BY THE END OF the day, Isaev, Popov, Lady Melissa, Pennington, and Goryanin had finished their working version of the contract, which covered the delivery and processing of crude oil to Global Oil. The remaining work, including copyediting, typing, and translating, was left to Boris.

Then after a final review and corrections by all participants, the agreed upon contract was faxed to the legal offices of Leber & Associates, LLP, in New York, representing the interests of Pennington International, Ltd.

The main point of the contract was that crude oil would not be sold, but be delivered for processing to Global Oil refineries in Europe, where different fractions of crude oil would then be separated. This way, only the product extracted from crude oil would be the subject of sale, and not the oil itself.

The second main point of the contract was that Ural or Soviet-blend[44] crude oils would be sold, and that prices would be calculated based on the chemical content of the crude oil being sold or delivered.

---

44   Both "Ural" and "Soviet Blend" are types of Russian crude oil.

24

THAT EVENING BEFORE BED, Boris called the service desk and reserved the Lincoln Town car for next afternoon, which he would use to take Kravchuk and Yakubovsky to the airport.

Boris didn't care when Kravchuk left, but he couldn't understand why he was leaving so hastily when the contract had not even been signed. Clearly, Yakubovsky's game, whatever it was, was very important to Kravchuk. It was all the same to Boris, who knew that without Kravchuk, no business would ever be done, and there certainly would have been no contract with Global Oil. What a very complex person this Kravchuk was.

The next morning, Boris called Mr. Barker to see whether a fax had come back from Leber and Associates. "Not yet" was the answer. It wasn't until 1:30 that afternoon that Mr. Barker called back to say that the eagerly awaited fax had just arrived, and that the Muscovites were invited to his office to review and sign the final.

Boris knocked on Kravchuk's door, and after Kravchuk told him to come in, Boris entered to see Kravchuk and Yakubovsky sitting at a table. In the middle of the table was a small plastic bag. Yakubovsky, seeing Boris's gaze, snatched the bag and stuck it in his pocket.

"I hope I'm not intruding," Boris said diplomatically.

"No, not at all," was the answer, which for some reason, Boris now realized, had come from Yakubovsky and not Kravchuk.

"Well," Yakubovsky continued, "I shall go to my room now. And Gavrila Petrovich, please make it fast. We have to leave soon." Then turning to Boris, he asked, "Will you come see us off?"

"Actually," Boris said, "I just got a call from Jonathan. He has the contract from Eddy's lawyers and wants us all in his office. We just have to review the contract one last time, and if it's satisfactory, he would like us to sign."

"I really have to go," Yakubovsky announced peremptorily and, without another word, purposefully left the room.

"What a beast," Kravchuk spitefully hissed after the door closed. Throwing up his hands in exasperation, he added, "Who would have thought that I couldn't go to Global Oil with you to sign this contract? Instead, I have to nurse this son of a bitch. But, you know what, Boris? You prepared this contract, and it is between your company and Eddy's. I know you will not sign if there are any obvious problems. You really don't need me anyway. But shit ... No more! Never again in my life!"

Although Kravchuk was so indignant that he could hardly construct a complete sentence, Boris noted that he was careful enough to be indignant in a whisper. Obviously, this Yakubovsky had some serious kind of hold over Kravchuk, especially if he could drag him away from Washington on such short notice.

"You know what, Boris, go to Global Oil with Popov. Isaev will go with us. After all, Isaev is only the Russian lawyer. Just finish up this contract, and that will be that. Go. I'll wait for you in Moscow. By the way, when are you arriving?"

"I've made a reservation for Saturday, July 24, which means I'll be in Moscow on Sunday. I have to be home on our son's birthday."

"Well," Kravchuk stuttered, "see you in Moscow."

They embraced and Boris left, almost running over Yakubovsky in the hallway. He had likely been waiting for Boris to leave so that he could go back in.

"Well, farewell, Boris," Yakubovsky, said with an ingratiating smile and outstretched hand. "Maybe we'll see each other again. It was pleasant to get acquainted."

Boris shook hands, but instead of answering, he just bowed and left. On the way to his room, Boris knocked on Isaev's door and went in to see that Popov was visiting.

"We have to go to Global Oil," Boris said to Popov. "I spoke with Jonathan. He received the contract."

Boris then looked at Isaev. "Kravchuk wants you to go with him and Yakubovsky to the airport, so I have an offer to make. This evening, when we have all returned, let's have dinner in a Mexican restaurant."

"Excellent idea," Isaev said. "I imagine, Popov, that you would not mind accepting our friend's offer, either."

"What do you think?" Popov answered. "By all means!"

And with that, Boris and Popov left Isaev's room, and took a hotel car to Global Oil, where they met with the others in a corporate meeting room. In the solemn atmosphere, the five original copies of the contract were then signed in the presence of Global Oil's executive vice-president by the following representatives:

- Mr. Eddy Pennington, for Pennington International, Ltd.
- Mr. Jonathan Barker, for Global Oil Research and Sales Corporation
- Mr. Alexander Mihailovich Popov, for Agroprom
- Mr. Boris Goryanin, for Agroprom - USA, Inc.
- Mr. Alexander Mihailovich Popov, for the First Russian Oil Corporation

After the signing, there were handshakes all around, and a champagne bottle was opened in honor of the event. Yet, despite the high spirits, Boris kept thinking about his meeting with Kravchuk and Yakubovsky. It was even more disturbing than the unexpected absence of Lady Melissa at the contract signing. Something was wrong, even rotten. But what could it have been?

25

July 22, 1993

BACK AT THE HOTEL, Barker threw a little party to celebrate, but Lady Melissa was not present there either. Again, Boris was relieved. He knew Eddy would be flying to Geneva that night, but wasn't sure whether Melissa was going with him, and he did not want anybody to know how badly he wanted to say good-bye to her.

By four o'clock, Eddy and Barker, after doling warm farewells to Boris and Popov, had left on their flight, and Isaev had returned from the Airport.

"So, did you see them off?" Popov asked.

"I have to tell you, guys," Isaev said, "that Yakubovsky is a complete jerk. Before leaving the hotel, he gave Kravchuk a package wrapped in packing tape. Kravchuk didn't want to take it, but Yakubovsky insisted. Then, at the airport, Yakubovsky demanded to be checked in first, even though their seats were side by side, and practically ordered Kravchuk to wait ten minutes before he checked in. I can't imagine how angry Kravchuk must have been."

"Maybe so," Popov said, "but I bet Kravchuk just got on board, had a few drinks, and forgot about it."

"Still," Boris noted, "you can't call Yakubovsky's behavior normal."

"You don't know the half of it," Popov blurted. In fact, Popov seemed bursting with desire to tell them about his adventure with Yakubovsky, but Boris suggested they wait until dinner. So they agreed to meet at the hotel entrance at 5:30.

The second Boris opened the door to his room, the phone rang. It was Lady Melissa.

"Boris?" she asked, "I would like to say good-bye to you. It was a real pleasure to meet you. And I really enjoyed working with you on this project."

"Likewise," Boris said noncommittally, and then trying to lighten the mood, he added, "The next time you offer me your hand, I will kiss it. Furthermore—"

"No more," she interrupted. "Please. Say nothing more. Maybe, someday, we will meet again …" She sighed deeply and, Boris thought, anxiously. He wanted to say something reassuring in response, or at least say good-bye, but before he could utter another syllable, she hung up.

Boris lay on the sofa, again fighting thoughts of her, until, eventually, he fell asleep. A half an hour later, when he woke up, he took a shower to wash away the thoughts. The water helped, but not enough. Simply put, Lady Mel, as he had begun calling her in his head, turned him on. His thoughts and emotions then snowballed with force, and he knew he had to do something to make them stop; otherwise, it could only end by his falling in love with her, and that would be just absurd. Perhaps it was a spell she had cast on him, he thought.

He dressed and went downstairs, the warm air of the evening restoring order to his thinking. By the time Isaev and Popov arrived, he was able to walk up to them jauntily and say, "Okay, guys. Let's go get some Mexican."

The Grill & Cantina was on Leesburg Pike, a few minutes' walk from the hotel. On their way, the three men enjoyed the unaccustomed sight of sprinklers watering luxuriant green vegetation. They arrived early enough that the restaurant was not even a quarter of the way filled, and asked for a window seat so they could watch the traffic outside. Although the 495 Freeway was near, the restaurant was so cozy, they couldn't hear it.

While they perused the menu, a waiter brought them chips and salsa, and three bottles of Corona. Living in California, Boris had become an expert in "south of the border" cuisine, so it was under his guidance that they ordered.

When the appetizer came—chicken wings marinated in vinegar and a huge amount of pepper, and a spicy Menudo soup, which burned their mouths—Isaev said, "Alexander, so tell us, what happened?"

And so as the three men worked on their appetizers and beers, Popov told them about his adventure with Yakubovsky, including the paranoid driving maneuvers and the "spy novel" incident at Sears. Clearly, neither companion found anything funny about the event; what each did find, however, was a distinctly unpleasant feeling in his stomach.

"Obviously," Isaev said with a sigh, "what happened was a transfer of the cash we brought from Moscow, in return, I assume, for information from the agent. Now the reason for his behavior is clear— before the trip, on the flight, and in the hotel. I am very worried, my friends, about the obvious conclusions we must draw."

"Do you think I'm in danger?" asked Popov.

"I have no doubt," Isaev answered. "Whether it's from one side or the other, you're hooked. I know those people very well."

"What do you suggest I do?" asked Popov, the fear in his voice now compounded by anxiety.

"What can you do?" Isaev threw back a shot of tequila. "Your best chance is to ask God that the consequences not be too serious."

Boris, who was experiencing a creeping feeling of depression, suggested, "Just to protect yourself, prepare a written statement tonight and have it notarized first thing in the morning."

"But, but … h - how can we find a notary at such short notice who knows Russian?" stammered Popov.

"Don't worry," Boris assured him, "A notary doesn't guarantee the truth of a document, just the fact that the signature is yours, so language isn't a problem. You can use your passport to prove your identity. In addition, Isaev and I will be witnesses."

"Yes, good idea," Popov said, his courage sounding at least momentarily plucked up. "First thing tomorrow morning, I will do it."

"By the way, young man," said Isaev, turning to Boris, "I trust that you haven't forgotten whose car Popov drove during his escapade."

"Good point," Boris said. "But I have an alibi. Remember that at Global, you always have to check in and out, and list the time of your arrival or departure. I will ask them to send me computer printouts of the registers on the days I was there."

"I'm afraid I won't be able to hide," Popov said. "Whatever I do, they can likely track me down with some kind of radar."

Boris smiled uneasily. "Speaking of this whole episode with Yakubovsky, I'd like to know whether either of you trusts Kravchuk. And maybe more important, do you think it is less likely that he will betray the three of us together than each of us separately?"

"I do not trust any of them," Isaev answered, emphasizing each word.

"I don't know who to trust anymore," was Popov's answer.

"Well, guys," Boris said, in a tone he hoped would raise their spirits, "let's agree here, then, before stepping into an uncertain future, that, at the very least, we will not betray each other. None of us doubts that Kravchuk would step on any of us if he felt it was in his interest. And though he might also be all too glad to betray us, I take the position that it will be much more difficult for him to do so if we stick together."

"And how can we be sure?" asked Isaev.

"There's no way to be sure," Boris answered, "but if we agree that none of us will betray another, that should be quite enough. It's the best we can do."

By this time, the main dish arrived: meat fried with vegetables and a variety of spices, and a half-liter of tequila with a lemon garnish.

They had already fortified themselves with three shots of Mexican tequila each, and Boris was about to fill up their glasses a fourth time when Popov protested. "Please, no more for me. I can handle three shots, but no more."

"But in Russia, shots consist of fifty grams, and in America only thirty," Boris pointed out. "So if your normal limit is a hundred and fifty grams, you still have sixty to go!"

"I don't care," Popov said, his voice filled with resolve, and his face growing red with frustration. "Three glasses, independent of their size, is my limit tonight. If you wish to have me in your company for the rest of this meal, please, three glasses only—no more."

"Boris, do not insist," interceded Isaev. "Just think. You and I can take care of the additional thirty grams ourselves! Each of us has his principles and, as you must have learned from your years in the States, respect for principles is the basis of democracy."

With that, the tension was relieved and the gloom was lifted, so the three men enjoyed their meal, joking, laughing, and telling funny stories.

As Boris paid the bill, however, he noticed that two athletic young men, upon seeing them pay, had hastily asked for their bill and paid as well—but not with a credit card, as Boris had done, but with cash.

Walking back to the hotel, Boris noted that the young men followed them, about a hundred feet behind. Once inside, he shared his observations with Isaev and Popov.

"It's good we're leaving tomorrow," Popov said, plunging again into despair.

In an attempt to reassure his friend, Isaev asked, "Are you really sure you have to be scared of these people, instead of Yakubovsky's? I don't think these people need you, Comrade Popov. All the more reason, however, for you to get to work on your statement."

"I will write it now, for sure," said Popov, looking down. "No doubt about it, I'm in trouble."

Reaching their floor, they found the tables covered with delicacies and the bar filled with a veritable paradise of liquid delight. But Popov went straight to his room to think and write.

Seeing it was only nine, Isaev suggested that he and Boris have a shot or two, to which Boris readily agreed. So, they downed a shot of a very smooth Irish Cream followed by one or perhaps two more of a delightful Amaretto.

"I have to say," Isaev said, almost sadly, "people here know how to live."

"Well, maybe when we finish this oil deal, we'll live better, too," said Boris.

"And you're so sure that the contract will go through?" Isaev asked, skeptically but affectionately.

"Why not? After all, Global has already committed to making the down payment."

"When the money is safely in your account, young man," Isaev cautioned, "only then will the money be yours."

"I am still optimistic," Boris insisted.

"We'll see," Isaev said. "We'll see."

Next morning after breakfast, Boris went to Global Oil and returned in less than an hour with printouts of the official record listing his, Isaev's, and Popov's arrival and departure times over the last several days. The three men then went to the business center and made copies of Popov's statement and had them notarized by a staff member at the front desk, with Boris and Isaev as witnesses.

Then, after returning to the business center, Boris took three heavy envelopes and put a copy of Popov's statement in each. Popov glued them shut and, in lieu of seals, pasted small pieces of paper over the closed flaps. All three signed their names on the seals and dated them as follows: "July 23, 1993. Saturday. The city of Washington, USA."

Popov gave one of the envelopes to Boris. "Please, save it for me. In case there are questions."

"Don't worry," Boris answered, taking the envelope.

Boris then made copies of the contract signed the day before, keeping the original and one additional copy for himself. Isaev put two of Popov's originals and three additional copies into his briefcase.

They returned to the lobby just in time to leave for the airport; Boris's plane was scheduled to take off for California in two hours, and the Moscow flight was scheduled in about three. So with their things packed, and with bittersweet feelings, they walked out of the lobby, leaving behind the luxury of the Ritz Carlton.

26

Moscow, Russia
July 25, 1993

AS USUAL, THE EX-OFFICER of the Ninth Division of KGB, and the head of
Agroprom security, retired lieutenant-colonel Dmitry Cherkizov, met Boris
at the terminal. Boris had arrived in Moscow via Frankfurt, precisely at six
p.m. They went through passport control in the VIP section, where Boris'
passport was stamped, and a porter brought his luggage: a single garment
bag containing a suit and a few other items. He carried the briefcase with
contract documents only.

On their way to the car, Boris noticed that it was hot and stuffy, typical
for the season, and ideal for a July thunderstorm. "Dmitry Vasilevich," he
addressed Cherkizov. "I have a gift for you. I have brought you a pair of
American running shoes."

"Many thanks, Boris," Cherkizov answered. "That is just what I wanted.
Every morning, I run cross-country to stay in shape, and as you know, the
quality of Russian shoes is not so good. But they say American shoes last a
year or two." He was obviously pleased with his gift, and Boris was glad, as
he always wanted to please those who were good to him.

In the car, they headed for the Hotel Mir, which was a favorite of Boris's
because it was in downtown Moscow, just a block from Tchaikovsky Street
where the US embassy was. To boot, many of its rooms overlooked the
Moscow River and the Russian White House, where the Russian Supreme
Council was located.

Before discovering the Hotel Mir, Boris had stayed at a hostel provided
by a former high school of the Communist party, located on Leningradsky
Prospect. But the Hotel Mir was much better. It adjoined the building

previously used by the Commission of Economic Cooperation of former Soviet bloc countries, which was now occupied by Moscow city government. Because of that, the hotel's dining room was of excellent quality, and had rather reasonable prices. In the mornings, a buffet was served, while the main restaurant opened in the evening.

As they drove, a powerful peal of thunder announced the beginning of a storm, followed by a real Moscow downpour. The dry ground greedily absorbed the moisture, and streams of water washed dust off the foliage bringing the huge city alive with color and good health. The driver asked if he could pull over for a few minutes until the front edge of the storm passed, and while they were waiting, Boris and Cherkizov opened their windows and enjoyed the clean, cool air. Soon, raindrops were bubbling in pools, a sign that the heavy showering wouldn't last long, and in about ten minutes, the rain was gone, and traffic started moving again. Boris and Cherkizov made good time, reaching the hotel about forty minutes later.

After breakfast the next morning, Boris left the hotel at 8:00 and asked the driver of the waiting car to take him to Agroprom, where his scheduled meeting with Popov and Isaev was to take place. It was a short drive, so fifteen minutes later, Boris was riding the elevator up to Kravchuk's reception hall, where Valerie said, "Gavrila is at the Kremlin now, but he will be back by lunch."

So Boris went to Filimonov's office, where he and Ivan shook hands like the good friends they were, talked a bit, and agreed to meet for dinner at the Mir's restaurant that evening.

Next, Boris went to Isaev's office, where Popov was also waiting for him. After greeting one another, the three took Popov's car for a visit to the SpetzMorTrans, the cargo-shipping company with whom Agroprom was about to finalize a contract for managing the transportation of the crude oil, as a part of the deal with Pennington and Agroprom - USA.

SpetzMorTrans, LLC, was located on Fourth Street at Izmaylovsky Zoo,[45] within easy reach of both the Izmayovsky Park Metro Station and Enthusiast's Road. The director of SpetzMorTrans, Mr. Andrey Viktorovich Zhukov, was a tall, strong man in his late fifties and a former commercial sea captain. Zhukov had managed SpetzMorTrans practically from the time it had been created, to coordinate shipments of cargo to Cuba. In 1963, after a confrontation between the USSR and the USA was resolved in the Caribbean, Zhukov helped build the so-called sea bridge from harbors in the Black Sea for the transport of weapons, equipment, and goods to—and of sugar, rum, and tobacco from—Cuba.

---

45 An area of Izmaylovsky Park, located in the central part of Moscow, where the city zoo was once located. Though the zoo is gone, the name remains.

Zhukov had graduated from Odessa's[46] Seaworthy College in 1960 and advanced quickly. He went on his first voyage as third assistant to the captain on the fifty-thousand-ton cargo ship *Freedom*. A year later, he was promoted to second officer, and in 1963, he became the first officer. When the Caribbean crisis ignited, the ship on which he was serving was re-equipped with two four-barrel, high-speed, twenty-millimeter machine guns on the bow, and two forty-five-millimeter cannons on the stern, to equip the vessel to resist an attack by sea.

By late 1964, Zhukov, expecting to be named captain of the *Freedom*, was instead assigned as deputy director of SpetzMorTrans in Moscow. The reason for such an important assignment was simple: Zhukov was the nephew of the legendary Captain Solyanik, the hero of Socialist work, the deputy of the Supreme Soviet of the USSR, and the well-known captain-director of the whaling fleet *Slava*.[47]

Captain Solyanik's popularity had been so great that songs were written in his honor. Composer Isaac Dunaevsky even wrote a musical, *White Acacia*, for him and the *Slava*. And each year, toward the end of May, when the *Slava* returned to Odessa from its hunting expeditions in the far-off Antarctica seas, the city went to the pier to meet the fleet. You can imagine the envy stirred by kids whose parents served on the whaling fleet, who would bring home whale mustaches, scarecrows of flying small fishes, and the ultimate object of desire—chewing gum. Not just any kind of chewing gum, but actual sticks of mint gum, wrapped in silver paper, and really made in the USA.

Mr. Zhukov received neither a whale mustache nor a pack of chewing gum, but he did receive the job as SpetzMorTrans's deputy director, along with a three-bedroom apartment in Moscow. And two years later, when the firm's director retired, the four stripes on Comrade Zhukov's sleeves were replaced with only one stripe—but a very wide stripe—for he was named the new director general.

So by the time the Agroprom trio walked into SpetzMorTrans, Zhukov had been managing for twenty-seven years. Their arrival at his reception hall on the second floor of the small building obviously had been anticipated. Zhukov's secretary, a middle-aged woman, graciously opened the door to the director general's large office, where the imposing Mr. Zhukov, sitting at his huge desk, stood, walked around, and embraced Isaev. The two had worked together many years ago on joint projects involving Cuba and, later, at the Commission of Economic Cooperation of former Soviet bloc countries.

After introducing his old friend to Popov and Boris, Arnold retrieved the contract, which was ready for checking and signing. So Zhukov called his

46   A city on the Black Sea.
47   Russian for *Glory.*

secretary, who brought in a tray of cookies and a jar of instant coffee, and then left and returned with a samovar of steaming hot water. While the business associates made their coffee, the secretary made four copies of the contract, one for each of them.

Having found no problems with the contract, Goryanin and Zhukov signed, after which Zhukov called in his secretary and asked her to apply the company seal and issue a corresponding confirmation number. He also asked her to have Mr. Victor Zakharov come in to supervise the execution of the contract.

In a short time, Mr. Zakharov came in and was introduced to their three visitors, with whom he exchanged business cards. And then, having all wished one another success, Popov, Isaev, and Goryanin left Zhukov's office and returned to Agroprom.

27

THAT EVENING, FILIMONOV MET with Boris. As mentioned before, Filimonov was previously a member of the central committee, an associate member of the ruling Politburo of the Communist party of the Soviet Union, and the Head of the Leningrad Region Communist Party Committee.

He was a real apparatchik,[48] clever and competent, but also honest and passionate about his work. He had never been involved in any scandals or bribes, let alone blackmailing, excessive drinking, and womanizing. He dressed for work in clean, ironed suits purchased in ordinary stores, and his shirts were always freshly cleaned.

It was a well-known fact that Ivan Filimonov tried to be fair with everyone, regardless of his or her ranking in the party. And in his position for the Leningrad region, he was respected not for his title as much as for his work ethic. The bosses, however, all too aware of his integrity, blocked him from rising too high on the party ladder.

In the beginning of 1991, when the country's political situation was reaching a boiling point, he did not hide his party membership as many others did, but, instead, resigned from his job. Still, he managed to maintain his relationships with the party and government elite.

Then in mid-1991, Filimonov was recommended for work at Agroprom. Recommended by leading government officials specifically to supervise the fulfillment of the Revival of Russia program, he was hired by Kravchuk just after the program had been approved by the Kremlin.[49] Thus, Filimonov was

---

48 A common name for professionals in the USSR Communist party.
49 A fourteenth century fortress in downtown Moscow and the official residence of the Russian president and presidential staff.

the one to obtain the necessary funding from the state government for the program.

Thanks to Kravchuk, Boris had met Filimonov the time he had come to Russia with private investors from the States who'd been looking at the Russian economy. Since then, Ivan and Boris often went on business trips to the Saint Petersburg, Arkhangelsk, and Karelia region, where, in Andropov's[50] time, the wood-processing industry was actively developed, including facilities for manufacturing veneers, plywood, wood paneling, furniture parts, and particle board.

In Saint Petersburg, they organized for a US investor an enterprise that repackaged, for export, furniture-quality plywood. The plywood was purchased at the Baltic wood-processing plant, whose identification and packaging processes were operating in accordance with old Soviet standards but did not meet international requirements, which kept them out of the States. So Boris and Ivan set up a private warehouse for remarking and repackaging the plywood, and soon it was being loaded onto cargo vessels and shipped to the Atlantic ports of Savannah and Galveston.

The investor had put down less than one hundred thousand dollars for the start-up, which included two years' worth of employee salaries, and then withdrew his money. He quit paying for rent and utilities at the warehouse, stopped compensating the workers, and never paid his Russian partners for the plywood that had already been delivered. As a result, his activities—at least those in Russia—were shut down.

Now, after two years of working together, Boris and Ivan enjoyed a warm relationship, spending even off-hours discussing personal and political matters. And so, it was about seven that evening when Ivan knocked on Boris's hotel door. The restaurant wouldn't open until seven thirty, so they decided to take a walk along the Moscow River. Although the sun was not at its zenith, it was still high above the horizon, and it was hot. Compared to Southern California, where at eight p.m. you needed to turn on the lights, Moscow during the summer remained light even at ten and only started to get dark around eleven.

The two friends walked along Bolshoi Devyatinsky Drive toward the Moscow River and turned left on the embankment. Other than the music from a tourist riverboat, all was quiet; few pedestrians braved the streets of Moscow those days, having long grown tired of the seemingly perpetual mob fights.

They approached the former building of the Commission of Economic Cooperation, crossed over to New Arbat Street, and went down it until they

---

50   Yuri Andropov was the head of the KGB, and, later, the secretary general of the Communist party of USSR, before Michael Gorbachev.

crossed the bridge and reached the Russian White House, where some kind of tense situation had developed. Reinforced groups of special security forces and police were in place to defend concrete block barriers intended to prevent through traffic. It was a clear sign that all was not peaceful.

Filimonov briefly summarized for Boris the building tension and possible impending confrontation between President Yeltsin and the Supreme Council of the Russian Federation led by Vice President General Rutskoy and the speaker of the Supreme Council, Ruslan Khazbulatov. Filimonov's view was that it would not end without serious complication and even traumatic events. Filimonov's words would soon prove prophetic.

After strolling to the end of the Russian White House, Boris and Ivan made a final right, completing their circle and returning to the Hotel Mir. As they talked, Boris got the feeling that Ivan regretted not having been in the Washington meetings. Ivan made it clear that he'd had time to hear Isaev and Popov's impressions of the proceedings, but that now it was Boris's turn to talk. And, Ivan said, it wasn't just simple curiosity. There was a behind-the-scenes power struggle at Agroprom that made having a hand on the pulse of new developments not only amusing but also essential to keeping his head in such a volatile environment.

So Boris told him about the negotiations, but also mentioned the strange appearance of Yakubovsky, as well as the agreement he'd made with Popov and Isaev to take precautions. Ivan thanked Boris for his interpretation of the events and said that, though he'd already had this information from the other two, he was now completely satisfied.

At the hotel restaurant, Ivan and Boris were the only diners. They had a little snack, two bowls of borscht, and a cup of tea before parting, after which Boris, due to jet lag, fell quickly asleep, and Ivan went home to his family.

The next day, Ivan and Boris went together to Novokuybyshevsk. Ivan had arranged a meeting there with the managing director of the dispatch unit of Transneft,[51] the organization responsible for pumping crude oil via pipeline from Tyumen to the port of Ventspils on the Baltic Sea.

During their trip, Ivan told Boris about the deepening conflict between him and Strelov. Ivan did not go into details, and Boris asked no more, but later, on the elevator to his floor, Boris remembered that the previous winter, when Ivan and he had been in the city of Petrozavodsk on some business for Agroprom, Strelov had gone with them. Boris had sensed the tension between Ivan and Strelov even then, but hadn't mentioned it, as he figured it was none of his business.

To boot, Strelov had no purpose on the trip. He seemed just to tag along, as if he were an observer, and behaved strangely the entire time. His face was

---

51 The Russion term *transneft* roughly translates to "crude oil transportation."

always red and he seemed perpetually tense and angry, coming to life only when he'd had a drink. In fact, there had been one episode during dinner, when Strelov had ordered three glasses of triple shots. When Ivan and Boris had declined theirs, Strelov consumed all three.

Then drunk, Strelov, without asking his dinner companions, invited three girls from a nearby table to join them. Ivan and Boris felt uncomfortable with the arrangement, not because the women weren't presentable—in fact, they were very pretty, and quiet enough—still, everything had its own place and time. And so after paying the bill, Boris and Ivan left for their rooms. Little did they know that a few minutes later, Strelov also went to his, accompanied by the three young women.

At about two in the morning, however, Ivan was knocking on Boris's door and telling him that Strelov was in trouble. The girls' pimp was demanding payment from Strelov, who, because he had no money, was making a scene, shouting that he was the Communist party boss from Leningrad and asking for the police. When Boris arrived, he immediately understood the situation and, because Strelov was so out of control, asked Ivan how much money was needed. Then hearing three hundred dollars, without a word, Boris reached into his pocket and retrieved the cash.

When the ruckus had subsided, Ivan called for an ambulance to take the still-raging Strelov to the hospital. Subsequently, they learned that Strelov had had a serious drinking problem and had already been treated for three weeks.

After Ivan and Boris left Petrozavodsk, Strelov's wife came from Moscow to retrieve him from the hospital, and Boris hadn't seen him since. As for his three hundred dollars, Boris never bothered asking for its return; in any case, Strelov probably would never be able to pay it back.

28

July 28, 1993

BORIS ARRIVED AT AGROPROM a few minutes before nine. He, Isaev, and Popov had to be at VneshtorgImpex, LLC, at ten to sign the contract between VneshtorgImpex and Agroprom - USA for the delivery, processing, and sale of crude oil, and the sale of processed oil products. The exact language of the contract was as follows:

> The firm, Pennington International, shall wire to Agroprom - USA's bank account the pre-agreed-upon amount of money for forty thousand tons of crude oil. Agroprom - USA shall pay VneshtorgImpex for its services in US dollars. VneshtorgImpex is licensed for its export and has the necessary quotas for the sale of crude oil exported for processing.
>
> Also, VneshtorgImpex converts US dollars into Russian rubles and will pay First Russian Oil Corporation in rubles for each shipment of forty thousand tons of crude oil. First Russian Oil Corporation and Tyumen Oil & Gas Association, having neither license nor quotas for the export of crude oil, is consequently able to operate in only Russian rubles. Thus, First Russian Oil Corporation will buy the crude oil from Tyumen Oil & Gas Association and, using the services of TRANSOIL and SpetzMorTrans, deliver this crude oil to the harbor terminal for loading on tanker vessels, which will subsequently deliver the crude oil to Global Oil's refinery plants for processing and future sales of petroleum products.

Although Transoil and SpetzMorTrans were to have been paid in rubles, neither company wanted rubles, which were daily losing value relative to other currencies. Therefore, while the contract arranged for payment in rubles, both associations anticipated finding a way to convert the payments to US dollars. A second problem had been to find a company with the necessary license and quotas to export the crude oil. VneshtorgImpex was this company.

A foreign trade association, VneshtorgImpex, LLC, was conveniently located on the sixth floor of the high-rise building on Smolensky Plaza, where both the Ministry of Foreign Affairs of the Russian Federation and the former Ministry of Foreign Trade of the USSR had their offices.

It was about a ten-minute drive from Agroprom to Smolensky Plaza. So when Popov had not arrived by twenty to ten, Boris and Isaev proceeded without him. For all they knew, he might already be there. After all, Mr. Nikolay Grushin, who was signing the contract for VneshtorgImpex, had been Popov's schoolmate.

Arriving at VneshtorgImpex, Isaev told their driver to keep an eye out for Popov and, if he saw him, to deliver the message that they would be in the security department. Inside, Isaev and Boris presented their Agroprom IDs to the security office and received two of the three temporary passes that had been reserved for them. Popov, however, was neither there nor in Grushin's office.

Something must have happened, they thought. Popov never was late, especially when he had to sign an important contract, and especially this contract, for which, just the day before, he and Grushin had prepared the particulars, such as the conditions surrounding delivery, payment, quantity, and quality.

Regardless, the men decided not to wait any longer. It took three hours for Boris and Isaev to review and sign the contract, and for the VneshtorgImpex secretary to finalize the accompanying paperwork. By then, it was already one o'clock p.m., and there was still no sign of Popov. Isaev called Agroprom, but Popov wasn't there, nor was he in his apartment.

So with their copies of the contract, Goryanin and Isaev said good-bye to Grushin, returned their temporary passes, and in less than fifteen minutes, were back at Agroprom.

They went again to see Kravchuk, who had, at last, returned to his office, and now warmly greeted them with embraces. They told Kravchuk that practically all of the contracts had been signed and that the next day, August 1, Boris and Ivan would take the train to Novokuybyshevsk to finalize the details of pumping through pipeline the crude oil from storage to the loading facilities at the harbor.

All the while, Kravchuk appeared fatigued, with a strangely reddish-blue face. It didn't look like he had been in the Kremlin; it looked like he had been drinking, steadily and heavily for days. Though his speech was precise and coherent, his florid face, alcohol-laced breath, and strong body odor gave him away.

After leaving Kravchuk's office, Boris felt the jet lag set in again, so after saying good-bye to Isaev and agreeing to check in with him and Popov later, he went back to his room. On his bed, Boris spread out all the signed contracts, sorted them into marked folders, and put them back in his briefcase. Then he lay down, staring at the ceiling.

The ringing of his phone a few hours later woke him up. It was Isaev. "Popov didn't show up in his office, and he's not in his apartment."

"Where could he be?" Boris asked.

"I'd better alert our security services," Isaev said. "We have to find him. I'm worried."

"Maybe ...." Boris hinted.

"That's it. That's what got me worried."

"I'll be at your office tomorrow morning at nine."

"When are you and Ivan leaving for Novokuybyshevsk?"

"Train number ten, the Zhiguli Express, leaves at 18:50 from Kazansky Railroad Station. It arrives at Novokuybyshevsk the next morning at ten. They'll send a car for us."

"Well, then, I'll see you tomorrow at nine," Isaev said and hung up.

Undressing, Boris lay back down and turned on the TV.

29

ONE MONTH HAD PASSED since Fedorov had directed Mr. Peter Veresayev to investigate what had happened in Tyumen. During this time, Veresayev had met with his friends, and friends of his friends, the chief of geological services for the Tyumen region, and the senior geologist of Tyumen Oil & Gas. He interviewed local business executives, railroad workers, and dispatchers.

During this time, a lot of vodka was drunk, enough food to satisfy a military brigade was served, and many a liberal monetary bribe was made, until, gradually, "Kazemirich" was able to construct a comprehensive picture of the state of affairs at Tyumen Oil & Gas. This picture included information regarding the local criminal organizations that had their eye on the association. It also included a copy of the agreement, by which the association acquired the right to sell its crude oil in exchange for the delivery of foodstuff and consumer goods not only for its workers but also for the entire Tyumen region. Under the terms of this agreement, the association would be handed over to its new owners upon completion of the crude oil sale and delivery of goods.

Most important, Veresayev had discovered that the waste-storage tanks, after being cleared, were not refilled with waste but with crude oil, in the unrecorded amount of about five hundred thousand tons. All of this meant that the association's real value was considerably higher than its book value—in fact, about fifty million dollars higher—though after the sale of the unrecorded commodity, the two values would become equal; you see, the association's devaluation was planned to coincide with the sale.

So it was armed with this knowledge that, after lunch on Wednesday, July 28, Veresayev called Fedorov and requested an immediate meeting.

They met at Fedorov's summer residence in the small village of Valentinovka, where, upon learning what "Kazemirich" had discovered,

Fedorov showed no emotion, but instead left the meeting room without a single word. He returned a few minutes later with three bundles of one-hundred-dollar bills, a total of thirty thousand dollars. He handed the money to Veresayev and suggested that he immediately take two weeks of vacation to Spain or France, and "properly" spend his time there, saying, "You must begin your vacation tomorrow. You deserve it."

Next day, Veresayev left for Paris, and then later traveled to the French Riviera. He did his work well, elated that his boss appreciated his efforts; but, as his vacation schedule called for, he had to return Sunday, August 15, to Moscow.

30

FIRST THING NEXT MORNING, Boris arrived in Kravchuk's reception room, hoping to coordinate their activities for the next few days. There, he came face to face with a beautiful young woman who also happened to have an appointment with Kravchuk, so they entered his office together.

Kravchuk stopped what he was doing and looked at them with raised eyebrows. "Do you two already know each other?" Kravchuk asked.

"Not yet," Boris answered.

"Well, let me introduce you," Kravchuk offered gallantly. "Boris Georgievich Goryanin, meet Lydia Ostapovna Selina."

Lydia extended her hand, not as Lady Melissa had, with the back turned up to invite a kiss, but as men did, for a handshake. And when Boris touched it, he felt not only the softness of her skin, but also the strength of her personality.

Kravchuk, noticing the wedding ring on her finger, lifted an eyebrow and said, "When did you have time to get married?"

"I made time," she answered, diplomatically shading her pride with a coquettish smile.

Kravchuk's face beamed. "When do we celebrate?"

"Let's finish the contract first," she said. "Or, at least, let's start work on the contract. Then we can celebrate."

"Ms. Selina organized the contract for the sale of crude oil from Tyumen," Kravchuk told Boris. Then turning to Lydia, he said, "Mr. Goryanin organized the negotiations and contract-signing in Washington. Now he's setting up a system for pumping crude oil to the port of embarkation and will organize the various financial flows."

"I am very pleased to meet you, dear Lydia," Boris began, but then she

132

looked at him in such a way that any impulse he may have had to flirt instantly vanished. Further, Boris was surprised to learn that Lydia had a PhD in economics; it hardly matched her exquisitely feminine appearance, with its delightful touches of the provinces. This woman, he thought, was definitely worthy of attention.

After updating Kravchuk and Selina on his recent work, Boris told them that on Sunday evening he and Ivan Filimonov would leave for Novokuybyshevsk, where they would sign the contract for pipeline transportation. They were scheduled to return to Moscow the very next day, after which Boris would then fly to Geneva to meet with Eddy Pennington.

Boris stood to say good-bye, and as Lydia had no further business, she did likewise. As they left the office, Boris added that, from her accent, she sounded as though she was from the Volga. Then he told her that he once lived on the Volga, but had traveled east of Volga only once, and a long time ago. When Selina told him that she had been born in Togliatti, Boris expressed intrigued; he, too, had lived for some years in Togliatti. When he asked her where in Togliatti she had lived, Lydia answered in VCO-5.

"You know," Boris said, "I had a friend who lived in a barrack in VCO-5. Her name was Svetlana Alexandrovna Sedelnikova."

"Sedelnikova?" Lydia asked, and now it she who was intrigued. "Svetlana Alexandrovna was the mother of my best girlfriend, Irene. We lived in the same barrack."

Boris suddenly remembered that, in 1970, Svetlana had told him that a neighbor had frozen to death in the street, less than a hundred feet from his house.

"That was my father," Lydia answered quietly.

"How small the world is," Boris said.

"You're right," she said. "I meet a stranger from America, and he turns out to know my former neighbor."

With this new information, Selina looked at Boris in an entirely new light. It was as if he were one of her kind. So when Boris announced that he needed to stop in and see Isaev for a moment, she decided to accompany him.

Boris asked Isaev whether he'd heard anything from Popov, but there was no news, so he reminding Isaev that he would be leaving for Geneva as soon as he returned from Novokuybyshevsk, and told him he would see him when he got back.

Isaev smiled. "Some people are lucky—here today, Oslo tomorrow, and we will never catch them." he was paraphrasing the refrain of the popular Russian bard, Vladimir Visotsky.

"Not them, but her," Boris corrected, with a smile.

When Boris and Lydia got into the elevator, she said, "We both agree that the world is an awfully small place, but you have no idea how small it is, in my case. When you return from your trip, I'll tell you my story and you will understand."

"Is this an invitation for a date?" Boris flashed her a sly smile.

"Don't be a bad boy, Boris. I am recently and very happily married. In fact, you will get to meet my husband on the main floor. He's a colonel in the paratrooper forces." At that very moment, the elevator opened to the lobby, and a strongly built man, of the same height as Boris but physically far more imposing, approached them.

"Boris Georgievich," Lydia said, "please meet my husband, Vladimir."

"Vladimir." The man gripped Boris's hand like a vice.

"Boris," Goryanin answered, a shade paler than before.

"Boris is our contact with Global Oil in the States," Lydia explained, and quickly said, "Good-bye, Boris." And with that, Vladimir with Lydia, arm in arm, left the lobby.

On the way back to his hotel, Boris thought more about Svetlana Sedelnikova. He had not told Lydia that he had become acquainted with Svetlana while preparing for his PhD exams. They'd met at the Kurumoch Airport, while waiting for the same flight to Moscow. Both were on business. Boris was heading to an annual trade show, and Svetlana, who headed the computer center at her institute, was to visit the computer center at the USSR Academy of Science.

They had registered at the terminal and checked in their luggage together. Their flight, as it was customary with Russian airlines, was delayed. Having free time on their hands, Boris and Svetlana wandered around the airport, leaving the terminal proper and walking across the plaza to a small park. After a pleasant walk through the trees, they returned to the airport as friends. They sat next to each other in the plane. In Moscow, Svetlana told Boris that she would be staying with her aunt and gave him her phone number. It's not hard to figure out what happened next. During their time in Moscow, Boris and Svetlana became more than just close friends.

When Boris arrived at the hotel, he asked the driver to pick him up and take him to the Kazansky Railroad Station at five p.m., this Sunday, August 1. Boris went up to his room. He left his briefcase there and went back down to the dining room for dinner. He spent the next two days by himself. He did not want to see anybody. He needed to be alone and get some rest.

On Sunday, at a quarter to four, Boris went down to the registration desk, left his luggage with the concierge, and left for the railroad station, taking only a briefcase full of documents and a small bag of toiletries. He met Ivan Filimonov at six and the Zhiguli Express left promptly at ten till seven.

In Russia, trains usually arrived and departed on time, not like airplanes, which were often delayed by weather or technical reasons. In fact, it was widely believed that taking a train often took as much time as it did to fly. Goryanin and Filimonov had reserved a double sleeping compartment. Once the train was underway and out of Moscow proper, a waiter brought them traditional hot tea, and they found themselves rolling pleasantly across Russia toward the Volga River.

Boris knew that Ivan had chosen to take the train because it would offer them not only more time to talk, but also more privacy. And the relaxed ambience of the train was conducive to thoughtful, detailed discussion. Boris was convinced that Ivan was an honest and fair person, and he trusted him completely.

During the next few hours, they thoroughly discussed and analyzed the Washington meetings and negotiations. After reiterating his account of the events, Boris answered many of Ivan's questions regarding particular participants' behavior. He also reminded him of the conversation that had taken place in the Mexican restaurant. Considering that Popov had now, apparently, disappeared for good, the implications of that conversation overshadowed even the scheduling of the first shipment of oil.

Though Boris had also recounted Popov's adventures with Yakubovsky, and the resulting tension between the two, he couldn't decide whether to report about the affidavit that Popov had sworn to in Washington. Then, as if reading Boris's thoughts, Ivan asked whether Isaev could confirm what Boris was saying. Boris's answer—that Isaev was a lawyer whose word would carry substantial weight—was met with a shrug that indicated doubt.

"Boris, are you able to keep a secret?" Ivan asked, seemingly out of the blue. Then as Filimonov had done a few moments before, Boris answered with an ambiguous shrug of his own. "Probably. I can. I think."

"So," Filimonov began, "I don't think you know that I began working for the Communist party straight from the city prosecutor's office. By education, I am a lawyer. I graduated from the Leningrad University Law School in 1961, while working as a detective, of all things, on the side. When I returned to Leningrad, I worked in the city prosecutor's office and was quickly promoted to senior inspector, a rank equal to major, and recommended for more advanced training.

By graduation, I had advanced to assistant prosecutor, which is sort of a colonel of the legal service. I soon earned my Jurum Doctor[52] degree, but in 1979, when I was named Head of the Leningrad regional Communist party branch, I left legal work behind. However, I have never lost my interest in law enforcement, though."

52   Doctor of Laws (Latin)

Ivan fell silent for a few minutes, and continued. "In those years, the concept of legality in our country was rather, shall we say, original—though, personally, I tried to remain fair and act in accordance with the law. You probably know what I mean about the legality and integrity of our country then, otherwise, you might not have left for the States. Perhaps, now, for your ethical stance, you might be able to occupy a place of honor in your native land. And there is no need to protest. I am very good at reading people."

Filimonov broke off again, but Boris stayed silent, understanding that Ivan's words had been only a preamble.

"I recently receive an offer to work in the office of Prosecutor General for the Russian Federation. The position is important enough that I have chosen to leave Agroprom shortly. As for you, I'd advise you to be more cautious, particularly with Kravchuk. Simply put, he tells big lies and he tells them frequently. He does not go to the Kremlin. And if he does go, it is only to drink. Agroprom's financing happens, basically, because of Isaev, Theodora, and yours truly—the obedient servant. In any event, I will report to my new office at the end of September. And if Mr. Popov has not been found by then, I will become personally involved in the investigation. Your help will, probably, be required."

Boris looked Ivan in the eye. "Is your new appointment somehow connected with the activity we observed at the Russian White House just recently?"

"You're on the right track, my friend," Ivan said.

"Does this mean new developments are expected by the end of September, beginning of October? Developments that might be reflected in our ability to deliver on the Global Oil contract?"

"I do not think so."

"So, what is going on?" Boris again asked.

"That is a reasonable question," Ivan said, folding his hands. "What you need to realize is that both financial and political power is increasingly being concentrated in the hands of mobsters. It is more complicated than that, but ... well, I might as well fill you in the hows and whys. After all," he said with a sigh, "It's a long way to Novokuybyshevsk."

"Certainly," Boris said with great feeling.

And with that, Mr. Filimonov began his story. For about two hours, Boris listened to Ivan, without a single word. Ivan unloaded what had apparently been accumulating on his heart. And even after Ivan had finished, Boris remained silent. Quite simply, there was nothing to add.

In the morning, they looked silently out the window, enjoying the beauty of the Russian summer as they passed the small towns of Syzran and then

Chapaevsk. At about ten o'clock, the attendant came with their tickets and they paid for the bedding.

"The train arrives precisely on schedule, at ten twelve," the attendant said. "We'll stop for only two minutes, so be ready."

"Always ready," they both answered, quoting the well-known Young Pioneers'[53] chorus, and bursting out laughing.

"You never forget what you have learned at your mother's breast," said Filimonov.

As the train approached Novokuybyshevsk, Boris said, "Considering your new position, will you even be allowed to have contact with me?"

"I know what you're asking," Ivan answered. "Don't worry. I can always communicate with honest, decent people. But God forbid that you ever need my services as an investigator." Filimonov added significantly. "I am not talking about you, of course. I know you and believe in you. But there are others in our business who may find themselves in trouble."

It wasn't two that afternoon that they reached a crucial point in the negotiations at the Novokuybyshevsk Oil dispatching center, at which point, the head of the center, Mr. Peter Anisimov, was very straightforward.

"Payment in the amount of 2 percent of the entire amount of the contract," he said, "is expected in advance. And from there, as they say, onward and upward."

At Boris's request, the secretary then brought them a signed invoice for the sum of one million dollars.

---

53   The USSR scout organization for school children.

31

AFTER ARRIVING AT THE Kazansky station at precisely 7:31, Ivan and Boris went straight to Agroprom, which they reached shortly before nine. They quickly ate breakfast at the dining room on the thirteenth floor and then went their separate ways.

While Ivan attended to his own affairs, Boris went to update Kravchuk on the Global Oil contract. Time was short, however, as Boris was scheduled to leave that afternoon for Geneva to open special accounts with the Swiss branch of the Banque Nationale de Paris. So upon learning that Kravchuk had not yet arrived, Boris asked Valerie to tell him that he would be waiting Isaev's office.

Again, Isaev's answer to Boris's question was negative; Popov had not yet reappeared. So with a resigned air, Boris reported the results of his trip to Novokuybyshevsk.

Upon hearing that the dispatch center's management was adamant about receiving cash in advance, Isaev responded with a shrug. "Your friend Eddy has said that he is handling the down payment, and you will see him tomorrow. As they say, the ball is in his court."

"Yes, it certainly is," Boris has answered. "But one million dollars. That's a lot of cash. How will they get so much into Russia?"

"There is no restriction on the import of hard currency into Russia," Isaev said, adding with a smile, "of course, if it were the other way around, there might be a problem. Anyway, before entering Russia, cash has to be declared at the customs offices. Just be sure to keep the declaration in case the customs officer wants to see it before you cross the Russian border on your way out. If you do that, there should be no problem."

So with the currency issue solved, they began to discuss the increasingly serious political situation. The tension between the president and the Supreme Council seemed to increase by the hour. However, Valerie knocked on the door just then and informed Boris that Kravchuk was in his office waiting.

"I hope Gavrila is sober today," Isaev said. "Boris, before you leave, please come back and say good-bye to the old man."

"What are you thinking?" Boris said. "Of course I will." With that, he closed the door behind him.

Gavrila was sitting in the armchair at his desk, shouting at a terrified-looking Mrs. Theodora. "Why do you never inform me of these things in advance?" The veins on his neck were bulging, and he punctuated his exasperation by jumping up and stamping his feet.

His behavior only emboldened Theodora, who went on the offensive, shouting even louder. "Look at him! A drunken bum, shouting! Who are you shouting at, you swine? If you did your job, you would know what is going on! Instead, you are running around, telling people you left for the Kremlin, when you really went to visit your favorite bar. I will let everyone know about you. I have seen rascals like you before."

The whole thing made Boris uncomfortable. It was obvious that Theodora had no intention of stopping her tirade anytime soon, so assuming Kravchuk would not be available for at least an hour, Boris left and motioned for Valerie to follow him into the hallway.

"What are they discussing?" Boris asked, half in jest.

"Oh, that? They do that every morning. Gavrila borrowed fifty thousand dollars from Theodora and hasn't returned it. So naturally, she's upset."

Boris grimaced. "I'm going to Isaev's office. When they calm down, please call me, okay?"

But Boris hadn't even reached Isaev's office before Valerie caught up with him. "Boris, Gavrila is ready for you now."

Boris returned to see Kravchuk in his armchair, quiet and affable, as if nothing had happened. He was a totally different person than he had been literally a minute ago, and Theodora was nowhere to be seen.

"Would you like a cup of tea?" Kravchuk asked.

"Thanks, but Mr. Filimonov and I already had breakfast."

"By the way, where is he?"

"In his office," Boris answered. "We returned from Novokuybyshevsk this morning, and Ivan plans to be here the rest of the day."

"I know how much he likes to work," Kravchuk said icily. "The idler. He'll see. Those lawyers in the prosecutor's office will teach him how to work and how to respect freedom. Those stinking democrats."

Boris knew that on the one hand, Kravchuk envied Ivan, but on the other, was glad that Ivan was leaving, so he would no longer have to share profits.

Having, by chance, witnessed the argument between Kravchuk and Theodora, Boris now also knew how important the contract was to Kravchuk. But that was not Boris's problem, so he preferred to stay out of it; he already had enough problems of his own.

"So, where are we with the contracts?" Kravchuk asked. "Can we get to Ventspils[54] and load the tankers?"

"I think so," Boris answered. "As of today, we have the contracts with Global Oil, VneshtorgImpeks, and SpetsMorTrance. I also have the Novokuybyshevsk Oil invoice. I hope that's all we need."

"And what's the situation with the prepayment?"

"I am leaving today for Frankfurt, and will be in Geneva tomorrow morning to open special accounts for Agroprom - USA. An irrevocable letter of credit in the amount of five point five million dollars will be deposited to fund the first delivery.

Kravchuk hesitated a second before saying, "I have a huge request for you. When you open the account, please send me a power of attorney for withdrawing the money." He caught himself and quickly changed his request. "Excuse me. No, that's not what I wanted to say. What I'd like is a power of attorney for managing the Agroprom - USA account."

Boris knew that what Kravchuk had first blurted out was what he had meant to say—it was no use trying to backtrack. The bottom line was, he wanted to put the responsibility for the money on Boris. But, contrary to his thoughts, Boris said, "Certainly, certainly. What kind of question is that? We are partners, aren't we?"

"Certainly," Kravchuk answered. "Well, then, I won't detain you any longer. By the way, when are you returning to Moscow?"

"As soon as I resolve all of the unanswered questions, probably mid-September, when payment to Novokuybyshevsk and the first delivery of crude oil are due."

"Well then, good luck and have a successful trip."

On Boris's way out, he stopped at Valerie's desk and said, "Keep well, Val."

"Are you leaving again?" she said. "When are you going to bring something for me?"

Boris laughed. "That depends on when you'll go out with me."

"I will go, for sure, if you bring me something," Valerie said, laughing back.

Boris went to Isaev's office, but the door was locked. So, he went to Ivan's office. That door was also locked.

---

54   The commercial harbor on the Baltic Sea.

"Well, okay," Boris said to the empty hallway. "I guess I'll see you guys, later." Heading for the elevator, he ran into Mrs. Selina.

"How are you, pretty lady?" Boris asked with a welcoming smile.

"I should be the one asking you," Lydia said with a smile of her own.

Boris told her that nearly all was ready for pumping the first delivery of crude to Ventspils. He also told her about his going to Geneva to open the bank accounts.

"And concerning preparations," Boris said, "Do you have anything to deliver?"

"Yes, sir," Lydia said, feigning a military salute that was so coquettish and adorable that Boris again realized how beautiful she was.

Lydia, reading his thoughts, said with a note of affection in her voice, "I know what you're thinking, young man." Then she shook hands with him, and left.

At the Moscow Sheremetyevo-2 Airport Boris went to the VIP desk and, without any customs inspection, continued to passport control, a service for which he had paid two hundred rubles. He was so pleased that he asked the cute girl at the VIP counter how he could arrange the VIP service again in the future.

"Just call me," she said. "I'll be happy to help you."

"Is it possible to do that from outside Russia?" he asked.

"Why not?" the young women said. "By the way, my name is Vicky Koval and here is my phone number."

Boris had the feeling that he seen this girl before, with her blonde hair, which fell in curls around her shoulders, and blue-blue eyes and succulent lips. She was a bit chubby; it was true. He tried recalling where he had seen her, until she asked him for his passport, at which point, he abandoned that train of thought.

After passport control, Boris realized that he was hungry, so he went to the second floor and ordered a bowl of Udon soup at the new Japanese restaurant. At nine dollars a bowl, he felt like he was already home.

32

BORIS ARRIVED AT HIS hotel in Frankfurt just before dinnertime; he had an overnight layover en route to Geneva. After dropping his things off in his room, he went to the sauna. This had become his routine after every trip to Moscow. The sauna warmed his soul and relieved the fatigue he always accumulated in that city, where disorder and discomfort were the order of the day.

Refreshed and invigorated, Boris awoke the next morning feeling like a new man. He ate breakfast and took his time getting to the airport. He took only a well-traveled briefcase and a travel kit of toiletries with him. The luggage, he left in his room, since he would be returning that very night.

Flight 4592 left shortly after noon, and in just over an hour, Boris had landed in Geneva, breezed through passport control, and was walking into the arrival hall, where, to his great surprise, he saw Lady Melissa.

"I don't believe what I'm seeing. Dear Lady Melissa, is that you?"

"It's me," she answered, smiling and offering Boris her hand as she had the first time they'd met.

"I am glad to see you," Boris said, shaking her hand in mock unawareness.

"Okay. Please, that's enough. Try to be serious now. I only came to pick you up because all the others were busy."

"And you are free?" Boris teased.

"If I am not good enough for you, should I live?" she said, feigning an insult.

"You don't understand," Boris said, now looking her in the eye, completely serious. "I never dreamed I'd see you again. You know, I had become quite fond of you."

Ignoring his comment, she said, "Do you have any baggage to claim?"

"No."

"So, let's go."

As Boris followed her out, he impishly tried to hide his interest, which now seemed not only genuine but totally out of his control. Then, suddenly he understood what was attracting him; it was the extraordinary depth and beauty of her eyes, which radiated with warmth and trust, sparkled with charm, and glowed with attention and care. That's not to say, however, that Boris found her body any less attractive than her eyes.

They got into her car, a large 400E Mercedes, which moved smoothly with its powerful, silent engine. As they drove, Boris kept to himself in an attempt to calm down after their unexpected meeting. He was relieved that Lady Melissa stayed silent as well. He mentally reviewed his day's schedule, which he had arranged before leaving Moscow: after his trip to the Banque Nationale de Paris, the bank suggested to him by Eddy, it was on to Pennington International, to see how people lived on the right side of the tracks.

A half-hour later, they arrived at the bank's downtown office, located on the shore of Lake Geneva on the Quai du Mont-Blanc, which was just in front of the lake's famous fountain.

Melissa pulled into the underground garage and parked masterfully in one of its tiny spaces. Then they took a small elevator to the third floor, where the bank office was located. When the elevator opened, a security guard opened a heavy metal door and led the visitors through to a small meeting room. A few minutes later, a tall man who was too nicely dressed in Boris's opinion, entered the room. He greeted Lady Melissa in a very elegant manner, putting her outstretched hand briefly to his lips.

Boris was again drawn to way Melissa offered her hand, while shyly turning her head to one side, and he was impressed by how expertly this dandy responded, showing gallantry that Boris was sure he could not have duplicated, even after a hundred years of training.

Then, after shaking hands with Boris in the conventional fashion, which relieved Boris a great deal, the man introduced himself. "Dominique de la Perie, executive vice president of BNP. I am pleased that you have chosen to rely on our institution and its two hundred forty-two years of tradition and respectability."

"How do you do, sir," Boris answered.

"How do you do," the man echoed. "As I understand, you have only a few hours in Geneva, so let's get to business."

Boris opened his worn briefcase and retrieved a beautiful red leather folder, which he had borrowed from Kravchuk and promised to return when he got back from Geneva. From the folder, Boris pulled copies of the

Agroprom - USA corporate filing papers, a resolution from the board of directors to open the checking account with Banque Nationale de Paris, and a general power of attorney issued to Boris Goryanin as president of Agroprom - USA authorizing him for management of this account. Meanwhile, Lady Melissa, acting uninterested, asked for a cup of coffee.

Boris then filled out forms provided by Mr. de la Perie, but did not write Kravchuk's name once, as if he had totally forgotten the request. In addition, Boris provided the executive vice president with the previous year's tax returns, both for Agroprom - USA and for himself.

After looking over Boris's personal tax returns, Mr. de la Perie said, "I don't think we'll need these."

Boris protested in mock embarrassment. "I brought them just in case. Would you mind including them in your file anyway?"

"Of course, if you wish," de la Perie agreed pleasantly without further discussion.

Boris knew full well what he was doing, however. His personal tax returns reflected his modest income, which would lessen his risk of being sued should anything go awry. With any business transaction, there was always a chance that something could go wrong, and no one was likely to sue him if he had no money.

Mr. de la Perie took all the documents and left the room. Now alone with Lady Melissa, Boris looked at her unabashedly. When she looked back at him, he realized he could not take his eyes off of her. So, both of them sat and looked at each other eyes. All the while, Boris examined her face, which was so dear to his heart, thinking the delicious words, "Lady Melissa!" and wondering, if she weren't so distant, whether he would be so brave as to cover that beautiful face with kisses. Then suddenly feeling a bit shy, he grinned crookedly and turned away, just as Mr. de la Perie returned with a book of checks for the newly opened Agroprom - USA account.

As Melissa and Boris were saying good-bye to Mr. de la Perie, Boris changed his plan to go to Pennington International. Suddenly ashamed by his poverty, he had lost the desire to see how Eddy's people were living. He became flushed with anger at his life, his motherland, and even his sweet Lady Melissa. He thought, defensively, that he was no worse than they.

Lady Melissa saw the rush of emotion on Boris's face, but lacking worldly experience, assumed that Boris' sudden change in emotion was caused by her. She found this curious and amusing. She suggested they drive around and see the city, but Boris asked if she would mind walking instead, telling her that he'd like to find a cafe where they could relax, drink coffee, and eat sweets. He further told her that sharing such simple pleasures with Lady Melissa had become his dream.

Hearing this, Melissa was delighted. She liked Boris's frank manner. So they did walk, and they stopped at the first small restaurant they came to, sitting at a small table that offered a view of Lake Geneva's famous fountain.

Then Boris excused himself and went to the men's room, where he took out a small travel-size shaving set, took off his shirt, lathered up his face, and gave himself a particularly smooth shave, all in less than three minutes.

As soon as he had returned to the table, Lady Melissa noticed that he had shaved, and knew it was for her. She appreciated that a relative stranger had made such a nice gesture.

When the waiter brought their coffee, Boris asked Melissa whether she would refuse a cocktail or glass of wine. In response, she ordered a glass of a Californian white zinfandel. Boris asked whether her choice was intended to symbolize friendship between America and Great Britain, since they were in the former home of the League of Nations, but then, without waiting for an answer, told the waiter, "In that case, I must have the Russian national drink." And with that, he had ordered a triple shot of vodka. They also ordered some ham sandwiches and then sat, joking with each other as they gazed out at the beautiful lake.

"If, Lady Melissa, you are familiar with *War and Peace*, do you know who Tolstoy's favorite character was?" Boris asked.

Lady Melissa was first surprised and then flattered by his question. "Was it Countess Natasha Rostov?"

"In my personal opinion," Boris said, with a note of triumph, "it was Princess Maria Bolkonskaya, because Tolstoy so many times noted the depth and beauty of her eyes." Then looking into Lady Melissa's eyes, Boris told her that they reflected the same radiance, at the same time lightly touching, as if by accident, one of Melissa's lovely hands.

She did not withdraw. On the contrary, she put her other hand over his, and, as such, they sat for what seemed like an eternity.

"My hands are always cold," she quietly admitted.

Boris took her hands, pressed their palms to his face, and closed them against his lips. Melissa luxuriated in the heat radiating from his gentle kisses. It was a pleasant, good feeling that seemed to epitomize the Russian proverb he then told her, "Whoever has a cold hand must also have a warm heart."

"Boris!" she said with a smile. "You are seducing me like the serpent seduced Eve."

"First, I am not seducing, but trying to please you," Boris reasoned. "Second, in accordance with Leo Taksile ..."

"Leo Taksile? Do you know him?" Melissa blurted. "He is my favorite writer. In the boarding school I attended, his books were prohibited, but the girls considered that merely a challenge and read them at night. Of course," she added with a smile, "it was good homework for our French lessons. So, what did you want to say about Leo Taksile?"

"I wanted to say that, according to Leo Taksile, it was Adam who tried to seduce Eve, not the serpent. And the serpent was not the serpent, but the most private part of Adam's body, which he gave Eve to hold. And the apples were not apples, but other, no less private, parts of Adam's body; indeed, the most delicate. But of course," and now it was Boris who smiled, "it was only for educational purposes."

Shocked, Lady Melissa caught her breath. She did not know what to do. First, it was a joke; second, it was this man's obvious attempt to put their relationship on more intimate terms; and third, and most pressing, it was in bad taste. Consequently, having pretended that she was embarrassed, she said that it was something she did not remember from Leo Taksile's books.

Incidentally, neither did Boris, for, under the influence of the vodka and the presence of Lady Melissa, he had made it up.

"I am sorry," he said. "If I said something wrong, it must have been the Russian translation."

"I understand," she said with honeyed irony. "Simply a translator's error."

"So let me recite something else to you," Boris said, hoping to change the subject, even if just slightly. "This poem is by the great Russian poet, Alexander Pushkin. It is called 'The Tenth Commandment,' and I recently translated it just for you."

Then, still gently holding Melissa's hands, Boris began:

"Don't covet things of other beings!
My Lord, have You commanded so?
There is a limit of my soul, You know …
I am unable to manage feelings.
I do not wish to offend anyone.
I do not need his land and village,
Do not need his horse and bull,
I look around me, very cool,
His slaves, his house and even cattle …
You know me. I'm not a fool.
But his girlfriend …
O! She is pretty …
My Lord, I'm weak, My Lord, I'm rattled.
She possesses the face of an angel,
That means: I've lost this battle!

My Lord, I ask You for forgiveness!
Who's able to command his feelings?
I covet my good friend's enjoyment,
I can't control my heart's employment,
I look. I languish. I'm depressed.
But … I'm a slave of my conviction.
I am afraid my heart's eviction.
So, I'm keeping silent … and suppressed."[55]

Lady Melissa's eyes grew larger and more shining with every word.

When Boris finished, she whispered, "Nobody ever said to me what you just did. Boris, did really you mean it?"

"I always mean what I say."

"Always?"

"Almost always."

And from that point on, they looked at Lake Geneva no longer. They had eyes only for each other.

As all good, however, quickly ends, the time to leave had come. Boris, no longer awkward in his love for Melissa, brought one of her hands to his lips and said, "I do not know what else will happen in my life, but I will never forget these few moments I have spent with you on the shore of Lake Geneva. I will never forget the warmth of your hands and your heart, both of which you have given me." He deeply sighed.

Lady Melissa sighed also, saying, "Nor I. I will not forget this time with you, Boris."

And with that, they returned to the garage, and took Melissa's car to the airport. When Lady Melissa switched off the engine, Boris said, "Because I do not know whether we will meet again … may I kiss you?"

Melissa looked at him with a silence that bore no refusal, so he gently took her face, and kissed her eyelids. Then feeling her respond with tenderness, he could no longer control himself and covered her face with kisses. Then while one hand held her face, the other undid the buttons on her dress. Reaching her breasts, he gently stroked her velvet skin.

Melissa felt out of breath, not from the absence of air, but from the surge of feeling that ran through her, paralyzing her will. Suddenly a shiver ran through her body.

Feeling her shiver, Boris realized what had happened, and if he had any suspicion left, it was confirmed by her heavy breathing. Boris then began

---

55   The poem was written by the greatest Russian poet Alexander Sergeevich Pushkin in 1821. This poem was translated from Russian into English by the author of this novel, and is not really corresponding to its original.

to kiss below her neck, and was soon covering her breast with kisses, when suddenly, she momentarily stopped breathing; the pleasure was so great, and so foreign to her, that she had nearly fainted.

When she finally came to her senses, Boris was gone. She smiled. He'd had to go to catch his plane, but she knew that if she ever met him again, she would not be able to resist his charms. She wanted to see Boris again.

Back at the corporate condo, Melissa rode the elevator up to Eddy's Penthouse, and seeing that he was not in yet, she let herself in, undressed, and filled the bathtub. Then soaking in the steaming water, she dreamt of making love—not to Eddy, her future spouse, but to Boris, the man from nowhere. The relaxing water and erotic fantasies led her to experience another orgasm, after which she fell into a state of melancholy at being alone.

When Eddy came in, Melissa was still bathing, her beautiful, glistening body still thirsty for love. She called out for Eddy, and he quickly undressed, without a word, and made love to her. He proceeded as always, dominating her and emphasizing his male superiority. He painfully pinched her exquisite nipples and squeezed her supple waist until it burned. And though Melissa had been ready and willing before, Eddy's roughness now cooled her desire, and the result was anticlimactic.

Later that night, for the first time, Melissa silently began to cry, knowing that she was not in love with the man she was obliged to marry. In fact, more aware than ever of the hopelessness of her situation, the unfortunate young woman cried all night long.

33

AFTER TWO WEEKS ON the French Riviera, per Fedorov's recommendation, Veresayev was one his way back to Moscow. He had spent time in Nice, Cannes, Monte-Carlo, and other watering holes, and had diligently visited all of the small towns along the Riviera. Of the thirty thousand dollars he'd gotten from Fedorov, he had left in his pocket only two twenty-dollar bills and a few Russian rubles.

And though his trip was nearly over, he had not yet stopped drinking, because he knew all too well that any man with information about fifty million dollars that didn't belong to anybody was not going to live for too long. Veresayev was celebrating his last days. In fact, having expected a visit in France—in hotels, on the beach, or at the bar—he was surprised to be on his way back to Moscow at all.

In the airport terminal, however, was a presentable young man, holding a sign with Veresayev's name. The man, who called himself Vadim and was extremely polite, introduced himself as Solvaig's new driver. Then he took Veresayev's bag and escorted him to the car.

The young man put the bag into the trunk of his Zhiguli, which Veresayev was surprised to find completely empty instead of full of junk as was usually the case in Russian escort cars those days. Veresayev waited while the young man opened the front passenger's seat door. Veresayev said he would prefer to sit in the back seat, but the young man told him that the seat next to the driver would be more comfortable. At this, Veresayev sighed deeply and got in.

As they drove away, he looked around the trash-strewn parking lot in front the airport from which he had left and returned so many times, carrying out various assignments for Fedorov. He watched an empty Coca-Cola can rolling in the wind, chased by a torn plastic bag. He sighed again. He understood it all.

"Kazemirich" never returned to his apartment. He did not report to work on Monday, And nobody ever saw him again.

34

FOR A FEW DAYS after Veresayev's disappearance, Arkady Fedorov felt remorse. It was the remorse he always felt when an enemy, or even an insider who knew too much about Solvaig's activities, disappeared. Then, somehow, he calmed down; knowing that what had been done was in the name of some higher purpose. And so it was this time.

By the end of August, using the report in which the "nowhere man" had precisely identified all names, positions, addresses, and telephone numbers of those involved with the Tyumen Oil & Gas Association, Fedorov arranged a meeting with the general director of the association, Mr. Nikolay Vasilevich Sviblov.

For his meeting, Fedorov took the YK-40 corporate jet chartered by Solvaig. There were six security guards aboard, including Vladimir Shkolnikov. Two drivers and two additional security guards had left earlier on an AN-12 cargo plane, carrying Fedorov's personal Mercedes S-600 and a Chevrolet Suburban for the bodyguards. All of this was done with a single purpose in mind: to flex both Solvaig's corporate muscles and Fedorov's personal ones.

In Tyumen, autumn had begun. Low, heavy clouds covered the sky to the horizon. Deciduous trees had dumped their foliage, and the dry leaves, blown into heaps by the wind, flew relentlessly. Rain and sleet had fallen, but not enough to create mud, and though temperatures were often below freezing, one's foot could easily step through into the pools of water that hid under the ice.

When Fedorov and his entourage approached the building, the employees flocked to the windows to see. This was not Moscow; in the remote province of Tyumen, their arrival was arguably as exciting as that of the Russian president.

When they arrived in Sviblov's reception room, a meeting was already in progress. Sviblov's secretary started to stand, but one of Fedorov's bodyguards ordered her to stay put, while another of the guards let himself into Sviblov's office. Meanwhile, Shkolnikov and two more guards were stationed in the hallway, blocking entry to the reception room. Still two more guards were at the entrance to the building, and on the street, their drivers were waiting, with engines running.

Fedorov stepped forward. "My name is Arkady Fedorovich Fedorov. I must discuss a matter with the general director alone. I do not have much time, which is why I have interrupted your meeting. I must ask all of you to leave us with Nikolay Vasilevich."

The chief of the planning department objected: "Who are you? What do you mean: to leave?" the chief of the planning department objected. He was stopped by the menacing voice of a security guard. "Didn't you understand? I'll be glad to demonstrate what he meant if you'd like."

After exiting Sviblov's office, the others were ordered by guards to remain in the reception area. So they sat around on the chairs, waiting for their collective fate to be decided. Sviblov's secretary reached for the phone, but a guard ordered, "Don't touch it, or I'll cut the wires."

Sviblov was a tall man in his seventies. He had accepted the leading position in the association in 1967, when he'd been forty-four, and was, to this day, in pretty good shape. Fedorov's blunt manner, however, put him into at least a figurative state of shock. Blood rushed to his face, but somehow he managed to calm himself down.

"You needn't worry, Mr. Sviblov," began Fedorov. "I will not occupy too much of your time. You will listen to me, and then make your own decision. I hope I'm speaking clearly? Good! Then I will continue. I have come here with the purpose of taking over the Tyumen Oil & Gas Association. I am offering you one million dollars for fifty percent of the shares, plus one share. In addition, I am offering you, personally, an additional three million dollars. This money will be transferred to your personal bank account within three days of your signing an agreement for the transference of control of the association."

"May I think about your offer?" Sviblov asked, his voice calm.

"Yes, of course you can think. Thinking is free; no money needed. But, there is no way you will be able to keep the association. Either I take it over or someone else will. It is merely a matter of time."

"I really should think about it," Sviblov said in a weak voice. "And consult."

"My dear friend, Mr. Sviblov. I know what is torturing you. It is the five hundred thousand tons of stored crude oil that remains unrecorded, but which you plan to sell."

"But the money we'll receive for it belongs to the labor collective. The people will receive the money. The workers."

"What do you care if the workers get any of it? And how much will you skim off for yourselves? Look, I know that this is what is torturing you. My offer is straightforward and unconditional, without the problems connected to transferring money, without bribes, and without consequences. Perhaps, my offer is half of what you were hoping for. But it is now. Today. Not later."

"But still, I should think about it."

"You have ten minutes. That should be enough time. Just answer me one simple question: does Selina know that the five hundred thousand tons have not been recorded?"

"I'll answer that question after I have answered your first one."

"Thanks, but you have already answered it. So who else besides Selina knows? Oh, wait. I don't care if somebody else knows! Okay, your time is up." Fedorov looked deliberately at his wristwatch, and seeing that eight minutes had passed, he sat down.

Sviblov remained motionless at his desk. He had sat at this desk for twenty-six years in an armchair that had almost become his extension. He was so used to this place. And now, after so many years, he was being asked to make the most important decision of his life without consulting his deputy and friend, Mr. Joseph Kozitsky.

"I cannot make a decision without talking it over with my deputy. Anyway, I am not the one who should receive the money you are offering."

"That's not my problem, and I did not ask for your opinion on the matter anyway. It will be yours, so you can do with it anything you want. The amount I am offering will last you and your deputy until the end of both your days."

A storm of passion raged through Sviblov. He had just been asked to betray his friend. Suddenly he recalled a phrase from a movie he had recently seen, called "The Roads We Choose," in which one hero said to another, "Bolivar [the name of his horse] cannot bear the weight of both of us."

And suddenly the storm subsided and, surprising himself, Sviblov said, "I agree."

Fedorov rubbed his hands together. "Wonderful. I will have the necessary documents prepared, and you can come to Moscow to sign them."

"Perhaps you could bring them here," Mr. Sviblov bargained.

"Well, let it be your way," Mr. Fedorov conceded. "The head of my security team will bring them here for your signature. You will be notified in due time, but from this moment on, not one drop of oil can be sold. It is no longer your property. I hope you understand."

"I understand," Sviblov said gloomily, for he hated himself for betraying a friend of twenty-six years.

35

WHEN THE HEAD OF Agroprom security, Mr. Dmitry Cherkizov, phoned to tell Lydia that her driver had resigned at the end of July and that it would take time to find a replacement, she was not surprised. Her driver, by the last name Gusev, had constantly complained to her about the managerial problems at Agroprom. In particular, he'd been tired of the constant delays in receiving paychecks. Lydia thanked Mr. Cherkizov for his concern, but told him to not worry, because she did not need a car.

A few days later, Lydia was walking from the metro station to Agroprom when Mr. Cherkizov drove by and spotted her. He stopped and offered her a ride.

"Thank you," Lydia said, "but I need to walk as much as possible."

At first baffled, Cherkizov then realized that her smile was full of the happiness of a woman expecting, so he wished her luck and a healthy baby, and went on his way.

The news didn't take long to spread. In fact, it happened only a few days later, when Cherkizov met with Kravchuk to settle personnel matters. In particular, Kravchuk had asked Cherkizov to cut costs by ridding the company of any "excess baggage," but, naturally, Cherkizov wanted to make a case for each person on the chopping block. So when he brought up Gusev's name, Cherkizov told him that the driver had already resigned.

"So, who drives Lydia?" Kravchuk asked.

"Nobody. She is at the stage when women need to walk as much as possible," Cherkizov said with a smile.

"And who is the lucky one?" Kravchuk asked, remembering when she had rebuffed his own advances. He already forgot that he had noticed her wedding ring before.

"Well, most likely a man," Cherkizov said, laughing.

"Listen to me," Kravchuk said, suddenly serious. "You, Mr. Cherkizov, are responsible for the safety of our company. And here is a case that directly concerns your department. Please find out who the man is and report to me. Do you understand?"

"Understood," Cherkizov answered.

It wasn't that Kravchuk cared about Lydia, but the circumstances were such that he needed to exert his power, which he routinely did by ordering his subordinates to engage in work of some kind, whether it was important or not.

And so Cherkizov, with a surge of enthusiasm, hurried to carry out the order, directing one of his staff to begin surveillance on Lydia.

Stephan Kuleshoff was a former officer of the KGB's 7-th Division — the KGB subdivision engaged in external surveillance. He was a member of the special group that, in the summer of 1962, had followed Mrs. V., the wife of a senior diplomat attached to the UK embassy in Moscow. Mrs. V. and her little son often strolled down Tsvetnoy Boulevard in downtown Moscow, and the officer watching her on one such stroll noticed a man who had twice appeared in close proximity to them. Disobeying orders, the officer left his surveillance post to follow the man, who turned out to be Colonel Oleg Penkovsky, a senior officer in the Soviet Army's intelligence agency, called GRU. Not long after, the colonel was arrested and executed.

Cherkizov, although being sure that Kravchuk's suspicions were groundless, assigned Kuleshoff to conduct Lydia's surveillance. He asked him to find out where and with whom she lived, with whom she communicated, and where she went, and to supply any pertinent names, addresses, and telephone numbers.

When Kuleshoff called and asked for a meeting to report his findings, Cherkizov could hardly believe that he had engaged himself in such nonsense, but because he had been the one to give Kuleshoff his orders, he obliged, setting the meeting for the next morning.

Kuleshoff gave his report by reading from a large notebook he had brought with him. Cherkizov was barely listening until Kuleshoff reached the part about Ms. Selina working for Solvaig. Cherkizov, who knew that Solvaig was involved in deliveries of crude oil, mineral oil, and petroleum products to the countries of the former Soviet Union, immediately interrupted him and called Kravchuk, requesting an urgent meeting.

Since he had already forgotten his order to establish the surveillance, Kravchuk was, first, surprised by the call, but more so by Cherkizov's urgency. So Kravchuk asked that both of them come to his office right away.

After ordering Valerie not to let anybody see or disturb him, Kravchuk found himself stunned by Kuleshoff's report. He instantly realized that the Tyumen Oil & Gas Association had been storing unrecorded crude oil. He could also see that Ms. Selina, on behalf of the management group she represented, had negotiated two contracts simultaneously: one for the delivery of oil to the countries of the former USSR, and the other to its delivery abroad. In this way, nobody would lose, and the delivery paths would not cross. But Kravchuk thought, "What if a receiver didn't make payments for the delivered crude oil?"

Kravchuk decided not to rush into a decision. He needed to carefully consider all the possibilities. So he gave himself several weeks, collecting all of the available information he could before setting up a meeting with Mr. Fedorov. As part of his research, he asked Valerie to call Boris to find out when either he or Pennington would bring the one million dollar cash payment.

It was five in the morning when Boris received the call in California, but Boris told Kravchuk that he'd planned to arrive in Moscow on Sunday, September 19, and that Pennington was scheduled to arrive on Wednesday, September 22. Then on September 23, the both of them were to travel to Novokuybyshevsk and make the cash payment directly to Anisimov. Immediately after that, they would return to Moscow, and Boris, in turn, would leave for California and wait for the money to be wired. As soon as the money was deposited into the Agroprom - USA account, he would take off again for Moscow, and then go on to Ventspils to get the financial paperwork. Thus, by the end of September, the first delivery of crude oil would be on its way. And after that, both money and oil should start flowing on a regular basis.

Boris then asked Kravchuk his opinion on the deepening confrontation between the Russian Supreme Council and President Yeltsin, saying that his own main concern was how it might affect the pumping of crude oil and the security of the banking system.

Kravchuk didn't know how to answer, without revealing what he knew. But he figured out a way: He told Boris that his wife was celebrating her birthday on Sunday, September 19, and that there would be some very important people attending her party. So they agreed that, as soon as Boris arrived in Moscow, he would come to the party directly from the Airport.

"And there, we will talk," Kravchuk said.

36

AFTER LONG THOUGHT, KRAVCHUK realized that Lydia, and those who had sent her to Moscow, meant business and were planning to fulfill their contractual obligations both with Agroprom and Solvaig. In that sense, their intentions were honest. He also believed they would use the money from the sale of crude oil to purchase food and consumer goods not available in Tyumen, and that anything left over would be distributed to employees. He felt sure that Lydia had worked hard for whatever advance she had received, and that Agroprom would legally report whatever they paid her in commission.

It was the thought they were planning to sell *unrecorded* crude oil that kept Kravchuk awake at night. Rationally, he knew that it was they, the oilmen, who deserved this money; Mother Russia, for which they had been working so long, day and night, in freezing cold and blistering heat, had not been paying them or supplying their stores and markets. Still, the oil had not been recorded.

So, the first thing Kravchuk did after arriving at the office Monday, September 6, was to consult a special directory of "hotlines." Solvaig was not listed, but Kravchuk was, which pleased him in a smug sort of way. On the other hand, he thought sourly, Solvaig had paid for the crude oil with its own money, while Agroprom—or, to be precise, Agroprom and Kravchuk—had no money at all. Of course, Agroprom was listed in the directory too, but that was no help.

Kravchuk groaned under the weight of his emotions, as he located Solvaig's telephone number in the report that Kuleshoff had left and dialed.

"Hello?" Tamara answered.

"Hi. This is …" Kravchuk began, and then hung up, immediately buzzing Valerie. "Dear, please come in for a moment."

When she did, Kravchuk gave her a piece of paper on which he had written the phone number of Mr. Fedorov. "Please, get him on the phone. I'd like to discuss some business with him."

"I am calling already," she said, rushing out.

"Hello?" Tamara answered again.

"I am calling from the industrial-financial company Agroprom," Valerie announced. "Our president, Mr. Gavrila Petrovich Kravchuk, would like to discuss some business with Mr. Arkady Fedorovich Fedorov."

"He's away on business," Tamara said, "but he is expected back in a day or two." And with that, without asking for name or number, Tamara hung up.

——— 37 ———

Two DAYS LATER, KRAVCHUK again asked Valerie to call Fedorov. This time, Tamara put the call through.

"How may I help you?" Mr. Fedorov answered.

"Sorry to bother you, but this is Gavrila Petrovich Kravchuk, president of the industrial-financial company, Agroprom."

"Did we do something wrong?" Fedorov joked, momentarily putting Kravchuk in an awkward position.

"The thing is," Kravchuk countered, recovering his poise, "that both you and we are in the business of delivering crude oil. As a result, there are certain questions which I would like to have the chance to … how do I say it … sort out."

"Sort out, did you say? Does that mean you would like to schedule a personal meeting?"

"Very much."

"Well, alright, then. Let's meet and sort. You just name the time and place."

"Anywhere. I don't care. We can meet at your office or mine. We can meet in the Vorobyovy Mountains[56] for all I care."

"Why don't you come here tomorrow? We'll have dinner together, break some bread, and have a few drinks. We should have no problem resolving any difficulties."

"Exactly my sentiments," Kravchuk enthusiastically replied.

---

56 Formerly called the Leninskie Mountains, this is an area in Moscow where mobsters used to meet to "discuss" disputes, which often ended in bloodshed.

"Well, if that's all for today," Fedorov said, "then I'll see you tomorrow at one."

"See you tomorrow," Kravchuk answered, though Fedorov had not heard him, as Arkady had already hung up.

——————— 38 ———————

IN THE PAST THREE days since his meeting with Fedorov, Kravchuk had been drinking nonstop. It was his only consolation after such a stunning rejection. Imagine, he kept thinking, Fedorov did not require any partners in his upstart; he could take care of his problems with no outside help.

But then, what difference did that make? The fact still remained that money that should have been Kravchuk's was flowing to this Fedorov guy.

Finally, on Sunday afternoon, Kravchuk stopped drinking. And on Monday morning, September 13, he arrived at his office with a fully detailed plan. He began by asking Valerie to find Yakubovsky. Then he invited Cherkizov to his office.

In a minute, Valerie reported, "Vladislav Ivanovich Yakubovsky is on the line."

"Ivanovich?" Kravchuk said as he picked up the telephone. "How is your sporting life?" Kravchuk was now talking in the honeyed tones he used when he wanted something. "How? Ah, that's good. That's perfect. By the way," he continued, more honeyed than before, "I have a gift for you. Do you remember, when you were in Washington, we took some photos? Yes, those. Well, it turns out that you are in them, too. So I'm sending them to you in an envelope by messenger, and they shall be—how do you say it—for your eternal memory. Be well, now. Good-bye."

In all actuality, the envelope on Kravchuk's desk contained only one picture—a picture that had been taken by Boris, per Gavrila's request, of Kravchuk, Popov, Isaev, and Yakubovsky. He was delivering it to Yakubovsky to show that he had proof of a meeting between Yakubovsky and Cherkizov.

Kravchuk instructed Valerie to write a letter to Yakubovsky, which she was to register with the appropriate reference number and then attach to the photo.

Valerie indicated that she understood, and then, as soon as she had left his office, she called him and, in her usual angelic voice, announced, "Dmitry Vasilevich is here."

"Dmitry Vasilevich," Gavrila Petrovich greeted him as he walked in. "Here is a package for Vladislav Yakubovsky. He is the ranking officer of an organization that I think you know about. Valerie will go and register the letter now, and it must go with this package. Please deliver it to Yakubovsky personally."

"Don't worry," Cherkizov answered, "I have known Vlad personally for many years. I will do it immediately."

"By the way," Kravchuk added, "Boris will be in Moscow on Sunday, September 19, and Pennington is arriving the Wednesday after. On Thursday, September 23, they will fly to Novokuybyshevsk together, to deliver one million US dollars to Mr. Peter Anisimov, the head of the oil pipeline dispatch center. One million dollars cash! You understand me? *Cash!* It would be very sad if this money fell into a stranger's hand, so you will take the proper steps to make sure that it does not. Do you understand, Dmitry?"

"I understand, boss. Don't worry. Everything will be done as you wish," Cherkizov answered.

"Yes, and may the Lord forgive you," Kravchuk said, and crossed himself. Then he looked at Cherkizov for a few long seconds, until Dmitry crossed himself as well.

Several minutes later, when Cherkizov arrived at Yakubovsky's office, they greeted each other as old friends, after which Cherkizov handed him the envelope. "It's from Kravchuk. He told me to deliver it to your hands only."

"What is it?" Yakubovsky asked.

"I don't know."

"No?" Yakubovsky raised an eyebrow. "Then, what do you know?"

"I know that Boris is arriving in Moscow on Sunday, September 19, and that Eddy Pennington is arriving the Wednesday after. And I know that they will be going to Novokuybyshevsk together on Thursday, to take Mr. Anisimov one million US dollars. Cash."

"Cash, did you say? One million dollars?" Yakubovsky whistled.

"Yes. One million dollars in cash," Cherkizov repeated.

"So, what do you make of this matter?"

Instead of answering, Cherkizov crossed himself.

Yakubovsky shrugged. "So that's the way it is. Well, then, good luck to you. And let's plan to meet tonight at eight, at our place, shall we?"

"See you then," Cherkizov said.

39

AS PLANNED, BORIS ARRIVED in Moscow on Sunday, the nineteenth, and as usual, Cherkizov met him at the terminal, where they warmly greeted each other.

"Dmitry Vasilevich," Boris said, shaking Cherkizov's hand. "I am glad to see you."

"How was your flight, Boris?" Cherkizov said. "Are you carrying your toiletries with you?"

"I know, I know. I have my shaving kit with me. I'll change here at the airport. I should have time to clean up, while the porter is bringing the luggage and handling the passport."

"You know, don't you, that we are going directly to Kravchuk's place in Arkhangelskoye?"

"Certainly I know. I even have a birthday present for Alevtina."

They walked to the VIP room, where the attendant recognized Boris and gave him a warm hug. It was Vicky. She reached out her manicured hand with its long fingers, and once again, something about her seemed familiar. And those eyes! But where would he have met her, he wondered, and when?

"Vicky, I have a gift for you," Boris said, taking from his briefcase three pairs of panties and box of American See's chocolate candies, which, unseen by others, he gave her, along with a hundred dollar bill. He always had such gifts ready for chance meetings with girls like Vicky.

"Thank you," she whispered, "but it's not necessary. And why would you even do such a thing?" Nonetheless, she quickly took the gifts and hid them in her desk.

"Boris," she said, "I am very touched. If you ever need something, please do not hesitate to call me. In the VIP room, we are always glad to serve good people."

"Thank you," Boris said, looking into her clear blue eyes and thinking he wouldn't mind spending more time with such a beautiful girl.

In the men's restroom, Boris quickly brushed his teeth and shaved off the shadow he had grown during the eighteen-hour flight from Los Angeles via Frankfurt. Then Cherkizov knocked on the door and handed him his collapsible garment bag, which the porter had just brought. Boris put on a nice suit, a tie, and a fresh shirt, then rolled up his jeans and shirt together and stuffed them in the bag. Now he was ready to go.

About a hundred guests had gathered to celebrate Alevtina's birthday, all of them either friends or important contacts, and all of them carefully screened. Among the visitors was the chairman of the board of the Central Bank of Moscow, Mr. Vasily Shorohoff; the senior adviser to the Russian president, Mr. Konstantin Belenko; the operating manager of the Ministry of External Economic Relations, Mr. Alexander Volosnoj; and the deputy minister of Foreign Affairs, Mr. Ivan Veliky. There were also several senior Agroprom employees, including Mr. Albert Isaev and his wife, and Mrs. Theodora Vasilieva and her husband. A few famous actors, athletes, and even writers were scattered among them, as well.

At the time, many were crowded around a particularly well-known Russian, who was saying, "Decree Fourteen Hundred, concerning dissolution of the Supreme Council, which is, to be more precise, the only purpose of this decree, was first discussed in Ogaryovo.[57] Mr. President Boris Nikolaevich Yeltsin had invited Mr. Tchernomyrdin, the prime minister; Mr. Kozirev, the minister of foreign affairs; Mr. Grachev, a four-star general and the defense minister; and Mr. Erin, minister of the police, to this meeting.

"Everybody approved the decree. The only sticking point was the date of dissolution. We wanted to do it on September nineteenth, but after thinking about it, decided on the eighteenth, instead, because it was a Sunday. With presumably no one in the Russian White House that day, it would be easier to arrange security forces to block entry to any Supreme Council deputies who might try to get in the following work day.

"On September sixteenth, however, the president decided to delay commencement to the twenty-first, which worked against us. First, it was more complicated to prevent deputies from coming to work on a weekday. Second, someone leaked the information, so when the deputies learned about our plans, they did not leave the White House on Sunday. In addition, the press made a big fuss and scared people with the possibility of one more putsch.

---

57   President Yeltsin's residence outside of Moscow.

So with no point in delaying any longer, the president ordered enforcement of Decree Fourteen Hundred to begin on Tuesday, September twenty-first."

After that, all talk focused on the upcoming press publication intended to explain to the public the decree itself, along with the concept of constitutional reform, accomplished in stages. Many partygoers also speculated on the Supreme Council's reaction to the decree, which most agreed would be to convene an emergency session and try to remove President Yeltsin from office, the consequences of which could lead to a full-scale civil war.

The political conversation did not prevent the guests from amicably and cheerfully drinking and eating to their hearts' content. Toasts were made, wineglasses were clinked, and all became tipsy.

At ten, Boris slipped out and had his driver take him to the Hotel Mir. Although it may not have been the least dangerous place in the country, given its proximity to the White House, at least it was momentarily quiet. And with beefed-up police squads surrounding the building and standing guard in the adjoining streets, at the moment, it was the second-most protected place in the whole country, except for, naturally, the Kremlin.

Boris awoke at five the next morning. It was still cloudy, and a fine mist was falling. Boris turned the TV to the English-language channel, where a political commentator was presenting the same points of view that Boris had heard the previous night, directly from high-ranking officials. None of it promised anything good.

By seven o'clock, Boris was down in the dining room having breakfast. His car pulled up to the hotel at eight, as scheduled, and Boris asked the driver to take him to Isaev's house, which was near Frunze's[58] Embankment. When they arrived, Boris saw Isaev walking his big standard poodle, Marquis. They greeted each other and since, at Alevtina's birthday party, they had had no opportunity to talk freely, the first question Boris asked was whether Popov had ever reappeared.

"Don't tell me you haven't heard," Isaev responded.

"What are you talking about? I'm only in Moscow periodically, and my only contacts are through Kravchuk."

"Popov, or rather, what remained of Popov," Isaev reported gloomily, "was discovered by his neighbors. They noticed ravens flying around the roof of his building, making a racket like you've never heard, and when the workers got up on the roof; they found an almost totally decomposed corpse. The only way authorities were able to identify him was by his name on an Agroprom ID card. The most surprising thing, though, was that near his body was an empty bottle of vodka. You remember, don't you that his normal rate was

---

58   Named after the Red Army commander considered a hero of the civil war from 1918 to 1921.

166

only three small shot glasses? And yet the cause of death was determined to be excessive intoxication!"

"I guess nothing else could be told from the coroner's examination," Boris said, suddenly serious. "Do you suspect anybody?"

"Yes. Either one or the other."

"You mean either Yakubovsky or Kravchuk?"

"Yes," Isaev said emphatically. "And do you know what—are you planning to see Mr. Filimonov before your departure?"

"If necessary," Boris said.

"Please give him my copy of the affidavit that Popov made in Washington, remember? I'll have to go in to get it, so in the meantime, do you mind taking Marquis for a little walk?"

Boris took the leash until Isaev returned a few minutes later, holding the sealed envelope. As Boris put it under his jacket, Isaev told him that two weeks earlier, Kravchuk, on his return from somewhere or other, was so beside himself that he not only was screaming at employees, but also smashed a chair to bits.

Boris remarked that a story about destroying chairs was part of every schoolchild's required reading.

Isaev did not share Boris' playful attitude; instead, he said that he was going to resign from Agroprom.

"If you resign, how can you benefit from the crude oil contract?" Boris asked.

"Are you so sure, my friend, that the contract will be executed?" Isaev cautioned.

"I understand," Boris admitted, "that I am not here in Moscow very often. But my part of the contract has been executed, and money for the first delivery should be wired by the first or second of October." Then, taking a more cautious tone, Boris added, "I will not transfer one dollar without receiving confirmation from the captain of the tanker."

"And you are so sure that you will be in charge of the money."

"It is to be deposited in the Agroprom - USA account, which I have full control of."

"Well, let me just tell you one thing, my friend. Be extremely cautious. I would not want you to disappear like our good friend, the late Popov. And do not go to Agroprom today. There is nothing to do there anyway. Kravchuk will sleep until noon, arrive at four, and claim he was at the Kremlin. If only you knew how upset I am by all of this. How I envy Filimonov. He found a real job!"

"Even considering the present situation and tomorrow's presidential decree?"

"What's the difference? Is that something new?" Isaev said sarcastically.

Boris thought for a moment and then said, "Yes, you are probably right. Anyway, I'd better be getting back."

And with that, they shook hands and parted.

40

FEDOROV BEGAN HIS WORKWEEK by enjoying Tamara's simple pleasures, followed by a short nap. Then he pulled himself together to deal with routine business. First, he checked up on new mail, and he signed various business documents prepared for him by different departments. Finally, he discussed business with the chief accountant, and then asked Tamara to summon Mr. Shkolnikov to his office.

With a joyful smile on his face, and a spring in his step, Shkolnikov entered the chief's office. All of Solvaig's employees had seen the changes in Shkolnikov after his marriage to Lydia. In fact, the only person who had not noticed that was Shkolnikov himself. He was a completely different person; he was happy, in love, and loved. It was as if the whole world were at his feet.

"Arkady Fedorovich, may I come in?" he said.

"Yes, please, come in, Vladimir. And don't stand on ceremony." Fedorov directed his chief of security to a chair next to his desk. "Sit down, please. Sit down. How are you?"

"Perfectly well," the smiling Vladimir answered in a hearty voice.

"Is that so? I'm delighted to hear it. So how about a business trip to Africa?"

"For how long?"

"Just for a few days," answered Fedorov. "Ivan is flying to Tanzania on October second. Go with him and bring back what Mr. Veresayev used to bring back, before he disappeared. Do you believe it? He left for vacation in France, and there has been no sign of him since!"

"You're absolutely right," Shkolnikov said, shrugging. "I checked that through my channels, and there has been no sign of him. We know only that he landed at Sheremetyevo-2 and went through passport control. After that, nothing."

"I didn't know he had returned from France," Fedorov said sadly.

Though Fedorov's response had been dripping with insincerity, Vladimir didn't notice. In his newfound happiness, he had lost his sense of caution, the one quality necessary for a commando officer and, even more, for a chief of security.

"So, coming back to your trip," Fedorov mumbled. "You must go to Cyprus and deposit our product in the bank's safe. Afterwards, go to Tanzania and pick up the set of stones that is waiting for you. If there's any downtime, Ivan will entertain you. The hunting season has begun in Tanzania, as well, so take a day or two off if you want and then return with the stones. I know it's not your job, but since Veresayev's disappearance, I don't have anyone I can trust. I'll find a replacement, eventually, but for now, I need your help."

"If it has to be done, it has to be done," said Vladimir.

"Okay. Coordinate your schedule with Ivan, and if you both can, take a couple of days off."

Vladimir left, slightly upset by this forthcoming separation from Lydia. She was already suffering occasional bouts of morning sickness, and he wanted to look carefully after his beloved wife. On the other hand, he thought, just a few days off couldn't hurt.

Alone again, Fedorov called in his son, Ivan, and said, "Here's how it is. Shkolnikov will go with you to Tanzania, but he must not return. Take him on a hunting trip. As you know from long experience, anything can happen on a hunting trip, and hunting accidents are, well, a routine thing. In any case, he must not return to Moscow, under any circumstance. Otherwise, he and his wife could make a lot of trouble for us."

"Understood." Ivan smirked. "Don't worry, I've got lots of experience in this area."

— 41 —

ON TUESDAY, BORIS AND Dmitry Cherkizov arrived at the airport, expecting to meet Eddy Pennington, due in from London on Aeroflot. But to Boris's surprise, he saw, instead, a smiling Lady Melissa. He felt the same strike of lightning that he had the first time he'd seen her.

With Cherkizov next to him, however, Boris controlled himself. He simply greeted her and then introduced her to Cherkizov.

Obviously, she announced, the plan had changed. It was now she, not Pennington, who would accompany Boris, first to the Airport in Kurumoch, serving Samara and Togliatti, and then to the dispatch center in Novokuybyshevsk to deliver the one million dollars to Mr. Anisimov.

"And where is Eddy?" Boris asked.

"Aren't you happy to see me again?" answered Lady Melissa playfully.

"That is not the point. Eddy should have brought the money himself."

"The money's all there," she said, and then informed them that both Eddy and his assistant, Mr. Anthony, one of whom usually undertook such operations, were both preoccupied. Mr. Anthony was in Latin America, and Eddy had just received word that his long-awaited meeting with Her Majesty's chief of staff had been confirmed for September 23.

Today, Melissa did not resemble the woman Boris had met in Washington, who announced her presence with bright, trendy clothes Instead, she was dressed from head to toe in the low-key European fashion: light black shoes with low heels, a black camel hair coat, a black woolen scarf around her neck, and a pair of sunglasses pushing back her hair. In her hand she held a large travel bag, while a smaller bag was thrown over her shoulder. Only her confident bearing and radiant eyes remained the same.

Taking the large bag from her, Boris said, "One more question. Where is your luggage?"

Melissa explained that she was planning to return to Moscow from Kurumoch tomorrow evening and, from there, fly back to London the following morning.

"Besides, I am a very low-maintenance person," she said. "Do you have any more questions?"

With that, they walked out of the terminal, and as soon as Cherkizov was out of earshot, she mewed, "Instead of asking how I am or how my flight was, you're concerned only with business. Doesn't this lonely little girl mean anything to you?"

Boris wasn't sure how to respond. They hadn't spoken since Geneva, and though he wanted to see Melissa more, Eddy was his partner, and a secret affair with Melissa could spoil the completion of the contract and overturn his whole life. For all these reasons, Boris had almost even hoped that he would never see Melissa again. At least that way, he could avoid having to make a decision. But, now, here she was. Such a meeting, and at such a time! Yet, somewhere inside, he uncontrollably ached for her.

In the VIP lounge, Vicky, seeing the three of them, discreetly asked Boris, "Is she your daughter or your niece?"

"She's our English partner," Boris said, equally discreetly. "But do I really seem old enough to have a daughter her age?"

"Oh, don't get upset. I was only kidding. Peace?"

Boris shrugged. "With beautiful women, it's impossible to be at war." Then he snuck a one hundred dollar bill into her hand.

"You are spoiling me," Vicky whispered, coquettishly wagging her hips.

"I am not spoiling you, Vicky. I'm just trying to get you to go out with me."

"Maybe I will. But only if you promise to behave yourself."

"Of course, I promise."

"Then call me. You have my number."

"Yes, I do. And I definitely will," Boris promised.

Then approaching Melissa at the bar, he asked, "Do you want something to drink?"

"No, thanks. I was just killing time while you were enjoying yourself with that ... that Russian girl."

"Are you jealous?"

"Yes, I am. I often become jealous on circumstantial evidence."

"Her name is Vicky. She works here in the VIP lounge, so we're well acquainted."

"I can see that," Melissa whispered.

Changing the subject, Boris offered to take care of the customs declaration form that allowed her to bring one million dollars into the Russian Federation. The customs officer on duty looked at the declaration, then signed and stamped it, without bothering to count or even look at the money. He then tore off the bottom half of the declaration form and put it in a desk drawer.

As they left the airport, Boris noticed that it was unusually warm. Lining the road leading downtown, trees touted their leaves painted the colors of autumn, as they waited for the approach of the cold. Melissa looked out the car window at them in awe. And though she had visited Moscow before, Boris's anecdotes about some of the places they passed kept her interested.

They reached the Hotel Mir in about fifty minutes, and agreed to meet back in the lobby at seven the next morning. Then, having nothing better to do, Cherkizov left. Boris waited while Melissa registered, then as he carried up her bags. As it was still early, he suggested they stroll down Old Arbat Street before supper.

Walking of the hotel, they came out on New Arbat just opposite the Aeroflot office. After a while, they came to Old Arbat and walked toward Vakhtangov's Theatre.

Accidentally brushing Melissa's cold hand with his, Boris took the opportunity to remind her that women with cold hands have warm hearts. Melissa, remembering, smiled and impulsively decided to show Boris just how warm her heart still was. Taking a deep breath of the warm Moscow air, she took Boris's hand and pressed her body against his. They walked like this, almost hugging each other, until they reached a restaurant called the Prague, then turned and headed back to the hotel. They turned left and again reached New Arbat, but when they came upon a Melodiya[59] store, which was still open, Boris couldn't help himself.

"Let's go in," he suggested.

"Okay," Melissa laughed, "it could be fun."

The store's shelves, which even six months earlier had been less than half empty, now seemed almost full of merchandise. Customers were eagerly crowding the counters. Boris wandered over to the section of string instruments, and Melissa followed.

"Maid,"[60] he said to a young, but tired-looking saleswoman. He pointed to one of the inexpensive violins. "May I see that one?"

The saleswoman took the violin from its stand and, holding it by the fingerboard, handed it to Boris.

He took it and deftly fingered the strings with his right hand, using precise movements born of long practice to see whether they needed tuning.

---

59   Russian for *Melody*.
60   A common way to address a young woman in Russia.

Encouraged by the familiar feel of the instrument, Boris spoke to the saleswoman again, but this time asked for a bow.

"Are you going to play right here?" the saleswoman asked despondently.

"No," Boris answered. "I just want to try it."

"Do you promise not to break it?" she said. "Because if you do, I'll be in trouble with the manager."

"Boris, please, let's go," Melissa urged, feeling self-conscious. "Don't you see? She doesn't want to help us?"

"Don't worry, my dear," Boris said softly, "this is my territory. I know how to deal with nice but overworked girls."

Looking up at the saleswoman, who was half-listening to their conversation, Boris realized that she understood English, as her face suddenly softened, reflecting her appreciation of Boris's consideration. The girl selected a bow and handed it to Boris.

"But, please," she added conspiratorially, "don't ask for rosin. That, I cannot give you."

Boris smiled, put the violin on his left shoulder, and tucked it under his chin. Then using the bow, he stroked the strings individually, and the sound that came out made it clear that he was not playing for the first time. At first, of course, there was a certain amount of scratching and scraping, but as Boris became accustomed to the instrument, it obeyed his mastery and began to make the music it had been crafted for.

After several minutes of tuning and adjustment, Boris turned to Melissa and drew the bow across the strings, and the violin began to sing. He played Fritz Kreisler's "The Torments of Love" while looking directly into Melissa's eyes. Melissa's breath stopped; it was one of her favorite melodies, and she understood exactly what it meant. Boris then played Schubert's "Night Serenade" and people began to be drawn to where he and Melissa were standing. Boris, however, could see no one but Lady Melissa. He looked at her and at her only, and she returned his adoring gaze with one of her own, a soft light shining from her radiant eyes.

When Boris had finished the melancholy, love-drenched Schubert, his small audience began clapping, and so he played more, this time, "Ochi Chornie."[61] It was so moving that many quietly sang along:

...*Eyes passionate and fine.*

As I love you.

As I am afraid of you...

This time, when Boris stopped playing, people actually applauded. Boris smiled, returned the violin to the saleswoman, and with a gallant bow of thanks, he and Melissa left the store.

---

61   A famous Russian song meaning "Black Eyes."

Outside, Melissa again gently pulled Boris against the warmth of her body. "I know you were playing for me, Boris. Thank you. It was very kind of you. You made me feel good."

"I was just playing," Boris said. "But yes, it's true, I was playing for you. And I am glad you liked it."

Boris now knew for certain that he was falling for Melissa. And it seemed that she, too, was falling for him.

Returning from their walk, they dined in the hotel restaurant together, and then Lady Melissa left for her room, saying she needed to make some calls. Boris watched her walk away, and considering the circumstances they were in, knew it would be sheer folly for them to continue such a mad dance.

42

ON SEPTEMBER 23, BY order of Moscow's mayor, Mr. Yuri Luzhkov, acting with the authority of Decree Fourteen Hundred, all electric power, other utilities, and all means of governmental telecommunication were disconnected to the building of the Supreme Council. From that point on, its deputies were cut off from the outside world.

That same morning, Boris left his things in his room, taking only a briefcase with documents and some toiletries. Neither he nor Melissa would check out of the hotel, since they were planning to return to Moscow that evening.

When Melissa and Cherkizov arrived in the lobby at exactly the same time, Melissa from her room and Cherkizov from the hotel's driveway, Boris was already waiting. After nine hours of sleep, a hot shower, and some light makeup, Melissa looked very attractive.

They loaded the car and began the drive to Moscow's Airport Domodedovo for the short flight to Airport Kurumoch. Overnight, the weather had changed. Autumn still had not completely displaced summer, but its relentless approach could certainly be felt. With increased humidity and a light mist, the result was a rather gloomy morning.

They arrived at Domodedovo in just under an hour, and after receiving their boarding passes, Boris and Melissa said good-bye to Cherkizov, asking if he could arrange for a car to pick them up when they returned. To Boris's surprise, Cherkizov announced casually that he'd be flying with them. This was a sudden change of plan, but, after all, Cherkizov was Kravchuk's chief of security and must know what he was doing. In fact, as they were carrying one million dollars in cash, Cherkizov's presence gave Boris a sense of safety.

In the plane, Melissa was seated next to Boris. Taking his hand, she nestled into his warmth and closed her eyes. When breakfast was served, Boris refused it in order not to wake her, and she did not awake until the plane landed at Kurumoch, and Boris awoke her by gently rubbing her hands. He was surprised for the second time that day when she put her hand over his, squeezed it, and quickly let it go.

It was much colder in Kurumoch than in Moscow, with sharp gusts of wind. Wearing her camel-wool overcoat, Melissa shivered, while Boris in his leather jacket felt the cold all too fiercely. Many oaks, birches, and aspens already stood naked, although some trees remained dressed in the red and yellow of autumn.

Leaving the terminal, they met two waiting cars. Cherkizov peremptorily announced that he would go in the BMW 540 with Melissa, while Boris would take the red Zhiguli.[62] The arrangement seemed odd to Boris, and Cherkizov's demeanor came off somewhat more forceful. But he was, after all, the chief of security, so he must certainly know his business.

The driver of the Zhiguli was a huge Caucasian man, and another man with dirty teeth sat in the back seat. In the BMW 540, where Cherkizov and Melissa were seated, there was a third Caucasian man seated next to the driver. All of them were suspiciously dirty, sullen, and ill-tempered, which seemed very strange. But as they drove away from the Airport, the BMW in front, followed by the Zhiguli, there didn't seem much that anyone could do about it.

At the intersection of highways M-5 and E-30, leading to Samara-Togliatti, Boris saw that the BMW turned not toward Samara, as he'd expected, but toward Togliatti. When he asked where they were going, the driver said, "Just wait and you'll see."

After about thirty minutes, they reached a small village on the Samara-Moscow Highway called Vintay, at which point they suddenly turned right. A few minutes later, on a road sign, Boris read, "Village of Novomatyushkino."

They turned right again, passed a pigsty, and then came to what looked like a country estate. Then reaching a dead end at the edge of a grove, they pulled into a gravel driveway. They were at a surprisingly new-looking house surrounded by a fence.

"Get out. We're here," said Boris's driver gruffly.

Boris began opening his door when one of Cherkizov's henchmen seized him by his jacket sleeve and dragged him onto the porch. It had happened so quickly and unexpectedly that Boris had had no chance to resist.

After the gorilla pushed Boris through the door, Cherkizov, who was already inside waiting, walked up to Boris and slapped him in the face.

---

62   A poorly designed Russian-made car.

"You son-of-a-bitch," Cherkizov snarled. "You've come to the end of the road." Then turning to one of the gorillas, he said, "Shamil. Kill him. But keep the bitch alive. I have to find a phone, but I'll be back in twenty minutes, and then we'll get busy on her. I hope you got the kerosene!"

"Keep your pants on, boss," the brute answered. "I'll take care of everything, just as we planned. There are eight cans of gas upstairs and two downstairs. It'll be plenty to do the whole house." Then laughing horribly, he asked, "Do you want me to make him watch while I rape his bitch, or just kill him first?"

The other two mobsters laughed with primeval delight, showing their dirty, rotten teeth.

"That's your business," Cherkizov answered offhandedly, "but don't touch her before I get back. I must be the first. Understood? Just put him in the bathroom for the time being. I have to go." Then looking at the other two men, he said, "And you. What are waiting for? Go to the store and pick up some drinks and food. We'll have a good time later today!"

Then with the shrill voice of an animal, Cherkizov let out a terrible cry of exultation and left, with the other two mobsters on his heels. Meanwhile, the huge Caucasian man grabbed Boris by his jacket and dragged him toward the bathroom.

43

THE BRUTE FROM CAUCASUS stuck a wooden dowel through the top part of the bathroom door handle, unlocking it from outside. Then he opened the door, pushed Boris in, and slammed the door shut again.

Under the dim light of a single bulb, Melissa sat on the edge of the dirty bathtub, sobbing.

"What they did to you?" Boris asked, with a combination of anxiety, suffering, and sympathy. This had nothing to do with her. She did not deserve to be in this situation.

"Th-th-they w-w-will r-r-r-rape m-me!" she sobbed. "I'd rath-th-ther be d-d-dead." Apparently desperate with fear about what she was sure would soon befall her, the unfortunate girl could barely speak.

Boris looked around the bathroom, as if searching for an answer. "I must do something before they tie me up, then beat me or worse," he thought, but he knew time was running out. Cherkizov would soon return, and that would be the end. And even if Cherkizov didn't return, that Caucasian thug was capable of snapping Boris's neck like a chicken's. And then there was the question of Melissa.

Boris noticed the unwashed tile floor, which bore traces of an unfinished repair job: cleaning clothes, pieces of wire, and nails. Then, looking up, he saw an electric socket on the wall, and an idea struck him.

Taking a long piece of naked wire, he firmly tied it to the door's metal handle and then pushed a second wire under the door, bending it over the threshold so that the long bare end was lying just in front of the door on the other side. Then he took the thick, dirty glass on the sink, filled it with water from the faucet, and then poured some of the water onto the threshold, hoping it would pool also on the other side of the door. Next, he carefully put the

179

other ends of both wires into the electric socket, filled the glass once more, and poured water on the bathroom side of the door.

Lady Melissa, who had been absorbed in her distress until now, stopped crying and watched him, although she was in such a shock that she had little idea what he was doing.

Boris, however, knew exactly what he was doing. He knew that Cherkizov would be gone for fifteen minutes or so, and that he had told his thug to "get to work" while he was gone. In fact, the Caucasian brute was already returning to the bathroom in his stocking feet, as was the Caucasus custom while indoors. He brought with him a ten-foot-long nylon cord. When he stepped into the water, he cursed, pulled the wooden dowel from the door, and grabbed the metal handle.

He never knew what hit him, as two hundred twenty volts of electric current ran from his hand down through his legs. His huge body began to shake, and when he tried to free his hand, the spasm paralyzed his muscles. In a few seconds, he lost consciousness, his hand still on the door handle. His body lay silent, slumped on the floor.

Boris carefully removed both wires from the socket, then opened the door, which, to his relief, swung into the bathroom, which meant it was not blocked by the thug slumped on the other side.

Then, afraid that his victim might regain consciousness at any moment, Boris struggled to turn him facedown and tied his hands behind his back with the nylon cord that had been intended to kill Boris. Boris used the same cord to tie his legs together, and then tied his legs to his head, and to his hands. After that, he wound the naked end of one of the wires around the man's neck and wound the other wire around his hands.

He finished just in time, as the brute, regaining consciousness, started moaning. At that point, Boris reinserted the ends of both wires into the socket, and the man's huge body again shook and went limp.

Boris carefully pulled the wires out of the socket, turned over the man's body, and took from his side holster a Makarov military pistol. Boris pressed the release button of the ammunition holder. He removed the ammunition holder and checked it: there were four cartridges. Boris then pulled a casing of a shutter and looked inside. There was a fifth cartridge. He inserted all of the cartridges back into the holder, and then secured the pistol in his pocket, without the safety lock, in case he needed to make a quick draw. Finally, Boris went through the man's pockets and took his passport.

Just then, Melissa crept out of the bathroom, white as a sheet and staring in horror at the scene before her.

When the Caucasian thug quietly moaned again, Boris picked up a dirty cloth from the bathroom floor and stuffed it into his mouth. Then he dragged him into the kitchen and left, closing the kitchen door behind him and heading back to the bathroom.

"Please," Boris begged Melissa, "go in the bathroom and stay there. I will let you know when you can come out."

She obeyed mutely, returning to the bathroom and closing the door. Boris went to the front room and sat down on a couch directly opposite the front door. Cherkizov could be back any minute, and Boris wanted the advantage. He had one ally: the element of surprise. And he had only one chance to make the first shot.

At home in California, Boris had a six-cartridge Colt Agent with point thirty-eight special cartridges. He had the nine-millimeter automatic fifteen-cartridge Brazilian-made pistol Taurus. Sometimes—about once a year—he went to a shooting range, but he was not professional like these mobsters were. He'd never killed; to do that, it was necessary to overcome something inside of you. Not to mention that pulling the trigger far enough was not simple, and for that reason, it was necessary to be trained.

Time seemed to stop. The longer Boris waited, the more his fear and uncertainty reduced the strength in his hands. After a few minutes, Boris decided he did not like his position opposite the door, but he didn't want to move any furniture. Cherkizov was a trained professional who could likely feel any change in the setup. So, Boris moved behind a low wooden cabinet near the front window. He knelt and put his hands on the cabinet counter, intending to use it as a firm surface from which to shoot.

As he resumed waiting, he could hear each beat of his heart, and was sure that each was his last. The pistol became slippery as his hands dripped with sweat, so he laid the weapon on the counter and wiped his hands on his pants. At that precise moment, he heard footsteps on the front porch. It had to be Cherkizov. Boris took the pistol in both hands, every muscle in his body straining in anticipation.

The front door opened softly, and Cherkizov very deliberately entered, turned, and closed the door. Then turning again, with the intent to walk in, he stopped, eyeing the pool of water in front of the bathroom door. He reached for his gun, but he was a split second too late. Boris had already fired.

Taking the hit in his stomach, Cherkizov was ejected from his standing position and thrown against the front door. In shock, he reached for his pistol, but Boris shot again, missing. He quickly fired a third time, and got Cherkizov in the chest. Slowly, Boris watched the strength drain from Cherkizov's body.

Then Cherkizov began to howl, not from pain but from the consciousness that this was his end … and from whom? From this … amateur! From a schmuck.

Boris left his hiding place and fired a fourth shot, from close distance, at Cherkizov's head. The bullet went straight through Cherkizov's skull, leaving a stream of blood and brains in its wake.

In the bathroom, Lady Melissa's sobs turned to howling, and her body wretched with hysterical spasms.

Having tasted blood, Boris turned into a wild animal. Grabbing a rag from a hallway hanger, he went into the kitchen, where the large Caucasian, with the gag still in his mouth, looked straight up at Boris, his huge eyes filled with hate as he groaned and struggled, trying to break loose. Boris threw the rag over the gangster's head and, using his last bullet, fired a single shot. Then he lifted the blood-soaked rag to make sure the Caucasian was dead.

As he did, Boris was hit by the realization of what had just happened. The smell of fresh human blood combined with the presence of two dead bodies made him vomit right where he stood. While gasping for air in recovery, a second wave of vomiting hit, the convulsions causing him wild pain that compelled him to hold his stomach.

With the second wave of vomiting over, Boris felt almost immediately better, and his first instinct was to run, until he remembered that Cherkizov had ordered his two remaining henchmen to return and burn down the house. Little did they know that their fate would be changed soon. Now that Boris knew he could fire shots, and kill, he was sure he could do it again.

Boris rinsed out his mouth under the kitchen faucet, and then, slightly reeling, left and went back into the main front room. Slowly approaching Cherkisov's body, he took the bloody pistol from his victim's hand and then returned to kitchen, where he took the Caucasian's gun. He found a clean towel in one of the drawers, used it to wipe both pistols, and then checked them each for ammunition. The Caucasian's magazine was empty, but Cherkisov's was full. Boris reinserted the holder in Cherkisov's gun, and then secured it under his belt in the back.

Opening the bathroom door, Boris found Melissa hunched in the corner, covering her face with her hands, and shivering in horror. "Is that you?" she whispered without looking up. Her voice shook from the specter of death and the sounds of gunshots, which still echoed in her mind. Then looking up and seeing Boris, she exhaled loudly. "I thought they killed you. You've saved us both. I was praying for you, and the Lord helped you. You are my knight! You are my knight." She sobbed, shuddering, and resumed covering her noble face. It was the face, Boris thought, of a true English lady.

Instructing her not to leave the bathroom, Boris then returned to the living room and, as best he could, trying to avoid getting blood on himself, he turned over Cherkizov's body and went through his jacket pockets. He found a passport and a notebook, both of which he put in his pocket that held the

Caucasian's passport. He could not find the BMW keys. He did, however, find a thick wad of money, which, without counting, he put in his pocket.

Then he searched the house. He found some plastic bags in the closet, so he took one and put in the Caucasian man's pistol and two passports from both men. Melissa's travel bag, which contained the money to pay off the contract, was nowhere to be found. Cherkizov, Boris figured, had probably taken it with him when he'd left. However, he did stumble over a bunch of keys on the floor, and taking a closer look, saw that one of them held the BMW emblem.

So Boris took the plastic bag with the pistol and the passports, along with his and Melissa's coats, out to the BMW. When he opened the door, he saw Melissa's travel bag sitting on the floor in the back seat. He put the coats in the back seat, and opened up the travel bag. Wads of money were there. He put the plastic bag inside. He returned to the house, retrieved his briefcase and Melissa's handbag, and took them out to the car as well. Then he returned to the bathroom, and gently took Melissa by the hand, covering her eyes with his other hand; the poor girl did not deserve to see such carnage.

Boris felt so sorry for this lovely, goodhearted girl that he tenderly kissed her hand before leading her into the corridor and out of the house. He led her to the BMW, opened the passenger front door, and helped her in.

He told Melissa to stay put, and went back into the kitchen, found a box of matches, which he put into his pocket, and turned on the stove's gas burners and the oven. Then going to the hallway, he grabbed a plastic canister with gasoline, took it to the kitchen where a strong gas odor had already started to build, and then poured the gasoline on the floor and on the Caucasian's body. With a second canister from the hallway, he emptied more gas into the front room and on Cherkizov. Finally, he picked up wires from the bathroom floor, lifted wires from the floor, fastening one of them to the bathroom door handle and the other to the kitchen door handle. He inserted the other ends of both wires into the socket in the bathroom and then left the bathroom door open, knowing the slightest movement of the door would excite the wires and create a spark.

Boris reached into his pocket for the matches, but then remembered the two other mobsters who were not there. He didn't know what to do then, until he went out to check on Melissa, at which point, he saw dust rising from the road ahead. He knew immediately that it was the Zhiguli.

Boris opened Melissa's door and literally pulled her out, dragging her away from the car and into some nearby bushes. Then, ordering her to lie down and stay silent no matter what happened, he crouched low and ran across the gravel to a hidden spot behind the porch. He then took the pistol out of his belt, ready to kill, should either one, or both, of them approach him or Melissa.

The Zhiguli pulled up to the house, and the driver got out and walked over to the BMW. After giving the car a once-over, he said something to other gangster in their language, and then opened the trunk. Together, they took out four canisters and headed toward the house.

Boris ran at once to the Zhiguli and stood behind it so that its wheels hid his legs. He took the pistol in both hands and, using the roof of the vehicle as a platform, aimed at the porch. If the mobsters left out the front door, he was certain that not only would he shoot, but he would not miss. He had already killed two gangsters, and he was confident he could kill two more.

Inside the house, the smell of the gas stove was so strong that it concealed the smell of the gasoline on the floor. Seeing Cherkizov's body immediately inside the door, the thugs assumed that Shamil had killed Cherkizov after killing Boris and Melissa first. They called out to their buddy, but there was no answer. They looked in the front room, which appeared in order. The bathroom door was slightly opened. One of the mobsters wished to get by on his way to the kitchen. He instinctively pushed it with leg. The naked wires touched each other. A spark ran between them. The resulting explosion instantly killed both of them and engulfed the house in fire.

Boris ran over to Melissa and dragged her back into the BMW. Then he ran to the Zhiguli and took car registration and other papers from inside the glove compartment and behind the driver sun visor. He also took the keys, which were lying on the driver's seat.

Back in the BMW, he put everything that he had taken from the Zhiguli and put it in the plastic bag, along with the unloaded pistol and the other documents, and then slowly drove away.

Melissa sat silent, looking straight ahead. Boris was silent, too. After passing the gate of a summer residence, they turned left following the road. Boris looked back at the house. Fire had completely engulfed it. Abruptly, one more explosion erupted and the sounds of windows breaking shattered the air. The gas tank had caught fire. Even if firefighters arrived shortly, Boris reasoned, the amount of gasoline in the canisters in addition to what the gangsters had stored, not to mention the steady wind that was already feeding the fire, would, together, ensure that there would be nothing left to save.

The sharp pain in his stomach had become worse, but right now they had to get as far away from this place, and as fast as possible.

After driving for a few minutes, Boris and Melissa had passed no other vehicle or living soul, but they were not safe yet. And Boris knew they could not use the car much longer; if it wasn't already bugged, someone would come looking for it soon. On the other hand, they both badly needed rest, even if for just a half an hour. So taking an unpaved road before the first turn into the woods, Boris pulled into an area of dense foliage and parked behind some high bushes covered in crimson leaves.

He turned off the engine and whispered to Melissa, "Please, close your eyes, my lady."

She did, and Boris went around to her door and lowered her seat to the lying position. He then returned to his seat and lowered it level with Melissa's. He put his hand on hers and closed his eyes. Melissa squeezed his hand in reply. They had no energy left. Both of them felt as if they had fallen through a hole to nowhere.

44

AFTER ABOUT TWENTY MINUTES, the pain in Boris's stomach began to subside, and he opened his eyes. Melissa was breathing steadily and seemed to be asleep. He looked for a long time at her face. Suddenly, a single tear ran down her cheek, and Boris realized that she was not asleep. He got out, opened Melissa's door, and leaned over and kissed her salty cheek. Then he embraced her, softly pressing her body to his, and greedily but tenderly kissing her forehead, eyes, and lips.

She moved into his arms and responded with open-lipped kisses of her own. Both of them felt as if they were suffocating. Boris knew that he must not continue, but he could not stop; the ordeal through which they had gone demanded release. These were kisses of desperation more than love.

An urgent sense of danger, however, returned them to reality, and they stopped. They had to get away from this place as soon as possible, and they needed to get rid of the car. The only question left was how, and their lives depended on the answer. Suddenly, Boris remembered seeing a sign for a hospital on the highway a little before they had turned off toward the village. They could go to the hospital, hide the BMW, and hope to bribe an ambulance driver to take them somewhere.

He went over the plan in his head while Melissa left the car and went behind the bush. When she returned, Boris got into the driver's seat and they took off. Soon, they were back on the country road driving toward the settlement of Vintay, and about ten kilometers later, they saw the sign for the Samara-Moscow road, and the hospital sign that Boris had remembered. They found the hospital just around the corner and parked behind a high pile of construction debris.

Boris took the car registration and other papers from inside the glove compartment, as he had from the Zhiguli and put them in the same plastic bag. Taking their things, Boris locked the car and put the keys in his pocket. As he walked up to the hospital with Melissa, he noticed some minivans marked as ambulances. A group of drivers sat nearby, smoking.

"Hey, guys," Boris said as they neared the group. "We need a ride to Syzran." As this is a common practice in Russia, nobody was surprised.

"What are you going to pay?" one asked. "Syzran is not close."

"A hundred greenbacks," Boris suggested, an amount many times more than was necessary.

"Agreed," another guy said. "I can use the money. Get in." He led them to one of the minivans, and Boris and Melissa made themselves comfortable in the back seat. Discreetly, Boris moved the pistol to a front jacket pocket, just in case he'd need to use it. Then they took off in the direction of the Samara-Moscow road.

45

THE AMBULANCE DRIVER TOOK a pack of cigarettes from his shirt pocket, lit one, and then offered the pack to Boris.

"Like one?" he asked.

"Thanks, I don't smoke," Boris said.

"What's your name, buddy?" the driver asked.

"Boris."

"Call me Gennady. And what's your name, little sister?" he asked Melissa.

"She doesn't speak Russian," Boris said. "Her name is Mila."

"Way to go, brother!" Gennady said, acting both surprised and a bit jealous.

"What are you two talking about?" Melissa asked.

"The guy asked your name," Boris told her.

"What did you tell him?"

"I said that your name is Mila. Melissa is difficult to say in Russian. Milaya, however, in Russian, means 'pleasant to my heart,' or even, you might say, 'my love.'" Boris's voice was slightly hoarse from their recent adventure.

"Do you really mean that?" Melissa asked, her voice softer.

"Have I ever lied to you, Mila?"

"Do you really mean that?"

"Yes, I really mean that. You are my mila."

"You are my mila, too," Melissa said, now whispering. She put her head on Boris's shoulder. He took her hand and gently squeezed her fingers.

"Are you talking about me?" the driver asked, laughing. "For all I know, you are, since I don't understand a word you're saying!"

"We're not talking about you," Boris said. "We're just talking."

After passing the village of Zelenovka, the driver resumed his conversation. "So, Boris, where do you work?"

Boris thought for a moment and then came up with an answer that would set in motion a plan for their escape. "At Diamond Bank. Have you heard of it?"

"Of course. My brother-in-law works there. His name is Sergei. He's the driver for the director of security."

"I know Sergei!" Boris exclaimed. "The director is a friend of mine."

"Really!" Gennady slapped his knee. "Small world."

"Listen, Gen," Boris said. "Could you please take us, instead of Syzran, to the Diamond Bank on Banikin Street in Old City? It will be closer for you. And it will be more convenient for us."

"But it's late now. Nobody will be there," Gennady said.

"It's okay. We'll find somebody to let us in," Boris answered confidently, and then he saw Gennedy shrug his shoulders, turn right, and drive on toward Old City.

It was eight o'clock when they reached Diamond Bank, and cold enough now that they could see their breath. Boris paid the driver his greenbacks and he and Melissa said good-bye, although Gennady said he would wait ten minutes in case the security guard didn't let them in.

Diamond Bank occupied what had once been a five-story residential building put up during the construction of the Volga Hydroelectric Power Plant. Upon learning that the building was equipped with an elevator, Diamond Bank had purchased it, moved all of the tenants out, and converted the apartments to bank offices. Some of the one-bedroom apartments on the top floor had been remodeled, furnished, and put into service as living accommodations for the occasional visitor, as well as for some of the management. A maid came once a day, changed the linens, did some light cleaning, and brought food.

Boris, hoping to stay in one of those apartments, knocked at the bank's front door. A security guard came and asked brusquely through the glass, "What do you want?"

"I need to call to one of the bank managers," Boris said in a firm, official-sounding voice. "Either Mr. Kislov, the chief of security, or the executive vice president, Mrs. Kozlova. Or, Mr. Paul Moiseevich."

Seemingly impressed by Boris's knowledge of all the bank managers' names, the security guard nodded. "It's late, but I'll call Mr. Kislov."

As soon as the guard made a connection, he handed the receiver to Boris. At the other end was Kislov's wife, Tatiana.

"Tanyechka, I hope you weren't asleep yet," Boris said. "Is Leo there?"

"Boris!" Tatiana answered, delighted to hear his voice. "Just a minute, let me get him. Leo, it's Boris, calling from California!"

"Boris!" Leo answered playfully. "It's good to hear from you. How are things in California?"

"Hi, Leo, things are okay," Boris said, "however, I am not in California. I am here, in Togliatti, at the Banikin Street branch. And I'm not alone. I'm with a girl. So, please tell the security guard to give me a key to one of the apartments." Boris paused. "I have a lot to tell you, Leo. A lot. But it will have to wait until tomorrow."

"Got it," Leo said. "Please give the receiver to the guard, and I'll see you tomorrow."

Boris did as Leo has asked, after which the guard uttered only, "Yes. Sir." Then after hanging up, he unlocked a key cabinet, retrieved a key from inside, and handed it to Boris. "Do you want me to show the way?"

"No thanks," Boris said. "I know where to go."

And with that, Melissa and Boris gathered up their things and went to the elevator. For the moment, they were safe. No mobsters would dare to attack Diamond Bank, which was protected by other, far more powerful, gangsters.

Boris unlocked the fifth floor apartment, followed Melissa in, and turned on the lights in the entryway. He removed his jacket and hung it in the closet, then assisted Melissa with hers. Then they took off their shoes and padded across the carpet into the bedroom, which had two beds and, instead of nightstands, simple chairs. There was no TV or radio.

Melissa sat down heavily on one of the chairs. She was too tired to talk, but the warmth of the apartment and the knowledge that she was safe quickly brought her back to life.

"Mila, if you'd like to take a shower, I'll fix some dinner for us," Boris suggested.

"You said mila," Melissa said. "Do you still mean it?"

"Of course I do," Boris answered, and the two stared into each other's eyes.

As Melissa picked up her small bag and went to the bathroom, Boris left and went to the kitchen and washed his hands first. In the refrigerator, awaiting their large appetites, he found eggs, oil, butter, smoked sausage, a small piece of cheese, and a large piece of real Ukrainian bacon. There was also a bottle of vodka, a bottle of Riesling wine, and a few Cokes. Boris got out a frying pan and put it on the stove, but hesitated before turning it on, suddenly envisioning himself pouring gasoline on the floor and blowing up that damned house.

Boris found some bread in a breadbox and cut a few slices. He buttered the pan and cooked the eggs. He sliced the bacon, cheese, and sausage. From an upper cabinet, he took two wineglasses. And in a drawer, he found a few bags of Earl Grey tea along with some utensils. So he put a teapot on the stove and spread everything out neatly on the kitchen table. Then he sat and waited for Melissa. Just as he heard the shower turn off, she called to him, "Mila, please come in and give me a towel."

Boris opened the bathroom door and saw Melissa, like Venus, looking at him, unashamed and magnificent. Her wet, dark copper hair fell around shoulders, and her gray-green eyes radiated tenderness. The brown circles around her love-hardened nipples contrasted beautifully with her white marble skin. Boris looked down at her girlish tummy, which held the slightest, most charming reminiscences of adolescent fat. Her hips and knees were so womanly that Boris was seized by a desire to make love to her without a second's delay. He took out a towel and wrapped her in it, drying her with soft pats.

Melissa responded by wrapping her arms around him. "This is what I promised when I prayed for you," she said in a barely audible voice, "when you fought for our lives, my mila."

"What would you have done if they had killed me?"

"I would have killed myself. I could not have lived any longer if they had taken my body. Please," she said, pushing him away, "say nothing more about this ordeal. Just take a shower and make love to me. Please, be my mila for real."

"But I'm right in the middle of fixing dinner," Boris said, though without much conviction.

"Come on," Melissa said, laughing. "Is there something you don't like about me?" She kissed Boris on the mouth.

Boris tried to hold the line. "I'm sorry. I didn't mean it. But I thought you would be hungry."

"Yes, I am. Hungry as a lioness. But first things, first."

Boris could resist no longer, and so sent her out of the bathroom. He undressed, shaved, took great pleasure in soaping his body and, then under the hot streams of water, he washed off the terror of their bloody day. As the horror went down the drain with the soapsuds, Boris became more and more hungry for Melissa. He dried himself, wrapped the towel around his waist, and walked out of the bathroom to find her lying in bed, covered in only a sheet, waiting for him. He turned off the lights and lay down beside her. Then feeling their hearts beating together, he gently kissed his mila. She hugged him with her entire body and showered his neck, his arms and shoulders, his chest and stomach, with kisses.

It is always impossible to know how long the ecstasy of love lasts, but even the best and finest lovemaking eventually comes to an end.

While Melissa lay motionless, savoring the magical moments of quenched desire, Boris gently punctuated her stomach with kisses.

Shyly, she laughed. "Am I a good lover?"

Not one to waste time on comparisons in such delicate matters, Boris led her into the bathroom, where they washed each other under kissing and caressing. Drying off, they went into the kitchen, where Boris fried some more eggs, poured vodka into the wineglasses, and opened one of the Cokes. He made two large but very delicious Ukrainian bacon sandwiches, raised his glass, and proposed a toast.

In the Russian tradition, after clinking their glasses and exchanging kisses, they drank the vodka in one gulp, washed it down with Coke, and ate their sandwiches. They repeated this ritual again and again, as they fed each other eggs and hot tea.

It didn't take long for Melissa to get tipsy, and with a fuzzy tongue, she declared that she was now an English Russian who would not think of drinking diluted vodka and who would regularly snack on Ukrainian bacon.

It was two in the morning by the time Boris and Melissa made it to bed, and then, uncomfortable lying together on one narrow mattress, Boris moved the mattresses of both beds to the floor and lay them side by side against the wall. On their new queen-sized mattress, he came to her, embracing and caressing her, and they fell asleep in each other's arms.

At eight o'clock the next morning, they awoke to the ringing telephone. It was Leo calling from the lobby. He had brought breakfast for them and was on his way up.

Boris asked Leo to give him thirty minutes, and then continuing to joke and caress each other, he and Melissa showered, dried with the same towel, and dressed. At precisely eight thirty, Mr. Leonid Kislov knocked on their door.

46

WHEN BORIS OPENED THE door, Leonid was standing on the threshold holding a heavy plastic bag. The two friends embraced, after which Boris introduced Melissa to Leo.

Boris and Leo went into the kitchen, and Melissa, understanding that her presence would be a distraction, excused herself. Back in the bedroom, she looked forward to a nap to help her recover from the intensity of the previous night. She dressed in Boris' T-shirt and lay down, covering herself with a blanket and embracing a pillow fragrant with the memory of Boris. Then smiling, and feeling like an angel, she fell fast asleep.

In the plastic bag that Leonid had brought was a bottle of vodka, a few bottles of Coke, two cans of pork, one can of vegetable salad, a can of pickles, one package of pirozhkies,[63] and a large loaf of bread. Leo told Boris that, in the enclosed deck, were also a bag of potatoes and a bag of onions. The two men quickly set the table, opened the vodka, and filled two wineglasses.

"Should we invite your young lady to the table?" Leo asked. Then looking directly at Boris, he added, "Have you separated from your wife and left home?"

"Where did you get that idea?" Boris asked in surprise.

"How else am I to understand you're being here with this young woman? And who is she, anyway?"

Boris had no option but to lay out the whole story. So he told his companion the whole story, from the visit to Washington, to the creation and execution of all the oil contracts, and ended with the events of previous day. He told Leonid about everything except for the money in Melissa's travel bag.

---

63   A traditional Russian food; a deep-fried sandwich.

"Why you didn't tell me about this crude oil deal before?" Leo asked incredulously. "Are we friends or not?"

"I didn't think it was necessary." Boris shrugged. "Everything was going great before yesterday."

Seeing that Leo was still not fully convinced that his story was real, Boris left. He walked back in a few minutes later carrying the plastic bag with the pistols, the car keys, and the documents, and put it on the table.

Leo nodded in affirmation.

"There's more," Boris said. "Cherkizov made a few phone calls from the village of Novomatyushkino. It would be interesting to know who he called and what he told them."

"I'd say so," Leo said, already considering the possibilities. "By the way," he added thoughtfully, "I received some information this morning. Early yesterday, as he was leaving his house for work, the head of the Novokuybyshevsk Oil Pipeline dispatch center, Mr. Peter Anisimov, was killed by two shots fired from a Makarov pistol. The third shot, the control shot, was fired point-blank into his forehead."

Boris shook his head. "We were just on our way to meet him."

Now Leo had no doubt that Boris had told him the real story, which meant that he and Melissa were in serious danger with both the gangsters and the feds. "One thing's clear, Boris: it was a gangland hit. Moreover, Anisimov's office was set on fire and all his files were destroyed. Also of interest, the time of the fire coincided with the time of the murder, which means that at least two groups were operating in sync. Federal security is looking for suspects."

Leo picked up the phone and called his driver, Sergey. "Sergey, listen to me. Please go to both Novomatyushkino and Zhigulikha and find out from the local gangsters what they know about the events of yesterday. Then go to a telephone station in Novomatyushkino and find out the recipients and the nature of some phone calls made yesterday by someone with the name of Cherkizov. Did you get his name? Cherkizov. Between one and four in the afternoon. As soon as you find out, let me know."

Leo paused before continuing. "No, that's all. But Sergey, please come back here as soon as possible. Understood? And one more thing, stop in at the hospital and ask the guys there if they know anything."

After hanging up, Leo said, "So, what are your plans now?"

"The most important thing is to get Melissa safely out of Russia. Considering the political situation just now, I think it would be better to go through Kazakhstan. It's quiet there, at least for now. I need to call my niece, Maria, in Alma-Ata."

Leo dialed his secretary. "Nadia, please put through an intercity call from this apartment." He looked at Boris. "What's the phone number in Alma-Ata?"

Boris retrieved the number from a notebook in his briefcase and gave it to Leo, who dictated the number to his secretary. A second later, they were waiting for the connection.

"As I see it," Leo said, "it will be impossible for you to leave this place until we have an understanding of the situation. I think Sergey will clear it up, but certainly you do not need to keep the pistols. I understand they're your battle trophies, but your life will be less complicated without them. I'll clean them and store them in a warehouse somewhere."

"No," Boris said. "That's exactly what I should not do. I'll put them in an envelope and leave it in a safety box at a railroad station. I have a friend in the state prosecutor's office. He is the assistant to the prosecutor general."

"You're right," Leo agreed. "Well, you speak to Maria. Then, when Sergey returns, I'll come back and let you know what's going on."

When Leo left, Boris quietly opened the door to the bedroom and saw Melissa asleep. He lay down next to her and gently pulled up the blanket to cover her. As he did, the large for Melissa Boris' T-shirt slide to one side, exposing her breast. Boris gently kissed her side and, having inhaled the intoxicating aroma of her skin, began to kiss her more passionately. Melissa woke up, opened her eyes, and, turning her head, watched Boris. For an instant, she lost consciousness, and then simply melted from the ecstasy that engulfed her.

At that moment, the phone rang in the kitchen. Boris, who could tell from the ring that it was the intercity call, ran and answered it.

"Masha!" he said, "it's me, your Uncle Boris. Masha, dear, I need your help. Can you call Lady Melissa's father in London now? You remember Lady Melissa, don't you? She's the girl you met in Washington this summer. Remember? That's right, at lunch! Her father's name is Sir Charles Spencer.

"The thing is, Melissa and I are in Russia, and we're in a difficult situation … right, I am calling you from Togliatti. The telephone is not bugged and we are safe here. I'm pretty sure that I can get her safely into Kazakhstan, to Uralsk, or even a little further south, but wherever it is, she must be met by a representative of the British embassy accompanied by full security. Otherwise, I will not let her go."

Then Boris called Melissa and asked for her father's telephone number in London.

"Tell him that his daughter, Melissa, is in grave danger," Boris told his niece. "He must contact the foreign office or the British ambassador to Kazakhstan, or … he should find out, and give us instructions for providing Melissa with safe passage from Uralsk to Alma-Ata, and Alma-Ata to London.

If they have any questions, they can call this number. We will be available. In fact, we cannot leave. And Masha, please don't call my wife in California. It would frighten her."

Masha promised to call London as soon she hung up, and then to call back with the information.

Boris hung up and went back to the bedroom, where Melissa was sitting in bed barefoot, with her toes curled shyly under her, and wearing only the T-shirt. Without saying a word, he embraced her and then playfully fell over on top of her. She did not resist; on the contrary, she encouraged his advance, and was more than ready to return it.

But they were interrupted again. It was Masha on the phone. "Uncle Boris? I phoned London. The connection was awful and I didn't speak with her father, but with his secretary, a complete idiot. He did, however, seem to understand the main point, that Melissa is in danger and has to be rescued. He said they would call you."

Bearing in mind that the phone could be bugged, Boris simply thanked Maria and hung up, then returned to Melissa, who was on her knees.

"Boris, my love," she pleaded sweetly. "Please, pray with me."

"Melissa? Darling! What are you doing?"

"Don't you remember yesterday? In that house of horror, I prayed for you, my mila, and our Lord helped you. Don't you know that the Lord protected you? Without him, on your own, you would have never been able to fight those bandits and win. As of yesterday, I know how and why my great-grandmothers loved their knights at the tournaments. Because they were protected by the Lord. And, through his protection, they won. Today, you are the greatest warrior. If I were Queen, I would make you a knight."

"Why not a king?" Boris said, laughing.

"Oh no, my love. You are not my king. You are my lord! I do not know how I could continue to live without you." She laughed, but then suddenly she ceased her joking tone, and said, "Seriously, though, please get on your knees and give me your hands."

Acquiescing, Boris fell to his knees opposite her and they joined hands, forming a circle.

"Please close your eyes and repeat after me," Melissa instructed. "Oh, great Lord, savior and ruler of the universe, please grant us your protection. Please make our love for each other as endless as this circle. Please help us in all our thoughts and activities. Amen."

Boris repeated each word after Melissa, and then they rose from their knees.

Melissa nestled in Boris's arms, kissed him, and whispered, though there was nobody to hear but him, "Now, I wish you to be my lord. Please, take me in your arms and make love to me." Then she took him by the hand and led him to their bed.

A great rush of love surged from Melissa to Boris and back again, as she spoke no words, but moaned from the tides and torments of pleasure.

Boris continued to kiss his young lover until she relaxed and released from her embrace, then he went to the kitchen for a drink of water. When he returned, to his surprise, he found Melissa still lying on her back, covered with a blanket. "Melissa? Darling? What are you doing there? You may get pregnant."

"Yes, I know," she said. "I wish to have your child. My mila, you always will be with me: first, inside me, and after, as my baby, to the end of my days. This is what I prayed for, and you were with me. This is what I asked the Lord for, and you were with me. Please kiss me. Please, kiss your mila."

Only then did Boris understand the true depth of Melissa's affections and it made him feel like a young man again, full of strength and full of power. Once again, he made love to her, but this time as a young warrior taking a slave. Melissa, understanding that she had provoked him, accepted him obediently, and when he exploded inside of her once again, holding her tightly, she exulted in his wild passion and strength.

Finally, having given Melissa everything he had, Boris lay down on her, supported by his hands, and fell asleep. Several minutes later, he woke up, and, seeing that Melissa was sleeping, quietly rose from the bed. His head was spinning from fatigue, and he felt slightly nauseated. Now that he was totally, physically empty, he was forced to face reality.

He quietly dressed and went into the kitchen, where he put the teapot on the stove, sat at the table, and tried to make sense of it all. He suddenly remembered that Melissa's panties, bra, and tights were lying on the chair so, thinking she should have clean lingerie, he got them and, while the teapot was warming up, washed them in the bathroom sink. After hanging her underwear on the warm radiator in the bathroom, he returned to the kitchen and made a fresh cup of Earl Gray.

He sat again and resumed his thinking. His affair with Melissa, despite the intensity of their feelings for each other, was improbably complex. What *was* their future together? But after a long while of sipping and thinking, the only conclusion he drew was that there was no answer.

Boris went to the entryway closet, took out the pack of money that he'd gotten from Cherkizov's pocket, and counted it. There were twenty-one thousand US dollars and ten million Russian rubles, which made it about two thousand dollars more.

So he went back to the kitchen, found a pen and a clean piece of paper, and wrote, "My dearest mila. I love you with my entire heart. Please, do not forget me. With love, your Boris."

He opened his briefcase and took out a two-by-three-inch color photo of himself, which he had made as a spare, perhaps if he were to need an additional visa. Then taking twenty thousand dollars from the wad of cash, he wrapped it, along with his photo, inside his note. It made a good size package. He took Melissa's handbag out of the closet and deposited the package into a zippered pocket where she had her keys, putting the rest of the money in his jacket.

"Who knows?" he thought. "She might need it someday."

The clock showed 4:30 p.m. Boris dialed Leo and asked if they could go shopping for a few things. "We have nothing with us," he explained. "Melissa didn't bring any clothes with her, and I left all my things in Moscow at the hotel."

Leo said he couldn't do it that day, but that tomorrow would work, as long as they went late enough in the day to ensure that everybody except security had left the bank.

Hanging up, Boris noticed that it was already dark out. The day had flown, as had the week, and in that time, so much had happened to him. In the next room, a woman twenty years younger than he was sleeping, and a noblewoman, no less, who was obsessed with having his child; the woman's fiancé was the oil-dealer and multi-millionaire, and her father was a British aristocrat.

Boris, meanwhile, had been married to the same woman for thirty years. They had met in a students' construction brigade working in virgin territory in the North Kazakhstan, and had married when they were in their second year in college. Their grown child was twenty-nine. They had once loved each other. Now, they still respected each other, though they had no money.

In contrast, he thought, his relationship with Melissa was not a casual one. He adored this beautiful young woman who loved him. Yet, all of it was beginning to seem like a nightmare.

He heard Melissa stirring in the next room. He made a second cup of tea and took it to her. She was already up, looking for her underwear. Boris raised her pillow and asked her to lie back down. When she did, he tucked the blanket around her, and held the mug to her lips. After she had taken a drink, he asked if she could remain in bed a little longer, until her underthings had dried. Unbelieving, she ran playfully into the bathroom where she found evidence that Boris was telling the truth. She ran back into the bedroom and embraced him, and then lay still in his arms. When Boris grew tired, he moved away from her, and saw tears running down her cheeks. He knew that the same questions he had about their future were also tormenting Melissa.

Boris spread his fingers, brushing the hair from Melissa's forehead. He then lifted her head and studied her, as though impressing every feature of her noble face on his memory for all time. "I love you so much," he whispered in Melissa's ear as he took her into his arms once again.

"Me, too," she said. "But what we will do?"

"I don't know."

"But you're a grown-up."

"Yes, I am. But this situation doesn't seem to have a reasonable solution."

"I know," Melissa said with a small smile. "I studied philosophy."

They remained in their embrace a while longer, looking deep into each other's eyes.

At last, Boris let go. "I am going to put together a statement for the attorney general, and I think you should do the same. Is that okay with you, my dearest mila?"

"Yes, that's okay," she said soberly.

Boris went to the kitchen and got out the notepad and pen he had used to write Melissa's note, then he sat at the table, and began writing.

To the Office of the Attorney General

Of the Russian Federation

From a citizen of the USA

Goryanin, Boris Georgievich

THE AFFIDAVIT

I, the undersigned—Goryanin, Boris Georgievich, citizen of the USA, born in 1945, living at —being in full capacity, am making this affidavit as follows:

On September 23, 1993, having arrived from Moscow to Kurumoch Airport, I and the subject of Her Majesty The Queen of England, Lady Melissa Spencer, were scheduled go to Novokuybyshevsk Oil Pipeline Dispatching Center for a meeting …

Boris then recorded every detail that he could remember of the events of the past few days, explaining the death of Cherkizov and his direct reports, and ending with the burning house in the village of Novomatyushkino. He then wrapped up his report with the following:

… By informing the Office of the Attorney General of my actions, I ask investigators to consider that these deeds were provoked by the gangsters' kidnapping us and keeping us against our will for the purposes of rape, robbery, and murder. I acted to protect my life and the life of the young woman. If I had not been able to prevent

these crimes, Lady Melissa Spencer would have been subjected to sexual violence and murder through torture.

In accordance with the above, I ask that my actions be identified as those I made within the limits of self-defense and for the protection of Lady Melissa Spencer.

The documents withdrawn from the gangsters, along with the aforementioned weapons and car keys, are attached.

Signed: Goryanin, Boris Georgievich. September 24, 1993

Witnessed by: A Subject of Her Majesty

The Queen of England,

Lady Melissa Spencer.   *September 24, 1993*

After Melissa had provided her signature as a witness, Boris sealed the affidavit along with the evidence into a manila envelope, put it in a plastic bag, and hid it in his briefcase.

47

THE NEXT EVENING AT about seven, Leo knocked on the door. "There is no one left at the bank," he said as soon as Boris opened it. "Let's go shopping!"

Boris was walking back to the living room to tell Melissa that he was leaving, when the phone rang.

"This is Mister Spencer speaking," said the voice on the line. "May I trouble you to ask my daughter to pick up the phone?"

"Certainly," Boris answered. "It's my pleasure, Mr. Spencer." He went into the living room and told Melissa that Leonid had come and that her father was on the phone. Then he and Leo left the apartment.

"I'm very grateful to you for helping us in this situation," Boris said to his friend.

"Come on, you'd do the same," Leo said. "By the way, do you know who you killed back there in the village?"

"I know that one of them was Kravchuk's chief of security," Boris said. "There was also one huge Caucasian, and two commonplace thugs."

Hearing only silence from his friend as they reached the street, Boris looked at him. "I guess you'd better tell me what Sergey found out."

"Well to start with, nothing's left of the house but ashes. It took the fire department forty minutes to arrive after a neighbor called them, so the house burned for at least an hour.

"The neighbors reported that there was possibly some ammunition, too, because they heard an explosion, but authorities couldn't find any evidence. No corpses were found either. Probably completely burned up. There was so much gasoline, it must have been part of their plan to burn you both up after they killed you. They had to hide the evidence somehow, and considering the current political situation, they must have figured nobody would search for you.

"As for that Shamil guy, as well as his two gangsters, they've been reported missing. I don't remember their surnames right off, but they were apparently infamous gangsters, topping the federal Most Wanted list for murders and robberies committed in Caucasus and Russia."

Leo shook his head. "I can't figure out how you managed to handle such professionals. Oh, and I'm not the only one—gangsters are assuming that what you did was the work of federal agents. In fact, they actually suspect Cherkizov. Their reasoning is that Cherkizov liquidated Shamil and the others after taking care of you and Melissa, which probably makes even more sense to them, because it's been announced that Cherkizov is the object of a special federal search."

"What about Gennady?" Boris said.

"When he asked around at the hospital, Sergey was told that Gennady drove two Muscovites, a father and a daughter, to the Syzran railroad station. Don't worry. Gennady won't say anything about bringing you and your girlfriend here."

Boris sighed. "That's good to know. Thank you, Leo."

"You're welcome, but there's more," Leo said. "In Novomatyushkino, a red Zhiguli was found next to the burned house, and near the hospital, a BMW. Both cars were listed as stolen. The BMW belonged to Mr. Anisimov, the murdered director of the dispatch center."

"What happened to the cars?" Boris asked.

"The cops confiscated them." Leo paused. "So, what are you going to do now?"

"I'm going to get some rest," Boris said. "Oh, but one other thing: did you find out who Cherkizov called?"

"He called two numbers. One was to Agroprom and one was to the KGB. I have to tell you, my friend, this is way over my head."

"For sure," Boris answered. "Cherkizov must have called Kravchuk and Yakubovsky."

In the street, it was cold and dark, and a fine drizzle mixed with light snow. They went into a clothing store where Boris bought Melissa a medium-sized, dark violet, insulated sports suit and two pairs of warm panties. The same kind of sports suit, but in extra large and black, he bought for himself. He also bought two pairs of long-sleeved T-shirts, some warm socks, and two pairs of thin cotton gloves—one in large and the other in medium.

When he picked up a pack of playing cards, Leo looked at him and said, "How long do you expect to be here?"

Boris told Leo that it depended on how quickly they could get Melissa out of the country through Kazakhstan. "First of all," Boris said, "she doesn't have a Kazakhstan visa. Second, she needs to get safe passage to Alma-Ata."

"And how are you going to get out?" Leo asked.

"As soon as she's safe, I'll go back to Sheremetyevo International and take the first flight I can to anywhere in Europe. I don't think they'll search for me there. Although, who knows."

"Listen to me, Boris. I got an idea." Being excited with this idea, Leo even stop in the middle of the street. "As the matter of fact, you could consider another possibility. The bank is sharing the lease of a corporate jet YK-40 with AutoVAZ[64], which both companies are using to fly employees from the factory Airport in Toglyatti to the Moscow Regional Airport Bykovo."

"This is the best way out. This alternative route seems much easier. For one thing, it would no longer be necessary for Melissa to go to Alma-Ata. For another, it would make it possible for both of us to fly to Moscow and we could be driven by the bank's car to Sheremetyevo." Boris immediately recognized the positive solution to the main problem—to secure Melissa safe way out of Russia. They agreed that Leo would check it out and touch base with Boris the next evening.

Leaving the clothing store, they crossed the street and went into a grocery store, where Boris bought six cartons of cream, three packs of pelmenies, a package of butter, and a loaf of bread.

When they left, they discovered that in the few minutes they had spent in the store, strong winds had moved in. It seemed a blizzard was brewing, as though it were already winter.

Boris bought whole stock of large, thick white mushrooms from a woman selling from the bucket on the street corner. Then they went to a newsstand and Boris bought some recent newspapers.

"It will be interesting," he thought, "to see whether recent events match what experts at Alevtina's birthday party predicted."

The first paper he looked at was the *New Times*. On the front page was printed "Presidential Decree No. 1400." The experts, as always, had been right. It really looked like civil war could explode at any moment. Boris couldn't stop thinking, "If Melissa and I had been killed by those gangsters, nobody would have looked for us. The war would have covered over everything."

Back at the bank, Boris felt the chill as he walked into their fifth floor apartment. The windows were not insulated, and wind was blowing in through the cracks.

The door to the kitchen was closed, which meant Melissa was still talking to her father. Taking off his jacket, Boris knocked gently at the door, interrupting Melissa just long enough to tell her about the possibility of their

---

64   A car manufacturing company in Togliatty.

flying to Moscow's Bykovo Airport, so that she could relay the information to her father. Then he went into the bedroom and spread his purchases across the adjoined mattresses.

Soon, Melissa came in. Boris put one of the T-shirts on her, pulled her close, and embraced her. Then, sitting her gently on the bed he took her right foot, kissed each toe, and then after tickling her heel, pulled on one of the new socks. A laughing Melissa pulled her foot back, allowing Boris to see that she was not wearing panties. It was too much for him. He threw the merchandise from the bed into the air and stripped off his clothes, making love to Melissa, who wore only the T-shirt and a right sock.

His passion soon spent, Boris looked down at Melissa to see her face wet with tears.

Seeing his quizzical expression, she burst out crying. "You are ... you are ... I do not ... I cannot live without you. I need you, I need you every moment." She stopped talking to release the sobs. When she had calmed, she said, "I told my father that I want to cancel my engagement to Eddy."

"What did he say?" Boris asked.

"He wasn't happy. Eddy's appointment with Her Majesty is scheduled for the twenty-ninth." Melissa wiped her wet face and stood up. She put on the sports suit, while Boris dressed in the trousers and a T-shirt. Now they looked like a hundred thousand other couples of no particular nationality living in the former USSR.

Both silent now, they took each other's hands and walked into the kitchen. Boris poured cream into two cups, and suggested that Melissa have some, telling her it would restore her energy. Melissa, looking at Boris, took a few sips and made a face of disgust. But then seeing him drink with obvious pleasure, she sighed and downed the whole cup herself.

Hearing the wind rise up again, Boris said, "It's urgent that we seal up the windows. Otherwise, we'll freeze to death in this apartment."

"But how? We don't have any paper or glue."

"Trust me," Boris answered. "I'll do it."

Boris walked to one of the kitchen cabinets, where earlier he had seen a package of wheat flour. He diluted a cup of the flour in two cups of cold water, poured the mixture into a saucepan, and put it on the stove. Constantly stirring, he brought it to boiling.

He then took pages from one of the newspapers he had bought, folded them lengthwise, and, using a kitchen knife, cut along the folds to make strips approximately three-and-a-half inches wide. Melissa watched with undisguised interest, and immediately offered to help. Boris accepted. He was ready to paste now, but first, the most difficult part had to be done.

Boris went into the hallway and got both their coats. Once they were both well-insulated, Boris opened an internal window frame, and then the external window frame, which had been very loosely closed. Wind rushed through the open window and blew snow on Boris. He then closed the external frame, tightly this time. Still, the wind and snow continued to blow through the cracks.

Taking tablespoons, he and Melissa smeared the glue mixture onto the newspaper strips, and pasted them onto the inside frame. Once this was done, Boris tightly closed the internal frame and repeated the process. Upon finishing the kitchen window, they went into the living room and the bedroom and did the same.

When they were finished, Melissa was delighted and a little bit proud when their apartment warmed up.

Now they were ready to eat. Boris took out a few potatoes and a piece of onion. He peeled the potatoes, cut them into small cubes, and threw them into a saucepan with boiling water. Then, finely slicing the onion, he sautéed it in a frying pan with a pat of butter until it turned a beautiful golden color. The kitchen became as warm and appetizing as any meal.

Boris asked Melissa to set out the plates, wineglasses, and utensils. Then he put a teapot on, and announced that the potatoes needed about twenty more minutes to simmer. As they waited, their jokes and light conversation took the place of radio and TV.

When the potatoes were ready, Boris poured them from the saucepan into the skillet with the onion. Then he opened a can of stewed pork and put approximately half of it over the mixture. He smeared the rest of the pork over two slices of bread, which he then salted and peppered with the confidence of an expert chef.

As he filled their wineglasses with vodka, Melissa watched him with great pleasure. Men in her circles had always considered cooking below them. How wonderful it was, she thought, when a man took his responsibilities seriously.

By the time they sat down to eat, it was already nine o' clock, and the storm outside was raging. The wind groaned and whipped tree branches against the windows. Snow formed into banks on the street below and into ridges on the outer window frame.

Boris took a candle from one of the drawers, along with a small saucer. Lighting a match, he then slightly melted the bottom of the candle, deftly stuck it onto the saucer, and then lit its wick on top. For a few minutes, the two of them watched the flame silently as they ate. And then Boris got up and turned off the kitchen light.

Now sitting in candlelight, Boris took Melissa's hands and recited a poem in Russian, which he then repeated in English:

"The snow blows through the earth,
From all four corners.
Candle is burning on a desk.
Candle is burning.
Like an asphyxiating summer night,
With insects flying to the flame,
Snowflakes accumulate
To window's frame.
The light is forming on the desk
Rings and a cross—like warning.
Candle is burning on the desk.
Candle is burning.
Shadows are dancing in the glow
On vaulted ceiling.
Crossing of legs, crossing of hands
Signals of destiny's meaning.
Small shoes fallen on the floor
With a loud sound.
The candle is dropping waxy tears
On the virgin's gown.
The world is lost in snowfall
Without warning.
Candle is burning on the desk.
Candle is burning.
Seductive heat blows the flame out
As love confessing.
The angel raises both wings
In holy blessing."[65]

Fascinated by the rhythms of the Russian poem followed by the emotion of its English translation, nearly deafened by the howling wind, realizing the complexity of their situation—being stranded somewhere between the Volga River and the horrors of Siberia, and knowing that each moment was bringing her nearer to separating from the man she loved—Melissa began to cry. She cried as bitterly as an overwhelmed child.

Boris got on his knees and tried to console her. Eventually, she calmed down, at which point Boris decided to resume their supper with a toast. He did so by listing Melissa's charms and taking a sip for each.

---

65   From "The Winter Night," by Russian poet Boris Leonidovich Pasternak. This poem was translated from Russian into English by the author of this novel, and is not really corresponding to its original.

When he was finished, she refilled their wineglasses with vodka, and, in turn, offered the same toast for Boris, which she ended with a tribute to their future child.

At this, Boris felt like a traitor, not only to Melissa, but also to his potential future baby, whom he might possibly never see. It was then Melissa's turn to soothe his pain.

After dinner, to wash down the vodka and stewed pork, Boris served hot tea. Instead of cookies, he offered a crust of bread. And it was thus—taking bites from the same piece of bread and washing it down with tea—that they finished another day in Togliatti.

48

WHEN BORIS AWOKE THE next morning, it was still dark. For a long time, he lay looking at Melissa's face, which in a few short days had become so familiar and close.

All day they did nothing. Boris taught Melissa to play the Russian card game called Fool. Boris quickly began to cheat, dumping unwanted cards into the center, and, eventually, feeling the urge to make love to Melissa again. When they had finished, Melissa told Boris that both cream and cards were forbidden. Later, the cleaning lady came. She replaced the sheets, made the beds, and left them four large towels. Then Boris gave her five dollars and gave her a short list of things to buy. When Melissa asked Boris what he had asked the maid to get, he told her he'd asked for another deck of cards and two more cartons of cream. But when she returned, the cleaning lady brought them two cartons of cream and a loaf of bread.

At dinner, Melissa asked Boris about the small birthmark resembling Australia that sat just above his right elbow. Boris told her that his father had had the same mark. Melissa probed further into his past, asking about his parents. Boris said that his father had died a long time ago, but that his mother was still living in the States.

"What was your father's name?" she asked.

"George."

"Like Saint George?" Melissa said. "Then, if it's a boy, I will name him after your father. George." She sat for a moment, thinking, and then asked, "Is it possible to name a baby Mila?"

"Yes," Boris said, "but Mila is the short form of Ludmila or Milana, which are both very pretty girls' names."

"So," Melissa said, "You are my mila, aren't you?"

"Yes." Boris smiled. "You are my mila, too."

"Yes. I know. And so if it's a girl, I will name her Milana, after both of us."

After they had cleared the table and washed the dishes, Boris again took out the paper and pen from his briefcase, and began writing.

To the Office of the Attorney General

Of The Russian Federation

From a Citizen of the USA

Goryanin, Boris Georgievich

THE AFFIDAVIT

I, the undersigned—Goryanin, Boris Georgievich, a citizen of the USA, born in 1945, living at—being in sound mind, am making this additional affidavit as follows:

In addition to my affidavit dated September 24, 1993, I wish to inform you that, as a result of the questioning of the employees of Novomatyushkino's telephone station, it has been established that on September 23, 1993, between 1:00 p.m. and 4:00 p.m., Mr. Cherkizov made two telephone calls from the Novomatyushkino telephone service center. One call was made to the city of Moscow to an officer of the Federal Security Service of the Russian Federation, Mr. Vladislav Yakubovsky. The second call was made to the president of Agroprom, Mr. Gavrila Kravchuk.

Signed: Goryanin, Boris Georgievich.   On September 26, 1993

Mr. Boris Goryanin's Signature, Witnessed by

A Subject of Her Majesty the Queen of England,

Lady Melissa Spencer.   On September 26, 1993

Boris attached the second affidavit to the first one, and then they went to bed, making love for the final time that day. And why not? Amid the development of a Russian civil war, they were the epitome of love, and this was their true honeymoon.

—————— 49 ——————

THE NEXT DAY, AS promised, Leo came over to relay the information he'd gathered regarding the bank's corporate jet. Its first flight to Bykovo was scheduled to leave October 2 at 9:00 a.m. and arrive at 10:30. Subsequently driving from Bykovo to Sheremetyevo would take another hour, putting them at the airport in plenty of time to catch any flight leaving after one in the afternoon.

"The ticket office is located here in the Old City," Leo told them, "just a few blocks away, near Hotel Zhiguli. Sergey's in the car waiting."

Melissa rushed to the bedroom to dress, and Leonid went downstairs to wait for them. Boris went into the bedroom where Melissa was sitting on the bed, looking downcast.

When she saw Boris, she said quietly, "I would give up everything in order to live here in this apartment with you, my mila!"

"Look, mila," Boris said, "please, please, do not tear my heart apart. You know how much I love you. But I also respect my wife of thirty years. I cannot betray her either. It is nobody's fault that I was born twenty-three years before you. When we met the first time, neither of us knew what was going to happen. But now, after all we have been through, we are in love. You know that we would be not able to survive in Russia. Think about our future. Let's enjoy the time we have together and trust that God will see our happiness and find a way to bring us together again."

At the ticket office, they reserved two seats on a Lufthansa flight from Moscow to Frankfurt on October 2. Boris and Melissa decided they would spend the night together in Frankfurt, before leaving on October 3, after which Melissa would fly to London and Boris to Los Angeles.

Melissa, Boris, and Leo returned to the apartment, where Boris and

Leonid quickly fixed a simple supper of fried potatoes with onions and sausage. All of them at the meal with great pleasure and washed it down with vodka. Afterward, they had tea and cookies.

When Leo left, Melissa told Boris that she wanted to discuss a serious matter. Boris tried to laugh the matter off, but she would not be deterred. "What are you planning to do with the money I brought to Russia?" she asked.

"What do you mean? Of course, we will return the money to Eddy."

"In my opinion," Melissa said firmly, "that would be very foolish of you. Eddy handles hundreds of millions of dollars. But you, with all respect to your skills, qualifications and achievements, you are a poor man. You may have done a lot of work on this deal, but Eddy will make sure you get nothing out of it."

"Eddy, too?" Boris asked. "I knew that Kravchuk, of course, would try, but I thought Eddy was a man of his word. How do you know about this?"

"I was present when Eddy spoke to Kravchuk on the phone, using Kravchuk's interpreter."

"And all this time, even back in Moscow, you kept silent?"

"First of all," Melissa explained, "I did not know you. Secondly, at that time, you were not yet my mila. And third, I may be carrying your baby—and just in case something happens to me, you will have to take care of the child. And who knows what else might happen? But the point is, this money is ours. We earned it.

"Let me put this way: I am giving you our money in trust. I know that you will take good care of it. When we get to Frankfurt, please open an account in your name. I will leave the rest to you."

"How you can trust me?" Boris asked, "You do not know me."

"I am in love with you. I have trusted you with my whole body. Part of you will be with me for the rest of my life. And you say that I do not know you? And think of how you risked your life to save mine."

"Yes, yes. You are right. So I will do as you say. But what will you tell Eddy?" Boris asked, embracing her. He kissed her hair, thinking life was unfair.

"That we were kidnapped by bandits," Melissa casually answered.

Sighing, Boris said, "I have to thank destiny that I was blessed with the opportunity to know such a wonderful lady. A lady is what you are, my mila." And with those words, Boris took Melissa's right hand and gallantly kissed it.

"Ah," she responded in mock surprise. "So you know how to kiss a lady's hand after all! Why didn't you kiss my hand in Washington, when I offered it to you? I wanted you to kiss my hand then."

"Maybe, if I had kissed your hand there, I might not have kissed all of you here. Which would you have preferred?"

"Everything," Melissa squealed. "I wish you would kiss me here, there, always, and everywhere." She then coyly turned her bare back to Boris, lifted her skirt, and bared her beautiful bottom with its two dimples. "Would you kiss me there?" she asked coquettishly.

"Your ass? I can, indeed. And I will not just kiss it, I will also bite your ass." Boris grabbed Melissa.

"Don't!" Melissa said, laughing. "You are such a traitor. I trust you with the best part of my body, and what do you do with it?"

"A-ha!" Boris said. "Now you know who you are dealing with." And with that, he seized her and started kissing her everywhere. And how it ended requires no words to describe.

And so they passed the next three days. They fried potatoes with mushrooms, made stewed pork sandwiches, ate pelmenies, drank cream and vodka, and played cards. And they loved—they loved each other, enjoying every moment. Trying to live a whole life in just a few days, they needed nobody, and nobody existed for them. They enjoyed only each other.

The afternoon of September 29, Boris called Vicky Koval, the friendly girl at the VIP service desk at the Sheremetyevo Airport. At his request, she agreed to be on duty when Boris and Melissa arrived, and to help them with check-in, customs, and passport control.

Later that evening, Melissa fell ill. Her body temperature rose. Her breasts swelled, and her nipples became hard. She felt a slight pain in her abdomen. Boris realized that Melissa was pregnant. When he shared his thought with Melissa, she asked him to join hands with her and then she silently prayed. In her prayers, Melissa thanked the Lord for bringing their destinies together, for rescuing them from the gangsters, and for the mutual love, happiness, and joy over their future child.

Melissa remained ill until October 1, and on that night, their last night together in that room, they lay awake for a long time before falling asleep, basking in the mutual feelings of love.

50

THEY GOT UP AT six o'clock the next morning. Luckily, Melissa felt healthy again. They ate, left a tip for the cleaning lady, gathered their things, and left with Leo for the AutoVAZ Airport.

The flight to Moscow passed without incident. Except for Boris and Melissa, there were only two other passengers, both strangers. In the plane, Boris and Melissa held each other's hands and passed the entire flight without a single word. As they say, what words could replace such feelings? When they landed at Bykovo at 10:30, they noticed a disabled YK-40 nearby, with one of its wheels missing.

After the landing, Boris asked the bank's driver make a short stop at the Savelovsky Railroad Station on their way to the Airport. Passing through Moscow, noting the heavy presence of armed troops, Boris chose not to talk politics with the driver. Under such critical circumstances, such talk could be dangerous.

Once at the railroad station, Melissa stayed in the car, while Boris rushed off to the self-storage section. He put the plastic bag with two pistols, both cars' keys, and the sealed envelopes in a free compartment, and wrote down the compartment number and lock code.

Twenty minutes later, they reached Sheremetyevo Airport, where Boris tipped the driver. They had little more than an hour until boarding. They went to the VIP lounge where Vicky met them with a friendly smile. She took their passports and processed them, returning in about ten minutes to lead them through the control gate.

Looking at Vicky, Boris once again caught himself with a thought he was trying unsuccessfully to place, where he had seen or could have seen this sunny girl with deep blue eyes. He had a memory from many years before,

213

when he was in a construction brigade on virgin territory in Kazakhstan and had become involved with a local German girl named Frieda. He would have asked Vicky where she was from, but in Melissa's presence it would have been tactless to both girls. Boris would have definitely asked the girl about her mother if she had not been dressed in her long-sleeved uniform blouse. In the kind of short-sleeve casual blouse she usually wore when off duty, he would have seen on her right arm above her elbow a small birthmark with a shape very much like that of Australia, and exactly like the one Boris had carried since birth on his right arm.

Boris asked Vicky to help them to take the travel bag (the one where the money was!). Boris carried his own briefcase and Melissa took her handbag. So, the three of them together went through the customs without checking their luggage or customs declaration form.

Then bidding good-bye to Vicky, as usual, Boris pressed two hundred dollar bills into her palm. Excited by the delivery of such a generous present, Vicky kissed, with great pleasure, both Boris and Melissa, and then left gracefully and proudly swinging her hips.

Upon landing in Frankfurt, and at each subsequent point in their travels, both had to keep their emotions in check, and they knew they were growing nearer to their last farewell.

Boris and Melissa went to the Deutsche Bank branch in Terminal A, where Boris opened a checking account in his name and deposited the one million dollars. As she had promised to do, Melissa categorically refused any right of attorney over the account. Her name did not appear anywhere on the account, and neither was she listed as a beneficiary.

"If you wish," she explained once again, "you may consider this money as a personal loan. Who knows, someday I may come and ask for it back. But for now, please use it wisely. I will not give you any advice. You know what to do with it."

Leaving the terminal they hailed a minivan to the cozy Hotel Astron near the airport, which Boris knew from his previous trips. Once inside their third floor room, they nestled in each other's arms for what seemed like a very long time. Tears rolled down Melissa's cheeks, and Boris was deeply moved. But at last they shook themselves free, dressed, and went down to the restaurant for a snack. When they returned, they fell silent again, only looking at each other, knowing that these final impressions might have to last them the rest of their lives.

Suddenly, Melissa could take it no longer and she broke down, sobbing uncontrollably. "Don't make me let you go," she begged inconsolably. "I love you. Don't you understand?" She fell to the floor, and wrapped herself around her lover's legs.

Boris could not take such an outpouring. He lifted Melissa and carried her into the bathroom, where he washed and dried her face. Then he took her to bed, where they both lay down, completely exhausted. Boris drew the blankets over them, and then, embracing, they fell asleep.

When Boris woke up, the room was dark. He looked at his watch. Suddenly aware of the fact that they had only nine hours more together, his mouth got dry. He went to the refrigerator and took a few sips from a small bottle of Coca-Cola. When he returned, she too had awakened, so he handed her the Coke.

Melissa took a few sips and resumed crying. "Nobody has ever taken care of me the way you have, and no one ever will again. There has never been any need to ask you for anything. You have always known how to fill my needs. Please, tell me what I can do to keep you always by my side."

Boris, almost at his wit's end, suddenly had an inspiration. "We shall wait," he told her, "and if we find we cannot live without each other, then we shall leave everything behind and go back to Togliatti." Melissa, perhaps also just seeking relief from her emotional torment, quickly agreed.

They went back to sleep and woke up at five the next morning, undressed, and expressed their mutual love yet again. Then quickly washing and dressing, they ate a quick breakfast and checked out.

Since neither had any luggage to check, they passed quickly through passport control, and went to the terminal to wait for Melissa's flight to London. When her flight was announced for boarding, Melissa could shed no more tears. She was dry. So they simply stood and embraced, without passion, and she left to board. At the last minute, however, she turned back to Boris and said, "Remember me, please. Do not forget me, my mila. I will remember you until the last day of my life."

"Melissa, darling," Boris answered. "Please call me if you ever need me. I will come to you, my mila, at once."

51

Moscow
October 2, 1993

VLADIMIR SAID GOOD-BYE TO Lydia at the Bykovo Airport. The YK-40 jet chartered by Solvaig was waiting for him.

Lydia, for some reason, did not want to let him go. She kept hugging and looking at him, and once she even burst out sobbing. The young woman shone with the natural beauty that develops during motherhood. Her outlines softened. Her breasts became larger. She became visibly tenderer. But what could they do? A job was a job. So they said good-bye, and Vladimir promised to return her as soon as possible. Lydia walked him out to the landing and took advantage of her last chance to hug her husband before his departure.

As agreed, Shkolnikov had arrived at the airport at nine, but Ivan Fedorov was not there and had not appeared even by ten. Vladimir called Solvaig several times, but they didn't know where Ivan was, and Tamara hadn't come into the office yet. The responsible person he was, though, Shkolnikov decided to wait for Ivan until eleven, at which point if he didn't show up, Vladimir would return to the city. Ivan finally appeared at 10:45 a.m., his breath reeking of alcohol. He muttered a token apology, took his seat in the jet, fell asleep. He had spent the night and morning with Tamara, and now needed rest.

The crew took their places and, having received permission to take off, taxied from the hangar. However, the plane drove over a hub and then carelessly left the hangar with its bolts sticking up. As a result, one of the wheels suffered not only a flat tire, but damage to the wheel itself.

In an attempt to replace it, the technicians discovered there was no such wheel in the warehouse, and they couldn't simply borrow a wheel from another YK, because it was a chartered plane that did not belong to any of the local companies. By the time an order was placed at the factory, the day was pretty much gone, and as its delivery could not happen until the following morning, everyone agreed to return to the city and meet again the next day at ten.

Heading home, Shkolnikov drove, as usual, not by the shortest route, but by a roundabout way that passed a park, by which he could see any cars coming to or leaving his building. He immediately noticed that one of Solvaig's security vehicles was driving away from the parking entrance. Shkolnikov didn't think that anyone at Solvaig knew that Lydia was now his wife, not to mention that she was in the fourth month of her pregnancy.

So, when he came to the front door of his apartment and found the door unlocked, a feeling of dread and foreboding gripped him. He waited a minute, hoping to shake off the feeling, and then he took out his pistol, which was equipped with a silencer. He also unfastened the strap on the holster, which carried a spare pistol. He then silently opened the door and entered the vestibule, his pistol at the ready. On the right, in their bedroom, Vladimir heard a noise. So pointing his pistol into the room, he pushed open the door with his leg.

"Commander, it's me, Khromoff," came a voice. It was one of Solvaig's security guards.

"You?" Vladimir said. "What for? I mean, what are you doing here?"

"Don't you know? The owner ordered us to clean up. We terminated the chick."

"Who have you have terminated? What chick?"

"As the owner ordered. Tamara was there and his son Ivan, too."

"Did you kill Selina?" Vladimir asked, and as the words came out, his soul broke. He began to understand that this was not a nightmare. After Fedorov's trip to Sviblov in Tyumen, Vladimir realized, he must have ordered to kill Lydia. And his men carried out the order, not suspecting that Lydia was their chief's wife.

"Yes," the guard answered. "The owner ordered us to do so. I assumed you knew."

Suddenly understanding that he had offended Vladimir, the security guard reached for his holster, but Vladimir was faster. Using the edge of his free hand, he came down with fierce impact on the hand of his wife's murderer. Khromoff cried out, and Vladimir took the man's throat in a vise-grip.

"Shut up," Vladimir ordered. "Who else was with you?"

"Kurdyumov and Shapovalov." Then understanding that his end was near, Khromoff begged, "Forgive me, commander. It was the owner's order." The vise tightened, and Khromoff begun to gasp for air.

"Where are they?" Vladimir asked.

"They will return shortly. They went for gasoline. We were told to burn the apartment down."

And with that, Vladimir, with a short chop to the man's chest, stopped Khromov's heart forever. Then he went into the vestibule and waited for Kurdyumov and Shapovalov to return. Soon after, he heard them enter, and he jumped on them out of the darkness. He took them both by their necks and struck their foreheads with such force that they crashed to the floor with broken skulls. He took their car keys from their pockets, but did not touch their weapons. He had his own.

Vladimir went into the living room. Lydia wasn't there. Nor was she in the kitchen. Finally, he found her body in the bathroom, hanging over the tub. What he saw shook even this combat-hardened officer of special-force commandos. Lydia's naked body, with her hair loose and her head facedown, was lying over the edge of the bathtub, her legs spread apart and lifelessly resting on the bathroom floor. Blood and sperm was still dripping from her womb and anus.

After that moment, there was no longer a happy man named Vladimir Shkolnikov, the husband of a beautiful woman and a future mother. There was no man preparing to become a father. That person existed no more. Instead, there was only a monster inhabiting Vladimir Shkolnikov's body, without either sense or desire to live, capable only of revenge for the terrible torment his pregnant wife had experienced.

The zombie named Vladimir removed his jacket, rolled up his shirtsleeves, and turned on the shower. He lifted Lydia's legs over the edge of the tub and put her body under the water. Then turning over the body of his beloved wife, he saw what no man should ever have to suffer. Her mouth been torn into a terrible permanent smile, and one eye, beaten from its socket, hung by a thin, bloody vein. Her beautiful round breasts, which he had once so gently caressed for fear of causing her the slightest amount of pain, had no nipples. They had been cut off.

After the first shock passed, he took a very deep breath, and without emotion, took the shower handle and washed the blood from the body of his beloved lady. As he did, he asked God to save her soul, which, he said, was already the soul of an angel.

He returned to the bedroom, opened the credenza, and took out some towels and a bed sheet. He returned to the bathroom where he carefully dried Lydia's body with the towels and then wrapped it in the bed sheet. Then he carried her to the bedroom, where the bed was splashed with his wife's blood. From the closet, he took her white wedding gown, which she had worn in the registry office when they had married, and dressed her in it. He put a white veil over her face, and on her feet, which he had caressed only yesterday; he put on white socks. Finally, Vladimir took the coverlet off the bed, spread it on the floor, and lay Lydia's body on it. He tenderly wrapped her in the coverlet, and secured it with a clothesline, which he had cut from the balcony.

He checked the phone on the entryway table for reception, and then dialed Joseph Kozitsky in Tyumen. After the first ring, Joseph answered, and immediately said, "Vladimir, Vladimir. What has happened to our Lyd? I was talking to her when she cried out terribly."

"Our Lyd no longer exists. Forgive me, grandfather, but I could not save our Lyd."

"Who did it?" the old man asked.

"Fedorov and Sviblov. Sviblov sold you, our Lyd, and the association to Fedorov, and Fedorov ordered to kill our Lyd because she knew too much. Forgive me, old man. Please, forgive and pray for us. Farewell." He hung up to Joseph Kozitsky's sobbing.

It was about nine that evening when Vladimir took Lydia's body out onto the staircase, and closed the door to the first and the last apartment of their life together. Taking the elevator, he carried his dreadful package down to the car, setting it on front seat in a way that it would remain erect while he was driving. Then he went back in and grabbed the gasoline canisters, which Kurdyumov and Shapovalov had so industriously obtained. There were eight canisters, more than enough to burn the whole apartment building. Vladimir no longer required money or papers. He had everything he needed, so he turned on the engine and drove to Solvaig.

The security guard at the entrance, a young guy named Viktor, recognized Vladimir.

"What are the conditions here?" Vladimir asked the guard.

"Nothing new," the guard answered. "As usual, Ivan is fucking the boss's secretary."

"I'll check up," Vladimir said impassively and walked in the building.

On his way to the elevators, Vladimir ran into another security guard, Felix Kolesnikoff. Vladimir said to him "Go to my office and wait for me. I need to speak to you."

Then Vladimir walked to the second floor and went into Fedorov's reception room. The lights were still on. From Ivan's office, located opposite his father's, Vladimir heard Tamara squealing. He kicked the door open, to see Tamara standing, leaning over the desk, with her skirt lifted and her panties down. Ivan, in only his shirt, was doing her from behind.

Disentangled himself from Tamara, Ivan turned around, and seeing who it was, yelled, "What are you doing here? Get the hell out!" He raised his fist as if to strike, but Vladimir struck first, landing a punch right into Ivan's solar plexus, doubling him up in pain.

Vladimir pinned Tamara to the desk with his elbow. "Who order Lydia to be liquidated?"

When Tamara squealed instead of answering, he pinned her more forcefully and repeated the question. Choking, she said, "Arkady Fedorovich."

"Did Ivan and you know about this?"

She was silent. So Vladimir increased the pressure further, until, in a barely audible voice, she said, "Yes."

And with no sign of emotion on his face, he raised his elbow and brought it down into Tamara's spine so powerfully that her bones audibly cracked. Tamara lost consciousness and was silent forever.

Vladimir turned back to Ivan, who was beginning to come to his senses. "This is for you, Lyd," Vlad said, jumping on Ivan's chest. The impact crushed the young Fedorov, sending blood trickling out of his throat.

Vladimir went to his office, where Kolesnikoff was still waiting. A young guy who had returned from the army, Kolesnikoff had married in June, like Vladimir, and now his wife was expecting their first child.

"Listen, Kolesnikoff," Vladimir said. "If you want to live, run home. If anyone asks, say that I ordered you. Understand?"

"Yes, sir?"

"Remember. Do not walk. Just run," Vladimir ordered. "And take Viktor with you."

Vladimir went to his weapons safe, and took out the American-made sniper rifle, equipped with a silencer and laser-optical vision, which would enable him to shoot in total darkness. He checked the ammunition magazine; it was full. From the bottom shelf of the safe, he then got two hand grenades and two antitank grenades.

He took his weapons to the car, and then carried four of the gasoline canisters back inside, placing them in different offices. He returned to his office, took out four antitank mines, and placed three of them throughout the building. The final one, he carried to his car.

Then walking through the building, Vladimir poured gasoline in streams around the floor and over the mines. He left grenades in Fedorov's and Ivan's offices, their shared reception room, and the accounting department. In the kitchen, he opened the gas valves on all six-range burners. On his way out, he grabbed a towel that he wound around his assault knife to create a torch. He drenched it in gasoline and then dumped what was left of the last canister on the floor, leaving a pathway to the exit.

Certain that the building was empty, except for the bodies of Ivan and Tamara, Vladimir stood inside near the front entrance, lit the torch, and threw it as far as possible. As fire flashed, running down a pathway of gas and mines, Vladimir ran out to his car and drove away. He was already at Zubovsky Plaza, when he heard three powerful explosions followed by several smaller ones.

Later at the night, when firemen arrived, there was nothing to do except look at the remains of what was once called Solvaig.

For Fedorov's summer residence in the nearby village of Valentinovka, Vladimir had personally developed the security plan. On the premises, in addition to the main house, there was a smaller residence for the security guards and guard dogs, the latter of which were released at midnight. But none of this made any difference to Vladimir, whose plan was fool-proof. He knew where the property was vulnerable—and, tonight, that was where he would attack.

The main house was at the end of a street from which a one-hundred-and-fifty-foot-long driveway formed a T-shaped crossroad. Normally when the caravan of cars left out this driveway, the front car was a Chevrolet Suburban, protecting the Fedorov's Mercedes S600. In turn, the Mercedes was followed by another Suburban, preventing any opportunity of attack.

With the street having no lights of its own, and the moon shining weakly through the clouds, the night was Vladimir's ally. He drove up with the headlights off, going past the end of the driveway to park in the cover of some elder tree branches. He retrieved the antitank mine from the trunk, sprinted silently back to the driveway, and put the mine in the middle of the driveway in clear view. After looking around for an instant, he armed it.

Vladimir returned to his car, put one grenade on Lydia's lap and another under her legs. He stood up one of the gas canisters between her and the driver's seats, and two more in the back seat, leaving the last canister in the trunk, next to car's gas tank. He took out the case with the sniper rifle then, and assembled it, installing both the silencer and the laser device. Finally, he was ready.

He climbed onto the roof of an abandoned storage shed, which adjoined the old house, and admired the view. From here, Fedorov's summer home looked like a shooting gallery. Then settling into position for his grisly work, he used his gun to focus in on the dining room table at which Fedorov was seated, along with his wife, his granddaughter, and his sister-in-law.

For a second, Vladimir hesitated. That little girl was not guilty. But then remembering what was in his car, he slowly cocked the rifle. He couldn't see Fedorov clearly, but the two women and the child were in plain view. Vladimir took a few practice sightings, inhaled deeply and then exhaled, and fired three shots. He did not have to take another look. He knew he had left three corpses. Now it was Fedorov's turn.

Vladimir climbed down from the shed, ran to his car, and quickly got in, hearing screams from the summer residence. He opened the canister between him and Lydia, and waited. Then switching on the ignition, Vladimir started to pray. He prayed for himself and for Lyd. And for more. But mostly, he thanked God for the last four months of happiness.

Then he heard the dogs being let loose, followed by the sound of one Suburban engine, then the other. Vladimir knew that the Mercedes was completely silent, but he also knew that the security guards were panicking, and would try to escort Fedorov to a safe place. Little did they know that by letting him drive away, they'd be exposing him to maximum danger.

Vladimir's body and senses tightened like a spring as he heard the scratching sound made by the front gate opening. He pushed down on the brake and put the car in drive, until he saw the first Suburban turning left into the driveway, followed slowly by the Mercedes. Then, filling his lungs with air for once last superhuman effort, he shifted his foot from the brake to the gas, pressing it to the floor. His BMW was at the driveway before anyone knew what was happening, and the antitank mine in the driveway blew up under Suburban as soon as it was hit by the BMW. Simultaneously, the BMW plowed into the Mercedes on the side where Fedorov was sitting. Vladimir was gone on impact, as fire consumed the BMW.

Security guards from the rear Suburban ran out, and seeing Fedorov's seat compressed by safety pillows, tried to open the door opposite him. Just then, the explosion of the first grenade thundered, followed by the second, scattering splinters, penetrating vehicles and safety pillows, annihilating Vladimir and what was left of Lydia, and crushing Fedorov and his security guards.

Outside this little theater of war, frightened neighbors called for emergency help. An ambulance arrived in a half an hour, and requested help by radio.

Next morning, investigators from the office of the public prosecutor arrived, along with police, firefighters, and various other emergency vehicles. They collected the bodies of the security guards from the rear Suburban, pulled out the scorched Fedorov from the Mercedes, and gathered the corpses of Fedorov's personal security guards and driver.

Except for its scorched frame, nothing remained of the BMW, which had become a shared crematorium for Vladimir and Lydia. And the front of the Suburban, having unsuccessfully tested the destructive power of an antitank mine, served as the final resting place for its five security guards.

Meanwhile, a military courier arrived at the site of the former Solvaig with a locked leather dispatch bag addressed to General Major Vladimir Shkolnikov. The manila envelope inside contained an official communiqué from the minister of defense of the Russian Federation announcing the promotion of Shkolnikov to general major. It also contained an order directing him to report to military headquarters, to pick up his new ID card and papers, and to receive his formal assignment for a six-month training course with the joint staff of the armed forces of the Russian Federation.

The courier asked around, and not finding anybody who could give him a distinct answer concerning the whereabouts of General Major Shkolnikov, returned to headquarters, where he handed the envelope to a clerk. He said that the letter was to be placed in undeliverable, and ultimately stored in the archives.

52

Tyumen/Moscow
October 2, 1993

JOSEPH KOZITSKY WAS IN his office talking on the phone with Lydia, when she told him that someone was knocking at the door and asked him to wait while she went to answer it. The clock showed 6:15 p.m., Moscow time.

What he heard next, however, was not his darling Lydia's voice over the receiver, but her shouting from a distance. It was the heart-rending shout of a dying animal, followed by a muffled groan and men's voices, cursing and laughing. Then a dial tone.

Joseph immediately redialed Lydia's number, but nobody answered. Cold fear for her safety gripped the old man's heart, as he dialed again and again and got no answer.

He called a Moscow operator and asked for the police. The officer on duty, in response to his request to check on Lydia, said, "You want me to do what, father? Aren't you watching TV? Don't you see what's going on? This is war, father. Civil war. All our staff is now under martial law. I am sorry, but I can't do anything to help you."

Joseph Kozitsky knew exactly what was happening in Moscow. At home and in his office, he had not stopped watching the news for three days. Yes, there was a war. But he had a feeling his granddaughter's problem was unrelated.

Joseph called his secretary. "Maria," he said, "Lydia is in trouble, terrible trouble, in Moscow. I must go there as quickly as possible. Please make arrangements."

As Maria left, Joseph feverishly went over the events of the last few weeks. Fedorov had visited from Moscow, representing Solvaig, the company with whom the association had contracted to deliver the crude oil, and for whom Lydia had worked as a consultant. Vladimir, he knew, was also working for Solvaig as its head of security. He'd better call Vladimir now. He got Solvaig on the phone, but was told that Vladimir had left for Africa, and would not be back for days.

Joseph thought some more. When Fedorov had been in Tyumen, Vladimir had accompanied him, but had pretended he did not know Joseph. Instead, he gave the old man a sign that he would call later. He did call later, and apologized, but said that his actions had been necessary, because Fedorov had made a proposal to Sviblov to buy Tyumen Oil. But then Sviblov had never discussed that conversation with Joseph.

That's when it hit him. For the first time in their friendship of twenty-six years, Sviblov had not invited him to take part in a high-level meeting, and had not consulted him on an important decision—in fact, the most important decision.

Maria returned, saying that the airlines in Moscow were still functioning, so she had booked three tickets for the first available flight—one for Joseph and two for his security guards. His plane was scheduled to leave at ten p.m., Moscow time, however, so he had just enough time to pull himself together, change his clothes, and pack a small travel bag.

Joseph was shaking, and his heart was pounding, so Maria accompanied him home, where he could prepare for his trip. The driver had just left to fill up the tank when Vladimir called.

He said that Lyd was dead. He said that he was sorry he had not saved her. He said that Fedorov and Sviblov had killed her. Then he hung up. The old man's heart nearly stopped.

Maria hurried to give gave him his heart medicine, and shortly after, when the security guards arrived, she gave them the entire bottle to take in case he needed it on the plane.

When the plane finally landed at Moscow's Domodedovo Airport, Kozitsky walked into a terminal full of people, shouting and crying. He and his guards promptly grabbed a taxi.

To get to the apartment, the taxi driver had to take a considerable number of detours, as there were tanks and armored cars stationed on all of Moscow's major highways and crossroads. Combat firepower and personnel also were evident downtown. If it had been any other time, Joseph would have stopped and discussed the current events, but the world was only starting to fall apart in Russia, while his world had already been destroyed.

By the time they reached the building where Lydia and Vladimir lived, a new day was dawning. In the distance, an artillery cannonade could be heard.

"Sounds like artillery firing at the White House," the driver said.

As they left the taxi, Kozitsky handed the driver an amount ten times the regular fare. "Please do not leave. We will not be here long. We will let you know if it is okay, and then you may leave. But if it is not ..." Joseph began to cry.

"I understand," the driver said and promised to wait.

On the sixth floor, Kozitsky took out his copy of the apartment keys and tried to open the door, but his hands were shaking so badly that he could not get the key into the keyhole. One of the security guards then tried the door, which turned out not to be locked. They went into the apartment to find the bodies of three men on the floor and the entire apartment spattered in blood.

Kozitsky faltered and began to slip on the floor. He was caught by one of security guards, while another guard went to survey the kitchen. When he saw part of a female breast in the kitchen sink, the guard didn't feel so well himself. He then left and went into the bathroom, and what he saw made this Afghanistan soldier think he might need heart medicine for himself.

The guard called his companion from the other room, and said, "Please, get Kozitsky away from this apartment. There is nothing for him to do here."

So while he removed a weakening Joseph from the floor and escorted him out to the landing, the other went through the pockets of the three dead men. To his surprise, they appeared to have been security officers for Solvaig

The fresh air on the landing calmed Kozitsky. He gathered his strength, becoming, once more, the strong leader, he returned to the apartment, and approached one of the guards.

"Kid," he said. "Please, give me one of these gangsters' pistols. And can I assume you are both armed?"

"Yes, we are," the guard, said.

"There is nothing for us to do here; it's all police work," Kozitsky said as if commanding his old regiment. "We must go to Solvaig and see if someone there can tell us what happened."

The guard gave Kozitsky a pistol, as requested, and with the practiced movements of a former military officer, Joseph checked the ammunition and the casing, and then put the pistol on safety before securing it in his belt. Seeing the guards admire his professionalism, Kozitsky said, "I participated in both the Finnish and the Great Patriotic wars. And when my parents were arrested and executed, by the time I was sent to a labor camp, I had already seen too much death. For my granddaughter, I will be ruthless. In my granddaughter's memory, I will take revenge on the reptiles who did this, even if it is with the last breaths of my life."

When they left the apartment, Kozitsky locked the door and then rang the doorbell at the neighbor's. From behind the door a small, senile voice answered timidly, "Who do you need?"

"We are looking for a neighbor who can help us," Joseph answered.

The door opened, but upon seeing three men, the elderly woman immediately slammed it close, crying out, "Get out. Leave at once, or I will call the police. The police!"

"My lovely woman," Kozitsky said to her in the calmest voice he could muster, "I am putting the key from your neighbor's apartment in front of your door. Yesterday, gangsters killed my granddaughter, Lyd. Perhaps you knew her. May I *ask* you to call the police? The keys from her apartment are on the floor."

As Kozitsky and his guards walked away, they heard the neighbor open her door and take the keys. Outside, the driver, as Joseph had beseeched, had waited.

"To Zubovsky Square." Kozitsky said, climbing with difficulty into the back seat.

When they arrived, they heard machine guns and canon fire from Smolensky Square.

"They are on the Moscow River Quay," the driver explained. "They must be storming the White House."

They tried reaching the site of the former Solvaig by its private driveway, but found burned rubble in place of a building. There was one fire truck and one policeman.

Kozitsky asked some Solvaig employees who were standing around where it might be possible to find Mr. Fedorov. They said he lived in the village Valentinovka, but that the phone there was not answering. So Kozitsky and his guards took down the address of Fedorov's summer residence and headed for Valentinovka.

They reached Valentinovka quickly. A few police cars and other emergency vehicles were around the residence. A policeman showed them what was left of a BMW, a Mercedes, and two Suburbans. Joseph knew exactly what had happened. He knelt silently in front of BMW, where, for a while, he remained, until his security guards lifted him up and put him back in the taxi.

"Where to now?" the driver asked. "Looks like we're tracking down some crime."

"Yesterday, gangsters killed my granddaughter," Kozitsky said. "And her husband revenged them. He committed suicide and cremated his body along with the body of his wife—who was my granddaughter. He has taken his revenge. But now my turn has come. So, please, take us back to Domodedovo. There is nothing we can do here in Moscow."

Next morning, after arriving back in Tyumen, Kozitsky took the company car to headquarters and walked straight into Sviblov's office. He asked the chief accountant to leave and locked the door.

He sat in a chair opposite the general director, and said, "I had a dream that we were trying to extract crude oil from the ground, but were pumping up blood instead. We were pumping blood through the pipeline." Joseph paused and looked his former comrade in the eye. "For what did you sell out my granddaughter to Fedorov? She should have lived a long life and had children. She was pregnant, you know—and still you sold her. And because of you, she suffered a horrible death, and her husband, Vladimir, was also killed. Well, at least he died as a hero, unlike you, who has betrayed our friendship. So now it is my turn to get even with you."

Sviblov, seeing Kozitsky's face, understood that he was not joking, and knew that his own end had come. In his desk drawer, a loaded Nagan revolver,the model of gun used in Gulag to execute "enemies of the people," he had kept for quite some time. Sviblov reached for it, but at that precise moment, Kozitsky, who'd had his pistol aimed under the desk at Sviblov, pulled the trigger. The bullet penetrated Sviblov's liver, but still conscious, Sviblov shot his revolver. At the same time, Kozitsky pulled the trigger a second time, and both shots thundered simultaneously.

The bullet from Sviblov's revolver had put a neat hole in Kozitsky's forehead, and he fell back into his chair. The bullet from Kozitsky's pistol had gone deep into Sviblov's stomach, and he cried out in terrible pain. He pressed himself into his armchair, trying to hold his stomach together, but his lifeblood flowed out between his fingers. So while the security guards summoned by Sviblov's secretary were attempting to open the office door, Sviblov died.

53

California
October 3–7, 1993

WHEN BORIS WENT THROUGH passport control, the absence of any luggage made the customs officers suspicious. He had been out of the country for more than two weeks and was now returning with nothing at all. However, all their questions were answered when Boris showed the customs officer his claim check from the Hotel Mir, just as the TV in his office showed a live broadcast from the very same hotel, reporting that it was occupied by supporters of the Supreme Council.

"Welcome home," was the only thing the customs officer could say as he stamped Boris's customs declaration.

From the shuttle stop, a minivan with an Orange County sign on its windshield picked him up. He was home forty minutes later, but his wife was at work; after all, someone had to be earning a living. Their grown son was not at home, either.

Boris undressed and settled into an armchair. He switched on CNN, to see a direct report from Moscow where it was currently one o'clock in the morning. The streets were full of people, and in front of the Supreme Council building, where he had so recently walked with Melissa, tanks patrolled. The Supreme Council building was burning.

Boris became inspired and carefully prepared his account of their kidnapping: Lady Melissa had appeared absolutely by chance. In fact, her arrival had been totally unexpected, not only to Boris but also to Cherkizov. Eddy Pennington had been scheduled to come, but because he was busy, or because his assistant was busy and did not want to endanger his precious life, Eddy sent Melissa instead.

Now to figure out exactly why there were four gangsters. For this, he had to answer one question: who sent Cherkizov, Kravchuk, or Yakubovsky? And why had Cherkizov called both of them? As he pondered, the jet lag together with the fatigue from his "honeymoon" put the still sitting Boris to sleep.

His wife Ruslana woke him at 8:00 p.m. In Moscow it was 7:00 the next morning. Boris greeted her and apologized that he had not met her with supper tonight, but explained that he had only just returned, was half asleep, and could not explain anything clearly to her. She left understanding only that there was civil war in Russia, that he had miraculously escaped death, and that, with Leonid Kislov's help, he and another woman had escaped the country.

Boris woke up again at four in the morning, California time. In Moscow, it was three in the afternoon. The first call that he made, after taking a shower, was to Ivan Filimonov's home. Ivan's wife, who Boris had never met but who knew about him, answered the phone. Her husband was not at home, she told him. Boris asked her to leave the message that Boris Goryanin had called from California about a very important matter.

Boris's head was full of disturbing, incoherent echoes, so he walked around the house a bit before going back to bed. He woke up again that evening, having slept the entire day. Boris got up, made some hot tea, and took two sleeping pills. The next thing he knew, he was waking up at about nine o'clock the next morning. Finally, his head had cleared.

He called his wife at work and asked her to come home earlier than usual. She did, and over the supper that he had prepared, Boris told her everything about the past several days. He told her about the kidnapping and about how he and Melissa, with Kislov's help, had hidden in the bank. He also told her that Melissa had opened a bank account for him in Germany. The only thing he didn't tell his wife was his relationship with Melissa.

Ruslana's response was emphatic. "Don't ever go to Russia again. It is too dangerous for you."

Boris understood this truth better than his wife would ever know. He might even be on the Most Wanted list in Russia. And if not, the Russian police would probably be delighted to frame him for some unresolved crime.

Next morning, he received a call from the local Bank of America branch manager, who told him that Agroprom - USA had received a money transfer from Switzerland in the amount of five million, five hundred thousand dollars. Boris immediately left for the bank, which was directly across the street from his house, and met with the branch manager, who gave him a receipt for the transfer from Pennington International, Ltd.

While Boris was scanning the receipt, a bank employee handed the manager a telex in which Kravchuk requested that all of the money in the account be immediately transferred to the Agroprom account in Panama. However, since the telex did not confirm that the crude oil had been shipped, Boris asked the bank to put Kravchuk's request on hold, pending receipt of just such a confirmation.

As soon as Boris got home, he called Captain Zhukov, the head of SpetzMorTrans to get a status update on the shipment. Zhukov told Boris that the tanker vessel was in port at Ventspils, where it was waiting to be loaded, but that they were having trouble contacting Mr. Anisimov to find out where the crude oil was.

"You're trying to contact Anisimov?" Boris asked in surprise. "He was killed on September twenty-third."

"He was killed?" Zhukov said. "But Kravchuk told me they were in constant contact." And from his words, Zhukov suddenly understood what Boris had known for quite some time. So without explaining further, Boris said good-bye and immediately returned to the bank, where he asked that all five million, five hundred thousand dollars be wired back to Pennington International.

"What about Kravchuk's request?" asked the manager.

"It's been cancelled," Boris answered categorically. "It turns out he's trying to embezzle this money."

The man warned Boris that Pennington International would demand indemnification for the remittance.

"If they demand," Boris said, "then we'll pay."

By Friday morning, October 7, the deal with Mr. Ruslan Khazbulatov and General Alexander Rutskoy was over. Both of them had been arrested and both had testified in the Matroskaya Tishina Prison.[66] Boris phoned Mr. Filimonov again. This time, Ivan picked up.

Considering his friend's new position, Boris tried to be as brief as possible. "Dear Ivan Fedorovich," he began. "Following up on our last conversation, please write down the following: SV, the fourth car, the twenty-sixth place. The ticket number is 2-4-8-1-6. That's all."

"Understood," Filimonov said. "So long, Boris. Take care."

What Mr. Filimonov had understood was Boris's reference, in the local manner, to the Savelovsky Railroad Station, self-storage section 4, and locker number 26 with a lock code of 2-4-8-1-6. It was where Boris had left the bag with the envelopes he had prepared in Togliatti, including Mr. Popov's

---

66 Moscow's prison for high-ranking officials and VIP suspects.

affidavit. Now Boris felt secure in knowing that the state office of the public prosecutor would find out about Yakubovsky and Cherkizov. The rest would be up to them.

Less than half an hour had passed when Monsieur de la Perie phoned. "We received our money back from you. What does it mean? Don't you understand that you are in breach of contract?"

"It means that I saved your money for you," Boris answered. "If I had not sent it back, your money would be in Panama by now, or even farther."

"But because you did not fulfill your obligations per the existing contract," de la Perie whined, "you'll have to compensate us for all expenses related to wiring the money to your account."

"My dear friend," Boris said smugly, "please listen carefully. Number one, there are "force majeure" conditions in Russia right now. Number two, check my tax returns for 1992. I don't think you'll consider legal recourse. Now, if there are no more questions, good-bye, my dear friend, and thank you for calling. Oh yes, and please say hello to our dear friend, Mr. Pennington." And with these words, Boris hung up.

54

October 3–7, 1993

As Melissa flew back to London, away from Boris, she knew that while this was the end of their present relationship, it could also be the beginning of a new, different kind of relationship. What kind, exactly, she did not know. She knew only that she and Boris would be connected by destiny until the end. And this alone made their separation much easier.

On the TV screen, CNN was broadcasting from the Hotel Ukraine across the Moscow River. She remembered when she and Boris were there the evening before their trip to Kurumoch. Only now did she understand why Boris had called Vicky to facilitate their safe boarding on the plane to Frankfurt. She again started to thank God for sending Boris to her rescue.

Later, at the baggage claim, she was pleased to see her father's secretary. "Mister Wiggins!" she exclaimed, smiling.

"How did you manage to escape?" he said, with outstretched arms. "I am amazed at what's happening in Russia."

She walked into Mr. Wiggins's arms, embracing him. "We were protected by our Lord."

"We? You were not there alone? But I thought Mr. Pennington was not there with you."

"It's probably fortunate that he was not," Melissa said. "If he had been, I would most certainly have suffered an awful death."

"So who was your savior?" Wiggins asked.

"A very, very good friend of mine."

"And how is it that you've returned without any luggage?" the elderly gentleman asked.

"You're right," confessed Melissa, "all I've got is this one bag. The rest is still over there."

"Just thank the Lord, Lady Melissa, that you're home, baggage or not!"

"Why didn't my father come to the airport?" Melissa asked as they left the baggage claim. "Is he okay? I've missed him so much."

"Sir Spencer is not feeling well."

"What's wrong?"

"Sir Spencer apparently had a very unpleasant conversation with your fiancé, and, afterwards, he took ill."

"Yes," said Melissa, "well, I can understand that. Let's go see him at least for a short while. I very much want to see him, but you cannot imagine how tired I am. I must take a bath, and get some sleep. A lot of sleep."

As Mr. Wiggins's Jaguar rushed them from the airport, Melissa opened a window, greedily inhaling the London air she was so accustomed to. Summer was gone, but this day reminded her of summer, drizzling just a bit, with the sun appearing now and then through a light cloud cover. Melissa loved London. It was the city of her childhood.

Fatigue took over, then, and watching the road float by, she found that her thoughts were jumping from one subject to another, although most of them focused on Boris. What was he doing? Sleeping on the plane, she decided. Melissa smiled at the thought and closed her eyes. When she opened them, they were in front of her father's house.

Like a little girl, Melissa ran up the familiar steps and rang the doorbell. Ms. Doughty, small and neat as always, opened the door, and upon seeing Melissa, she began to shout, cry, cross herself, and kiss and hug Melissa all at once.

It seemed that Ms. Doughty had been with them in this house since Queen Victoria's time. She had nursed Melissa from birth and had long since become a substitute grandmother.

After escaping from Ms. Doughty's iron embrace, and without taking off her coat, Melissa rushed in to see her father.

Dressed in a warm robe over a shirt, tie, and sweater, with a scarf wrapped around his throat, Melissa's father sat in his old leather armchair, his legs extended and his back straight as a ruler. On a little table next to his armchair were a telephone and a silver bell to call Ms. Doughty.

When Melissa had burst in, she had noticed her father's hand resting on his heart. He had quickly moved it as soon as he saw her, but she'd caught him already. She ran and knelt down next to him, putting her head on his knees. In immediate response, he put his right hand on her head. Both were silent for some time, and then started talking simultaneously, excitedly asking each other questions—Melissa about his health, and he about her adventures in Russia.

After some discussion, Melissa told her father how badly she needed to rest, and, promising to return that night, warmly said good-bye. Her apartment was on the next street, a five-minute walk.

Finally at her door, Melissa dug in her handbag for the keys, and felt something unfamiliar. So after going in, she looked through her handbag to find Boris's note, his photo, and a pack of money. She read the note, smiled adoringly at the photo, and put aside the money. When could he have put all that in her bag? They'd been together the entire time. He could not have done it in Moscow or Frankfurt, so he must have done it in Togliatti.

She counted the money: twenty thousand dollars. But when they had opened his account at the bank, all of the money had been accounted for. That meant he'd had some other money—his own money, which he'd put into her handbag in Togliatti, before they discussed what to do with the million.

Melissa put the money back in her bag, and put his photo and note on the kitchen table. While the tub was filling, she went into the kitchen for a snack, but she was so tired, she didn't want to eat so much as have a drink of cream. But in her refrigerator there were only a few cans of juice and a few bottles of water.

Grabbing a water, Melissa returned to the bathroom, and having done so, remembered how she and Boris had run together into the bathroom. Once in the bath, she began to sob, but the relief it brought caused her to doze off momentarily. She forced herself to get out of the tub and go to bed.

The phone woke her up. It was dusk and her father was calling, wondering if he should expect her for dinner. She murmured something incoherent and fell asleep again. All night long, Melissa dreamed that she was drinking cream directly from a carton, and eating pickles, which she pulled out with her fingers straight from a tall jar.

Next morning, she was feverish and felt pain in both breasts. Her nipples had swelled to the point that the slightest touch caused them sharp pain. After a while, she forced herself to get up to go see her father.

In the same armchair, and in the same pose as the day before, Sir Charles John Spencer met his daughter with outstretched hands. He loved his little girl, though in his own way, of course. The members of his beloved Shakespeare Club were each expected to report on the successes of their children, and Sir Charles John had proudly announced the forthcoming wedding of his daughter with Baron Pennington. And when his daughter had returned from Russia, having experienced some amazing adventures, he was looking forward to telling his friends all about them.

Melissa told her father about her adventures in great detail. Of course, she did not tell him about her relationship with Boris, but said only that "the Supreme" had helped her. He told her how he had tried without success to contact the British ambassador to Kazakhstan, as well as some people from the embassy and the Ministry of Foreign Affairs. He was embarrassed to admit that his requests to arrange help for Melissa had fallen on deaf ears. But, Glory to the Lord, everything unpleasant was behind them, and she was home, alive, and safe.

Sir Spencer then told Melissa what he had been doing while she was away, but left out the part about his financial problems and the most recent conversation he'd had with Eddy Pennington.

In this way, they spent the next few hours talking and drinking tea, until a phone call came for her at lunchtime.

It was Eddy Pennington, and he started in on her immediately. "Melissa, dear, I really don't understand why it was so difficult for you to call your little Eddy when you were in Russia. I worried a great deal about you, alone in that awful country. I heard that you came through some ordeal. Good for you, of course, that you successfully survived the situation."

"Eddy, it was you who didn't find the time to call me. And I didn't *get* into the situation, as you call it; it's more like I was betrayed into it. Don't forget that it was *you* who put me in this situation, my 'little Eddy.' And it was not I who managed to survive the situation. It was Boris who rescued me from certain death."

"Ah, that little guy from California. Who would have thought he'd be capable of such?"

"Of such what?"

"Well ... of such heroics. To save you."

"Do you have any idea what you are talking about?" Melissa asked. "We were kidnapped by Caucasian gangsters at Kurumoch who took all our money and said they would kill us."

"How you know what they said?" Eddy said. "Do you speak Russian now?"

"You don't have to speak Russian to get a message like that, and besides, Boris was there—he knew what they were saying. You're just lucky if you never have to experience what we went through."

"I don't believe you. Something's not right here. Are you sure Boris wasn't in cahoots with the gangsters?"

"Eddy, this conversation is becoming very unpleasant to me. Please call Moscow and speak to the assistant to the general prosecutor of Russia, a Mr. Ivan Filimonov. Call and check on what I have just told you. Until you do that, there's nothing more I can say."

"So does this mean you didn't get the money to Anisimov? If that's the case, then where is the money now?"

"Eddy, don't you know Anisimov was assassinated?"

"Oh, I see. Now Anisimov has also been killed. You and Boris were about to be killed, and then Anisimov was killed. That's sounds just a little too convenient, I think."

"Just call Mr. Filimonov."

"Okay, okay, listen. Take it easy for a day or two and then I'll be waiting for a full and complete report from you, here in Geneva, let's say the morning of the seventh. I'll meet you at the Airport.

"Now, here's the main thing. I placed an announcement in the *Guardian* about our wedding. We won't get married in a church, but in London City Hall, just to avoid any possible complications. Your father has agreed."

"Do what you like. But if you do not call the public prosecutor in Russia, my coming to Geneva will be senseless. In fact, you might as well go ahead and fire me. In fact, I'm not coming back to work for you anymore. If my boss doesn't trust me, I may as well have been fired."

"Melissa, baby. Okay, calm down. I'll call Filimonov. All I did was ask about this stranger, and suddenly I become your enemy. By the way, do you have his phone number?"

"Call the embassy," Melissa said, resigned. "They'll get you his number. I'm sorry. I simply can't speak to you anymore. I'm too tired. I'll see you in Geneva on the seventh." And with that, Melissa hung up.

When she hung up, her father, who had remained silently by her side the entire time, looked at her, but seemed only to manage a deep sigh. Now Melissa understood why her father had become so upset after his last conversation with Eddy. Likely, Eddy had told her father that if they got married in church, a divorce would be rather messy, probably requiring the intervention of Her Majesty. But the cancellation of a civil marriage would be a much simpler business. Additionally, children from a civil marriage were considered differently than those from a marriage consecrated by the church. The question of inheritance, for example, was much more complex.

All of this meant that her father understood how very tangled things were becoming for his daughter. He must have wondered whether she even needed such a marriage.

Melissa approached her father, kneeling next to him and putting her head on his shoulder. Then she whispered to him that she was in love, with all her heart, with another man, a married man who was considerably older than she. She told him that she was pregnant with his child, and that it was the man who had rescued her in Russia. She told her father that she intended to have his baby, and not marry Eddy. Finally she reminded her father she loved him too."

Without saying a word, the old man made a fist with his right hand and brought it up to his mouth. He, the great Sir Spencer, who had once thought he could handle anything, could not imagine how to deal with what he had just heard, even in his wildest, most terrible nightmare. And to think that it had all happened to his daughter. Well, what would the fellows at the Shakespeare Club think now?

55

AFTER ALL THE TERRIBLE events in Russia, the anxiety about her pregnancy and the constant thoughts of Boris, she needed to sleep, chat with her best girlfriends, and spend quality time with her father. And that's exactly what she did.

Four days had passed since she and Boris had bid farewell in Frankfurt, but she still could not help feeling, with each cell in her young body, that he was there with her. She felt his presence at the bank where she deposited the money he had put into her handbag. She expected at every moment that he might appear and make her life easy again. It was hard for Melissa to be without Boris and gradually face the reality that she might never see him again, that he might never embrace or kiss her again. She wanted so much to be with him.

As her thoughts came into focus, however, she understood one main thing: she would have to struggle for her happiness. She also knew that it would not be enough to struggle for just one day. But then, for how many?

On October 7, she took an afternoon flight to Geneva via Frankfurt. She had chosen this route so that she could spend a night in the Astron Hotel, where she and Boris had been several days earlier.

When the Astron shuttle arrived at the airport, Melissa took a seat and her heart started beating faster. She felt Boris's presence. At first she was sorry that she chosen to come here, but then she understood that she must have chosen it because, in some way that she did not understand, it was the way that would eventually bring her to her lover.

To Melissa's surprise and pleasure, the hotel clerk recognized her, so they exchanged several casual remarks, after which Melissa requested the same room in which she and Boris had spent their last night together.

In her room, Melissa, overwhelmed by her memories, lay down on the bed. She mechanically took off her jacket, remaining in a sleeveless blouse. Then she took off her stockings and, in a sort of daze, went to the bathroom and washed them, exactly like Boris had done. As she spread them out on a towel and wrung them dry, she felt funny and sad at the same time. But when she was through, to her surprise, she somehow felt more confident. She still didn't know what the future would hold, but she was certain that she could make the decisions that would lead her there.

Next morning, however, she awoke with searing pain in her breasts. Her nipples were on fire. When she touched the left nipple, the sharp pain pierced her body. Melissa knew that these were symptoms of pregnancy, however, and would soon pass. In about fifteen minutes she felt better. She got up, washed, put on her clothes and prepared to leave.

A couple of hours later, she arrived at Geneva, where her close friend, Frau Marika Globke, was waiting. They warmly embraced, and Melissa was glad that Frau Globke, and not Eddy, had met her. An exceptionally sweet, older woman, Frau Globke was Eddy Pennington's secretary. And during the two years that Melissa had worked at Pennington International, the two had become friends. Raised without much maternal attention, Melissa quite naturally reached out to a woman who would have made an excellent, nurturing substitute. Frau Globke, who with her husband raised three daughters, recognized Melissa's emotional need and gave her both attention and love. When Melissa came back from a business trip, she always brought a souvenir for Frau Globke who, in turn, often brought Melissa cakes and cookies that she had baked.

Although Frau Globke knew absolutely everything that went on in the office, she did not gossip and kept all she knew to herself. She did not like her chief, but never showed it. With Melissa, however, she was frank. When Melissa told her what had happened in Johannesburg, the deeply religious woman made it clear that she was disturbed that Pennington had acted so reprehensibly with such a lovely young woman as she. In fact, she was the only person who had told Melissa that she was not happy about her forthcoming marriage to Eddy Pennington.

"You will shed many tears from this marriage, girl," she had said.

On the way to the office, they stopped for lunch at the small restaurant where Melissa and Boris had eaten. Melissa went to the same small table at which she had sat with Boris, and proceeded to give Frau Globke a detailed account of everything that had happened in the last two weeks.

Frau Globke warned her, "Don't go to the office, girl. Run away from here. You don't know who you are dealing with."

"Don't worry," Melissa said. "I've decided to quit my job at Pennington International and will fly back to Frankfurt tonight."

"Well …" Frau shook her head. "Then please let me take you to the airport myself. Anything might happen to you on the way there. He is not a human. You do not know him. He is a monster."

When Melissa and Frau Globke arrived at the office, the door to Pennington's office was closed. He was on the phone speaking to someone. As Melissa sat on the chair next to Frau Globke's desk, her breasts started burning again, and the pain became intolerable. Melissa could barely keep from moaning in pain. At just that moment, the door to Eddy's office opened and he came out.

He went to Melissa and, taking her chin, turned her face toward him and kissed her on the mouth. "How was your flight, baby?" he said quickly, followed by a nervous laugh. "I hope Frau Globke didn't feed you too many pastries on the way here. Remember, you're going to have to get used to starving. I don't love fat women." He helped Melissa stand and guided her into the office.

After closing the door behind him, Pennington said, "I called Filimonov, and everything you told me about Goryanin and Anisimov was the truth. He also confirmed that the money was not recovered. That son-of-a-bitch Kravchuk lied to me! I believed him and wired the money on Monday. But guess what happened? The little Russian Goryanin, instead of stealing five-and-a-half million bucks and taking off for Brazil, sent back the entire amount. It's pleasant to deal with an honest person," Eddy said, adding with a sarcastic smile, "I hope you didn't sleep with him in Russia."

Before Melissa could answer, Eddy pinched her left nipple with enough force to bring tears to her eyes. Although that was not unusual, this time, this time, a lightning bolt of pain pierced through her. She cried out and reactively slapped Eddy across the face with her palm. Not expecting such a reaction, Eddy froze for a moment, and then viciously hit Melissa's face with a closed fist. His face now distorted with rage and madness, he seized Melissa by her shoulders and turned her around so that her back was facing him. Trying to keep Eddy off, she shouted, "No! No! You are hurting me! Please, Eddy! Boris! Boris! Where are you? Help me. Rescue me. Help me!"

Frau Globke, who heard Melissa's heart-rending cries, did what any Swiss woman would have done in her place. She called the police and told them that a man in her office was attempting to murder a woman.

Meanwhile, Eddy was pushing down a weakening Melissa against his desk. He pressed one of his elbows on her spine, crushing her last ounce of resistance. As she groaned in pain and terror, Eddy lifted her skirt and lowered her panties, exposing her bottom. Then excited by his sadistic attack,

Pennington unzipped his trousers and unloosed a penis excited as never before. He rammed it into Melissa, ripping everything in its path.

At that moment, two policemen ran into the outer office, where Frau Globke pointed at the door to Pennington's office. One of policemen kicked the door open, at which point Eddy released Melissa, and her limp, unconscious body slipped to the floor. Both officers, though they had witnessed many terrible things, were paralyzed by what they saw. The older one, however, launched a crushing blow into Eddy's solar plexus, doubling the rapist over. Then without pause, he struck a second blow to Eddy's neck and a third to his head. Eddy fell, incapacitated, and the police handcuffed him without effort. By this time, the other policeman had already radioed for medical emergency.

The ambulance from Grangettes, an exclusive private hospital considered one of the best in the world, arrived at Pennington International ten minutes after receiving the call. The attendants put the still unconscious Melissa onto a stretcher, gave her a painkilling injection, and rolled her out.

When detectives arrived, Eddy was still on the floor. He remained on the floor as they photographed the office and talked to employees and took blood samples from his trousers and penis.

When he finally came to, Pennington demanded that the police call his lawyer. In response to his request, the older officer waved his huge fist in Eddy's face and said, "This will be both your lawyer and your judge."

In the meantime, Melissa lay in an emergency operating room, where doctors were afraid that, from internal bleeding and peritonitis, she was on the brink of death.

56

Geneva
October 1993

ONLY THREE DAYS AFTER her operation, Melissa began to return to life. During this time, doctors had kept her sedated in intensive care. Penetrated by needles, and connected to various tubes, Melissa had hovered between life and death.

If it had happened in some country other than Switzerland, she would have been lost. But the artfulness of her doctors helped her survive the initial trauma, and after that she started to regain her strength.

The first question she asked when she came to was about her child. Her attending physician, a kindly older man named Dr. Krauss, told her that the term was still very early. Her rectum, however, as a result of the physical assault, had been ruptured in two places, necessitating temporary bypass tubing. Fortunately, her vagina, uterus, and fallopian tubes had not been damaged, so the doctor anticipated she could recover without any long-term consequences. If her recovery went well, he said, the bypass tubing could be removed within a week to ten days.

"But for now," he said, "it is necessary to rest and not worry, and to follow all of Dr. Krauss's orders." The old man touched Melissa's hand, and with kindness in his voice, told her, "The worst is over. You will recover and be a good mother."

When the doctor left, Frau Globke arrived, pushing open the door of Melissa's room. She was not allowed to go inside the intensive care room, however, so Frau Globke stayed in the hallway. She had been visiting her friend daily, and today, had brought Melissa a small bunch of flowers. She looked at Melissa for a few minutes through the open doorway, then after waving to her, she left.

Melissa could not see how violently Eddy had damaged her face—damage that had not yet healed completely. The entire left side of it was puffy, including her eye, which was swollen shut and covered in a hideous bruise. Owing to soothing balms and ointments, Melissa felt little pain.

Abbey Weiss, the clinic's chaplain, however, felt a great deal of pain. As soon as he had seen Melissa and learned why she was in such a condition, he had called a lawyer he knew, named Dr. Steinmaer, and requested he act as Melissa's legal counsel.

Melissa was still unconscious at the time, but Dr. Steinmaer had contacted the Geneva police and confirmed that, if Lady Melissa Spencer appointed him as her lawyer, he would receive copies of documents providing evidence in the case. Although the doctor was confident the judge would impose a bail amount high enough to prevent Pennington from getting out of jail and possibly fleeing the country, he wanted to be sure he would have all of the documents he'd need to press charges by Monday, October 18, when Pennington's court appearance was scheduled. Meanwhile, Dr. Steinmaer daily consulted the hospital regarding the state of Melissa's health, so upon learning that she had regained consciousness, he rushed to the hospital with Abbey Weiss, and together they went to see Melissa.

"Dear Lady Spencer," began the abbey, "I am the chaplain of this hospital. My name is Richard Weiss. I would like you to meet Doctor Steinmaer, an old friend of mine. He is an honest and knowledgeable lawyer who, I am fully convinced, would be able to fairly represent your interests in court."

"Thank you, Holy Father. But it is difficult for me to make a decision now. I don't know yet what to do," Melissa answered in a low voice, choosing her words with difficulty.

"My daughter," the chaplain responded, "at least I hope you understand that, despite the fact that our Lord and his son advise mercy, my sincere belief is that the harm that has been caused to you must be punished according to the laws of our country."

"Of course," Melissa agreed. "Only a gangster could have done what he did to me. And there was nobody to protect me."

"My daughter," the chaplain cautioned. "Do not forget about our Savior. He was there and he spread his hand above you. Frau Globke, who called the police, and the policeman who saved you from the claws of a devil, were your protection."

"Yes, yes, I agree with you, Holy Father." And so Melissa, with a trembling hand, signed a power of attorney giving Dr. Steinmaer the right to represent her in the canton of Geneva.

Abbey Weiss prayed for Melissa's recovery, blessed her, and left, together with Dr. Steinmaer, who told Melissa that he would return in a few days when she had become stronger.

Due to Melissa's youthful constitution, in combination with outstanding care from one of the best hospitals in the world, on October 13, she was transferred from intensive care to a private room. And though the bypass tube remained, so that she continued being nourished intravenously, Dr. Krauss told her that if she continued to be a good patient, it would be removed in less than a week.

Soon after, the lawyer, Dr. Steinmaer, returned and, after ensuring that Melissa felt well enough to speak to him, told her about the progress he'd made. He had received copies of statements made by Frau Globke and the policemen, as well as affidavits from Pennington International employees. He had obtained the blood-test results and other medical records from her doctor. And he had collected a large stack of photos from investigators, of everything from Pennington International and Eddy's private office to pictures of the victim in the hospital.

Dr. Steinmaer then suggested their plan of action: Melissa, he advised, should submit to the criminal court a complaint against the actions of Eddy Pennington, and to the civil court two claims—one against Eddy himself and a second against Pennington International, Ltd., on the premises of which the wrongful deed had happened and been performed by its principal. Dr. Steinmaer also asked Melissa whether she would object to notifying the offices of the Queen and the Prime Minister about what had happened, since Pennington was scheduled to be raised a baronetcy. Melissa agreed to both of his suggestions, on the condition that this very private information not is made public.

Dr. Steinmaer also asked Melissa what she would like to have printed in the *Guardian* as a retraction to the already-published announcement of her forthcoming marriage to Pennington. Melissa reflected, and, for the first time in many days, she smiled. In fact, she smiled with that mysterious kind of *La Giaconda* look, of which only women in love are capable. Then with an impish sparkle in her eye, she asked the lawyer whether he had a copy of the newspaper with the marriage announcement in it. When he told her he did, she asked him to send the page to an address in the United States, which she was able to dictate by heart. Dr. Steinmaer acquiesced, no questions asked.

After the lawyer left, Melissa thought for a long time about the situation she was in and considered her options for the future.

"It is absolutely certain that my reputation is stained," she thought. "In fact, if anything is certain, it is that my opportunity for future employment in this industry is slim to none; the trading companies monitor their competitors' employees as much as they do their own. So, I will have to make some changes.

"But I am pregnant which means that I will not be able to take on the responsibilities of full-time employment anyway. Then again, I won't stay afloat for long by doing nothing. Besides, I don't have a lot of money, just some personal savings in addition to what Boris left me. Add to that the medical expenses I'm incurring—and may incur from the pregnancy—and I could not survive for more than a few months.

"There is only way for me," she concluded with satisfaction. "I will go to graduate school. By doing so, I will be eligible to draw on my mother's inheritance, and won't have to bother finding, and then proving myself, at a new job. Of course, that opens up other questions: Where should I study? And what subject?"

A moment later she had the answer to both questions. "I will study the law! And, since the opportunities for women in the Old World are limited, I will study in the USA! Boris is there." Then turning her thoughts to the west coast of America, she silently cried out, "Boris, my darling, how are you?"

After a minute, Melissa returned to her primary train of thought. "So, it is solved. After I am discharged from the clinic, I will leave Geneva and return to my apartment in London. I won't have to pay for it, and I will be closer to my father. In London, I will pass the entrance exams for law school, and then I should be able to enroll for the fall semester at some university in California." Suddenly, another detail fell into place. "Of course! My school friend Sharon Smith lives in California now. She can help me get set up and orientated.

"It's an excellent plan," she concluded. "I will give birth in California, so the baby will be an American citizen. And I will give my baby a double surname, Spencer-Goryanin. George or Milana Spencer-Goryanin."

Having made her decision, Melissa laughed. Her future lay easily and clearly before her. Now able to concentrate on gaining strength for the forthcoming surgery, she fell asleep easily with a smile on her lips.

The surgery took less than three hours and was fully successful, after which Melissa was scheduled to leave the recovery room in just a few more days.

Meanwhile, in the Geneva courthouse, Pennington appeared before the judge strategically dressed in a magnificent Gucci suit and expensive shoes. While the assistant public prosecutor was presenting the details of the arraignment to the court, Eddy's friend Jonathan Barker, who had just arrived from overseas, entered. When Pennington spotted him, he briefly affected a Mussolini-like pose, lifting his head upward and inflating his nostrils. He suspected what was true—that Barker was in disbelief that his old buddy, the future Sir Eddy Pennington, had done anything criminal.

When the public prosecutor ended his opening statement, the floor was given to Pennington's defense attorney, Mr. Vito Laviterri, who spoke at length about his client's excellent reputation, about his generous and substantial contributions to the local community, about his forthcoming raise of a baronetcy, and about his engagement to Lady Melissa Spencer. At the end of his statement, Mr. Laviterri said that Lady Melissa had provoked her fiancé's rough outburst of passion, and asked the court to drop all charges against his client, releasing him from custody.

To conclude the proceedings, Dr. Steinmaer was given the opportunity to enter evidence. He gave the bailiff a photo of Melissa's battered face taken after her arrival at the clinic, and one of her lying naked on the floor in Eddy's office with blood flowing from her anus. He entered into evidence a copy of a letter received from the Prime Minister's office in London, in which it was specified that the awarding of a baronetcy to Eddy Pennington had been suspended pending the outcome of the trial in Geneva. Dr. Steinmaer did not need to mention Melissa's reputation. He simply asked the court whether the lady's plea to her fiancé to stop could be considered, under any circumstances, justifiable provocation for a violent sexual assault that resulted in a fractured cheekbone, a concussion, and a ruptured rectum.

Dr. Steinmaer then gave the court two civil claims. The first claim was for the indemnification of the Pennington International, Ltd., in which office the crime been committed by the principal of the company. The second claim was for indemnification of Mr. Eddy Pennington personally, for causing extreme physical and mental damage that disabled the company's employee from carrying out her work at the company.

The decision to arraign was quick and to the point. The accused, Mr. Eddy Pennington, was to be remanded in solitary confinement until the setting of a trial date. And effective immediately, all of Mr. Pennington's personal accounts and assets, as well as all those of Pennington International, Ltd., were to be frozen until the trial. The judge asked whether additional time would be necessary for the attorneys' preparation, then having received a negative answer from both parties, he scheduled the second court appearance for Thursday, October 28.

At this point, Pennington's head lost its altitude and his nostrils deflated. His old friend, Jonathan Barker, before arriving at the courthouse, had wanted to meet with Pennington, but after what he had just seen, he no longer wanted to do so. It was clear to him that Pennington was guilty on all charges and that Global Oil would be held responsible for the losses incurred.

Leaving the courtroom, Barker caught Pennington looking at him, but returned no acknowledgment; after all, he did not want to spoil his own reputation. Instead, he left the courthouse and went directly to Pennington International, Ltd. The situation with his company needed to be salvaged.

57

At about four in the afternoon, there was a knock on Boris's door. He opened it to a postman handing him a package. Boris signed the receipt for delivery, but was perplexed about whom it was from. He had agreed with Melissa that they would not correspond. And yet here was this large package without a return name or address.

Inside, he found the entire issue of the *Guardian* newspaper, dated October 7. Leafing through, he quickly came to page eight and a formal portrait of Melissa and Eddy, both in formal evening clothes. The caption explained that Pennington and Spencer were to marry on October 17 in London City Hall. Knowing how religious Melissa was, Boris was struck by the fact that the ceremony was not to take place in a church.

Melissa looked superb in her gown. The black-and-white photograph emphasized her classical nobility. The thin beauty of her face was enhanced by a beautiful diamond-and-white-gold pendant hanging on a slender golden chain. Her earrings were a matched set to the pendant, as was the delicate tiara that encircled her elegantly styled hair. As Boris stared at the photograph, he almost believed that Melissa was looking straight back at him, and for a moment he thought he heard her voice, although he could not understand what she was saying. He looked and looked at her. Alas, he thought, he could not look at her enough.

Boris examined the envelope in which the newspaper had been mailed. The postmark was from Geneva and dated October 18. Why had Melissa not put a return address on it? As a matter of fact, as far as he knew, she should be in London. Perhaps, Melissa hadn't sent it. But then who did? And why? And why had her wedding not been held in a church?

Boris's son Anton came into the room just then, and followed his father's intent gaze down to the photo.

Anton's eyes also became transfixed, as if he had just fallen in love for the first time. "Who is she, Father?"

"This is the woman with whom I escaped from the gangsters in Russia," Boris answered, still staring.

"Wow! Is she married?" Anton asked, and then added with a boyish confidence in his voice, "I'd marry her without hesitation."

"You're right, my son," Boris said. "In fact, if I were as young as you, and were not with your mother, I would marry her myself. And, as you said, without hesitation." Boris then closed the newspaper, and, very carefully, as if the *Guardian* were made of glass, handed it to his son.

"Would you introduce me to her?" Anton asked.

"Perhaps," Boris said philosophically. "It could happen."

"I will wait for her," Anton answered, leaving the room with the newspaper.

"Me, too," Boris whispered.

At 10:00 p.m. London time, Boris dialed Melissa's apartment in London. Nobody picked up. He called again four hours later. But again, there was no response. So at six the next morning, Boris called Pennington International in Geneva. He introduced himself to the secretary of the company who was none other than Frau Globke. But when Boris asked to be connected to Lady Melissa Spencer, Frau Globke told him that the lady was no longer with the company. Further, she asked Mr. Goryanin not to call again. Frau Globke firmly believed that Boris bore full responsibility for what had happened to Melissa.

Boris could wait no longer. He contacted his travel agency and reserved tickets on the first available flight to Geneva via Frankfurt, on October 31.

Boris arrived in Geneva as scheduled and took a taxi to Pennington International. As he approached the entrance to the building, Boris spotted Jonathan Barker and called out to him. Unlike de la Perrier, Barker seemed to appreciate that Boris had returned money for the unfulfilled delivery. He greeted Boris as an old friend, invited him into his office, and asked Frau Globke to bring them coffee.

After exchanging small talk about the political situation in Russia, Boris casually asked Barker what had happened in Geneva. Barker described how Eddy was being held without bail for physically assaulting Melissa, who had just been discharged from the hospital the day before and left Geneva. Barker did not know for sure where Melissa had gone, but figured she had returned to London where her father lived.

Boris tried to ask Barker cautiously for more details, but was interrupted by the telephone. It was the president of Global Oil, so Boris left the office and waited. About fifteen minutes later, Barker motioned him back in and told him that he could not reveal anything more because of the investigation in progress. Barker couldn't even give Boris the number to Melissa's lawyer.

On his way out, Boris tried to talk to Frau Globke, but she turned away and, after curtly informing him that he was keeping her from her work, asked him to leave. Boris sighed. There wasn't anything he could accomplish in Geneva, so he left for the airport, where, an hour later, caught a flight to Frankfurt.

In Frankfurt, Boris took a shuttle to the Hotel Astron, where, at the registration desk, he asked an unfamiliar clerk for the room in which he had stayed with Melissa. The clerk told him that the room was occupied by a British lady—a crippled woman in a wheelchair under the care of a nurse. Settling for a room on the second floor, Boris went down to the sauna to relieve his stress and to think about what to do next. He came to a reasonable decision: if Melissa might be in London, he would just have to fly there himself to find out.

Later that evening, Boris changed and went downstairs to the hotel restaurant. In the hallway approaching the restaurant, he noticed a nun pushing a wheelchair holding a crippled woman. If only he had known that the woman in the wheelchair was Lady Melissa!

Instead, Boris caught the Lufthansa flight to London the next morning, and took a taxi to the apartment where Melissa had lived. But she was not there, and the discrete concierge either knew nothing of her whereabouts or felt obliged to keep that information from a perfect stranger.

So Boris wrote a note to her, which said that, more than ever, he loved her with all his heart, that he didn't know what was happening to her, and that people were telling him all sorts of incredible stories. He finished by asking her to contact him at the earliest opportunity, and slipped the note into Melissa's mailbox.

As he left her building, rain started pouring from the sky, and his taxi driver had already left. So Boris found a telephone booth and called Melissa's father several times. No one answered, but Boris noticed that someone had left an umbrella in the booth. So he took it with him, and his life in London slightly improved.

Next, he decided to catch a taxi and take it to the nearest library, where he asked for a London telephone directory. He quickly found Mr. Spencer's address and went there, but was disappointed yet again when no one was home.

To stay in London made no sense, so Boris left back to California, via Frankfurt. By 8:30 that night, Boris was back at the Astron. Again, in the hallway, he saw the nun pushing the wheelchair but this time, they were going into the elevator ahead of him. He stopped and decided to catch the next elevator, as there would not be enough space for all of them in one.

The next morning when Boris was checking out, the desk clerk—this time someone he was familiar with—greeted Boris and then, out of the blue, asked him, "Why didn't you leave with your companion?"

"What companion?" Boris shot back. "What are you are talking about?"

"The woman you were with the last time, when you stayed on the third floor."

"In which room on the third floor?" Boris asked, confused.

"In the room where you stayed with your lady friend, at the beginning of the month."

"But I couldn't get that room this time. I was told that an elderly woman in a wheelchair and her nurse were in that room."

"No, Mr. Goryanin," the clerk said. "Lady Melissa Spencer was in that room. She just checked out this morning. And her nurse, Frau Gartvig, was in the room across the hallway. They got here three days ago, and Ms. Spencer had requested that room specifically. In any event, both of them left about fifteen minutes ago. I wished the lady a prompt recovery, but she said she was already better, and hoped for a full recovery soon."

Boris was in shock. He had traveled to Geneva and London searching for Melissa, and she had been here the entire time. He had even passed her in the hallway—twice! He couldn't believe something like that could actually happen.

"Where have they gone?" Boris asked in a fit of desperation.

"They were going to the airport, Mr. Goryanin, as far as I know. The shuttle will return in a few minutes—maybe the driver will know."

When the shuttle returned, the driver said that he had seen the two women walking toward Terminal A, and the next thing he knew, he was driving Boris back to the airport. Boris rushed to the information desk in Terminal A, where the clerk paged Lady Melissa Spencer. But it was in vain. She did not call. Lady Melissa had disappeared.

"Would they ever meet again?" Boris asked himself again and again during his flight back to Los Angeles.